Books by Ben Mezrich

Reaper
Threshold

Published by HarperCollins*Publishers*

REAPER

BEN MEZRICH

HarperPaperbacks
A Division of HarperCollinsPublishers

■ HarperPaperbacks
A Division of HarperCollins*Publishers*
10 East 53rd Street, New York, NY 10022-5299

This is a work of fiction. The characters, incidents, and
dialogues are products of the author's imagination and are not
to be construed as real. Any resemblance to actual events or
persons, living or dead, is entirely coincidental.

ISBN 0-06-109718-7

HarperCollins®, ■®, and HarperPaperbacks™ are trademarks
of HarperCollins Publishers, Inc.

A hardcover edition of this book was published in 1998 by
HarperCollins*Publishers*.

First paperback printing: December 1998

Printed in the United States of America

Visit HarperPaperbacks on the World Wide Web at
http://www.harpercollins.com

❖ 10 9 8 7 6 5 4 3

To Jon and Josh,
great brothers, great friends

ACKNOWLEDGMENTS

first, my deepest thanks to my mother, my extraordinary first reader, and my father, my tireless source of technical information. Also to Eamon Dolan, my brilliant editor at HarperCollins; Aaron Priest and Bob Bookman, agents who know what works; Or Gozani and Katrin Chua, who walked me through the details; Rick Horgan, a sharp eye in the early stages; Dr. Bill Carlson, generous with his expertise; Harriet Cohen and Dr. Arthur Feinberg, unfailing in their confidence and support; Aileen Boyle, my publicist; Scott Stossel, who knows his conspiracies. And Anthea Disney, whose faith in me has opened so many doors.

I'm also grateful to: Joanne Chang, Sandra Newman and Jack Kerry, Saumya Das, Erik Finger, Lucy Hood at Harper L.A., Paul Lance, Marina and Skadi,

Drew Tulumello (just for being Drew), Pete Jacobson and Lianna Orlando (spaghetti on the Vineyard), Dave Fox and Alex Wolfson, Simon Lipskar, and The Posse—Kate, Francesca, Liisa, and Courtney.

ONE

mitch Thomas dug his fingers into the leather armrests of his Tudor-style chair, as the other eight partners took their seats. The mahogany table was at least twenty feet long, polished so severely that Mitch could see himself reflected in the wood. His nostrils looked grotesquely large, a product of the peculiar angle, and he quickly turned away. He was nervous—scared, actually—and his five-hundred-dollar shoes bounced against the egg-white marble floor.

This was Mitch's first time in the enormous boardroom. The Room—as the associates at Alistar, Brodney and Falk referred to it—was deliberately imposing: high, leather-lined bookshelves, original Renaissance oil paintings, an extravagant tangle of crystal posing as a chandelier. Mitch felt completely out of place, the butt of some vast, practical joke. Did he really belong in this place that reeked of money? Or was someone, somewhere staring at him on a TV screen, laughing his ass off? Mitch Thomas, hotshot corporate lawyer. *Yeah, sure.*

He shifted his eyes around the table, trying his best to ignore the thickening tension. He was the youngest man in the room by ten years, and he knew his appearance didn't help. Wild ruffles of California blond hair, a trim, muscular body—he should have been sitting on a beach somewhere, not cowering in the boardroom of one of the most prestigious law firms in Boston.

He crossed his legs under the table, feeling the sweat under his knees. Four-thirty in the morning, and he was trapped in the Room, sweating his way through a Brooks Brothers pinstriped suit. He should have been at home, his arms wrapped around Alison's burgeoning waist. Three more months and the little turnip would finally pop out of there. Mitch would never say it to Alison's face—and risk a broken nose, or worse—but he couldn't wait to have her back to her normal, svelte self.

At least now, with the way his career was developing, they'd have the money for a nanny *and* a home gym. He smiled, spreading his fingers out against the mahogany, somewhat calmed by the cold smoothness of the wood. He had made partner barely two months ago—unexpectedly, but then, nobody had expected the accident that had taken the lives of three of the firm's biggest producers. Wind shear, pilot error—whatever the reason, at thirty-one Mitch had suddenly become the youngest partner in firm history. An office with a window, a new secretary, a hefty raise, and a four-thirty A.M. visit to the Room.

An important teleconference with a client in Washington, his secretary had explained. Mitch had almost canceled last night's touch football game to reflect on what that meant.

Washington. Mitch's stomach trembled, as his eyes shifted to the two senior partners sitting across the table from him. Michael Alistar had thick gray hair and an old-style charcoal suit; he looked like somebody's grandfather, his heavy lips ready to break into a smile at the slightest provocation. Next to him, Craig Brodney was his opposite: rail thin and angry, with ferret-like eyes and a permanently embedded frown.

Washington, and the presence of the two senior partners—there was no doubt, the teleconference had something to do with Client 297. Mitch had jumped right into the big leagues. Two months ago, he had been just another piddling associate, and now he was a partner who took teleconferences with Client 297.

As if on cue, the curved television screen squatting at the far end of the table suddenly flashed on, bathing the boardroom in cold blue light. The room went dead silent, all nine partners turning to stare at the glowing machine. Mitch laced his fingers together to keep them from trembling. He had never met Client 297, had never even heard his voice on a telephone. Rumor was only the senior partners dealt with him face to face. But everyone at the firm knew how much Client 297 was worth.

Billions. Not hundreds of millions, like the other corporate clients—the small computer companies and cable operators that were the firm's bread and butter. Client 297 was worth *billions.* Mitch sucked air through his teeth, thinking what he and Alison could do with just a tiny piece of that kind of money.

There was a sudden noise behind him, and he glanced over his shoulder. He spotted a janitor at the edge of the room, mop in hand. What the hell was he doing there? Brodney was going to have a fit if he noticed.

"All right, gentlemen," Alistar's thick voice interrupted, and Mitch turned his attention back to the table. "I don't have to remind you how important this client is to our firm. He's asked for this tele-conference to get to know our partnership, before we enter into a new stage of our relationship—which I'll explain in greater detail after the meeting."

Mitch shifted his eyes back toward the television screen. The blue light started flickering; any moment Client 297 would appear. The anticipation was intense, and Mitch noticed that his heart was really racing. He took a deep breath, trying to calm himself—and felt a sudden, tearing pain under his rib cage.

He gasped, his eyes going wide. The pain quickly went away, but now his heart was absolutely frantic, and he could feel the sweat breaking out across his forehead.

Christ, was he having a heart attack? He was in the best shape of his life. He worked out regularly, played in a half-dozen organized sports. And he was young—much too young for a heart attack. Maybe he had injured himself in the football game last night? He didn't remember getting hit, but the game had gone on for three hours. Then he and Alison had fulfilled their Sunday night quota of cautiously contorted, "pregnant couple" sex. Plenty of opportunity for injury.

He swallowed, trying to regain his composure. A torn muscle, that's what it had to be. Still, his heart was racing. He glanced across the table, inadvertently catching Brodney's eye. The senior partner was staring straight ahead, a strange expression on his face. Maybe he had noticed Mitch's discomfort. If so, he didn't seem happy about it, and Mitch was probably better off keeping it to himself. Client 297 was too important—

Suddenly, the pain was back, an umbrella of daggers spinning through Mitch's chest. His eyelids clamped shut. *Christ, a heart attack, it had to be a heart attack!* He dug his fingernails into the mahogany table and opened his mouth—but nothing came out. He couldn't get his lungs to work; he couldn't pull in air; his chest felt like it was full of concrete!

My god, my god, my god. His head started to spin. He was suffocating, and the pain was multiplying, spawning out from the center of his chest to his limbs. His muscles began to convulse and he felt his spine stiffening, his body arching back against the leather chair. *Alison, god, Alison!* Every inch of his being wanted to get out of that chair and out of that room and find her—but he couldn't get the commands to his body; he couldn't get past the immense pain. Something was turning him inside out and there was nothing he could do.

Why wasn't someone helping him? Where were the other partners? He used every ounce of willpower to force his eyelids up, up, up—

Christ. His stomach dropped and he knew immediately that he was going to die.

TWO

at seventy miles per hour, nothing is textbook. Nick Barnes braced his wide shoulders against an equipment cabinet as the sirens echoed through his skull. He could feel the tires screeching beneath him, each twist in the pavement tilting his world. His green surgical scrubs were soaking wet, and every inch of his six-foot-two, athletic frame ached from overuse. Even his impenetrable mop of unruly hair looked exhausted, plastered to his forehead by sweat and effort, a boyish gauntlet of thick dark curls.

"Time!" he shouted, leaning over the stretcher and inserting the thumb and middle finger of his gloved left hand into the patient's mouth.

"Twelve minutes," Charlie Pace answered from across the ambulance. Charlie's expression was grim, sweat beading above his overly round, deep-

6

set blue eyes. Under pressure, his weathered face seemed as cracked and rough as tree bark, fierce creases outlining his puglike features.

"Not good," Nick answered. One-fifth of the "golden hour" was already gone, and Boston General was still twenty miles away. Despite the driver's heroics, it was going to be a close race. Every emergency specialist knew that a seriously injured patient had sixty minutes to make it to the OR—and this patient was beyond seriously injured.

They had ripped her out of her car's remains a few minutes past four in the morning—unconscious, in respiratory and cardiac collapse, with severe trauma to the face and chest. They had immediately opened her airway, gotten her breathing—barely—and jump-started her heart. Then they had locked a cervical collar around her neck and had rushed her into the ambulance. Now they had to keep her alive until they reached the hospital.

"Orotracheal intubation," Nick shouted, reaching for the intubation tube. His pulse was racing, and he could almost taste the adrenaline. Rivulets of sweat trickled over his high cheekbones, down across the angles of his prominent jaw. Because of the cervical collar and the extensive facial trauma, he was going to have to do the intubation blind—a tricky procedure, but nothing he hadn't done before.

He pressed down on the woman's tongue and slid his fingers forward until he could feel her epiglottis. Then he inserted the tube into the left side of her mouth and pushed until it slid past the epiglottis. Carefully, he performed a test ventilation, watching and listening as the woman's chest rose.

"Still not getting much inflation," he said, taping the tube into place.

"Not surprising," Charlie said. "Take a look at that bruise."

Charlie was pointing at the dark blue crescent that covered three-quarters of the woman's chest. Nick sighed, tracing the bruise with his eyes. He could just make out the imprint of the steering wheel where it had hit her, smack in the center of her rib cage. Deceleration injury, probably forty miles per hour. A quick lesson in conservation of energy. A few broken ribs, but that wasn't a big deal. The real problems were underneath the rib cage. The lungs, the heart, the arteries.

"All right," Nick said, "let's get started. One hundred percent oxygen."

"Got it." Charlie attached the oxygen lead to the intubation tube and began breathing her, while Nick shifted forward on his knees. His mind became instantly alert, searching for signs, symbols, the language of his profession. He had been riding with the ambulances for almost two years and had seen a thousand patients like her. But every time it was like the first, a virgin experience.

"Rapid and shallow respiration," he began, gently running his hands up the center of her chest. "No open wounds. Trachea out of midline. Veins in the neck fully distended. Pulse . . ."

He paused, lightly palpating her carotid.

"She's going into shock. Damn it."

He whipped out his stethoscope and pressed it against her chest.

"Breath sounds diminished on the right side. Hyper-resonance on the left. Charlie, we got ourselves a pneumothorax."

Nick's voice was calm, but inside he was on fire. A hole in the woman's lung was acting as a one-way valve; air was entering the pleural space during inhalation, squeezing the lung and compromising ventilation. The superior and inferior venae cavae had become compressed, hindering the return of blood to the right side of her heart. If they didn't do something fast, this woman was going to die. Nick had no intention of letting that happen.

Beneath the bruises and the blood, she was young and pretty, maybe twenty-four years old. Nick clenched his jaw, a determined coldness filling him from the inside. There was a familiar tinge of pain in his right hand, which he balled into an angry fist. No fucking way was he letting this one go.

"Fourteen gauge angiocatheter! Stat!"

Charlie reached into an equipment cabinet with one hand while still breathing the patient with the other. The ambulance tilted thirty degrees as it took a high curve, but somehow Charlie kept his balance. Twenty years in a blue paramedic's uniform had given him an agility Nick could only marvel at.

"Here. The stylet's already been removed."

Nick took the catheter with his left hand and uncapped the needle at the end of the plastic tube. Then he leaned forward, identifying the site for puncture. He wanted to get the catheter in between the second and third ribs. Most importantly, he had to avoid the intercostal nerve and artery which ran along the bottom of the woman's rib cage. He braced himself, mentally closing out the scream of the sirens and the squeal of the tires, blanking out the growing pain that emanated across the palm of his right hand.

He pushed the needle into the woman's chest and felt a slight pop as it broke out into the pleural space. There was a sudden venting of air through the catheter, and the right side of the woman's chest deflated. Nick smiled, withdrawing the needle through the catheter, leaving the plastic tube in place. He capped the top of the tube with a rubber flutter valve and watched as the woman's breathing grew stronger.

Perfect execution. He leaned back, pushing his gloved fingers through his hair, letting Charlie check the vitals. The rush of adrenaline was like an orgasm. It felt so good that for the moment, his right hand didn't ache.

But a few seconds later Charlie looked up—and he wasn't smiling.

"She's breathing better," he said quickly, "but the veins in her neck are still distended. Her pulse is weak, and I'm not getting any capillary refill. She's still in shock, and her pressure's dropping."

Nick cursed to himself—it wasn't over. His right hand throbbed as he leaned forward, taking a closer look at the bruise on the woman's chest. Something about the bruise pricked at him, and he had a sudden thought. He went back to his stethoscope, this time placing it midline, over the woman's heart. As he suspected, her heart sounds were distant and muffled.

"What do you think?" Charlie asked, his voice monotone—a sure sign that the veteran was nervous.

"Muffled heart sounds," Nick said, thinking out loud. "Falling blood pressure, distended neck veins. Beck's Triad."

Charlie raised his eyebrows. Nick moved quickly, testing the woman's pulse on either side of her body.

"Pulsus Paradoxus. Damn it, no question. Pericardial tamponade."

"Christ," Charlie murmured.

Nick understood his partner's anxiety. Pericardial tamponade was a rare and usually fatal condition. Even more rare was tamponade secondary to blunt trauma; even a seasoned paramedic like Charlie would have likely missed the diagnosis. But Nick wasn't a paramedic. For nearly three years, he had been the top cardiovascular surgeon at Boston General—perhaps one of the top five surgeons in the entire country.

"There's an accumulation of blood in the pericardial sac," he said, cursing himself for missing the signs earlier. "Her heart's drowning in it. In a few minutes it will stop beating altogether."

"So we're going to lose her," Charlie said, his despair evident.

"No," Nick shot back. Even if he wasn't a surgeon anymore, he was still the best at what he did, damn it. "We're going to do a pericardiocentesis. We're going to drain the blood out."

Charlie stared at him.

"Here? In the ambulance?"

Nick didn't answer. Instead, he turned his head toward the open door that led to the driver's compartment. "Sully! I'm going to need you to keep it steady for five minutes. I don't care if there's a fucking cow on the highway, you don't turn the wheel."

He turned back to Charlie. Charlie's face was gray, the thick folds of skin over his eyes slick with sweat. He looked like a bulldog that had just been dragged through a rainstorm.

"This is going to be a little difficult because of the cervical collar," Nick said. "But we're just going to have to pray there isn't any serious spinal damage. We're going to need an eighteen-gauge cardiac

needle, a fifty-milliliter syringe, and the portable
EKG."

Charlie rushed to find the equipment. In a second he had the EKG out and ready. As he searched
for the needle and the syringe, Nick attached the
EKG leads to the woman's extremities. He put one
lead on the inside of each arm, one on each inner
thigh. Then he glanced at the machine, taking in the
reading. They had only a few minutes left.

Charlie returned with the needle and syringe.
Nick took them both with his left hand and worked
quickly to attach the needle to the syringe. His right
hand cried out as he pushed the needle into place,
but he gritted his teeth and ignored the pain. When
the needle was in place he turned back to the EKG
machine. He found the V-lead and used an alligator
clip to attach it to the hub of the 18-gauge needle.
Now he would be able to monitor the needle as he
inserted it; any jump in the EKG would mean he
had gone too far into the heart.

He took the needle and syringe out of his aching
right hand and quickly found the woman's ster-
num. He took a deep breath, steadying his wrist.
Even after two years, it felt funny using his left
hand for such precise work. He wanted so badly to
switch the needle back to his right hand—but he
knew that he couldn't. If it had just been the pain,
he would have worked through it. But the pain was
just a symbol of what he had lost.

Anger filled him, melding with the adrenaline
that coursed through his veins. Not now, he hissed
to himself. He bulldozed the anger away and jabbed
the needle into the woman's chest, just below the
xiphoid. He pushed until the tip was past the ster-
num, then angled the needle upward until it

pointed to the left lower tip of the woman's scapula. He kept his eye on the EKG, watching for any jump in the green line that monitored the woman's falling blood pressure.

Slowly, carefully, he advanced the needle into her chest. Thankfully, Sully was keeping the ambulance at an even pace—but still, the divots and bumps in the highway bit at the tires, making the curative procedure almost as deadly as the condition itself. One overlooked pothole, and the needle could hit a coronary artery. . . .

Nick felt a sudden pop as the tip of the needle entered the pericardium. He applied instant suction and watched, relieved, as the syringe immediately filled with blood.

"Wow," Charlie whispered, also watching the syringe. "Pretty neat."

Nick forced a smile. "And left-handed, too."

He clamped the needle into place to prevent it from moving and leaned back from the stretcher. A flawless pericardiocentesis. She was going to make it. Nick exhaled, absentmindedly rubbing his right hand with the fingers of his left. The adrenaline drained out of him, and a cold shiver moved through his shoulders. He closed his eyes as his fingers found the tangle of scars that fanned out across the back of his right hand. Even through the latex glove, he could trace the ridged legacy of that night two years ago.

She had been a young woman, too. Pretty, mid-twenties, dark hair, bleeding and bruised . . .

Nick opened his eyes. The ambulance was slowing as it pulled into Boston General's receiving driveway. He took a deep breath, cleared his mind, and reached for the ambulance doors.

*   *   *

Twenty minutes later he was leaning against the side of the ambulance, his hands jammed into the pockets of his scrubs. Next to him, Charlie was searching his paramedic's uniform for a cigarette. It took him a good three minutes before he found a loose single caught in the elastic of his slacks.

"Twenty-six-year-old woman with both a pneumothorax and pericardial tamponade," he mumbled, as he slipped the cigarette between his thick lips, "and she's gonna walk away. Her car's flat as a pancake, there's an imprint of a steering wheel across her chest, and because of you, she's gonna walk away."

Nick didn't respond. He watched as Charlie flicked ashes toward the sidewalk. A stupid, dangerous habit. Nick wanted one badly. He had quit when Jennifer, his wife, had first gotten sick. *His wife.* Amazing that he still thought of her that way. At least, now, her name could cross his thoughts without a suffocating thickness taking hold of his throat.

"Any other shift," Charlie continued, suckling his cigarette, "she would have died. No question."

"Come on, Charlie. It was as much luck as anything else."

"Luck?" Charlie coughed, flicking more ashes. "Yeah, right. So what if you are crazy? You're good. That's what matters."

Nick couldn't help but crack a smile. He liked Charlie, really liked him—and that was a surprise. They came from completely different worlds. Charlie rode a motorcycle, played in a midnight jazz band, and had never been married. He had dipped his hands in tragedy every day for the past twenty years, but somehow it had never truly affected him. He had only the barest knowledge of the scars Nick carried within him. Somehow, it didn't matter; at the moment, Nick counted him as his closest friend.

"Tell that to Pierce," Nick grunted. "See how much he cares about my abilities."

Rudolph Pierce was the hospital administrator. He'd had it in for Nick for a long time. The trouble had started shortly after Jennifer's death; Nick had been hauling enough repressed anger to level a city block, and Pierce had often played the part of punching bag. Perhaps justifiably, Pierce had labeled him a troublemaker, an angry hotshot with little regard for rules and regulations, and the label had stuck. When things had gotten bad again, two years ago, Pierce had been ready to pounce all over him. Although Nick had somehow survived the administrator's efforts, it still seemed like the bastard was always lurking around a corner, just waiting for him to screw up.

"Pierce is an ass," Charlie agreed. "But I'll tell you one thing—that fat fuck ever ends up lying in the back of an ambulance, I bet he prays it happens on your shift."

Nick laughed. Now that would be quite a scene. Obese, pasty Rudolph Pierce crushing the hell out of a stretcher as Nick worked to save the jerk's life. After everything Pierce had tried to do to him two years ago—the psychiatric reviews, the probations, the "gentle" requests for his resignation—"You think I'd raise a sweat for that scumbag? If it were up to him, I'd have lost my medical license years ago."

"You'd save him all right." Charlie coughed. "Because then he'd have to kiss your ass for the rest of the century. No more red-eye shifts, no more drunk-detail out in Dorchester. Just the peach calls."

Sully stuck his head out the driver's side window. His bright red hair was pulled back in a tight ponytail, and his face was covered in freckles. He had the CB mike in his hand.

"We got a call for a pickup in the financial district. Some psyche-job wandering down the middle of the street. It's nearly five—you want me to tell central to pass it on to somebody else?"

Nick looked at Charlie, who shrugged. It had been a long night—but they had enough left for one more call. Inside, Nick was glad.

As long as the sirens were screaming and the adrenaline was pumping, Nick was content. The pain of Jennifer's death had receded, and although the memories of his old life came and went, it was never more than a wistful longing. As far as his career was concerned, he had traded one consuming passion for another; when his heart was pounding with the excitement of a peach call, it was easy to pretend that the trade had been a matter of choice—not of circumstance.

He sighed, clamping his aching right hand into a fist.

THREE

Pulse Jockeys. That was what they called themselves: the hard-core paramedics, the EMTs, the emergency specialists who lived for the adrenaline, the vein-popping surge they got when the pavement was flashing by and the sirens were screaming in their ears. For Charlie, it had been a way of life for a long time; rough and weathered, he was what you expected to find beneath the dark blue uniform. But Nick was different. A medical doctor, a highly trained surgeon, thirty-five years old and formerly one of Boston's best scalpel men.

He reclined in the front passenger seat of the ambulance, his face pressed against the side window, eyes half-open, body dormant, waiting. Boston flashed by on the other side of the glass. Old, three-story town houses with ridiculously high

front steps gave way to more modern glass and
steel buildings as the South End became downtown.
The hum of the tires against pavement mingled
with the high chords of a familiar radio commercial,
and Nick watched as Sully changed the channel
with a freckled hand. The same commercial was on
the next channel, and Sully cursed, shaking his
head.

"Every five fucking seconds," he hissed, "they
gotta remind us that the world's changing. 'Turn It
On, With Telecon.' I hear that Telecon commercial one
more time, I swear I'm gonna puke."

Nick laughed, as the singsongy jingle echoed
through the ambulance. The melodic voice had just
gotten to the part about what Telecon Industries'
upcoming national fiber optic network was going to
mean for American business, when Sully slammed
his hand against the knob, changing channels again.
The voice disintegrated in a lick of heavy metal
music.

Nick turned his face back to the window. Fiber
optics, glass and steel buildings, heavy metal—it
was true what the melodic commercial voice had
said, the world was constantly changing. Certainly,
Nick knew more about change than most.

It was strange, how quickly he had learned to
adapt. After Jennifer's death, he had thrown himself
entirely into his work; for three years, his entire life
had revolved around the pristine world of the operating theaters. Sometimes it had felt like he had
been born a surgeon in dark blue scrubs with a
scalpel in his hand. He glanced down at the back of
his right hand, at the ridged scars that ran from his
fingers to his wrist—

"Christ, this is a mess." Sully was hunched close

to the steering wheel, a grim look on his face. They were at the edge of Boston's financial district, and the traffic was intense, cars five thick across the narrow street.

Nick cleared his thoughts, reaching up with his left hand and flicking on the siren. Immediately, the cars struggled to open a path for the ambulance, but still it was slow going. The intersection up ahead was completely snarled, a cholesterol clot lodged in the city's heart.

"We might have to ditch the wagon," Sully said, pointing. "The site is right on the other side of the intersection. My guess is, this snarl has something to do with our call."

"Great," Nick said. "Pass me the radio."

Sully handed him the receiver, and he dialed up central dispatch. There was a hiss of static, then a thick South Shore accent burst out of the dashboard.

"Go ahead three-thirteen."

"We're thirty yards from the corner of Milk and State," Nick said into the mike. "And it looks like we're not getting much closer. What are the stats?"

"A case eighteen. Two-seven-two, blues on the scene. Awaiting emergency backup."

Nick nodded, replacing the receiver. A case eighteen was a psychiatric case. Two-seven-two meant that the patient was bleeding, perhaps seriously. There were police on the scene, but they wouldn't do anything without paramedics around.

"Sully, just pull in as close as you can. Charlie?"

Charlie stuck his head out of the back compartment. He was already wearing his white mask and gloves. His thick, graying hair was sticking up at the sides, and Nick guessed he had taken a quick nap on the way from the hospital. Other paramedics slept on their off nights; Charlie sucked on a saxophone in a greasy bar in Cambridge. Nick had seen him play a few times, and had gained an understanding of Charlie's longtime bachelor ways. There was no way a woman was going to compete with that saxophone.

"We're gonna need the jump kit and the portable litter. Full restraints."

"Got it." Charlie disappeared into the back. A few seconds later, Sully pulled the ambulance to the side of the road and flicked off the siren. He left the lights running, blue and red reflecting off the glass of a nearby building.

Nick pulled his white doctor's coat out from under the dashboard and pushed open the side door. A cold wind bit at him, reminding him that it was already October. The summer had gone by too fast, a familiar Boston phenomenon. Soon winter would fall out of the sky and they'd start picking up the snow shovel cardiacs and the drowned kids with the rusting ice skates still strapped to their little feet. He pulled the white coat over his shoulders and reached in the pockets for his latex gloves. He left his mask in his front pocket; he didn't like to wear the mask, unless it was truly necessary. Especially with the psychiatrics.

Charlie came out of the back with the jump kit and the stretcher. The kit was bright red and waterproof, maybe thirty pounds. Charlie hefted it into the air and Nick grabbed it, tucking it under his arm like an oversized football. Game time, and the clock was ticking.

The scene on the other side of the intersection was worse than he had expected. Four police cruisers sat at odd angles, lights flashing, effectively blocking off the two-lane street. Behind the cruisers waited a fairly large crowd of onlookers, standing by their stopped cars. A pair of burly police officers stood at the front of the crowd, red-faced and obviously unhappy. There was the rhythmic sound of a traffic helicopter from somewhere up above; as time progressed, this was rapidly turning into a transit nightmare.

A smattering of ill-humored applause erupted as Nick and Charlie pushed through to the police officers. Nick grinned as he approached the larger of the two cops, a thickset man with a pug nose and gunmetal hair.

"Jack, looks like we got here just in time."

Officer Jack Beatty grunted, rubbing his fingers through his gray eyebrows. "Well if it ain't the great Doc Barnes. Looks like your talents are going to be wasted on this one."

Jack Beatty was a Boston standard; a rough-and-tumble Irishman, a cop who had seen everything but still managed to keep a sense of humor—although as he went gray and the streets progressively went to shit, he was much more inclined to go for his rubber baton or the heavy flashlight on his belt before cracking a joke. Nick had worked with him a half-dozen times over the past two years.

Beatty turned away from the crowd and led Nick toward the police cruisers in the center of the intersection. Charlie followed a few feet behind, still lugging the portable litter and the rubber restraints.

"What have we got?" Nick asked.

"Garden variety whacko. Found him wandering down the middle of the street about ten minutes ago. He's got cuts and bruises all over, bleeding pretty heavily. We've got six uniforms ready to take him in, but we want to do this by the book."

"Getting soft on me, Jack?"

The officer rolled his eyes. "New captain, new rules. Besides, nobody wants to go near the blood. Nowadays you bring in a bleeding suspect, ten minutes later you come down with a fever and your dick falls off. Times are changing, Doc."

They had reached the other side of the intersection, and Nick paused, sizing up the situation. A few feet away, six uniformed cops leaned against a police wagon, smoking cigarettes and drinking coffee out of covered Styrofoam cups. The two-lane street ahead of them was blocked off for fifty yards, a gray expanse of blacktop embraced on either side by glass-walled buildings. In the center of the street, straddling the yellow line, stood a man in an olive jumpsuit. The man was black and large, probably six three, with wide shoulders and graying hair cropped close to his head. His overly long arms were limp at his sides, and his entire body seemed to sway as he fought to keep his balance.

Nick took a few steps forward. The man saw him and his shoulders straightened, his head jerking back. Nick stopped, holding up his gloved hands, palms first. He was still a good ten yards away, but already he could see the streaks of blood that covered the man's face and the front of his jumpsuit. He could also make out little glowing specks all over the man's hair and clothes.

"Broken glass," Charlie said, coming up behind Nick. "Looks like he fell through a window or a plate-glass door."

Nick nodded, rubbing his jaw. Despite all the blood, the man's wounds did not look too bad. A few of the cuts would probably need stitches, but there were no severed arteries, no life-threatening punctures. It was just a matter of restraining him before he hurt himself or someone else.

"We'll take it from here," Jack Beatty said, pushing past Charlie. He flicked his hand at the six officers and a rain of cigarettes and empty Styrofoam cups spattered the pavement. Nick made a quick decision and touched Jack's shoulder.

"Hold on a second. I'd like to try to talk him down, if it's okay with you."

The officer raised a thick gray eyebrow. Then he shrugged.

"It's your skin, Doc."

He stepped back, his arms crossed against his chest. Nick turned toward Charlie. Charlie had a quizzical look on his face.

"You sure about this, Nick? He's a pretty big guy. And he looks nuts. Maybe we should let the cops handle it."

Nick shook his head.

"I don't think he's nuts, I think he's scared. The broken glass probably indicates an accident; maybe he's suffering from some sort of post-traumatic shock. And I'd rather not watch six of Boston's finest manhandle him. Take the litter and the straps, and follow me. Slowly."

He began to walk forward, each step calculated and slow, his palms still out ahead of him. He felt a familiar churning in his stomach; in truth, a part of him knew that Charlie was right. This was an unnecessary danger. The cops might break a few bones, but in the end the damage would be minor—the man would be restrained. And he certainly was big.

But Nick wasn't exactly a waif. He was a hundred and ninety pounds, had played tight end on his high school football team like his father before him, and would have earned a Varsity letter at BC if he hadn't chosen to concentrate on baseball instead. He could handle himself—although he hoped he wouldn't have to.

He closed in on the man slowly, keeping his palms up, his face as friendly as possible. Charlie was two paces behind him, clutching the rubber restraints, a look of sheer reluctance on his face. When Nick was ten feet from the man he stopped, motioning for Charlie to do the same. From that distance he could see that the olive jumpsuit was some sort of janitorial uniform, sporting a rectangular name tag above the right front pocket.

"Okay, Tarrance," Nick said loudly, reading the name tag. "We're not here to hurt you. We just want to take a look at those cuts."

Tarrance shifted his head back and forth. His eyes were bulging, and his teeth were clenched together. His entire body was trembling, and his chest heaved up and down. Blood trickled from a long gash above his eyebrows. Nick took a tiny step forward.

"Now, Tarrance, you're going to have to help us out here. You've got a pretty bad cut over your eye and I'd really like—"

Suddenly, Tarrance stumbled backward. His right arm shot up and his mouth opened and a loud scream exploded from his chest. Nick glanced at Charlie, then looked back at the screaming man. He wondered if his initial diagnosis was correct; perhaps the man was deranged. He'd never seen post-traumatic shock cause such severe symptoms. Still, the broken glass hinted at some sort of accident. He bit down on his lip, trying to figure out the best way to handle this.

"Fuck it," he said, finally, and walked forward, his motions fluid and determined. Tarrance stood his ground, his right arm still straight out, his mouth wide open. Charlie opened the litter and locked it into shape, readying the rubber arm and leg restraints.

"We're going to get you to a hospital," Nick stated, as he angled next to the screaming man. "We're going to get you some help." He put his left hand on Tarrance's shoulder and came around behind him. The man began to struggle, and Nick locked his arm around the man's chest. Suddenly, he felt something bite into his skin. He looked down and saw a small shard of glass sticking through his sleeve.

"Shit," he hissed, shaking the shard free. He couldn't tell if it had broken the skin, but it certainly felt like it had. Of all the luck. Now he had a dozen new things to worry about; hepatitis, tetanus, and worst of all, AIDS. Nick felt a chill even thinking about the blood-borne plague, his mind flashing back to Jennifer and the year of hell between her infection and her death. He had become an expert on the disease—and so, of course, he knew that the odds were against him contracting anything from a random puncture wound. As a surgeon, he had been stuck, jabbed, poked, and pierced many times. Still, the prick to his arm filled his head with unpleasant thoughts.

He tried to forget about the piece of glass and the sudden memory of Jennifer's final year as he tightened his grip around Tarrance's chest. Charlie added his strength to the battle and in a second they had the man halfway onto the litter. Still, he wouldn't give up. He lurched forward, his muscles straining as he fought them, his scream changing to a thick, guttural sound. And his right arm remained outstretched; every time they pushed it down, it came straight back up. It wasn't until they had the restraints around his legs and left arm that Nick realized the man wasn't struggling—he was pointing.

Nick followed the extended limb with his eyes. Across the empty street was the entrance to a posh black-glass building. The doorway was high and brass, and there were gilded letters above the arch. Nick shifted his eyes downward and saw a thin trail of broken glass leading from the brass doorway all the way to the litter.

"I understand," Nick said, turning back to Tarrance. "You want me to check out that building. Now just relax."

The man's arm fell, and immediately the tension left his body. Charlie tied the last restraint around his right arm, and the litter was ready to go. Nick turned his attention to the gash above Tarrance's eyebrows. The bleeding had slowed to a trickle. It would need a few stitches, but it wasn't bad.

"Charlie, clean up that cut and get him back to the ambulance. I'll be with you in a second."

He stepped back from the litter and took a look at his own arm. He didn't see any blood soaking through his sleeve, which was a good sign. He carefully opened his jacket and slipped it off his right shoulder.

Damn. The nick was tiny, but it was there, a dot of bright red blood. The glass had pierced the skin. Not very deep, but deep enough for hepatitis and AIDS. Again, he reminded himself that the odds were enormously in his favor. Even if he knew for a fact that the shard of glass was infected with HIV, his chance of contracting the disease from a puncture wound was less than one in two hundred and fifty. With Jennifer, he had taken risks many times worse. He'd clean up the wound and get some inoculations as soon as he got back to Boston General. In a few hours, he'd forget it had even happened.

He walked back toward the group of police officers. As he came closer, Jack Beatty separated himself from the others and held out a thick hand.

"Nice job, Doc. You made me five bucks—with thirty seconds to spare."

Nick laughed, pulling his jacket back over his shoulder. Then he pointed across the street. "See the brass door over there? There's a trail of glass leading right up to our guy. I think you might want to check it out."

Beatty nodded, signaling for two of the cops to follow. He started toward the door, and Nick couldn't help noticing how his hand rested on the butt of his revolver. He felt a chill of excitement and made a quick decision.

"Hey, Jack, mind if I tag along? That guy was pretty shaken up; there might be need for a doctor."

Beatty thought for a minute, then shrugged.

"Just stay a few feet behind, okay, Doc?"

Alistar, Brodney and Falk, Attorneys

Nick read the gilded lettering as Beatty pulled open the brass door and stepped through. The two officers came next, and then Nick, his shoes clicking against a brightly polished marble floor.

The firm's lobby was extravagant, to say the least. The floor and walls were carved out of the

same marble, glistening white in the light of an
enormous chandelier. A rounded obsidian desk
squatted in the center of the atrium, surrounded by
a bank of computers and fax machines. A ten-foot-
high ivory replica of Michelangelo's David stood to
one side of the desk, above a cryptic plaque:
"Perfection is the ability to embrace imperfection."
A few feet behind the statue was a glass revolving
door, which led to a long, carpeted hallway. The
room was devoid of life—not surprising since it was
still before five in the morning.

"Over there," Jack Beatty pointed, his voice echoing through the empty atrium. "Behind the naked
guy."

There was a trail of broken glass leading into the
revolving door. The door itself looked intact; obviously, the glass came from somewhere on the other
side.

The three police officers moved forward, cautiously. Nick watched as Beatty unlatched the strap
on his holster and lifted out his revolver. The gun
looked heavy and mean under his thick fingers.
Nick gave the cops a good ten-foot berth as they
passed through the revolving door.

The hallway was twenty feet long and ended in
what was once a milky glass door. All that was left
of the door was the frame and a few hanging
shards; there was a pile of glass spreading out
across the carpet, glistening in the low fluorescent
light that swept down from the ceiling. Beatty
cleared his throat as he got within a few feet of the
shattered door.

"Boston police," he shouted in his guttural Irish
voice. "Anybody home?"

There was no answer from the other side of the

shattered door. Beatty looked at his two partners and jerked his head to the side. The two men sidled back against the cream-white wall and took out their revolvers. Now all three were armed, and Nick felt a burst of tension move through his shoulders. He'd been in a shoot-out once; it was his third month with the ambulance, and he'd been terrified. He and Charlie had pulled a wounded police officer to safety while bullets ricocheted around them. Afterward, Nick hadn't been able to sleep for two nights—the adrenaline had stayed with him for that long.

He wet his lips as he watched the three officers disappear through the open doorway. A few silent seconds passed. Then he heard a sudden gasp, and Jack Beatty's voice: "Holy mother of God!"

Nick couldn't wait any longer. He jogged forward, his pulse racing. He angled his way through the open door frame, carefully avoiding the hanging shards of glass.

He entered an enormous boardroom lined with leather and wood bookshelves, and stopped dead. Orange light trickled down from a crystal chandelier, glancing off the pearly white floor and casting rainbows around his feet. In the center of the room was a long mahogany table, surrounded by nine high leather chairs.

The figures in the chairs used to be human.

Nick's stomach turned as he ran his eyes over the closest of the nine corpses. The man looked fairly young, perhaps thirty, but it was hard to tell. His skin was as white as ivory. His spine was arched backward, his body rigid. His eyes were wide-open, bulging. His lips were curled back, his teeth clenched as if in agony.

"Christ," Jack Beatty whispered, standing just a few feet from one of the corpses. "Looks like they just turned to bone."

Nick swallowed. He moved his gaze from chair to chair, corpse to corpse. They were all the same. Ivory-white skin. Bulging eyes. Contorted spines. Jaw-clenched grimaces. He had never seen anything like it. He rubbed his hand across his forehead and realized that his fingers were shaking. Then he felt a pinch and looked down at his arm.

He thought of the fresh cut from his struggle with the janitor. Suddenly, his heart stopped in his chest. Images of tiny, ravenous viruses flashed behind his eyes. He jerked his head up and saw that the cops were staring at him, waiting for his cue.

"Get back!" he shouted. "Stay away from the bodies! Back into the lobby! Now!"

He clamped his hand over his cut forearm and stumbled backward through the open doorway. The cops hurried behind him. Their expressions were a mixture of nausea and confusion.

If they had known what Nick was thinking, their faces would have shown nothing but sheer terror.

FOUR

marcus Teal closed his eyes and sucked in a deep breath of the liquid air, the back of his tongue flickering as the pungent sting of sweat, adrenaline, humanity twisted through his nostrils. *Oh my god*, it was like cocaine in his veins; it was every neuron sparking off at once. His eyes came open and both fists crashed down against the podium. The crowd trembled under his gaze, a thousand sweating black faces with eyes wide and lips curled back in proud, devoted smiles. They loved him—because he was one of their own. The prodigal son of South Central.

Boy-wonder Billionaire, Hero of the American Ghetto. Teal had only to glance behind himself to see what the crowd of brothers and sisters was seeing; at his own command, his publicity people had blown up the *Time* magazine cover to gargantuan proportions.

His face beamed through the Teflon gloss: wide
almond-shaped eyes, caramel skin, chiseled features, rounded, freshly shaved head, perfect teeth.
No one in this room would doubt his accomplishments. No one would walk out of this room without
knowing that it was possible, that one of their own
could rise so high.

"I look out across this room and I see hope," Teal
shouted into the shiny insectoid microphone. "I
look out into your eyes and I see a rising tide! I see
the ocean and I see the sky and I know, Jesus God, I
know it's gonna change! Together we'll make it
change!"

The crowd roared forward, fists and Amens
dangling in the air. Teal rubbed a sleeve across his
forehead and felt the sweat seeping through the
Armani. He laughed inwardly, as happy as he had
ever been. Just yesterday, he had addressed a congressional hearing while wearing a similar charcoal
Armani suit. He had come out of that amphitheater
without shedding a bead of sweat. He had spoken
quietly for forty-five minutes about life, change, the
future—the very same themes of today's lecture—
and he had never once raised his voice, never once
slammed his fists or felt the Amens splashing
against his proud black face.

But this was not Washington, this was South
Central, this was home, this was where it had all
begun. Marcus shifted his eyes back and forth, taking in the church-style auditorium, the carved oak
walls, the stiff, parallel pews, the oval stained-glass
windows, the large metallic fans in either corner.
Just seven years ago this spot had housed a burned-
out Korean supermarket, the very center of the
horrible riots that had torn this community apart.

Today, the MLK Youth Development Center was the most glowing example of a community pulling itself back together.

Marcus crossed his hands against his chest, his eyes fierce with pride. The center had been his gift to South Central. It had been his first act of charity after taking his company public—and he was doubly proud that not one penny for the center had come from the Presidential Task Force assigned to rebuild the riot-stricken area.

"Not long ago," Teal continued, leaning forward over the podium, "I was a kid on these same streets. I had nothing and came from nothing. But I wasn't going to end up a nothing. Now I'm here to give back. I'm here to help you do what I've done."

The Presidential Task Force. Teal's throat filled with bile at the thought. As if the president or any of his white-bread cogs had any right putting their dirty fingers in Teal's backyard. What the hell did they know about South Central? What the hell did they know about struggle, about the incessant strength it took to rise out of hell? What did they know about the barriers that kept South Central down, that had tried to keep Marcus Teal down?

"Life is about climbing walls," Marcus whispered into the microphone. "About breaking through the barriers. You rise by taking chances—and you never let the barriers hold you back."

Again, the room shook. Chances. Chances that had guided Teal to the top of an industry full of boy-wonder billionaires. Chances that had made his Telecon Industries the largest telecommunications company in the history of the world.

Teal paused mid-thought, as his eyes fixed on the back row of the crowded auditorium. Two of

them, far left corner, maybe sixteen, seventeen years
old. Dark, heavy jackets even in this heat, thick
wool caps, shades—gangbangers. Every time Teal
spoke in South Central they showed, maybe just to
see if he was real, maybe because of a grandmother
or an aunt who still cared—or maybe because of a
parole officer with half a heart still ticking away in
his chest. They showed, always in the back row,
always with the shades and the garb and the attitude, slumped down against the wooden pew, lips
curled in distaste.

Marcus stared at them, remembering himself.
The words weren't going to affect them. He was
standing behind the podium in an Armani suit with
manicured fingernails and in front of a massive, air-
brushed *Time* magazine cover—he seemed as foreign to them as Bill Cosby and Colin Powell. He
wasn't going to get to them with his words.

So he shut his mouth and stepped away from
the podium. As the crowd stared, he leapt down off
the stage and started up the center aisle. Every eye
was pinned to him, hands outstretched to touch him
as he came by. He was glad there were cameras in
the room—a crew from CNN, another from
Nightline—because this was going to be one hell of a
PR moment. A Marcus Teal moment.

He walked right up to the last row and faced the
two gangbangers. Their mouths opened in shock,
and they squirmed against the wooden pew.

"Take off the shades," he said, his voice firm but
not unkind.

The kids stared at him, then slowly complied.
Marcus felt a chill ride through his shoulders as he
looked into their eyes. It was a mirror from twenty
years ago. Before he had discovered the local Boy's

Club, before the part-time job in the electronics store, before the scholarship to UCLA, the meteoric rise. *The self-respect.*

He looked into those pitch-black eyes and saw himself, and that made him want to cry. "It isn't going to be fair," he said, quietly, as the cameras whirred around him. "And it sure as hell won't be easy."

He reached into the front pocket of his Armani suit and pulled out a small white card. *Marcus Teal, Telecon Industries, CEO and Founder, Washington, D.C.* And a phone number. A private phone, in a private office. He tossed the card onto the nearest gang-banger's lap. "You want to try, you give me a call. No bullshit."

He turned and walked back toward the stage. He could feel the applause around him, the sheer ecstasy of the crowd. You want to try? *You really want to get out?* Teal remembered the day he was asked that question. The day after his father was shot to death on the front steps of the housing project he had called home. The man who had asked the question had been a distant relative, one of the sponsors of the local Boys' Club, and the owner of the one electronics store in the area. *Do you really want to get out?*

It had taken every ounce of strength for the seven-year-old Teal to answer honestly—the street and desperation already had such a hold on him. But he *had* answered honestly, and things had begun to change. He had gone to work in the electronics store, discovering science and self-respect. Out of that came the scholarship to UCLA. Then the idea for the software company he had run out of his dorm room. And the rest was history, documented in a hundred magazines around the world.

But deep inside, Teal knew that his meteoric rise was only the beginning. The two gangbangers in the back of the auditorium made it as clear as anything—his mission was not yet complete.

There were still seventy-two hours to go.

Teal reached the stage and crossed back to the podium. If the president or his cronies had had any idea what Teal was hoping to accomplish—yesterday's congressional address would have gone in an entirely different direction. But even the president didn't grasp the enormity of the event that was fast approaching. Teal clenched his hands against the podium, his eyes pinned to the now-attentive gangbangers in the last row, a smile growing across his chiseled, model-sharp face.

In seventy-two hours, Marcus Teal was going to become the most important man in the nation. In that same stroke, America would begin to change. The barriers would fall.

All the barriers would fall.

FIVE

just take it easy, Nick."

Kim Harrington, Boston General's top virologist and infectious disease specialist, tried to appear nonchalant as she approached the examining table. She was holding a long hypodermic needle in one gloved hand and a thick cotton swab in the other. Half of her pretty, angular face was hidden behind a white mask.

"We'll take some blood, give you some inoculations, and everything will be okay. There's no reason to panic."

Nick unrolled his sleeve and tapped at the vein that ran up the front of his arm. "Kim, you didn't see the bodies. It was like nothing I've ever—ouch."

He clenched his teeth as the needle went into his arm. Dark blood filled the syringe. He looked away, concentrating on the stark white walls and furniture of the quarantine room. In twelve years at Boston General—two as a paramedic, three as a surgeon, seven more as a resident—he had never been in this room before. The air had a sharp quality to it, years of antiseptic scrubbing, chemical washes, disinfecting microwaves, heat sterilization. Nothing survived in this room for very long.

"What about the cops? Any symptoms yet?"

Kim pulled the needle out of his arm and pressed the cotton swab against his skin. "No, and we don't expect any. We've got them in the quarantine room next door. But from what you've described, this was a fast-acting agent. Nine people don't die in their chairs from something that takes its time."

"That doesn't mean—"

"Of course not," Kim interrupted, crossing to a nearby equipment shelf. She was a small woman, mousy, her body completely shrouded by her white doctor's coat. With the gloves and mask, she looked like some sort of futuristic acolyte, at home in this antiseptic sanctuary. "As you know, if we are talking about a virus, there could be a dormant form, mutations—with viruses, anything could happen. But there's no evidence that this was viral. It could have been some sort of chemical contamination, or perhaps bacteriological. We'll do a full run of tests, we'll play it as safe as we know how—and in the end, everything will be fine. You'll see."

Nick knew that she was right. But the tension inside him didn't ease. He could still see the bone-white faces, the bulging eyes. The thought that the disease could be lurking in him, waiting to twist him inside out—he looked down and noticed that his hands had started to shake. A ticking time bomb,

Jennifer had told him, that's what it feels like. *Inside my veins.*

"Nick," Kim interrupted, leaning close to him, her voice soft. "Come on. You're tired, your defenses are down. The odds are, this was a random, unusual contamination. Lethal, instantaneous—but it's doubtful that anything that could kill that quickly would still be around to cause more harm. You didn't touch any of the bodies, you didn't even get close enough to breath anything in."

Nick listened to her, unconsciously rubbing at the cut on his right arm. It was true, he was tired and he had a pessimistic streak. There were extremely few lethal airborne viruses. And any sort of bacteria that killed its hosts so quickly couldn't survive long. The connection between this disease and the horror that had taken Jennifer from him was in his head—not in the facts. Finally, he managed a half-smile.

"I'm sure you're right, Kim. Still, I want to take part in the autopsies. And I want to see a report the minute the microbiological team returns from the scene."

Kim sighed, shaking her head. "I'm not sure that's going to be possible. As of an hour ago, Boston General isn't in control of the investigation. The CDC took over as soon as we faxed your description of the scene to their offices in Atlanta."

Nick raised his eyebrows. The CDC was the Centers for Disease Control, a national watchdog organization that investigated disease outbreaks and directed the national struggle against various epidemics. Every possible new disease had to be reported to the CDC, but, usually, it took a few days before they jumped into an investigation—unless the disease was proven to be infectious, and spreading. The nine dead lawyers were a frightening mystery—but to Nick it seemed too early for the CDC to get involved.

"Wonderful," he mumbled. "As if I didn't have enough to worry about. Now I'm going to have those wonks from Atlanta sticking needles into me and telling me Ebola war stories."

Kim laughed. But there was a hint of concern at the corners of her eyes. She cocked her head to the side.

"Nick, when was the last time you got some sleep? I hear you've been doing double shifts and weekends."

Nick's smile drifted away. He knew that Kim was a friend, and that she was concerned. Lately, he had been putting in some extra shifts, perhaps working harder than he ought to. He was using his work to fill the voids in his life. It had been the same after Jennifer's death; he had pitched himself into the operating theaters with legendary fervor. Now that surgery had been taken away from him, he had found something new to fill the vacuum.

But ambulance shifts were relatively short compared to surgery. Since he did not have a social life to speak of—even five years after, how could he possibly date?—he often found himself alone in his apartment. That's when the memories usually hit him. Not of Jennifer—she had faded into something less vivid, a past he could not go back to, even in thought. The memories that bit at him had to do with his more recent loss.

He hated the memories. The accident was something he couldn't change. He was building a new life, now, with new thrills, new challenges. If putting in a few extra hours helped him forget about the past, there was nothing wrong with that. And he certainly didn't like the idea that Kim was checking up on him. There was little he disliked more than pity. Perhaps that was why he found it so easy to be friends with Charlie Pace. Charlie never got that look in his eyes, that edge of sympathy. Nick shifted against the examining table.

"Virologist by day, private detective by night."

Kim touched his shoulder with a gloved hand. "I'm serious. If you need to talk about something—"

"From spy to therapist. And you know how well I respond to therapy."

"I just want to help you, Nick."

"You can help me by just butting out. I'm handling it, damn it."

The room went silent, and Nick felt a cold guilt splash across his cheeks. His tone had been rough, and he hadn't meant to come off so strong. Jennifer and Kim had been friends; as Jennifer's condition had deteriorated, Kim had been there by her bedside, holding Nick's hand. Through the pancreatitis, the cryptosporidiosis, finally the fatal pneumonia— Kim had helped Nick stand by and watch his wife die. It had been hell for both of them; Jennifer had gone from a beautiful, athletic woman of a hundred and thirty pounds to barely a skeleton, less than eighty pounds at the end. She had lost control of her bladder, her bowels, she had been racked by fevers, vomiting, a dozen infections that had filled her minutes with constant pain. Kim had watched the effects of the horrible syndrome with him—but she *hadn't* lived through the feelings in his head. The anger, frustration, impotence, fear—and guilt. Guilt, because at the end, he wanted her to die, he practically begged her to just let go and die. He couldn't watch another minute of her pain.

So now he worked too hard and didn't get enough sleep. The accident that had taken his career away was nothing compared to what had happened to Jennifer—but he had every right to act out.

"Kim, I know what you're trying to do. But the last thing I need right now is pity. I can manage this on my own."

"Sometimes you can be such a shit," Kim responded, turning away.

"Look, Kim, I didn't mean—"

He was interrupted by the clanking of the quarantine room airlock. The heavy door swung inward, and in stepped a tall, lanky brunette in a stiff, form-fitting gray suit, buttoned all the way to the throat. The woman had dark, wavy hair swept back in a tight ponytail that fell between her shoulder blades, and there was a clipboard under her right arm. Her face was model-sharp and beautiful, with high cheekbones, minimal makeup, and a triangular, determined chin. But the first thing Nick noticed was her eyes: gray, intelligent—and brimming with lightly reined anger. The second thing Nick noticed was that she wasn't wearing a mask or gloves.

"Excuse me," Kim Harrington said angrily, stepping forward. "This is a quarantine room—"

"It's okay, Dr. Harrington. I'm Samantha Craig. From the CDC." She opened up her clipboard and took out a plastic ID card. Kim ignored the card, her anger rising behind her mask.

"I don't care who you are. This is a hot room."

Samantha Craig shook her head. She looked

directly at Kim with those dangerous gray eyes. "Not anymore."

Kim's mouth dropped open, but Samantha ignored her. She stepped forward, lifting the clipboard. When she got within a few feet of Nick, she paused.

"Dr. Barnes," she said, reading his name. "You're free to go. There's no need for further tests, or for continuing quarantine. I've already dismissed the three police officers."

Nick raised his eyebrows. She had "dismissed" the police officers? Who the hell was this woman? A wonk from Atlanta? It had been less than two hours since he had discovered the bodies in the law firm. Already the CDC was ending the quarantine?

"What the hell are you talking about?"

"Our team at the site has completed an extensive preliminary analysis," the woman continued, as if she hadn't heard Nick. "We've determined that there's no risk to you or to the police officers. The 'agent' which resulted in the nine deaths is no longer infectious, and you're in absolutely no danger. This matter is now under our jurisdiction, and we'll continue our investigation. When we know more, you'll be contacted."

With that, she turned on her heels and started toward the door. Nick couldn't believe what he had just heard. The CDC had completed its preliminary analysis in less than two hours? And that included mobilizing a team of field scientists and running chemical tests and microbiological scans—this was ridiculous! A preliminary analysis should have taken days, perhaps weeks. And still it would be difficult to conclude that the "agent" was no longer infectious. It was impossible for the CDC to know so quickly.

Unless this wasn't the first time the CDC had seen this disease. If they knew what they were looking for . . .

"Hold on a second," Nick interrupted as the CDC woman reached the door. "This isn't an isolated outbreak, is it?"

The woman stopped, but didn't turn around. Her voice remained official, controlled.

"I'm sorry, Dr. Barnes. This is a CDC investigation. I'm not at liberty to discuss the details."

Nick felt his cheeks flushing red. "Bullshit, Ms. Craig. I was at the scene. I saw the bodies. If this isn't the only outbreak, I think I have a right to know."

Samantha turned to look at him. He thought he saw her lip twitch.

"For the record, it's Dr. Craig. And I'm sorry, but there's nothing more I can tell you at this point. I suggest you go home and get some sleep."

She pulled open the door and breezed through. Nick stared at the spot where she had been standing, his anger growing. It was true, the CDC didn't have to let him in on the details of its investigation. But common courtesy would have dictated that she answer a few questions. She was probably worried about starting some sort of a panic—but he was a doctor, she should have been able to trust him. This simply wasn't right. Who the hell did she think she was, anyway? Some damn Ph.D. from Atlanta, waving her authority around.

He looked at Kim. She was across the room, fussing over his blood sample. Her mask was off, but she was still wearing her gloves. Obviously, she was accepting what the CDC woman had said—to a degree. But Nick wasn't going to give in so easily.

"Can you believe that?" he asked, loudly. "Have you ever heard anything so ridiculous? Since when does the CDC operate like the fucking CIA?"

Kim shrugged, not turning around. Obviously, she was still upset about their earlier exchange. He exhaled, frustrated. He didn't want to get back into that argument, not now. Two hours ago he had stumbled into a room full of dead bodies. Was he just supposed to forget what he had seen? He had spent a year of his life studying viruses, learning to hate them like only an insider could. A virus had ravaged Jennifer, tortured her to death. If there was a chance—even a tiny one—that he was infected by the thing that had killed the nine lawyers, he was going to get involved.

And besides, he didn't like being told what to do. Go home, get some sleep? The woman with the gray eyes might want him to pretend that nothing had happened—but he had no intention of taking her "advice."

He wasn't going to sit around and let the CDC have all the fun.

SIX

five minutes later, Samantha Craig exited through the front entrance of Boston General and slid into the backseat of a black stretch limousine. An unsmiling man in a gray suit shut the door behind her and spoke softly into a microphone embedded in the collar of his tailored jacket. Immediately, the limousine pulled away from the curb and entered the mid-morning traffic.

Samantha let herself sink into a plush leather seat. Her body ached, and her throat felt dry and scratchy. Her reflection glanced at her from the dark glass that separated her from the driver, but she turned away, afraid of what she might see. She could almost feel the anxious wrinkles rippling across her skin. Certainly, she no longer felt like a twenty-nine-year-old kid, a prodigy in charge of her first real assignment. The past two weeks had been a nightmare, and it looked as though things were just going to get worse.

Nick Barnes was going to be a problem. Samantha shut her eyes and tried to lose the thought in the quiet rumble of the tires against pavement. But she couldn't shake the arrogant man out of her head. Those fierce blue eyes, that curly mop of dark hair, those angry lips. The resemblance was uncanny; not solely his boyishly handsome appearance, but his attitude, his palpable impudence. He *was* Andrew—fifteen years later, with a few wrinkles and ten extra pounds of shoulder.

She opened her eyes and worked to undo the knot holding her hair in place. Then she shook her head, letting her hair fall in furious curls to her shoulders. If the similarities ran deeper than appearance and outward attitude, she knew what she could expect from Dr. Barnes. He wouldn't accept her as an authority figure, and he certainly wasn't going to just disappear.

A high-pitched chime echoed through the limousine, and she quickly reached into the front pocket of her Donna Karan business suit. Her Nokia cellular phone weighed barely four ounces and was fitted with the latest in security technology. She flipped it open and pressed the receiver against her ear.

"Secure line, priority one. Are you alone?"

She recognized the voice immediately. Sydney Foster, her immediate superior. Six feet tall, imposing, with thin gray hair and a scar from a Korean shell fragment perched a few inches above his right eye. He had a Ph.D. from Yale and a medical degree from Cornell.

"Priority one," she responded. "Go ahead."

As was his way, Foster cut right to the point.

"We've been running models all morning—and it doesn't look good. Is there any progress on your end?"

"I'm chasing a few promising leads," Samantha lied, her stomach churning. "But nothing I'm ready to report."

"We've *got* to see results. If we don't come through with something soon—well, I don't have to tell you what kind of a catastrophe we're talking about."

Samantha raised her eyebrows. She could tell from Foster's voice that something was really wrong. "What is it? Has something happened?"

There was a pause. When Foster's voice returned, it was barely more than a whisper. "Let's just say this is no longer an internal matter. There is now enormous concern at the highest levels. I repeat, the highest levels."

Samantha closed her eyes.

"I understand."

"I hope you do. I've seen a lot of shit come and go over the past few years—but this is beyond anything I could have imagined. People are scared. And I'm talking about people who don't get scared."

Samantha swallowed, turned off the phone, and shoved it back into her suit pocket. Her face was hot, her fingers shaking. She undid the top button of her suit, letting cool air touch her long, smooth neck. *The highest levels.* She knew exactly what that meant. She couldn't risk any setbacks.

She leaned forward and pressed a button on the divider in front of her. A three-foot section of the wall slid upward, revealing a curved Plexiglas computer screen. There was a track ball to one side of the screen next to a set of numbered plastic keys.

Samantha put her palm against the track ball and waited the necessary few seconds for the infrared scanner to verify her identity.

The screen flashed once, and suddenly the interior of the limousine was bathed in blue. Samantha grimaced, blinking rapidly to clear her vision. Her contacts were dry, and the blue light only made the glare worse. She wished she had remembered to pack saline solution when she had left Washington. But she had barely had time for a shower before her escort had arrived to whisk her to the waiting Lear jet. She would have to make do with dry eyes.

A numbered index flashed across the screen and she maneuvered the track ball, scrolling through options and commands. Above the screen, attached to the ceiling of the limousine, a small black box blinked as the cursor touched each option. Her Telecon Industries Set-Top Box was enormously more complicated than the common version that was now attached to 90 percent of the nation's televisions and computers, but effectively the technology was the same. *Interactivity.* She smirked, wondering if the word had made it into the dictionaries yet. Or were the boys at *Webster's* waiting seventy-two hours, with the rest of the nation, for the information highway to officially come into existence.

She pressed a button located directly above the track ball. A small fiber optic antenna rose a few inches above the trunk of the limousine. The antenna was curved, with a tiny mirrored dish attached halfway up its trunk. The dish began to spin slowly around the antenna, a high-tech miniature carousel. Samantha waited for the computer to verify a secure link.

"SATLINK 227 ESTABLISHED. PRIORITY AA7."

Samantha nodded to herself and went back to work with the track ball. She was now linked to the massive computer network in Washington; the information banks of a half-dozen federal agencies were at her fingertips. On a small scale, this was a working preview of the "Big Turn On" they were constantly talking about on the news—the much heralded birth of the information highway. In seventy-two hours, the entire nation would have access to a much vaster cyberworld—God only knew what was going to be possible with such awesome technology at everybody's fingertips.

Samantha shrugged, speeding through untitled directories and alphabetical lists. Finally, she found what she was looking for. She punched in a series of letters and waited for the satellite link to spit out the information she needed.

First came the pictures. "Good-looking bastard," she admitted, as she scrolled through the time-coded images. Nicholas Barnes as a high school student, holding a gold-plated football trophy, standing next to his father, a former star himself. Nicholas Barnes in a Boston College baseball uniform. Nicholas Barnes winning an academic award his senior year, wearing his baseball jacket and backwards hat. Nicholas Barnes at Harvard Medical School: more awards, more smiling pictures, more backwards hats.

Then the pictures were replaced by newspaper articles and corroborating documents from more than a hundred disparate sources. Samantha rolled her eyes as she read about the high school sensation, the .350 switch-hitter who could also play football, the kid all the college scouts wanted—and were willing to pay for. Full scholarship to BC, captain of the baseball team by his sophomore year. Barnes was a true athletic phenomenon.

But the Barnes story did not end there. Samantha could not help but be impressed as she read about his decision to attend medical school instead of heading to the pros. He'd breezed through Harvard Medical School, graduating near the top of his class. Then an internship and a residency in surgery, and soon he was in the papers again—this time, for his skill in the operating room. Over the next three years, he rose to prominence in the Boston medical scene, saving more lives than any other surgeon in town.

A fairy tale—if it had ended there. Samantha paused as an article flashed across the screen, wiping away the list of awards and accomplishments. The headline caught her eye:

Widowed Hero Recovering from Surgery,
Saved Life, May Lose Hand

She paused at the first word, surprised that this was the first mention of his widowed status. Then she continued past the headline, compassion rising as she read the story: A little over two years ago, Nicholas Barnes had saved a woman from a car wreck and had seriously injured himself in the process. Although surgeons had managed to reattach the torn muscles in his wrist, he would never be able to use his right hand in surgery again.

At this point, Samantha switched from library archives to FBI files, getting a full picture of the injured hero. First, she went back to three years before the accident, to Barnes's last year as a resident. She found his scrawled signature on the death certificate of Jennifer Barnes, his wife of four years. The cause of death was listed as pneumocystis carinii pneumonia.

Samantha pressed her lips together as she read the words; she was well aware that PCP was the most common cause of death of AIDS victims. Perhaps that explained why there was no mention of his wife's death in the press clippings—there was still a fair amount of stigma attached to AIDS then, and Barnes might have wanted to keep his wife's disease out of the papers. Samantha filed the information in the back of her mind, and pushed ahead three years, to the next tragedy in Barnes's life.

According to the FBI records, after the accident Barnes took a three-month leave from the hospital. Two arrests for public drunkenness, then a DWI two days later. It looked like the combination of his wife's death and the accident that took his career away had pushed him over the edge.

His problems hadn't ended there. Letters began to drift into the state medical board from Boston General's administrator, Rudolph Pierce, suggesting possible action against the faltering doctor. The medical board had rejected the administrator's requests, but it was obvious that Barnes's hero status could protect him only so far.

But somehow, Barnes had managed to pull himself together. He had begun riding with a Boston General ambulance team. According to hospital records, he had signed on to as many shifts as possible, plunging full force into dangerous, high adrenaline work. It was obvious he was a strong-willed man. His perfect life had been taken away from him, and still he had adjusted—after a brief flirtation with disaster. Samantha ran her hands through her hair, again struck by the similarities with Andrew.

When the doctors had told Andrew at fifteen that he'd spend the rest of his life on crutches, he had just about laughed in their faces; two years later, he was playing football again as if nothing had happened, as if spinal injuries were something you expected and ignored. And at eighteen, when they told him he was a long shot to make it as a Navy pilot, he had doubled his resolve; nothing was going to keep him from landing A6s on aircraft carriers.

She flicked the computer screen off and leaned back in her seat, rubbing her palms into her eyes. The limousine was still drifting through the city traffic, a moving command center with a staff of one. Samantha tapped her finger against her chin, then retrieved her cellular phone and dialed from memory. A rough voice answered on the first ring.

"Marco here."

"Marco, please organize a twenty-four hour tail on Dr. Barnes. Low profile, but make sure he doesn't wriggle through our fingers."

She slipped the telephone back into her suit. It still felt so new to her: speaking orders into a cellular phone, running computerized background checks while resting in the back of a bullet-proof limousine, commandeering a Lear jet at barely a moment's notice. A few years ago, she had been just another laboratory scientist, huddled behind beakers and test tubes. She was proud of the change she had enacted in her life, but immediately, her mood fell as she thought of the horror story unfolding around her. And now she had something new to worry about. A blue-eyed cowboy with dark curls and an attitude.

The spitting image of her brother, damn him. She winced, angry at her own lack of control, as she felt a fresh tear touch her upper lip.

SEVEN

*C*ome on, Britt. A little sweat never hurt anyone. Just a few more feet . . .

Britt Taylor gasped with near ecstasy as she broke through the woods, her Reeboks throwing up a fine spray of dust and gravel. The cabin was barely a hundred yards ahead, two beautiful stories of lumber and brick with wide picture windows and a quaint, shingled roof. Britt's baby blue Jeep Cherokee was parked next to the aluminum screened side door, two tires resting on the lawn. She had driven the thirty miles west from Burlington three days ago, and since then it had been just she, the Jeep, and the cabin. The perfect Vermont getaway, and no one had needed to get away more than Britt Taylor.

She took the last few yards at a jog and paused by the screened door, bending at the waist. She was breathing heavily, and beads of sweat fell like rain-drops around her shoes. Her long blond hair was pulled back into a tight ponytail, and her Walkman earphones hung around her neck. The batteries had run out two miles ago, but she had hardly noticed. Her mind had been too busy with the colors in the trees, the sheer splendor of the trail.

She stretched her long hamstrings one at a time, then raised her arms high above her head. Her sweatshirt rose up with the motion, and a brisk wind tickled her flat stomach, sending a shiver through her breasts. The sensation was somehow pleasant; lately, her nerves felt more attuned, and she could only assume it was another sign of recovery.

She threw open the screen door and ambled inside, a smile breaking out across her face. Today, she had gone seven miles. She was sweating hard, her legs ached—but inside, she felt great. For the first time in many years, she was truly clean. She hadn't had a drop of alcohol in nearly eight months.

She passed through a short hallway and into the kitchen, a brightly lit rectangle with finished wood cabinets and a long, Lucite counter. A row of brass and copper pots hung from hooks embedded in the ceiling, and the walls were covered with pictures torn from the latest issues of *Food & Wine* and *Gourmet*. Matthew and Jeannette were both accomplished chefs; sadly, Britt shared none of her brother's gastronomic genes, and in three days she hadn't even touched the cast-iron stove that lurked behind the counter. Maybe before she left for the city she'd try to cook something simple. There was a frozen chicken in the freezer with a recipe stapled to its wrapper, a present Matthew had left behind before he and his wife headed to the airport.

Britt sighed, picturing the two of them in Paris, wandering the cobbled streets or sharing coffee in an outdoor café. Matthew had such a perfect life; he probably never understood what had made his sister into such a screwup. Two husbands by the age of thirty, a half-dozen jobs that never amounted to anything—and of course, the alcohol. Britt had really made a mess of things.

But now she was finally on the right track. Eight months sober, back in the dating pool, in good health, and earning a decent living. She had gotten her real estate license a month ago, and had just closed on her first house, making enough to pay for her new best friend, the Jeep.

When Matthew had first offered to lend her the Vermont cabin for the week, she had been reluctant to accept; part of the recovery process was learning how to deal with real life—without running away. But after the closing, with a little money in her pocket, she had succumbed to Matthew's generosity. Despite what her AA group might say, a week alone in the woods sounded like heaven: no neighbors, no phone calls, nobody to bother her for seven full days.

She crossed to the huge refrigerator and tore open the door. Still pretty full; she wouldn't have to make a trip to the county store for another few days. She grabbed a jar of pickles off the front shelf and peered through the glass, making sure there were a few of the little suckers left. Then she closed the refrigerator and headed out of the kitchen.

The den was rustic to a point, but not to a fault. Exposed wooden beams, Indian weave throw rugs, a pair of antique rocking chairs, and a small, Crate & Barrel couch in front of a thirty-inch TV. Britt plopped onto the couch, the pickle jar braced between her legs, and searched for the remote. It was on the floor beneath the brass legs of a ridiculously ugly standing lamp—obviously a wedding gift, because Matthew and Jeannette had excellent taste.

She flicked a button on the remote and the television twinkled to life. Red numbers flashed across the digital display on the small black box sitting on top of the set, and Britt tried to remember the correct setting. The Set-Top Box was going to take some getting used to, that was for sure. On the surface, it looked like a cable box, but with rounded corners and a polished face. She had the same Set-Top Box attached to her TV in her apartment in Burlington, but hers wouldn't be working for another couple of days. Matthew and Jeannette had been lucky enough to be part of the Telecon test run, along with a few thousand other households across the nation.

The Information Highway. Britt pulled a pickle out of the jar and stuck it in her mouth. If you asked her, it was just a lot of bullshit. She had never been a big fan of the Internet, and she wasn't quite sure how the new fiber optic network was going to be different. So it included television sets, big deal. Would people really want to sit around inside, playing with remote controls, while the leaves were changing?

Then again, she did like the idea of being able to watch whatever she wanted, when she wanted to. It was eight o'clock Monday morning, and she was going to be able to catch this week's "Seinfeld" before breakfast. Forget interactivity, forget on-line banking or research or even real estate—now *this* was progress!

She laughed, hitting a button on the remote. The screen shivered, changing from blue to white. A green time code appeared in the upper right corner, and she plugged in numbers. A few more seconds and her show would come on. She settled back against the couch, her fingers searching the jar for another pickle—

"Ouch."

Her own voice startled her and she froze, her fingers still in the jar, her other hand clutching the remote. The pain had been sharp and sudden, rising right up between her breasts. Indigestion, maybe? She bit down on her lower lip, lifting her fingers out of the pickle jar. No more of the little suckers before breakfast . . .

Suddenly, her lungs clamped shut and a fiery pain erupted beneath her rib cage. The pickle jar slipped out from between her legs and shattered against the floor. Her eyes went wide and her shoulders lifted a few inches off the couch, her spine twisting under her skin. Her mouth came open but nothing came out. It was like a fist closing shut on her esophagus, choking her as broken glass tore through her insides.

It wasn't fair! She had stopped drinking; she was changing her life; she was finally going to be happy! But the pain was relentless, the truth undeniable. Something horrible was happening to her. She was dying. Her body arched back against the couch; her arms rising as her muscles stiffened. She caught sight of her left hand, still clutching the remote, out of the corner of her eyes. Her brain started to scream.

The skin on the back of her hand had turned ivory white, the color of bone. Her head jerked back with sudden force, and there was a crackling sound as the top of her spine shattered. The remote control slipped out of her lifeless fingers and clattered to the floor.

EIGHT

nick came awake suddenly and sat straight up on the tiny metal cot, eyes wide, wondering where the hell he was. Then the details of the gray intern room knocked some sense back into him; after leaving quarantine, he had stopped in the empty room to catch his breath. Even so many years after his brutal internship, the little metal cot had been too enticing to ignore.

He slowly raised himself from the cot and rubbed his eyes. Christ, maybe he *had* been pushing himself too hard. He felt like he was coming out of a deep coma. He glanced at his watch and quickly did the math: three hours gone, ten more to blow before his next ambulance shift. More than enough time for some investigative medicine.

A few minutes later he was showered and

dressed, choosing his clothes from his hospital locker in the blind fashion of a man who dressed quickly and for comfort: faded jeans, tan work boots, an old green sweater, and a leather aviator's jacket. His car was parked in the M.D. lot behind the children's wing, and he used the ten-minute walk around the outside of the hospital to banish the last vestiges of grogginess.

He paused when he reached his BMW, wincing at the scuffs and scratches that marred its sheer black body. He had bought the car at the end of his first year as a surgeon. He and Jennifer had struggled on two residents' salaries for so many years; then she died, and suddenly he had had money, more than an overworked widower could possibly spend. He had thought, foolishly, that the BMW could take some of the sting away. He had been wrong.

He slid inside and started the engine. The dull purr filled his ears, and he felt a sudden familiar tinge, a memory trying to grow. He quickly slammed the car into reverse and whipped out of the M.D. lot, narrowly avoiding a pair of residents in dark blue scrubs.

But the memory was persistent, urged on by the purr of his BMW, the squeal of the tires against pavement. He had been driving fast that night, too, his BMW cutting through sheets of gray rain like a pitch-black guided missile. Lane to lane, gliding, controlled precision. Maybe he had been thinking about Jennifer; the pain had still been fresh, barely three years old. Maybe it was the thought of her that had made him turn to look.

The other car had been upside down in a ditch, its tires spinning helplessly, black, oily smoke rising above licks of orange flame. Nick had skidded to a stop, hitting 911 on his cellular phone while searching his front seat for his doctor's bag. Then he had leapt out into the rain.

Cold, wet, the wind whipping at his face, he had charged toward the wrecked car, his thighs pumping, his teeth clenched against the frozen rain. He had headed straight for the driver's side, dropping to his knees in the dirt.

His heart had jumped when he saw her. Hanging upside down in her seat, still caught in her seat belt, her hands hanging straight toward the ceiling, her long black hair matted with blood. The side window had been shattered, and there were shards of glass everywhere, glistening in the orange light of the rising flames.

"Holy shit," Nick had mumbled, staring. The smell of smoke had been thick in his nostrils, and he could see the fire spreading in his peripheral vision. Any second, the entire car was going to erupt; he had realized immediately that he was all that stood between the unconscious woman and death.

Jennifer, beautiful, dying Jennifer. He had sat by her bedside and watched her struggle for each breath, had watched the infections ravage her, the dementia eat her alive. Not again, damn it, never again. It had driven him to be the best surgeon he could be, and it would drive him to save this woman no matter what the cost.

Nick's entire body had come alive, heated by an internal force. He had stuck his head and hands gingerly through the shattered side window, his trained eyes shifting over the woman's body. There was a deep gash above her eyes, and one of her arms was twisted at an unnatural angle, but the main threat to her life was the car itself. Any second, the flames would find the gas tank.

Nick had backed out of the window and grasped the door handle with both hands. The metal had been searingly hot, but he had ignored the pain, pulling with all his strength. His muscles had rippled as he fought against the car; finally, there was a loud tearing and the door came open. He leapt forward, his hands searching for the seat belt, oblivious to the rising heat and the thick clouds of dark smoke that billowed in from every direction.

The metal buckle had come apart suddenly, and the woman had dropped downward, slamming him back against the roof of the overturned car. He had gasped, straining against her weight as he worked his right arm around her chest, a fireman's carry. Then he had inched backward toward the open door.

He had heard sirens in the distance, but his world had become tiny, a man and a woman and a burning car, a race against fire and time. He cursed as her legs caught under the twisted steering wheel, and he yanked with all his might, aware that he was damaging her, perhaps ripping skin and bruising bone. Her legs came free and again he was pulling her through the smoke, inch by inch. Suddenly his free hand had touched wet pavement and he was halfway outside, gasping for air, his other arm still tight across her chest.

With an immense burst of strength he had pulled himself another foot backward, dragging her fully out of the car. He had kneeled on the pavement, sliding his arms under her prone body. Using his thighs and knees, he had lifted her into the air and stumbled forward. He had done it! He had saved her.

The explosion had been sudden and immense, a wall of heat and sound. Nick had crashed forward, covering the woman's body with his own. As he hit the ground he had felt a searing pain ricochet up and down his right arm. He had cried out, yanking his arm up in front of his face—and his eyes had gone instantly wide. A thin, metal rod was embedded right through the center of his wrist. Warm blood fountained out of the wound and his head spun, his mind screaming out in pain.

He heard shouts and voices and running feet. Hands had touched his shoulders and whispers had kissed his ears, words that he had recognized as a dark film enveloped him: *"Christ, the car antenna. Right through his wrist."* Then came the warmth of sleep, of unconsciousness. Perhaps he had dreamed of Jennifer. Perhaps he had dreamed of nothing at all.

Later, in the hospital, he had been told about the battle on the scene, about the incredible efforts of the pair of paramedics who had worked on the woman for twenty minutes, saving her life. She was going to make it—and Nick Barnes was a true hero. But there had been a steep price.

Nick shook his head, hard, trying to ignore the ache in his right wrist, struggling to concentrate on the road ahead. It was just a memory, he told himself. It had happened a long time ago. And despite what he had lost, he knew inside that he had done the right thing.

The traffic on Storrow Drive was slacking off, another morning rush hour disappearing into history. He slammed the steering wheel to the right, taking an off ramp at close to sixty-five miles per hour. The rear tires left the pavement for what seemed like a full second, then came crashing down.

The glass buildings of the financial district loomed up on either side, and he turned onto State Street, edging the speedometer down to fit into the constant stream of traffic. The cops had done a good job of cleaning up the intersection, and there was little hint of the earlier snarl. Nick slowed to a crawl, and a new tension filled him, his nerves snapping to life. Finally the memory was gone, chased away by a much more recent horror: nine corpses in high leather chairs.

He pulled the BMW up against the curb and put it in park. Although there were no empty spots—in Boston, the odds of finding an empty parking spot were roughly the same as getting hit by a meteor—he felt safe leaving the car in a yellow loading zone. He had M.D. plates and a Boston General sticker identifying him as an emergency paramedic.

He stepped out onto the sidewalk, pulling his leather jacket tight over his chest. It was cold and windy, and the air felt crisp against his skin. He started forward, determined; the CDC might have control of the nine bodies, but that didn't mean there weren't clues to be found.

There were two police barricades on the sidewalk in front of the doorway to the black-glass building, connected by a three-foot-high line of bright yellow tape. Nick approached the barricades slowly, searching the ground for anything he might have missed earlier. The flecks of broken glass had been cleaned up, and there was a thin smell of disinfectant in the air. The CDC people had been thorough, spraying the outside as well as the inside, but that did not make Nick feel any more comfortable.

Many viruses and bacteria could survive even the most sophisticated chemical disinfectants. Unless the CDC knew exactly what it was dealing with, even a thorough spraying was a shot in the dark.

He reached the police barricade and stepped over the yellow tape, fighting a sudden apprehension. He was a doctor and this was the scene of a medical tragedy; he had every right to be here.

"Doc Barnes, back again?"

The voice was unmistakable. Officer Beatty slid out of his cruiser, followed by a heavyset man in an expensive blue suit. The cruiser was parked along the side of the building, partially hidden by shadows. Beatty was smiling, but there was something strange in his eyes. Nick nodded, still moving toward the front door.

"Hey, Jack. I'd just like to check a few things out, if it's okay with you."

Beatty opened his mouth to respond, but suddenly the man in the blue suit stepped in front of him, pulling a leather wallet out of his pocket. The wallet flipped open and Nick saw a glint of polished silver.

"Marco Douglas," the man said in a gruff voice. "Federal marshal attached to the CDC. May I ask who authorized your visit to this site?"

Nick stared at the man. A federal marshal? Since when did the CDC post federal guards at its sites?

"I'm a doctor at Boston General. I was the first emergency worker at the scene, and I'd like to make a follow-up survey."

"I'm sorry," the man interrupted, still moving toward him. "That's going to be impossible. This is a closed investigation."

He took the last few steps at a quick swagger

and put a thick hand on Nick's shoulder. Nick felt red anger swirling behind his cheeks. He quickly looked the man over: five ten, maybe two hundred pounds. A scar under his left eye and a short military crewcut.

"Jack?" Nick said, still glaring at the stocky marshal. "You taking orders from this joker?"

"'Fraid so, Doc. Got it direct from the captain. These guys are in charge."

"Guys?" Nick turned his head just as he heard the voices. There were four more men in dark suits moving toward him. They were ten yards down the sidewalk, heading away from a pair of parked Pontiac sedans. They must have been sitting there, waiting for signs of trouble—or perhaps waiting for him? Nick felt fear mingling with his anger. What the hell was going on?

He turned back toward the marshal. The man was still holding him by the shoulder—as if keeping him from running for the brass door. Nick felt his lips twitch upward at the corners. He wondered what was going on behind that door. What was so important that they needed a team of federal marshals to keep him from finding out?

He flexed his fingers, feeling the muscles in his arms tighten up. He had a good few seconds before the four reinforcements reached him. He lowered his eyes, studying the man in front of him. He could hear his dad's voice in the background, Coach Barnes standing on the front porch with a bottle of Jack Daniel's in his left hand and a football under his arm: "You want that end zone, no way can he stop you. *Action* beats *reaction*. Always. You got that?" From sixth grade through the end of high school, Nick had run drills in the front yard, sometimes when it was so hot the sweat soaked through his sneakers. Action beats reaction. The coach had known what he was talking about. A college star at Iowa State, he would have gone pro if not for his knees.

Nick had no problem with *his* knees. He rubbed the back of his hand against his lips, hiding a grin. The CDC was a scientific watchdog. They couldn't arrest him for ignoring their precious authority. Besides, this was just the sort of thing that pissed him off: bureaucrats who thought they could control everyone around them, bastards like Rudolph Pierce and that woman, Samantha Craig, pushing him around.

"Okay, whatever," he feinted, still grinning, raising his hands in the air. "No need for the goon squad."

He took a small step back. The marshal lowered his hand, a smirk on his lips. Suddenly, Nick spun right and charged forward. The marshal opened his mouth, shocked, and tried to leap in front of him. He was fast for his size, faster than Nick expected, but he was reacting, and like the coach said, a reaction was never quick enough. Nick lowered his right shoulder and caught the marshal with a glancing blow, sending him sprawling to the side. Thighs pumping, head tucked low, he continued forward at full pace. He could hear the four suited men behind him, but he had a good head start. He hit the brass door and burst through.

His feet skidded against polished marble, and suddenly his eyes went wide. Before he could do anything to stop himself, he slammed headlong into a group of men in camouflage uniforms. Mean-looking assault rifles clattered to the floor, and sud-

denly the room was filled with shouting. Nick felt
hands come at him from every angle, and he struggled to protect his face.

He was dragged to his feet, tight arms around
him from behind. A half-dozen assault rifles were
pointed at his chest, and he felt the breath run out of
him. He couldn't believe what he was seeing.

The room was full of people. At least thirty, half
of them in military uniforms. The other half were
obviously scientists, in protective gear ranging from
white body sheaths to full-scale Racal space suits,
specifically designed for viral emergencies. There
was a makeshift airlock where the revolving inner
door used to be, and the reception desk was gone,
replaced by a portable laboratory.

Nick felt hands brushing up and down his body
from behind. Then a nervous voice: "He's clean."

A second later his arms were pulled behind his
back, and he felt cold metal handcuffs click shut
around his wrists. Still, the assault rifles remained
trained toward his chest. The men holding the guns
looked young, almost like teenagers. He could see
the fear in their eyes.

Suddenly, the camouflaged soldiers took a step
back, clearing a path. A space-suited figure stepped
forward. The suit was bright orange and made out of
thick plastic, with a shielded Plexiglas helmet. The
suited figure hit a button on the side of the suit, and
the helmet clicked upward. Nick's eyes widened as
he saw angry gray eyes.

"What the hell is this man doing here?" Samantha demanded, avoiding his stare. There was a
slight commotion from somewhere behind him, and
the federal marshal from outside stepped forward.
He had a sheepish look on his face.

"I'm sorry, sir. He, ah, got away from us outside. We tailed him from the hospital and were going to detain him, but—"

"Enough. Damn it, Dr. Barnes."

She turned back to Nick, and he saw conflicting emotions in her eyes. Part of her was angry, but there was something else there, an edge of sympathy. Nick was hypersensitive to the emotion, had seen it so much in the past few years that he could read it in the slightest twitch.

"What am I going to do with you?" Samantha asked, exasperated.

Suddenly, Nick's fear evaporated. He didn't care that there were men pointing guns at him. He didn't care that he had stepped into something he didn't understand, or that there were scientists in Racal space suits camped out in the center of a law firm in downtown Boston. How dare this woman feel sorry for him?

"First," Nick hissed through his teeth, "you're going to get these damn handcuffs off of me. Then you're going to tell me what the hell is going on."

Samantha raised her eyebrows. Color flashed in her high cheeks. "Are you just stupid? Or do you have a problem with your memory? I already explained this to you. This is a CDC investigation—"

"Don't play games with me," Nick growled, stepping forward. "I'm not an idiot. First you tell me that there's no danger of infection. Now you're walking around in a fucking space suit. Which is it, Dr. Craig?"

He hit the "Dr." hard, and watched as she winced. Then he saw a flame erupt behind her eyes and, despite himself, felt a tremble move through his knees.

"I do not have to explain myself to you. You're a walking train wreck, Barnes. Your own administrator has been trying to get rid of you for years. Well, perhaps now you've just given him the ammunition he needs."

She spun on her heels and shouted something at one of the uniformed men. Nick was bodily turned toward the door, and two men in dark suits took position on either side. The federal marshal stepped in front of him, pausing to flash him a wide, evil smile.

"Nice job, Doc. Thanks for making things easy for us."

Nick turned away, his lips tight against his teeth. As he was led through the brass door and outside to a waiting Chevy sedan, he wondered if he had finally pushed things too far. He cast a quick glance at the dark-suited man to his left. The man's face was hard and lined, and his eyes were cold, severe. Nick could just make out the bulge of a shoulder holster under the right side of his suit jacket.

These people had nothing to do with the CDC.

NINE

You wanted to see me, Ms. Parkridge?"

Melora Parkridge looked up from her notebook, startled. Ned Dickerson's oblong head bobbed through the air as he shuffled into her office. He was hunched forward, his hands jammed into the back pockets of his oversized blue jumpsuit. He was nervous, balding, and short, with round shoulders and a sunken chest. His saucer eyes were hidden behind a quarter inch of thick glass, and most of his piglike face was likewise obscured by heavy plastic frames.

Melora closed her notebook and rose out of her cushioned swivel chair. Her office was large and meticulously ordered: high metal bookshelves lined with computer manuals, thick white carpeting, a polished glass desk sporting a pair of smoke-gray, boxlike personal computers with oversized screens, and a single, rectangular window. For the moment, the shades were drawn, giving the room an orange tint. In a few hours the shades would automatically open, revealing a spectacular view of the National Mall. Everything in the Telecon complex was like that: levels of complex beauty hidden behind walls of simplicity, all of it controlled by computer software. And who controlled the software? That depended on whom you asked.

"I'm going to be leaving the office for a few hours," Melora stated, her voice official. "There are a few things I need you to look into before I get back."

Ned's glossy eyes drifted toward the ceiling, and he nodded distractedly. Melora felt her lips turning down at the corners. Ned had been her assistant for two years; a software engineer by training, he had worked out excellently for the first sixteen months. Then he had started to slack off.

Melora wondered if the poor fool was reaching burnout. It was a common occurrence in the industry, because of the long hours and the nature of the work. She scooped up her notebook and crossed the room in three steps, pausing a few feet in front of the piggish engineer. There were tufts of stubble around his thick, chapped lips, and what was left of his hair was greasy, as if it hadn't been washed in days. Also, he smelled. Melora squinted in disgust.

"I know we're all overworked with the big event coming so soon," she commented. "But you've really got to take better care of yourself. You're making us all nauseous."

Ned nodded, his glassy gaze shifting toward the floor. This, at least, hadn't changed. He hadn't looked her in the eyes in two years.

"Yes, Ms. Parkridge."

"Really, Ned. If Teal saw you, he'd fire you on the spot. You know how concerned he is with appearances. The man practically lives in a salon."

"Yes, Ms. Parkridge."

Melora sighed, heading through the doorway. A brightly lit, carpeted hallway snaked past in either direction, and Melora headed left, her low heels sinking into the thick white shag. Despite the carpet, she could hear Ned's shuffling step behind her; even his gait was piglike. The past few days had really taken a toll on his already diminished demeanor. He had become sluggish, his eyes often glazed, and his hygiene had gone to hell. He'd also begun to put on some weight, mostly in his arms and shoulders—inharmonious new muscles outlining his pudgy form.

They were truly a study in contrasts. Melora was close to six feet tall, with severe, jet-black hair cut close to her ears. Her legs were long and thin, her face chiseled, her skin the texture of buffed porcelain. She was also wearing blue, but her jump-suit was tailored to her angled form, sharp at the shoulders and jutting forward to compensate her conic, space-age bust.

She did not look fifty-eight; she could easily have passed for thirty, especially when she walked, her legs keeping determined stride as Ned struggled to keep up. Then again, she knew she was not conventionally attractive. Her mother used to tell her that men didn't approach her because they were afraid they'd cut themselves on her angles. That was the sort of thing her mother liked to say, right up until her death. *The jealous bitch.*

The hallway took a sharp turn, and they entered

the area of the fourth floor known as Software Alley;
this was where most of the Telecon Set-Box Top software had been developed. The alley consisted of a
necklace of plastifoam cubicles, the hibernating
coves of the software engineers. The alley was
crowded—as it always seemed to be—and gaggles
of young men and women huddled by watercoolers
and coffee machines. All of the engineers wore the
same blue jumpsuits, and Melora caught many
awed stares as she skirted by. She knew most of the
engineers by name, but none would dare speak to
her; she was Marcus Teal's right-hand woman, his
director of R&D. In a large part—larger than they
would ever know—she was responsible for Telecon's
ascension to the top of the industry. The Set-Top Box
would have been worthless without Melora's software addition, and even Teal, the consummate ego-
tist, would admit that it was her technology that had
pushed Telecon over the edge.

Her chin rose with pride as she passed the last
cubicle and entered another long hallway. Then she
heard a quiet murmur of laughter and quickly
glanced behind her. Her face blanched as she saw
Ned struggling with his jumpsuit; his pantleg had
somehow snagged on the corner of a nearby water-
cooler. There was a loud tearing sound, and he
stumbled forward, one leg bared from knee to
ankle.

Melora shook her head, hastening her pace. The
hallway took another sharp turn and ended in a
thick steel door. Melora placed her palm against a
panel halfway up the steel, and the door slid
upward. She stepped through, beckoning to Ned.
He rushed after her, barely making it before the
door slid shut.

Melora stood still for a few seconds, letting her eyes adjust to the change in lighting. They were in a short tunnel with curved, plastic walls. Tracks of tiny red lights ran along the ceiling, pointing the way. At the other end of the tunnel spun a mechanical glass revolving door.

"Honestly," Melora said, stalking forward, her eyes finally adjusted. "I don't know what's going on with you. Perhaps I *have* been working you too hard."

Ned didn't answer, just followed behind, his piggish face bouncing with each step. A dull hum filled the tunnel, as the infrared scanners embedded in the curved walls noted their body temperatures, as the motion sensors in the floor counted their footsteps and calculated their heights, weights, and relative speed. Somewhere in the base of the building a computer digested the information and overrode the alarm response system, allowing them to proceed.

"Just a couple more days. That's all I ask. Then you can take a long vacation."

"Yes, Ms. Parkridge."

Melora rolled her eyes as she reached the end of the tunnel and stepped into the spinning revolving door. She could see herself reflected in the glass; her expression echoed her disgust. She couldn't wait until she was rid of the little engineer.

A stiff wind tugged at her short hair as she stepped out of the revolving door. The helicopter bay was fifty feet across, an open rectangular glade of blacktop embraced on four sides by cinder-block walls. Melora's C-29 McDonnel Douglas helicopter was parked in the center of a red bull's-eye thirty feet in front of where she stood, its long rotors already sweeping in a slow circle. The helicopter was black and polished, with rounded Plexiglas windows and a Telecon emblem emblazoned on its tail. The emblem was bright blue, like the jumpsuits: two spherical eyes connected by a three-dimensional lightning bolt.

Melora shifted her eyes to the helicopter's cockpit, and saw the pilot wave at her. Then she turned toward Ned.

"I'll be gone for three hours. When I get back, I want to see everything we've got on the audio cache program. The techs are telling me the new Set-Top Boxes are having trouble recognizing words with lots of vowels."

"Yes, Ms. Parkridge."

"And then we're going to have to go over the beta test stats again. The big meeting with Teal is later this afternoon. So you'll have to find Dr. Benson and get the rest of the file from him."

Ned glanced at the blacktop under his sneakers. Melora knew he and Benson were less than friends. Benson was a practical joker at heart, and Ned was a congenital target. Last year, Benson had scanned Ned's yearbook picture into his computer, attached a Chippendale dancer's body to Ned's head, and e-mailed the image to everyone in the company. But despite his immaturity, Benson was a stellar programmer, and Teal had put him in charge of the statistics for the beta test.

"And requisition yourself a new jumpsuit," Melora finished, pointing at Ned's bared leg. "I'll page you when I'm back in the office."

She turned and headed for the helicopter. When she got within a few feet of the rotors she bent down, holding her hair with her hands. The pilot shoved the side door open for her, and she pushed through the wall of wind and sound, climbing into the cockpit. The door slammed shut behind her and she settled into a leather bucket seat, snapping the harness tight around her waist.

The pilot smiled at her from beneath his black visor. He had a pointed chin, a long neck, and an unfortunate underbite that made him look like an eel. Simon Mirand had been Melora's pilot for her entire tenure at Telecon Industries, also doubling as her driver. She had recruited him herself.

She nodded, and he pulled back on the throttle. The helicopter lurched upward. Melora's stomach jumped, and her hands gripped the leather seat. She didn't like flying, but it was something she would put up with—a necessary evil.

The helicopter slowly gained altitude. Melora stared down through the glass bubble; for some reason, Ned was still standing there by the revolving door, his hands in his pockets, a glazed look on his face. The wind from the helicopter tugged at what was left of his hair.

Melora grimaced as the helicopter continued to rise. Soon the entire Telecon building was visible; it was certainly impressive, a massive rectangle with glass and steel walls and a cinder-block roof, spotted with satellite dishes and huge, fiberglass antennas. A small crowd of tourists had already gathered by the front door; by mid-morning, five thousand people would pass through the front lobby of the complex, reveling in what Teal had created. Not one of those tourists would recognize the name Melora Parkridge. Even though it was Melora, not Teal, who was going to change the nation. *Seventy more hours.*

"I'm feeding the trip log into the system,"

Simon interrupted, hitting buttons on the control panel. "The usual, I assume?"

Melora nodded. Simon would tell the helicopter's computer that they were heading to Telecon's satellite complex in Baltimore. The helicopter, in turn, would transmit the information to the Telecon computer system.

"And we're moving out of radar range. Three, two, one."

Suddenly, Simon yanked on the throttle, and the helicopter banked hard to the left. Away from Baltimore. But the helicopter's computer would continue to transmit flight information to the Telecon system; as far as the computer knew, the helicopter was heading on to Baltimore as planned.

"We'll be at the lab in forty minutes," Simon said.

"Fine." Melora closed her eyes, the hum of the rotors echoing through her teeth. She trusted Simon to get her to the lab safely; in truth, she would trust the eel-faced man with her life. She knew his past, knew what hell she and her colleagues had saved him from. He would serve her loyally until the day he died.

"Should be a smooth ride," he murmured, checking altitude and windspeed. "The others have already arrived."

"Good. They'll sit there waiting for me, thinking that something's gone wrong. It will give them a chance to reflect on the gravity of what I've accomplished. On what Pandora will accomplish."

"You certainly know your business, Ms. Parkridge."

Melora smiled. By the time she arrived at the lab, the others would be clawing at the walls. Then her demonstration would blow them away.

She let her head sink back into the leather seat, her eyes still tightly shut. She knew that the view from the cockpit was supposedly stunning, the most beautiful section of Washington, D.C., laid out beneath her, the monuments rising up around the green glade of the National Mall. But to her, the view wasn't stunning at all. She knew about the fiber optic lines running between each building, the spider web of broadband glass connecting every television and computer in the city. She knew about the technology that was waiting, dormant, for Marcus Teal to flick the switch.

She knew where that technology would lead. She had helped develop it. A necessary evil, she thought to herself, like flying. A thin smile broke across her lips. Everything Pandora had worked for was so close.

And the best part of it was, Teal had no idea. He would stand by, staring in shock, along with the rest of the nation.

TEN

nick rubbed his wrists as he sat in the empty waiting room. His shirt stuck to the vinyl chair behind him, and he shifted, uncomfortable. He hated this place. His gaze trotted over the pretentious decor: oversized redwood desk; African wall hangings most likely purchased just over the river, in Cambridge; frayed Oriental rug, with the price tag still attached to one corner; and a bronze bust of Asclepius, the Greek god of healing, standing on a stone pedestal near the door to the inner office. What the hell did Rudolph Pierce know about healing? He was the hospital administrator, a lawyer by training with a Ph.D. in group dynamics.

Nick fought angrily with the vinyl chair, his teeth grinding together. It didn't take a Ph.D. to figure out the dynamics going on in the next room. He could hear them talking right through the heavy wooden door. Samantha's authoritative voice intermingling with Pierce's whine. And every now and then, the soft chords of the hospital chairman, old man Peterson. Peterson was Nick's only true defender at Boston General. The other doctors had backed away after Pierce's first round of requests for his resignation. They had considered him a marked man—and only Peterson had stood by him. Peterson had been one of Nick's favorite teachers at Harvard Medical School before he had ascended to the role of chairman at Boston General. The two men had built a bond of mutual respect. But this time, Nick suspected Peterson was seriously overmatched.

The door separating the two rooms swept open. Peterson came out first, and Nick could tell by the man's eyes that his intuition was correct. Peterson was short, stocky, with wild gray hair and pinpoint brown eyes. He looked a bit like Albert Einstein, but with better taste in clothes. Peterson didn't say anything, just shook his head, his fingers twisting through his curly hair.

Pierce came out next, rolls of fat jiggling under his light blue Oxford shirt, his oversized glasses balanced crookedly over his upturned nose. His thinning blond hair was pulled back in a trendy ponytail, and his thick, girlish lips were turned up at the corners, as if he had just swallowed something delicious.

Behind him came the woman, her angular chin turned upward. Her lips were a stiff line, her eyes cold atop those ski-slope cheeks. Her long hair flowed in sophisticated curls down her back, wisps touching the stiff shoulders of her gray suit. Her hands were clasped behind her back, her chest jutting forward. She did not meet Nick's eyes as she took position next to Pierce behind the redwood desk.

"You've really done it this time," Pierce started, dropping into a low cushioned chair. The chair squealed in metallic pain. "Crossing a police line, purposefully interrupting a CDC investigation—"

"Rudolph," Nick interrupted, raising his hands. "Don't I get a word in here?"

"Your actions have embarrassed this hospital," Pierce barreled on. "You're a risk, Barnes—to yourself, to us, to everyone around you."

Nick crossed his arms against his chest, glancing again at Samantha Craig. He could see the corners of her stiff lips inching upward. She was loving every minute of this. And she was bringing out the best in Pierce; Nick could tell by the way he was posturing that he was trying to impress the CDC woman. As if the fat, married jerk had any chance. Samantha was a good inch taller than Pierce, and she looked like she kept in shape. She could borrow half of Pierce's fat and still pass for shapely.

"She's the risk," Nick said, flicking his head toward her. "Running some sort of Reston cover-up, right under our noses."

"Reston?" Pierce scoffed, leaning back in his chair to get a better angle on Samantha's long legs. "What is Reston?"

Nick was disgusted by the administrator's ignorance. Peterson coughed, and Nick turned, watching as the chairman lowered himself into a chair by the outer door. It looked like the old man's arthritis was bothering him, and Nick felt a pang of sympathy; he had watched his father struggle with the pain in his joints every day for years, had helped him with his warm salt baths and cortisone injections. It was a large part of the reason he had chosen to play college baseball instead of football; Peterson had been a running back like the coach, though Ivy League football could hardly be compared with the real college experience.

"Reston is a small city about ten miles west of Washington," Peterson answered, his voice low. "In 1989 there was an outbreak of a form of Ebola in a Reston monkey house. The U.S. government moved in and sanitized the place; the whole thing was real hush-hush, a secret operation. They were afraid that people would panic if word got out."

"But this has nothing to do with Reston," Samantha interrupted, her voice quiet but commanding. All three men turned to look at her, and her face softened, her white teeth flashing; she could be charming, when she had to be. "The CDC is simply performing some equipment tests on the site. We're using this as a dress rehearsal. Or at least we were—when your Dr. Barnes came barging in and threw off all of our controls. Now the experiment is a total washout."

Nick's fingers twitched against his vinyl chair. Equipment tests? He hadn't thought of that. He assumed that the CDC had to test its equipment somewhere. But did they bring armed soldiers with them? And even if the CDC was conducting tests— that still didn't explain what happened to the nine lawyers, or how the CDC could be so sure that Nick wasn't infected.

"Dr. Peterson, I'm not buying this. I saw the bodies in the law firm. These men died of something that isn't documented anywhere; even if it wasn't viral or bacterial in nature, it was still something that has to be explained. I'm not going to accept some bullshit reassurances. I know what it's like to have something tick away inside you—I'm not going to live in fear because this woman wants to keep secrets."

He felt slightly ashamed at his ploy. Peterson had been one of the people he had confided in when Jennifer first got sick. He had been considering suing the hospital, and he had wanted to get Peterson's opinion. Peterson had offered to support him, whatever he decided. He hadn't sued, but he had gotten Peterson's help in keeping Jennifer's condition private.

Peterson gently shook his head, his hands massaging his pained knees. "I'm sorry, Nick. I have to think about the hospital. Dr. Craig has the proper authority, and if she says there's nothing to be concerned about, we have to believe her."

"Dr. Peterson—"

"Nick, I've received phone calls from the Massachusetts Council of Hospitals, the director of the CDC, and from two of the governor's aides. Dr. Craig is a highly respected expert. It's just not in my power to overrule her."

Samantha Craig had certainly put on the pressure. Nick had never had a chance. He heard Peterson's knees creak as he rose from his chair. Before the chairman could reach the door, Pierce's runny whine split the air.

"Dr. Peterson, considering Dr. Barnes's behavior, I think a suspension is in order."

Nick looked at Peterson. Peterson smiled at him, gently. "I think Nick understands the situation, and we'll have no more trouble from him. If Dr. Craig is satisfied, I'm satisfied. Dr. Craig?"

Nick shifted his gaze to the woman. She was straightening the line of her gray suit, barely paying attention. "There's no need for a suspension. As long as I can continue my work without interruption."

Nick's eyes narrowed. He was being railroaded. He stared at Samantha, trying to break into her head, to see what she was hiding. His intensity obviously bothered her, and she glanced up, then quickly turned away. *Fear.* Nick knew the look from his sport's days. He suddenly wondered: How far would she go to ensure that whatever was going on remained a secret? He leaned back in his chair, lifting his long legs.

"As long as everyone's satisfied," he said, letting the heels of his loafers slap down on Pierce's desk. "Maybe we can all go out for a nice lunch—well shoot, I already have lunch plans. A good friend of mine, Arthur Harrison. The nightly anchor on Channel Four News. Maybe you saw the special? Local hero saves the day, or something like that. Old Harrison is quite an investigative reporter. He always loves a scoop."

He looked right at Samantha. Her cheeks were turning white. The tip of her tongue slipped out and touched her lower lip, then receded between her icicle white teeth. "Can of worms, Dr. Barnes. You don't want to do something stupid."

Nick smiled, waving at Pierce. "I'm known for doing stupid things. Just ask Pierce. He can probably show you a pretty long list."

A gnarled hand came down on Nick's shoulder, and Peterson leaned close to his ear. "Nick, there's probably a better way to go about this."

"Dr. Peterson, I'm sorry but I don't agree."

"Nick—"

Suddenly, Samantha raised her hand, cutting the chairman off. She had instantly reclaimed her cool. She lowered her hand, and again went to work on the line of her suit. Without looking up she spoke, her voice firm.

"Dr. Peterson, Dr. Pierce, thank you for your time. Now, I'd like a moment alone with Dr. Barnes."

Pierce slapped his desk, staring at her. "You're not going to take this psycho seriously, are you?"

"We'll use your office," Samantha said sharply. "And please close the door on your way out."

When they were alone, Samantha slowly crossed to the desk and lowered herself into Pierce's chair. As she did, her body underwent a change. Her stiff features softened, her tight lips became fuller, her eyes lost some of their edge. She seemed to be losing a war against a bone-crunching exhaustion. Nick watched her carefully. There were many levels to this woman, and he did not want to underestimate her. It did not help that she was so physically intimidating: her good looks immediately put him on edge.

"Dr. Barnes," she said, finally. "I don't like you. I can guess that you don't like me."

She was direct, that was one thing in her favor. And there was a hint of the Midwest in her voice. He wondered why the slight accent was only coming out now that they were alone. Was she letting her guard down? Or just trying to get him comfortable? He was originally from Texas, a small town north of Dallas. Perhaps she had noticed his leftover drawl, and had chosen to ply him with a familiar dialect. *Now that's paranoia.*

"I have nothing against you," he finally responded. "I just don't like the shit you're trying to pull. You were up to something in that law firm."

"So you decided to barge right in? I'd never seen anything so ridiculous in my life. What the hell did you hope to accomplish? Were you even thinking? Was anything going on inside your head?"

Nick's cheeks turned red. He could hear the emotion behind her words. True, he hadn't really thought through his assault on the law firm. The federal marshal had pissed him off so he had charged. What did it matter now?

"That's the way I do things. Call it a character flaw. I don't like to be pushed around."

Samantha leaned forward over the desk. "We've got a real problem, Dr. Barnes. I don't want to have to put you in prison. It could lead to an embarrassing situation. But you're not leaving me much of a choice."

Prison? This was a new twist. Nick scratched at his neck, watching her face. She wasn't kidding. His eyes slipped to her stiff gray suit. Expensive. Probably some Italian designer he had never heard of. She wore almost no makeup, absolutely no jewelry. She did have a watch, though: heavy, steel, with a covered face. The kind of military watch that could withstand almost anything.

"You're not with the CDC, are you?"

Samantha reached into her suit and pulled out a black leather case. She tossed the case onto the desk. It landed open, and Nick stared down at the glistening metallic seal.

"United States Army Medical Research Institute for Infectious Diseases," he read. "USAMRIID. You're U.S. military."

"My official title is Director of Immediate Viral Response and Covert Reaction. The response proto-col was instituted two months ago, after an Ebola scare in Minneapolis. The scare turned out to be a false alarm, but we've kept the response team up and running. Now we're facing something real—and I have full military authority to do whatever's necessary."

Nick stared at her. As part of his general research into viruses, he had read about USAMRIID. It was a hard-core organization, shrouded in secrecy. USA-MRIID had run the secret sanitation in Reston, Virginia. USAMRIID had also coordinated the Ebola missions in Zaire. He had never heard about the response team before, but it sounded like it fit the times. With new virus threats cropping up all over the world, it made sense that USAMRIID would form some sort of protocol for dealing with danger-ous situations.

But Samantha did not look like a hard-core mili-tary scientist. She looked young, perhaps under thirty. And when he thought of USAMRIID, he pic-tured uniformed men with crewcuts and scars. Not runway models in tailored gray suits.

"So some virus breaks out, you come running?"

"Something like that. We estimate the threat, then decide what sort of action is necessary. We have full cooperation from the Pentagon, and have access to a number of FBI and CIA laboratories."

Nick thought of the Racal space suits and the armed soldiers in the law firm. It dawned on him—if what Samantha said was true, they were taking the deaths of the nine lawyers very seriously.

"So it was a virus. The thing that killed the lawyers."

"Right now, we're trying to keep things as quiet as possible. We don't need some cowboy doctor shooting his mouth off to the press."

Nick saw that she was serious. Still, he didn't want to walk away from this. *A time bomb, ticking away inside him.* He had seen the effects of this virus—and he wanted to be involved in the investigation. He knew what the families of those nine lawyers were going through. He wanted to help stop the virus from killing again.

"Maybe I can help," he tried, sitting up in his chair. "Have you begun the autopsies?"

"Dr. Barnes, we are quite capable of running this investigation on our own."

Nick exhaled, frustrated. "I can't just forget what I saw. And I know I can make a difference. I was the best surgeon at this hospital. Nobody knows the inside of the human body better than I do."

"We have plenty of capable physicians on our team. We don't need a surgeon—"

"You didn't let me finish. I'm a surgeon who can also tell you what viruses kill cells by complement-dependent cell-mediated cytotoxicity; that Natural Killer cells are among the earliest antiviral defenses; the relevant symptoms of the different strains of dengue virus—hell, I can go on for hours. And I haven't even gotten to AIDS yet."

The room went silent, and Nick realized he was halfway out of his chair, his face hot, both hands gripping the edge of the desk. He swallowed, dropping back into his chair. Samantha watched him, her long fingers tapping the shiny surface of her USAMRIID badge.

"You seem to know a lot about viruses."

Nick took a deep breath. His hands were shaking, and he placed them carefully on his thighs. He had never spoken so openly about his virus research before, but he did not want Samantha to push him out of the way. He raised his eyes.

"My wife died of AIDS. I spent a year researching the syndrome—and because of AIDS' nature, my research spanned a great many virus families. In the end, my wife suffered from cytomegalovirus and molluscum, as well as a number of other less documented viruses. After her death, I continued my research, as much as my career allowed."

He studied her face as he spoke. People reacted differently to the knowledge that his life had been affected by the modern plague. He had kept it a secret from most of his and Jennifer's peers—she had not wanted to die in a spotlight, nor had she wanted the disease to mark her memory. Since her death, he had told very few people what had happened. Peterson, the hospital chairman. The coach, in Texas. The handful of therapists he had abused during the rough times. And now Samantha Craig.

She pursed her lips, touching them with a long finger as she, in turn, studied him. He could guess the questions she wanted to ask. Everyone wanted to know the same two things: How did Jennifer get the disease? And was Nick HIV positive? If Samantha asked, Nick would tell her. But he would not offer the information on his own.

Finally, Samantha broke the silence. "This is personal to you. You saw a hint of a virus, something that reminded you of Jennifer, and you charged headlong through a federal marshal. Your research was guided by emotion—"

"But that's the point," Nick countered. He had noticed her use of his wife's name, but he did not let

it bother him. So Samantha had studied his background—that meant she knew about the accident,
as well. She knew that he did not—would not—give
up. "That's how it has to be. You have to look at this
like it's a war. These viruses don't give a damn
about us. They want to kill us, and we have to want
to kill them just as bad. Let me help, Dr. Craig. At
least let me take part in the autopsy. I won't disap-
point you."

His words had been passionate, and he could
tell that she was wavering. Her fingers had tangled
together over her USAMRIID badge, and she was
staring down at her short nails. Clipped, or bitten?
She was obviously under an immense amount of
pressure. Did she want to share that pressure? Was
she going to do something out of character? She
looked up, a decision made.

"This wasn't the only outbreak of this disease,"
she stated, speaking quietly. "Over the past two
weeks, there have been four incidents in four
widely separated locations. That we know of."

Nick felt a thrill—he had broken through. But
then his mind digested her words. *Four incidents in
four distinct locations.*

"That's impossible," he said. "There has to be
some link, some carrier."

Samantha shook her head, pulling her long hair
off of her shoulders with both hands. He could see
the lines in her face getting deeper as she spoke.
"Nothing we can find. We've gone over it and over
it. Just bodies. And every time, the same characteristics. Ivory-white skin. Twisted spines. Sudden
death."

Nick sank in his chair. No wonder she was
scared. A disease breaking out, at random, with

such horrible results. If word got out, there would be wholesale panic. And perhaps for good reason. Ebola had wiped out whole villages in Zaire.

"And you're sure the cause is viral?" Nick asked.

Samantha shrugged. "We've isolated a viral pathogen that has been present in the cells of every victim. The pathogen is inert, unresponsive, but present in enormously high quantities. We have not found it present in the air, nor on nearby surfaces, so we are not sure how it was spread from victim to victim. Even close cellular contact with the bodies does not reactivate the pathogen. As an example, as far as we can tell, your cells are completely clean. We checked the samples drawn from you in the quarantine room, and we screened the police officers who were with you at the site. We are convinced that the pathogen does not remain infectious after its initial outbreak."

"So you don't know how it's spread, where it comes from—do you know how it kills? What made the lawyers' skin turn white?"

Samantha nodded. She spoke as if she had told this story many times. Nick guessed there were a few dozen reports with her signature at the bottom already circulating through USAMRIID and the Pentagon. "Something—we assume it's our pathogen—sets off a process of calcification. Every cell in the body begins to pump out calcium. The skin, the lungs, the brain. The cause of death comes from more than a dozen simultaneous factors. Suffocation, because the lungs are too calcified to function. Cardiac arrest, because the heart has hardened. Renal failure, collapsed liver, brain death—all simultaneous from an immense overproduction of calcium."

Nick nodded. That explained the white color,

and the stiffness of the bodies. In a sense, they had turned to bone. "Have you compared the pathogen you've isolated to other viruses?"

Samantha seemed pleased—he had asked the correct next question. "That's where things get really frightening. As far as we can tell, CaV—as we're calling our pathogen—bears a striking resemblance to a rhinovirus."

The room went silent. Nick could hear his own peristalsis as he fought to get a few droplets of saliva down his throat. "You mean the family of virus that causes common colds?"

"One of the most ubiquitous virus families on earth. In this room alone, there are probably fifty million rhinoviruses floating through the air, clinging to every surface, being inhaled into our lungs. Rhinoviruses are everywhere, and from what we can tell, CaV may very well be a slightly mutated member of the family."

Nick felt a tremble move through his body. If that were true, if those bodies in the law firm had come from a mutant sister of the common cold . . .

"This can't be happening," he whispered.

"It's happened in four places already," Samantha responded, her voice equally strained. "Nineteen people have already died of CaV. But that's nothing, compared to what we could be facing. Viruses mutate all the time; flu viruses change daily, racing the antiviral drugs we create to fight them."

Nick nodded; this was an area of virus science he was familiar with. "There are some who believe that HIV is a mutant form of a monkey virus; that it is related to the simian immunodeficiency virus, SIV. One stems from the other, or they are both associated with some intermediary virus. Either way, a random change in a previously harmless virus's genetic material, and suddenly it turned deadly."

Samantha was watching him carefully as he spoke about AIDS. She was going after this virus because it was her job. For him, it was much more, the stakes absolutely personal. She had to agree— that made him valuable. She shoved her USAM-RIID badge back into her suit pocket. "As horrible as AIDS is, we could be facing something worse. If the rhinovirus is really changing . . ."

She didn't finish her thought. And she didn't have to. Every human being on earth came in contact with rhinoviruses. It didn't take unprotected sex, or a blood transfusion, or a prick with a conta-minated needle. Rhinoviruses were everywhere. But something still didn't make sense.

"You say there have been four discrete inci-dents," Nick commented. "Why would the virus be mutating simultaneously in distinct locations? The chance of that happening has to be close to zero."

"Which leaves us with one hell of a mystery."

Samantha rose from her chair, her hands stiff at her sides. She forced the exhaustion out of her fea-tures, and suddenly she was back to her chilly, com-manding self. Nick couldn't help thinking that she looked like some sort of beautiful machine; he pic-tured colorless, interlocking gears beneath that striking veneer.

"The autopsy is taking place as we speak," she said. "The odds are good that we're not going to find anything new, but we have to go through the motions. You can observe at my side. Then you can give your opinion—and we can go our separate ways."

She headed for the door. Nick rose to follow.

"And what about prison?"

She didn't look back. "That will depend on you, Nick. If you can accept the fact that I'm in charge, we'll get along just fine. If your ego—or your self-destructive urge—makes that impossible, well, we'll just have to see."

Nick stared at the back of her head. A remark she might have classified as "self-destructive" sprang to mind, but he kept his mouth shut.

ELEVEN

marcus Teal pressed his right eye against the rubber-lined lens, staring directly at the red crosshairs imprinted on the inlaid fiberglass screen. A bright light flashed behind the screen for less than a millisecond, too quick to cause a tear. Then there was a quiet whirring, and a metallic female voice echoed through the small steel chamber: "Retinal identification accepted. Please present audio confirmation."

Teal cleared his throat, stepping back from the lens. The lens was attached to a plastic console containing four rows of colored diodes.

"Melora, have you and Emile coordinated your beta test results?"

The rows of lights flickered with Teal's voice. The words themselves didn't matter; the software matched the frequency of his vocal chords against its computerized records, then correlated the findings with the retinal scan. After a two-second pause, the console clicked. A section of the steel wall a few feet in front of Teal slid upward. Bright, fluorescent light filled the chamber.

"I've got our stats with me," Melora's voice responded from behind him. He glanced over his shoulder, beckoning her forward through the chamber. The steel anteroom was a ten-foot by ten-foot cube, painted stark white, devoid of furniture. Melora was still at the far end of the room, a thin file under her right arm. Next to her slouched Emile Benson—blond haired, blue eyed, his oversized body gone to hell from a programmer's diet of cheeseburgers and late-night pizza.

"Excellent," Teal said, starting forward. "We can go over them as we inspect the system."

He strolled through the bright opening. Melora and Benson rushed to catch up. Both of them had been inside the main computer atrium before; Teal's director of R&D and his head programmer were the only other employees with access to the secure atrium. As a security precaution, when all three of them were inside the room at the same time, the door remained open. After the Big Turn On, Teal planned to have both of the others removed from the clearance system.

The main computer atrium was enormous and technologically awe-inspiring; the walls were curved and white, and the entire space was designed to look like the interior of a carved-out sphere. The floor was transparent Lucite, underneath which ran an almost infinite matrix of colored glass strings. The strings were incredibly thin, only visible because of their immense number; this was

the core of Telecon's fiber optic matrix, and the
strings were functioning broadband carriers, connected directly to the computer system and running
in long twists through the complex's walls, to a
junction in the front lobby. From there, the fiber
optic lines sped out under the city itself, linking into
the greater network, multiplying a hundred times
every mile, stretching out across the entire nation.
*The most powerful advance in manufacturing technol-
ogy.* Each strand of optical fiber was five times thinner than a single human hair, and could transmit
information at more than 2.4 gigabits per second. Its
broadband capacity was the key to the information
highway.

But at the moment, Teal was indifferent to the
amazing capabilities of broadband glass cables. He
hurried across the Lucite floor, ignoring the colored
strings a few feet underneath his feet. To his left and
right was a sea of file cabinets and computer counters, but his attention was completely attuned to the
massive computer system that curved along the
entire front wall of the atrium. The system consisted
of a rounded, waist-high steel cabinet sectioned into
a half-dozen different colored regions. Each region
contained more than a thousand microchip boards
stacked on inlaid mechanical trays. The trays resem-
bled the loading bays of conventional CD players,
though much thinner and tied into a centralized
locking system.

On top of the medial region of the vast computer
stood a three-foot-tall, high-definition, Plexiglas
screen. The screen was only two inches thick, and
rose up in front of the curved white wall, a stark con-
trast of color. The background pixels on the screen
glowed a magnificent dolphin blue, while crimson

lines of lettered and numbered code scrolled verti-
cally up the screen's face; as Teal approached, the
numbers and letters silently tracked the gigabytes of
light data flowing through the fiber optic strings
beneath the floor.

This was the hardware of the upcoming information highway, the supervising computer through
which all transmissions would pass. The center of
the web, the virtual tour guide to the network,
where each encrypted packet of data would receive
directions to its destination. That this machine sat in
the secure confines of a private complex, not in a
federal building somewhere, was a feat of corporate
maneuvering that biographers would try and piece
together for decades. The simple truth was, it was
Teal's technology and Telecon's capital that had
made the highway possible. By the time it was
decided that the network needed a centralized
directional system, Telecon Industries had a monopoly on the necessary patents for much of the hardware and software.

Of course, the simple fact that the information
passed through Teal's computer did not mean he
had *access* to that information; privacy was the cor-
nerstone on which the entire highway was built.
Each packet of data was encoded by the sending
Set-Top Box, only to be decoded by the receiving
Set-Top Box. Teal provided both Set-Top Boxes, the
fiber optic lines, the supervision computer, even the
encryption software—but the information itself was
sacred.

Teal came to a stop in front of the vast computer,
a chill moving through his shoulders. He felt this
way every time he entered this room. It had nothing to do with the high-powered air-conditioning

system, or the humming fans inlaid into the back of the steel computer cabinet. This was his throne room. This computer was the culmination of his journey, his climb out of South Central. Soon, too, this computer would be his gift to the world. And all of it, every inch of his ascension, was built on that single, simple concept: *Encryption.*

It was the source of Teal's billions, the true key to his meteoric rise. It was the core of the information highway itself. Without a foolproof method of encryption, there would be no true exchange of data. The highway would be nothing more than a curiosity, a tiny step up from the pathetic little Internet.

Teal could still remember the day the idea had first hit him. He had been a sophomore at UCLA, a scholarship student with the pressure of an entire community on his shoulders. He had been in his dorm room—avoiding a schoolwide dance, another lurching carnival of spoiled rich brats— reading an obscure computer magazine. The articles had sounded like science fiction, telling of the infantile Internet, from its beginnings in a government project called the ARPANET in the 1960s, to its expanding role as the first personal computers began to appear in American homes. The IBM PC had just been introduced, and reading the magazine Teal had instantly foreseen the network that would one day link the nation. Just as quickly, he had realized that the key would be a method of securing the information that passed from computer to computer.

Like his now-vanquished nemesis—Bill Gates, the former CEO of the famously defunct Microsoft— Teal had made an educated guess, and the guess had paid off. Gates had earned his billions because he had foreseen the personal computer revolution itself; he had stood at a turning point in technological history, and had prophesied that PCs would one day be ubiquitous.

Marcus Teal had stood at the same turning point in technological history. But he had taken Gates's guess one step further. Without perfect encryption, there could never be an information highway. Digital money, person to person interactions, exchanges of ideas and resources—without adequate protection, these were nothing more than pipe dreams. Every single packet of information had to be encoded and decoded. If one system of encryption could outshine all the rest, could be accepted as the industry standard . . .

"I see you've updated the interface," Melora's sharp voice interrupted, as the tall, angled woman came to a stop next to Teal. "High density, looks like a Toshiba. A good choice."

Teal nodded, forcing a smile. Melora had been his indispensable head of R&D since Telecon opened its doors, ten years ago. She had helped develop the encryption software and the Set-Top Boxes. It had been Teal's idea, capital, patents, and business sense that had made Telecon possible, but without Melora Parkridge, the encryption software itself would not exist. She and her former co-director, Eric Hoffman, had written the prototype of the program they had since named the Evolving Code.

Teal's strength had never been the actual programming—just the ideas. So he had had no choice but to rely on the emaciated woman. At first, he had enjoyed her briskness, her stiff mannerisms and quick, biting wit. But as the years passed, the differences in their personalities had eaten away at their relationship. She had no appreciation of the impor-

tance of form, only function. When Teal had instituted the blue jumpsuits, she had balked at the
notion of a corporate uniform. When he had
designed the next level of Set-Top Box with sleeker
curves and more display features, she had called it
wasteful.

And since Hoffman's death a year ago, she had
become almost unbearable. Her passion was as
great as Teal's, but she had no vision, no overarch-
ing mission. She was cold and enigmatic. For the life
of him, he did not know why she worked so hard
for Telecon. But for whatever reason, she had made
herself indispensable. He could dislike her, but he
couldn't get rid of her.

"It has twice the resolution of the old interface,"
he commented curtly, waving at the screen.

"Although I'm still not sure there's any need for
an interface at all. The computer is quite capable of
routing the data without human supervision."

There it was again, the lack of vision. "Melora,
do you realize how many federal watchdogs will
come through this room over the next few weeks?
Congressmen, senators, at some point the president.
What do you suggest we show them? A microchip?
They're going to want to see the highway in action."

His eyes followed the scrolling code as it
flashed across the blue screen. Each line symbolized
a hundred transmissions; the letters signified the
location, type, and duration of each transmission.
Teleconferences, video on command, data transmission—although the beta test was a mere shadow
of what was coming, the screen was an apt window
into the workings of the information highway.

"Why don't we forget about the interface for the
moment," Teal continued, leaning forward to check

a row of microchip trays. "And talk about the beta test."

Emile Benson came forward, rubbing his sweaty palms against his jumpsuit. Since Hoffman's death, he had taken on much of Telecon's general programming responsibilities.

"So far, we've had very few glitches. Six thousand residential and corporate subjects, and only two Set-Top Boxes had to be returned for small repairs. As expected, the highest use has been for video and television on demand; teleconferencing comes next, then interactive software such as games and corporate research. The more interesting uses of the highway—such as the universal marketplace or network banking—won't be available until after the Big Turn On."

Teal nodded, hitting a button next to one of the microchip trays. The tray slid out of the cabinet, and Teal stared down at the tiny microboard. Each board contained enough microchips to power a room full of personal computers.

"Sounds about what we expected. How are we looking in terms of Thursday?"

Melora pulled the file out from under her arm and glanced at its contents. "Telecon Set-Top Boxes are now attached to ninety-two percent of all televisions and personal computers in the country."

Teal looked at her. *Ninety-two percent.* It was a beautiful number. How could she remain so absolutely stiff? "And the other eight percent?"

"Some people refuse new technology no matter how free you make it. But I think we'll have nearly complete saturation by the end of the year. Every new television set manufactured in this country or imported from outside comes with our box. In urban areas, our customer service teams are making apartment by apartment sweeps. We have installed more than one hundred million boxes in the past six months. That puts the total at five hundred million, three hundred and fifty-seven thousand. That's more than one and a half Set-Top Boxes per person."

Teal pretended to concentrate on the microboard. Inside, he was on fire. It was really going to happen. Every household, every business, everywhere. No matter how poor or how fallen—there would be total and complete access.

And then? Teal felt his lips turning up at the corners. He turned his head toward the high-density screen. Line after line of code scrolled by. Soon, those lines would represent millions of transmissions, not hundreds. Soon, the entire nation would be riding the highway: banking, buying and selling, telecommuting, educating, even voting. And every transmission would pass through Teal's complex. Every transmission would pass right before his eyes—encrypted, of course.

He rose to his full height. He could see his beautiful features reflected in the screen. "Thursday morning at precisely ten, I will address a CNN camera crew from this room. Melora, you'll be monitoring the system from my office. Emile, you'll be down in engineering in case of any last-minute glitches."

He turned to face his two employees. They had no idea what he was really planning. Even Melora, who had helped make it possible, did not foresee the true leveling power of the network. Lack of vision. *Lack of mission.* He flashed her his trademark smile.

"Let's keep our heads up, our hands working. This is going to be a week for the history books."

TWELVE

the limousine pulled off of the highway onto a deserted dirt construction access, complete with red warning signs and the parked remnants of a road crew; discarded pickaxes, pile drivers, even a stalled bulldozer surrounded by weathered cement blocks. A hundred yards past the bulldozer squatted a windowless gray building, ringed by a nondescript chain-link fence.

"This is it?" Nick asked, peering through the limousine's window. "No security checkpoints? No armed guards?"

Samantha didn't look at him. She had a feeling that if she thought too hard about what she was doing, she'd realize how foolish it was. At the time, it had seemed like the best way to keep him from getting in the way.

Shoving him in prison would have been cruel

and inconvenient. And it couldn't hurt to have another set of eyes at the autopsy; God knew she had cut up enough of these bodies over the past two weeks on her own. Perhaps the combination of his knowledge of viruses and his former skill as a surgeon would give him a useful perspective. At the very least, his intense motivation to stop CaV would help her keep focused.

She didn't have to like him; the question was, could she control him? The more time they spent together, the more he reminded her of Andrew. She had worshiped her older brother, had loved him more than anything in the world, but she had always been powerless around him. She had watched him nearly destroy himself a dozen times while they were growing up; and when his dauntless attitude finally did get him killed, she completely fell apart.

Nick had that same drive, that same explosiveness. If he destroyed himself, that was one thing. But if he took Samantha's investigation with him—it would be catastrophic. Especially now. The death toll had recently risen to twenty. A half-hour ago, Samantha had been informed of another outbreak. Marco had brought her a Polaroid of the victim: a young woman, in an isolated cabin somewhere in Vermont. She had the Polaroid in her pocket—and intended to keep it with her until her investigation was over. *Another outbreak*. That meant another useless autopsy, as soon as they were done with the nine lawyers.

"I'd have thought there'd be a few federal marshal's running around," Nick continued, ignoring Samantha's silence. "Just to keep up appearances."

"The best way to hide something is to leave it

right out in the open," she responded curtly. "The less conspicuous the security measures, the less chance there is of anyone asking questions."

Nick seemed to accept that. In truth, the cubic building known as the Northeast Federal Quarantine Unit B12 had an extremely sophisticated security system. The nondescript chain-link fence was electrified and contained over three hundred fiber optic cameras making it virtually impossible to approach the complex unnoticed. The bulldozer was a computerized command station, hooked into an underground network of magnetized checkpoints and infrared scanners. At one time, Unit B12 had been the linchpin of USAMRIID's biological warfare efforts. And although USAMRIID was now mostly concerned with investigating and fighting domestic medical threats, the need for secrecy had not diminished.

Samantha cringed inwardly as the limousine grumbled past the bulldozer and headed toward the chain-link fence. If the newspapers got word of the situation that was developing, there would be a nationwide panic—followed by a rush on the airlines and train stations, and an exodus from the perceived danger areas. And there was nothing more dangerous in terms of virus control than widescale movement of populations.

The limousine slowed as it approached the chain-link fence. There was a ten-second delay, and then a section of the fence rose, revealing a paved driveway that gently sloped upward toward the front entrance of the windowless building. The limousine continued forward, and Samantha turned toward Nick, pushing the fear out of her features. She was determined to remain collected and in charge. *She was stronger now than she ever had been with Andrew.*

"You say you're an expert on viruses, and I'm willing to believe you. But before we go inside, I need to know how clear you are on the basics. Not the specific viruses themselves—we're dealing with something new, so we need to start from scratch."

"Depends how basic you mean. I know that they're tiny creatures that attach themselves to cells in order to replicate. I know that they contain strands of DNA that interact with their host cells, turning the cells into virus factories."

Samantha nodded, pleased. "Essentially, that's all anybody really knows. Viruses are parasites, microscopic life forms—neither truly alive nor the opposite—that sit around waiting for the proper host to come along. When an acceptable host comes in contact with a virus, the virus tricks its way inside and uses the host's cellular machinery to create copies of itself. Sometimes, the sheer numbers of those copies overwhelm the host, killing it. But that's not what the virus wants."

"What do you mean?"

"As I said, viruses are parasites. They can't reproduce without their hosts. So a virus that kills quickly is actually an extremely weak creature. That's why the more spectacular medical threats—such as Ebola and the Hantaviruses—aren't really as dangerous as they seem. Ebola turns its host into liquid, consuming from the inside. Horrible to think about, but in actuality, not that frightening. Ebola kills too fast to spread. Makes for great copy, but hardly the global threat that people think."

The limousine pulled to a stop in front of the cubic building, and Samantha reached for the door.

"In many ways, the most perfect virus is the one you're most familiar with—HIV. It hides inside its host—symptomless—for many years. This allows it to spread and reproduce. One host can spread the killer virus to sites across the globe. And then one day the full-blown disease springs up everywhere—impossible to trace, control, or cure."

She could see the determination in his eyes. She had purposefully chosen AIDS to get a rise out of him. If she was going to use his passion, she wanted him as personally involved as possible.

"And you think that CaV is something like HIV?" he asked. "That it has been lying dormant, waiting?"

Samantha took a deep breath. "I don't know what to think. It kills faster than Ebola. But perhaps it spreads like AIDS. It's hard to believe that the common cold is mutating everywhere, at the same time. But if CaV hides, like AIDS, it only had to mutate once. It spreads unnoticed, traveling like a normal rhinovirus, waiting for something to set it off. And then, bang." She slapped her hand against the top of the limousine. The sound reverberated through the cold afternoon air.

"All hell breaks loose. Twenty bodies become twenty million. They die too fast to spread the virus—but it doesn't matter, because the virus has already spread. Like AIDS. Like the common cold."

"Step into the stall and take off your clothes."

Samantha pointed toward one of the three steel dressing room doors on the other side of the room. The fluorescent lights seemed incredibly bright, stinging her eyes as she followed Nick across the glistening porcelain-tiled floor. This was the first stage in the safety procedure for entering Unit B12.

Samantha had been through this many times before, but still she felt a chill as she opened the door to her own dressing room. How many scientists had gone this same route, only to end up statistical certainties, numbered plastic bags in some classified biocontainment morgue?

She closed the door to her dressing room and listened as Nick did the same. The room was tiny, about six feet across, with sheer walls, a row of shelves, and a small closet stocked with hangers. Samantha slid out of her suit quickly. Her skin prickled as it touched the cold antiseptic air, and she undid her bra and rolled down her hose and panties. In a moment she was naked.

There was a green surgical scrub suit hanging from a hook on the changing room door. As she reached for the suit she glanced at herself, frightened at how thin she looked in the hard white light. She had been working hard lately, and it showed; her stomach was flatter than usual, and she could see the angles of her rib cage through her pale skin. She looked back over her shoulder, down the slope of her back to the round curves of her backside; at least that still looked right, heart-shaped and high.

She would have to be more careful as the pressure increased. Like alcoholism, anorexia was something that never went away. Even though it had been eight years since she had pulled herself out of the truly dangerous stage of the disorder, she knew how easy it was to go back to the old ways. Especially with a living memory of Andrew so close. She had to watch carefully for the warning signs, make sure she wasn't inadvertently controlling her caloric intake as she struggled for control of the investigation.

She quickly pulled the green pants up over her long legs. As she tied the knot in the front, she heard a thud and a quiet cursing from the other side of the steel wall. She smiled, unintentionally picturing Nick fighting his way out of his jeans in the adjoining cubicle. Then she yanked the green top over her shoulders.

She stepped out of her dressing room and crossed to a high set of shelves that stood next to the steel inner door of the compound. She took a cloth cap and a pair of thick white socks from the top shelf, and finished dressing. Then she turned and watched as the door to Nick's dressing room finally swung open.

"Could that room be any smaller?" he grunted, as she tossed him a cap and a pair of socks.

She ignored his comment, leading him to a metal airlock that led to the interior of the compound. She pressed her right hand against a pad next to the door, and there was a series of metallic clicks. The door swung inward.

"Step through the door and stand in the middle of the room." She followed Nick through and shut the airlock behind them. The interior room was small and white, with a low ceiling and rounded, plastic-looking corners. There was a brief pause, then a bright blue light filled the room. Samantha squinted, covering her eyes.

"Ultraviolet," she said. "Gets rid of any contaminants, anything you might be carrying with you."

"I thought the point of a quarantine unit was to protect us from the cooties, not the other way around."

"That's precisely why we want ourselves as sterile as possible," Samantha answered. "Viruses are resourceful creatures. They use the environment around them—incorporating DNA they come in contact with, piggybacking on bacteria. A harmless, or dormant virus can be activated by something it touches, and suddenly it becomes something else entirely."

The blue light went off, and a section of the far wall suddenly slid open, revealing a long hallway. Samantha started forward, ignoring Nick's raised eyebrows. She had grown used to the technological magic of the unit many visits ago.

She stopped halfway into the hallway. To her right hung a row of bright orange Gore-Tex suits, complete with gloves, boots, and clear Plexiglas helmets. She reached for the nearest suit, pulling it off its peg with the slightest effort; all together, the suit and helmet weighed less than six pounds.

"We got your measurements from your hospital file," she said, beckoning to the next suit over. "So hopefully it should be a snug, comfortable fit."

She stepped into her suit, pulling the zipper up the front. The orange material clung to her body, sheer against her long curves. In a moment she was entirely covered, except for her head, and she paused to check the sealed joints at her wrists and ankles. The gloves and boots could be removed if necessary, connected by a Velcro derivative that had been developed by NASA for protection in deep vacuum.

She tucked the helmet under her arm, then turned to help Nick. He had his legs in the suit, but was struggling to find the armholes. She couldn't help smiling as she held the material steady for him; the frustration in his cheeks reminded her of a kid trying to put on a snowsuit. *Andrew, on a ski slope*

*when they were in grade school, shouting at their father
that he didn't need a coat, didn't want a coat, wouldn't
wear a coat . . .*

Finally, Nick pulled the zipper shut, fixing the
clasp at his neck. Then he reached for his helmet. He
paused, glancing at the hard, clear Plexiglas. There
was a plastic tube fitted to the backside of the glass,
which led to a small cylinder, barely nine inches in
length.

"Doesn't look like much," he said, hefting the
cylinder.

"The art of compression," Samantha answered,
fitting her own cylinder into a built-in pocket on the
back of her suit. "It's enough air for three hours. The
suit is completely self-contained, fire-proof, puncture-
proof, and comfortable up to thirty-percent vacuum."

She slid her helmet over her head and sealed it
at the base. A cool rush of air touched her cheeks,
and she breathed deep, tasting something vaguely
metallic. She watched as Nick sealed his own helmet. Then she pointed toward the end of the hallway.

"Ready?" Her voice was barely a whisper, but
she saw Nick flinch inside his helmet. The microwave receiver was set barely an inch from the left
ear—another NASA design, developed to counteract
the loud interference of space launches and land-
ings.

"I feel like some sort of huge insect," Nick
chuckled. But Samantha could hear the nervous
edge in his voice. The suits had that effect: it was
hard to ignore the potential dangers when you were
shrouded in three million dollars worth of state-of-
the-art safety equipment. For all his bravado, for all

his boyish ego and cowboy attitude, Nick was
scared. *Was Andrew scared at the end? Or did he hold
on to that cocky smile all the way down . . . ?*

Samantha shivered, shaking the thought out of
her head. It was good that Nick was scared. They
both had reason to be terrified. The enemy they
were about to face was invisible, unreasonable, and
deadly.

"Keep your hands at your sides, no sudden
motions, and keep the pace slow, like walking on
the moon. No accidents."

Nick nodded, noting the seriousness in her tone.
"No accidents," he agreed.

The airlock clanged shut behind them, and they
paused to let their eyes adjust to the fluorescent
lighting. The room before them was octagonal and
huge, with high ceilings and a glassy, polished steel
floor. The walls were unmarked except for red emergency showerheads spaced shoulder high every ten
feet around the room.

Samantha felt a chill ride through her as she
moved forward, conscious of the noise her light
plastic boots made against the steel floor. In the center of the room were nine stainless steel autopsy
tables, complete with blood and fluid gutters. The
gutters were attached to plastic holding tanks,
where the dangerous liquids would be collected for
study and ultimate destruction. On each table was a
body, bluish-green skin glimmering under the
bright autopsy lights. Standing in front of the nearest table was a short man, suited. He acknowledged
them without turning around.

"Dr. Craig," his voice echoed in her ears, "and
Dr. Barnes, I presume. Alvin Stein. I'd shake your

hand, but then I'd have to find someplace to put this liver."

Samantha moved next to him, Nick right behind her. Her face blanched as she caught sight of the opened corpse. Stein, the pathologist, had already made the thoracic-abdominal incision—the Y-shaped cut across the chest from shoulder to shoulder, then down the middle to the pubis. The ribs had been cracked open to expose the heart and lungs. Stein had skipped removing the heart, lungs, and esophagus en block—the usual first step in an autopsy—and had instead turned his attention first to the abdomen. He was in the process of removing the organs one by one, after which they would be sectioned and studied.

"Amazing," he said, as he hefted the liver. "Absolutely amazing. Crystals, even in the fatty tissue. I've been digging into corpses for fifteen years, and I've never seen anything—Christ, Samantha, just a little article in the *New England Journal*? No names, I promise—"

"Dr. Stein," Samantha chided. She half-turned to Nick. He was trying to look over the pathologist's shoulder, confusion evident on his face.

"Why have you left the heart and lungs?"

"The calcification is too severe," Stein answered. "Learned my lesson the first time I cut into one of these poor bastards. The entire heart crumbled to dust in my hands."

Samantha watched Nick's cheeks turn pale. "Crumbled?" He leaned past the pathologist, peering into the chest cavity. His gasp reverberated through Samantha's helmet.

"Christ," he whispered. Samantha followed his eyes with her own. She had seen it before, but still it was a horrific sight. Even from a few feet away, the calcification was obvious. The lungs were startlingly white, and the heart was like a solid chunk of gray-white chalk, grainy crystals glistening in the bright fluorescent lighting.

"It's the most brutal thing I've ever seen," Stein said, his voice tinged with macabre delight. "The process is like a string of firecrackers going off—one cell flips out, starts spitting up calcium, then the virus jumps to the next and that cell freaks, and pretty soon an entire organ is turning into stone!"

Samantha nodded, her eyes unconsciously shifting around the room. She had grown used to the pathologist's colloquial style, but she had trouble accepting his detachment; there were nine bodies in the room with them, nine people who had died a horrible, painful death.

"Do these new cases shed any light on the mechanism?" she asked, conscious of the sweat beading up on the back of her neck.

Stein shrugged under his suit. "I've sent slides up to the lab for workup. But from what I see here, they look the same as the rest. The virus is now completely inactive—has been since the moment these organs stopped functioning. It's still in the cells—we can see it in the slides—but it isn't doing anything anymore. Just sitting there."

"Dead?" Nick asked.

"Was it ever alive?" Samantha responded. "Dead, dormant, maybe waiting for the trigger that brings it back to full activity. Until we find that trigger, there's no way to tell."

"What we do know," Stein said, "is that it's one hungry motherfucker. You think that set of lungs looks bad? You should see what CaV does to the brain. Come over here, I've already sawed one open. This is gonna blow you away—"

"Hold on." Nick said. He had paused, leaning over the open chest cavity. He outstretched an arm, gingerly, reaching for something. Samantha raised an eyebrow, moving next to him.

"What is it?"

"This is interesting," he said, barely noticing her presence. "Dr. Stein, I assume you've already taken chest X rays and MRIs?"

Stein nodded. "MRIs, ultrasound, X rays—the works. I've got the charts outside. Why?"

"Take a look at this," Nick said. Samantha and the pathologist leaned forward, almost knocking helmets. Nick's gloved finger was inches from the corpse's solidified heart, pointing at a spot on a pulmonary vein. There was a small raised bump, perhaps a centimeter in diameter, on the outer wall of the vessel.

"An accumulated crystal," Stein said, shrugging. "More evidence that this thing is a zealous monster—"

"No," Nick said. "I don't think so. I've seen this before. I'm going to need to look at the MRI, but I'm fairly certain this node isn't solid."

Stein glanced at Samantha. Samantha felt the skin above her eyebrows crinkle up. She wondered what Nick was getting at. He had been one of the top vascular surgeons in the country; she knew the pathologist would defer to his knowledge of the heart and the surrounding vessels.

"What do you think it is, Nick?" She asked, trying to read his face through the clear helmet.

Nick was certain. He didn't need to look at the MRI. "An ecchinococcal cyst, fluid-filled. Fairly rare. Especially this large, and so high up on the vascular wall. I've removed three in my lifetime."

"Does it have something to do with the virus?" Samantha asked.

Nick shook his head, but Stein was the one to answer. "I doubt it. It takes a long time for a cyst this big to build up. Congenital, right, Dr. Barnes?"

Nick nodded. "Could be. Perhaps just a symptom of the aging process. Most likely, the area resisted calcification because the cells in the area were already damaged by the cyst. If we're lucky, the fluid inside hasn't been contaminated by the virus or by bacteria in the air."

"Lucky?" Samantha asked, confused. "I don't understand. Why is this cyst significant? We know what killed this man, and it had nothing to do with a cyst. His lungs and heart are as solid as rock."

Nick's eyes flashed as he looked at her.

"Time of death," he said simply.

Stein clapped his gloved hands together, a motion that seemed completely out of place in this room. "He's right. Excellent catch, Dr. Barnes. I'll find something to tap that cyst with right away. Gotta make sure it's a perfectly sterile container—I think I have just the thing, one moment."

He scurried off toward the far wall. Samantha felt a tinge of excitement. It hadn't dawned on her before, but Nick was right: if this cyst was full of fluid, there was a chance it would give them information that the rest of the autopsy could not.

In any autopsy, one of the most important—and most difficult—things to determine was an accurate time of death. Just as dying was a process—a virus entering the body, the cells spitting out calcium, the calcium overwhelming the lungs and heart and brain—death itself was a process. Enormous numbers of factors caused the body to change after life stopped. A pathologist was, in many ways, a medical detective, using clues to backtrack the hours to the beginning of the process.

The most obvious clues were the ones visible to the senses: color, texture, smell. For instance, lividity, the purplish discoloration caused by gravity pulling against the blood inside the body usually began thirty minutes after the time of death. Six hours later, the lividity became fixed, no longer changeable by repositioning of the body. The muscles stiffened—rigor mortis, caused by the disappearance of the chemical energy source required for muscle contraction, adenosine triphosphate—within four hours, and the skin became waxy, greenish. During this time, the body cooled—a loss of 1.5 percent of body temperature per hour—and the eyes flattened out.

But these visual and tactile clues allowed little more than an estimate of the time of death; according to the files Samantha had looked at on the way over to the unit, Stein had already guessed that the lawyers had died some time in the early hours of the morning, but he could give them nothing more definite. He had even suggested the possibility of using forensic entomology—the study of predictable insect activity, such as maggot hatchings—to get a better estimate, but that too would have been an indefinite predictor.

Fluid trapped in a cyst, however, might just be the ticket to a precise time of death. If the fluid had remained sealed inside the cyst—uncontaminated by outside factors—they would be able to work backwards through the expected chemical reactions.

Stein returned with a small Plexiglas vial attached to a long hypodermic needle. He carried the needle carefully, keeping the exposed tip pointing straight up, away from his body. "This will take a second. Then the boys in the lab can have their fun."

Nick and Samantha stepped back, giving the pathologist room to work. As Stein used the hypodermic to suck fluid out of the cyst, Samantha glanced sideways at Nick's face, trying to read his expression. She expected to see a cocky grin; any second he'd break out with some of his cowboy attitude, reveling in the fact that he had seen something the pathologist had missed.

But there was no grin; his expression was laudably serious. Perhaps it was the space suit, perhaps the open corpse, perhaps the steel autopsy tables with their blood and fluid gutters—but Nick seemed to have accepted the severity of what was going on.

Samantha realized, with a chill, that this scared her as much as anything else.

Twenty minutes later they were sitting in a make-shift cafeteria, sipping muddy, overly aromatic coffee out of Styrofoam cups. They had traded their suits for clean blue scrubs, and the cool, soft material felt good against Samantha's overheated skin. Her hair was pulled back from her forehead, and she wondered if she looked as harried as Nick. There was an inch of scruff on his chin, and his dark locks were spiky with sweat. He seemed focused on the cup of coffee in his hands, as if the world around had somehow stopped, as if the silence waited for him.

Men. Nick Barnes seemed to embody everything Samantha had learned to hate about them: the arrogance, the attitude, the stubbornness. She knew she was scarred by Andrew's death, but she couldn't help the loathing she felt when confronted with those qualities—qualities that seemed to mark half of the males she met. She had been in relationships; right after college, one had been mildly serious, lasting nearly a year. He had been an FBI technical operative—brilliant, handsome, funny. But as always, the hated characteristics had cropped up. At least with Nick they were obvious from the start. He was about as subtle as an oncoming train.

But still, as much as she hated to admit it, there was something there. A knot in her stomach that refused to go away. It wasn't just that he looked like an older Andrew—it was deeper than that. Pity? Had his injury pricked alive some primal, maternal instinct, ticked off some uncontrollable chemical reaction? She hoped not.

There was a sound behind them, the airlock opening, and then Stein's voice broke across the room. "Finally," he grunted, pulling up a seat at the small steel table, "the lab boys aren't getting any points for promptness, I can tell you that."

Samantha felt a tinge of irritation; she wasn't in the mood for the pathologist's dramatics. Since Nick's discovery, she had had time to think about what it might mean. In truth, they were grasping at straws, getting excited over a cyst; sure, it could give them a more accurate reading of the time of death, but how much closer to understanding CaV would that put them?

"Ten hours," Stein said, pulling a sheet of computer paper out of his scrubs. "Give or take, ten, fifteen minutes. The fluid was deteriorating at a rate of five percent every half-hour; the lab boys are pretty certain the cyst remained intact, so we can be fairly confident in the number."

"Ten hours," Samantha repeated, stunned. "That puts the time of death at around four forty-five in the morning."

She paused, looking up. Nick was staring at her. She knew what he was thinking.

"That's only a few minutes before I found the bodies," he said.

Samantha nodded. Before, they had assumed that the janitor Nick had subdued in the street had discovered the bodies—that his post-traumatic stress had resulted from finding the corpses in such a horrible state. But if the nine lawyers had died only minutes before Nick had found them . . .

"He might have been there," Nick said, putting voice to her thoughts. "He might have been in the room when it happened."

THIRTEEN

the primary care unit was bustling with late afternoon traffic: nurses in white and pink uniforms clutching clipboards, orderlies guiding wheeled IV racks, exhausted young interns careening after overworked residents, and a smattering of attendings in white coats, standing by watercoolers and coffee machines—oases of calm in the landscape of pandemonium.

Nick worked his way down the narrow hallways, Samantha a few steps behind. Eyes followed him as he walked by, but he had long since learned to accept the attention. Sometimes it was pity, for what he had lost; sometimes praise, for his perceived heroism. Mostly just curiosity—everyone at Boston General either knew Nick Barnes or knew about him.

Despite the watching eyes, he moved confi-

dently, his athletic body loose and his stride long.
He was on the trail of something worthwhile. The
last time he had spent significant time in these hallways, he had been racked by impotence. He had
been helpless to stop the thing that had killed his
wife. Now he was part of an investigation into a
new virus, one that was just as deadly; he had a
chance to redeem himself, to help stop another
killer.

And this time, he was not alone. She was cold,
tough, controlling—but there was also depth to her,
something that he did not yet understand. He could
tell she was slowly starting to soften toward him;
the frosty looks had lost their edge, the angles had
begun to blur. But still, there was a tension that
went beyond a shallow dislike of his attitude.

He turned a corner and brushed past a pair of
bickering medical students standing beside a
wheeled echocardiogram cart. It was easy to spot
the janitor's private room; there were two burly federal agents leaning against the door frame—arms
crossed, faces stone. Nick recognized the closer of
the two as the thickset man who had accosted him
outside the law firm. Obviously, the man recognized him as well, his heavy lips drifting downward
into a snarl.

"Two out of three?" Nick jibed, referring to his
earlier end-zone run. "Or are we ready to kiss and
make up?"

"Pushing your luck, Doc—"

"Marco," Samantha said quietly. Nick was
impressed by how quickly the thickset man stiffened at her voice. Marco stepped aside, his eyes
spitting fire at Nick, but his lips tightly shut. Nick
opened the door and stepped into the private room.

The familiar smell hit Nick solidly in the face, and he paused, a slight tightness in his chest. He hadn't been in a hospital care room in a long time; as an ambulance jockey, he usually kept both feet on the pavement, handing off his patients at the ER front door. He took a deep breath, suddenly feeling like a doctor again; there was a strange sense of power standing in the doorway of the room—he was there to diagnose, to process, to cure. At the same time, he could not ignore the deep sense of sorrow in his stomach. Jennifer had spent her last days in a room just like this. Nick shook the thought away, stepping forward.

The janitor was lying on his back on the small white hospital bed, a spaghetti strand of IV wire leading out from under his covers to a steel rack beside the bed table. There was a plastic feeding tube attached to the man's nostrils, and a collage of bandages on his face and exposed upper chest. Coming closer, Nick couldn't help noticing how long and tall the man was. When he had first seen Tarrance in the intersection, he had guessed that the man was six three; but lying on the hospital bed, his head against the stiff pillows, the man seemed almost unreasonably large. His neck was long, his arms lengthy spindles under the white top sheet, and his legs seemed to go on forever. His ankles jutted out over the end of the bed, and his feet were huge, at least size fourteen.

There was a nurse standing at the IV rack, checking the plastic wire for kinks. A young intern—Asian, prematurely balding, with thick horn-rimmed glasses—was on the other side of the bed, staring down at a clipboard. Both the intern and the nurse were wearing masks and gloves; no more than they would wear caring for a patient suffering from AIDS or hepatitis. Nick had to remind himself that Samantha and the USAMRIID virologists had determined that those unaffected by CaV did not carry it in their cells, or on their person—that was the reason Nick himself was not in quarantine.

Samantha stepped past Nick and turned toward the intern. "Has his status changed since this morning?"

The intern shook his head. "Still sleeping off the sedatives. I've stitched up his cuts—nothing too serious."

"Good. If you don't mind, we need a few minutes alone with him."

The intern shrugged and followed the nurse out through the door. When the door clicked shut behind them, Nick motioned with his head. "How much do they know about the virus?"

"Almost nothing. They know there was some sort of contamination—that Tarrance was in proximity of some sort of tragedy."

Nick bit his lower lip. "Borders on unethical. They're treating him without understanding the possible consequences."

"Nick, you know what we're dealing with. Nurses talk. Interns have families. And besides, Tarrance is clean. As clean as you are."

She stepped close to the bed, looking down at the sleeping janitor. Nick came around the other side of the bed. The man's face was agitated, even in sleep. His upper lip twitched, some dream playing out behind his closed eyelids.

"Is there something we can give him to wake him up?" Samantha asked. Nick looked at her, surprised. He had almost forgotten that she was not, in fact, an M.D. She was a scientist—something very different. He shook his head.

"Not necessary. I doubt they gave him a serious dose." Nick bent forward and placed the palm of his hand against the man's cheek. With his right forefinger, he lifted up one eyelid.

Instantly, Tarrance shook his head to one side, his lips churning. "Gonna take me down," he suddenly hissed through his teeth. "Gonna take me down down down . . ."

Nick looked at Samantha. Obviously, Tarrance was still in a post-traumatic state. Nick had seen this sort of thing many times during the past two years. He knew it could last days, weeks, even longer. There were instances in which a trauma victim remained almost comatose for years—it depended on the circumstances that brought on the state, and the mental strength of the affected individual. Judging from the nine dead lawyers, they could only hope that Tarrance had immense fortitude.

"Tarrance," Samantha whispered, her voice suddenly gentle. "We're here to help you. We need to know what happened. We need to know what you saw—"

"Take ol' Tarrance down," Tarrance mumbled, his head shifting back and forth, pure terror emerging in his expression. "Gonna take ol' Tarrance down down down . . ."

"Tarrance," Nick tried. "Gotta help us out, here. We know it was horrible—"

"They all goin' down," Tarrance hissed, his voice louder, his expression more tortured. "Skeletons goin' down! I'm next, I know it. I'm next!"

"Listen to me," Samantha said in a strong voice. "Tarrance, you're all right. Nothing is going to hurt you—"

Samantha stopped. Tarrance had suddenly sat straight up in the hospital bed. His eyes were wide open. His lips quivered. "Didn't know what hit 'em," he whispered. "Right there in the middle of the tele-conference. Mouths wide open. Spit in the air, spit right in the air! They all went down! They all . . ."

Tarrance went silent, and a grimace tore across his face. His right hand went to his chest, and he lay back on the bed. Then he moved his hand up, to his right shoulder. He seemed to be in a fair amount of pain. Nick's training immediately kicked in.

"Christ," he mumbled, moving forward. He didn't have his stethoscope, so he leaned close to Tarrance's chest.

"What is it?" Samantha asked, frantic. "Is he having a heart attack?"

Nick ignored her, quickly crossing the room to the hospital intercom console near the door. He slammed the button with his thumb.

"Room 217! Crash cart, stat! And there's an echocardiogram in the hall—get it in here!"

The door swung inward almost immediately. The Asian intern leapt through followed by two nurses pushing the plastic wheeled cart Nick had seen out in the hall. The intern's face was bright red, his eyes wide.

"What is it?" he asked.

Nick ignored him, too, and headed for the cart. He grabbed the ECG leads from the ultrasound echocardiogram and unstrung the wires, working as quickly as his pained right hand would allow. Then he swung back toward the hospital bed.

Tarrance was lying quietly, but his head was arched back, a look of pure pain on his face. His hand was still massaging his right shoulder. Shit, Nick thought to himself. If he was right, this guy was in deep trouble.

He attached the ECG leads to Tarrance's bare arms, then pulled out the echocardiogram's dowel-shaped probe and pressed it against the line that ran up the middle of his rib cage. Then he nodded at the intern, who fiddled with the voltage. A small black-and-white screen on the top of the cart blinked to life. In a second, the inside of Tarrance's chest was visible. Nick carefully moved the probe back and forth, focusing high on Tarrance's chest. It took a fair amount of skill to find what he was looking for.

"What is it, Nick?" Samantha repeated, her tone a mixture of fear, frustration, and building anger at being ignored.

Nick pointed at a spot on the screen. "Son of a bitch," he said. "Just like the textbooks."

"Distended, swollen aorta," the intern mumbled. "Christ, I can't believe I didn't catch this."

"Could have just happened," Nick responded. "An adrenaline rush when he came awake, or the sedative wearing off. It's a time bomb—you never know what's going to set it off."

"Set what off?" Samantha asked, her anger getting the better of her. "What the hell is it?"

"Dissecting aneurysm," Nick stated in a quick voice, finally sure. "His aorta is splitting in half right in front of our eyes. We've got to get him to the OR right away."

The intern nodded, cursing himself. With the help of the two nurses and an incoming orderly, he gently lifted Tarrance onto a wheeled stretcher. In a flash the team was out the door, the crash cart and ultrasound echocardiogram left behind. The surgeon in the OR would simply use his eyes to guide the operation, as he stitched a graft across the ruined vessel.

Left alone with Samantha in the room, Nick stared at the open doorway. His heart was slamming, his body slick with sweat. A fierce pain emanated from his right hand, sliding up his wrist, his forearm. He clenched his other hand into a fist. Damn it. He wanted to be in that OR so badly. Diagnose, process—cure. That was the surgeon's job, the curing, the cutting that would save Tarrance's life. Nick longed to be in that operating room, his body bathed in surgeon's scrubs, a scalpel sure and shining in his hand—Goddamn it.

He shook his head. It didn't do any good to think like that. It hadn't saved Jennifer, it wouldn't bring his hand back. He just couldn't do it; he couldn't hold the scalpel. It was as simple as that. If he had tried to open the man up with his good hand, his left hand—he simply couldn't. Surgery wasn't baseball. Wielding a scalpel wasn't like swinging a bat. Damn it . . .

Samantha was looking at him. Her cheeks were flushed, and the look in her eyes could only be described as awe.

"How did you know?"

Nick felt his own face turn red. He was embarrassed by her tone. "There were clues," he finally answered, coughing. "I've seen it before—I've fixed it before. It's a common manifestation."

"Manifestation of what?"

Nick rubbed the sweat off of his forehead. "You get a look at Tarrance's fingers? How long they are?

And did you notice how tall and spindly he is?"

Samantha nodded. "Yes, I noticed. He looks like a basketball player—a little like Hakeem Olajuwan. What of it?"

"Marfan's. It's a fairly rare disease, strikes maybe one in every two hundred thousand people. Characterized by weak collagen in the connecting joint tissue, which is why they have such long limbs and fingers. A few players in the NBA are supposedly in the Marfan's club. If watched, it isn't categorically dangerous. Long fingers and legs, bad eyesight or blindness from slipped lenses. But the dissecting aneurysm is one of the very real risks. The minute I saw him indicate the radiating chest pains, I knew. Everything fit together."

Samantha whistled. "You're very good, Nick. You've surprised me twice in one day."

Nick nodded, pleased. "But I'm not sure what difference my brilliance is making," he said. "We didn't learn very much."

"I don't agree. Didn't you hear what he said before the pains struck? He was in the room. He saw them go 'down' during the teleconference. Tarrance was in the room, and he didn't die with the rest of them. I think that's pretty significant information. Now our big question is: Why didn't Tarrance die?"

Nick met her eyes. He knew immediately what she was thinking.

"Marfan's?" he asked.

She shrugged. But he could tell by the way her lips twitched up at the corners—she was convinced they were on the verge of a breakthrough.

FOURTEEN

*M*y cubicle is my castle. Here I am King.

Ned Dickerson slumped forward in his swivel chair, his eyes dull and glazed. Cubicle 9927-3 enveloped him, as it had for two marathon-long years: sheer white plastifoam walls, a small steel desk with an IBM workstation bolted to its surface, a black plastic phone next to the computer, and the swivel chair. There was a dead plant next to the phone, long brown tentacles curling down across the keypad.

Ned took a shallow breath, his body slumping lower in his chair. His neck felt tired and his head slid down, his chin touching his chest. His gaze trickled across the stiff blue material of his new jumpsuit, over his knobby little knees, down to his shoes. There was a kidney-shaped coffee stain on the carpet by his right Ked, surrounding an upside-down coffee cup shaped like a smiling cow. His mother had given him the cup when he had first gotten the job at Telecon.

My cubicle is my world. Here I am God.

He concentrated as hard as he could and slowly raised his head off his chest. His eyes focused on the black plastic phone. A red diode blinked above the dead twig–covered keypad. Blink blink blink. The message light had been blinking for two days. Ned knew there were thirty-nine messages on his phone; he had started to listen to them an hour ago, but had given up after number twelve. The first six were from his girlfriend, Mary Dober. She was trying to be strong, but she just didn't understand why he wouldn't return her calls. Was it over? Had he found someone else? By the fifth message her sobs wiped out her words.

The next few messages were from his mother in Baltimore. His mother who had given him the cow coffee cup. Who two years ago had helped him pack up his things in cardboard boxes and move to his one bedroom apartment in Georgetown. He no longer lived in the apartment in Georgetown. He did not know why.

The next two messages were from his dentist's office. He had missed the appointment to have his wisdom tooth taken out. He noticed that the pain had subsided from a dagger to a dull throb.

What the hell was happening to him? He slowly lifted his hands to his eyes, tried to rub the glaze away. His overmuscled shoulders ached, every muscle crying out in exhaustion. He could not remember the last time he'd slept. Every night, it was the same. The urge would hit him—and there was no way to fight the urge.

Even thinking about it made his stomach tremble. He watched his hands move forward, feeling under his desk—*there*, his fingers touched the cold edges and a thrill moved through his body. His fingernails found the strips of electrical tape and he tore at them, his forearms bulging with muscular strength he did not formerly possess.

The laptop came loose from where it was taped to the underside of his desk. He placed it on his thighs, glancing over his shoulder. His cubicle had a thin plastic door, enough to keep the prying eyes away. But he had to be careful. It was not his laptop.

He had stolen it from Ms. Parkridge's office the week before the beta test. He hadn't meant to steal it—he had just wanted to snoop through her files. He knew she was up to something; every day, she disappeared from the office for a few hours, claiming to be supervising a project at the satellite lab in Baltimore. Ned was in an online Doom tournament with two of the leading engineers from the satellite lab—and they had never met Ms. Parkridge.

So Ned had snuck into her office while she was on one of her secret journeys. Curiosity, boredom, cubicle fever—whatever the reason, he had intended to go through her files. He had found her laptop in the top drawer of her desk. He had opened the laptop and . . .

His heart raced and he felt an almost sexual energy build below his waist. The laptop felt heavy on his lap, and he reached forward with trembling fingers. There was a dull click and the laptop came open.

The colored lights were incredible. His head tilted back and his entire body began to shake. Mary could never make him feel like this. Mother could never make him feel like this.

Somewhere, deep in his mind, he knew that something horrible was going on, that the colored lights were bad, that they were making his life fall apart. He was not a stupid man: he had an engineering degree from MIT; he was Phi Beta Kappa from Johns Hopkins. He understood the term "addiction"; he knew about the mice and the adrenal glands and the electroshock therapy. He had once watched a video of those mice; the button that gave them a sexual high also zapped them with potentially deadly electricity, but the poor little creatures would press that button and press that button and press that button . . .

He leaned close to the screen, staring at the colored lights. His whole life revolved around those colors. Sometimes, he could see them when the laptop was off. He could see them when he closed his eyes. When he tried to sleep.

He was a mouse pressing a button, but he could not stop. The rush was too good. He didn't care about the blackout periods, the disorientation, the exhaustion, the strange changes in his life and body. He did not care that he no longer bathed, barely ate, did things he couldn't understand. All that mattered was pressing that damn button. His teeth came together and he swam through the colors, waves of orgasm moving through his groin.

My cubicle is my cage. Here I am Slave . . .

FIFTEEN

t he air in the small steel elevator was warm, and Nick pulled at his orange laboratory smock, conscious of how it stuck to his chest. Because of the confined space, Samantha's shoulder was barely an inch from his own, and the scent of her hair was strong in his nostrils. Flowery, scrubbed, probably conditioned—it had been a long time since Nick had pondered the intricacies of feminine hair-care products. In many ways, the social isolation of the past five years had made him stronger, more secure with himself, but the nagging discomfort of being so close to a beautiful woman pointed at something he had lost—rather, misplaced.

He flushed, telling himself it was the heat. Samantha Craig was a bureaucratic bitch—so what if she looked great and smelled like summer? He wasn't ready to think about any woman in that way—and especially not her.

The elevator stopped suddenly and the steel doors slid open, revealing an octagonal laboratory: speckled linoleum tiles on the floor, beehive plastic paneled gray walls, long marble counters, aluminum sinks, glistening test-tube racks, and half-filled beakers. Nick tried to guess how many feet below the autopsy room they were—somewhere between fifty and seventy-five, he couldn't be sure. Federal Quarantine Unit B12 was obviously much more than it seemed from the outside.

There were at least fifteen people in the room, all wearing the same bright orange smocks. Nick had held back a dozen comments when Samantha had forced him to don the stupid thing in the car; some nonsense about a personnel-tracking computer that used the color of the smock to keep tabs on the scientists in the lab.

"Follow me," Samantha said as she strolled into the laboratory with an exaggerated ease, and Nick chased after her, fumbling to balance a thick folder of computer printouts under his right arm.

After they had split up outside of Tarrance's hospital room, he had spent a good forty minutes coaxing paper out of the hospital research system. Marfan's was a well-documented syndrome, and he wasn't sure what he was really looking for—so he had adopted the shotgun approach. Anything and everything, he had told the computer. He had hoped that something would jump out at him, some gem of information that would explain why Tarrance had lived and the others had not.

Instead of a gem, he had a stack of computer pages: cases, synopses, broad generalizations. The

stuff of medical research, grants, and Ph.Ds. He had
gone through them back at his apartment, between
showering, changing, and tearing his way through a
box of leftover Chinese food. He had barely made it
to the last printout when Samantha arrived with her
pitch-black car, ready to take him back to the unit.
Her first words had been something like "The damn
chimps just won't die!" It was obvious she wasn't
having any better luck with her investigation of the
virus.

"We're running out of ideas," she said as she led
him through the shiny basement lab, frustration
obvious in her voice. "We've tried everything we can
think of to get the thing to reactivate. We've pumped
it directly into chimpanzees; we've used human tissue, cells from every damn part of the body—and
nothing. We've consulted with doctors, biochemists,
even biological weapons experts. And we're getting
nowhere. Some of my people are beginning to wonder if we've even got the right culprit."

She turned a corner in the lab and stopped in
front of a fifty-inch television screen attached to a
bank of oversized computers. Nick stared at the
monstrosity.

"What do you mean? They don't think CaV is
the killer we're looking for?"

"Finding a strange new virus is not the same as
proving cause and effect; until we actually see it in
action—in a laboratory or in real life—we can't be
sure. And if we're not sure, we may be wasting
valuable time."

Nick could hear the tension in her voice.
Something was bothering her, something she hadn't
yet told him. "The evidence might be circumstan-
tial," he said, trying to soothe her. "But it's still

pretty strong. We've got a mutant virus found in the cells of each of our victims."

Samantha took a deep breath, and Nick couldn't help glancing at the way her chest pressed out against her smock. "But there's a problem with the virus, Nick. Something I've been thinking about for a while."

"What sort of problem?"

"I'll show you."

She leaned forward and began hitting keys on the computer console. A few seconds later, the large television screen flickered to life. A black canvas turned green, then a picture formed in the center. It looked something like the traced outline of an enormous three-dimensional soccer ball, with twenty triangles fitted together, the attachments, or stitching, illustrated by bright red lines. Nick had an idea of what he was looking at, but he let Samantha explain it for him; it had been a long time since med school.

"This is a three-dimensional model of a rhinovirus," she said, flipping hair out of her eyes as her voice became clinical. "Rhinovirus 14, to be precise. To get this model, the rhinovirus was first crystallized; then we used an atom smasher to focus an intense beam of X rays directly through the crystal. The beam, deflected by the virus's structure, gave us images of the atoms which make up the virus. Our Cray supercomputer took the information and drew us this model."

Nick nodded as he ran his eyes over the giant soccer ball. He knew the rhinovirus was so tiny, that compared to a single skin cell it was the size of a period on a blank sheet of paper. In some ways, it was terrifyingly beautiful—but so completely alien, a parasitic creature that was both as primitive as

anything in the world and as fully developed and
capable as evolution allowed. Without thought,
unrelenting, devoid of soul: it didn't care about the
cells it destroyed, the lives it ruined. It followed its
genetic code, the perfect, incessant machine.

"Now this," Samantha continued, hitting more
keys. "Is CaV."

The screen blinked, and the picture was replaced
by an almost exact replica. The soccer ball was now
slightly more oblong, with five extra triangles
spaced across the front face. The "stitching" was
somewhat more pronounced, the red tracings
thicker, implying more structure, more intricate
strength.

"It looks pretty close."

"That's what bothers me. That's what's bothering all of us. It's so damn close, a virologist would
give it a number and add it to the rhinovirus family.
And that's where everything falls apart. That's why
some of us aren't sure we've got the right pathogen."

"I don't understand."

"Nick," Samantha said, pointing at the television screen. "Rhinoviruses aren't airborne. They can
live only in the cells that inhabit the mouth and
nose, and they're passed from person to person
through direct physical contact. Usually nose to
hand, hand to nose. They can't be carried on breath,
or by wind, or by ventilation."

"So that means—"

"That means we don't just have five distinct geographic outbreaks. In just that Boston law firm, we
have nine distinct and simultaneous outbreaks in a
single *room*."

"That's impossible," Nick said, staring at the
glowing soccer ball.

"Completely. But if this thing is what it looks like—a sister to the rhinovirus—there's no mode of infection that could spread it so damn quickly. So the only other possibility is that everyone in that room contracted it somewhere earlier and had it explode at the exact same moment. Which is equally impossible."

Her face was flushed with frustration. She leaned back against a marble counter, her fingers white against the stone. It was obvious she didn't like not having all the answers—it seemed almost a personal affront, an insult. Standing there, Nick had the sudden urge to take her hands in his, to touch her, somehow, let her know that she was not alone in this. He immediately regretted the feeling. He hadn't touched a woman in the way he was thinking since Jennifer.

"I think you're jumping the gun," he said, avoiding looking at her, at the way she absentmindedly rubbed at the silky skin above her collarbone. "Viruses can do some wild things. Chicken pox can resurface fifty years after an infection; measles can cause insanity; viruses can disappear and reappear and do whatever the hell they want—we really don't know what they're capable of."

"But we do know what they want to do—they want to reproduce and survive. Nothing else; these are the only two reasons they exist. A virus finds an appropriate host, inserts itself into appropriate cells, uses the cells to reproduce, then spreads to another host. But CaV isn't doing this. It appeared at once, killed, and seemingly died along with its victims."

She slammed her hands against the counter. "Makes no sense," she continued, stunning Nick with her vehemence. "From an evolutionary standpoint, it's ludicrous. This is a virus with no mode of infection—it completely destroys its host without being passed on!"

Nick held up his hands. "But if CaV didn't cause these deaths, what is it? A coincidence?"

"Maybe it's associated in some other way. Let me ask you a question. If we hadn't discovered CaV—if we took the virus out of the picture, how would you have characterized these deaths?"

Nick pondered the question. "Contamination," he finally said. "Some unknown chemical or bacteriological leak—except that still wouldn't explain the different geographic locations."

"Contamination would be one possibility," Samantha agreed. "But there's another, one that also doesn't make any sense, but is still worth thinking about. An allergic reaction."

Nick rubbed at the scruff that covered his jaw. He hadn't had time to shave in his hurried stop at home. "Why an allergic reaction?"

"Allergies are caused by the immune system misreading a signal—overreacting to a harmless substance, like pollen or insect toxin. So in some ways, an allergic reaction is actually a spontaneous assault from within. A danger created by the human body—like cells pumping out calcium for no apparent reason. Maybe our victim's bodies thought there *was* a good reason."

"That doesn't put us any closer to figuring this out. We've still got four isolated geographic locations and nine simultaneous allergic reactions in a single room—which makes no more sense than contamination. And it doesn't explain the presence of CaV."

"But it does jibe with the spontaneity of the situation. If the killing stroke came from within the victim's bodies—rather than from the outside—that would explain why we can't replicate the situation in the lab."

She pushed off of the counter and headed down the aisle. Nick followed, slightly irritated at the way she led him around without explanation.

Samantha took a sharp left when she got to the far wall of the lab, and Nick was immediately swept up by what he saw over her shoulder: an immense Plexiglas screen suspended from the ceiling, split into five distinct rectangles. In each rectangle glowed a holographic three-dimensional image of the CaV soccer ball. Behind the screen Nick could see a team of scientists in lab coats fiddling with computer consoles, hands waving heatedly as they argued about things he knew he'd never understand.

Samantha stopped ten feet in front of the screen, beckoning with her hand. "If the disease is coming from inside the victims, we can fiddle with the structure of this virus all we want, and it will never do anything but play dead."

"Amazing," Nick mumbled, staring at the screen.

"Genetic manipulation," Samantha said simply. "The computer allows us to replicate bioengineering without having to actually get our hands dirty. The results are plugged into an entirely automated laboratory upstairs. We can manipulate our virus, inject it into chimpanzees, see the results—without ever putting on a Racal suit. The system cost the taxpayers about two hundred million—so I hope we come up with something better than this dead end."

She turned to face him, pointing at the almost

forgotten folder under his arm. He could see the
hope in her gray eyes. "I think the key is still right
there. Why didn't Tarrance die? If it was an allergic
reaction of some kind, why didn't he succumb? If it
was the CaV virus, why didn't it activate in his
bloodstream? If it was contamination, how did he
survive?"

Nick handed her the folder. He was still half-
focused on the amazing display to his left; he felt as
if he had entered some completely alien world.
"Marfan's," he finally began, pulling his thoughts
away from the enormous soccer balls, "may not be
our answer, but it certainly is an interesting syndrome. Basically, it's an inherited disorder of connective tissue. It's characterized by musculoskeletal,
vascular, and ocular abnormalities."

Samantha glanced at the folder. "Musculoskeletal—the long arms, elongated torso, spiderlike
fingers. And vascular—the aortic dissection. What
sort of ocular abnormalities are we talking about?"

"The eyes are affected in fifty to eighty percent
of cases. The most common manifestation is ectopia
lentis, which means the lenses are displaced. Many
Marfan's patients suffer sever myopia, even blindness. But it's just a side effect, compared to the more
significant vascular dangers. Marfan's causes a mol-
ecular defect in the fibrillin of the blood-vessel
walls; this leads to the dilation, dissection, and
eventual rupture of the aorta. Now, why a molecu-
lar defect in fibrillin kept Tarrance alive in that
boardroom—that's a question I can't answer."

Samantha turned back toward the Plexiglas display. One of the soccer balls had begun to rotate,
slowly, its glowing red stitches shimmering. Two of
the scientists on the other side of the screen were

shouting at one another in angry, frustrated tones. Obviously, they were as stumped as Samantha and Nick.

"Fibrillin," Samantha repeated. "The basic component of connective tissue. How is it related to CaV?"

Nick shook his head. "It isn't. From what I saw of the autopsy, the calcifying process was most pronounced in the brain, a little less in the heart and lungs, and *least* of all in the fatty and connective tissues."

"But there's got to be something. We're missing something!"

"Samantha," Nick said, a little too harshly. "You can't control the facts by getting angry at them. Marfan's might have something to do with Tarrance's surviving the disease, but we may never make a true connection."

Samantha turned away. "Then we have to try harder—"

A metallic ringing interrupted her. She reached into an inner pocket of her lab smock and pulled out her cellular phone. Nick watched her, thinking back to all the spy movies he had ever seen. The more he learned about USAMRIID and Samantha Craig, the more absurd everything seemed.

"Call your administrator," Samantha interrupted, her voice low but full of energy. "Tell him you won't be in for a couple of days. We're going to Washington."

"What is it? I thought the most recent outbreak was in some cabin in Vermont."

"There's been another," Samantha said. "And, more important, there's another survivor."

SIXTEEN

the situation didn't seem any different at thirty-thousand feet: cradled in a leather seat, his long legs stretched out against a light blue carpeting, Nick felt his entire body tingling with fear and anticipation. Another outbreak meant that the disease was still out there, waiting, a monstrous time bomb that knew no geographical boundaries. But the news of the new survivor almost turned the outbreak into a breakthrough.

Nick looked around the interior of the Lear jet, trying to clear his mind. The jet was opulently appointed: six leather seats, carpeted walls and ceiling, built-in mahogany bar, projection television—more than Nick had expected when Samantha had shuttled him to the private airfield adjacent to Logan. But he had reserved comment; he was happy to be there, and slightly surprised. Samantha had already fulfilled her promise to let him sit in on the autopsy; she obviously thought he was worth something to her investigation, or she would have shown him the door a long time ago.

He glanced across the aisle to where she was sitting, punching away at her laptop. Her dark hair fell down around her face as she worked, and every few seconds she tucked the ruffled strands behind her ears. Her legs were unavoidable, crossed and bare from ankle to knee.

She looked good: slim, athletic, sophisticated. And she was smart. Smart in that hard-edged way— the youthful, arrogant intelligence of a prodigy. Nick wondered, looking at her, how much younger than he she really was. Ten years?

Nick, what the hell do you think you're doing? He felt his lips tighten. How many therapists had told him that he was being unfair to himself, that Jennifer would have wanted him to fall in love again? But what did the therapists know? Jennifer had not asked for the disease. She didn't choose to die and leave him alone—a virus had made that choice for her. What right did Nick have finding happiness without her?

"I don't mind if you stare," Samantha's voice suddenly swept through the airplane. "But the expression that just crossed your face makes me more than a little nervous."

Nick felt his cheeks flush. He had to keep his mind out of that dark place. "Sorry. I didn't realize I was staring. Find out anything interesting?"

Samantha shut the laptop and stretched her arms over her head. Her suit pulled slightly open under her throat, revealing more porcelain skin. "Nothing I didn't learn on the ride to the airport.

The disease struck the control room of a sewage treatment plant just outside the city. A crew of eight was watching a basketball game on TV when the thing hit. Seven died, one survived. Stanley Parker, sixty-two years old, a mid-level supervisor. They've got him isolated at George Washington University Hospital. His cells show the same immunity as Tarrance's; no CaV. If we can find some similarity between the two, we might be able to get control of this investigation."

Control. If Nick had to use one word to sum up Samantha Craig, that was it. She needed to be in control. Always, in everything. It was obvious in her appearance, in the way she dressed, in the way she led him around, not telling him anything until the last minute.

"The odds are, it won't be something obvious— if it's anything at all."

"I'm not an idiot, Nick. I don't expect to find out that Stanley Parker has Marfan's. But I think we're due for a little good luck."

Nick shrugged, turning toward the window to his left. The sky was just beginning to darken, night coming down in infinite sheets. The Lear jet was extremely quiet, almost like some sort of hot air balloon. "Bet this thing cost us taxpayers a pretty penny, too. You guys at USAMRIID certainly don't skimp."

Samantha laughed. "Not my jet, Nick. I'm borrowing it from the Pentagon. I think it's the secretary of defense's."

"Hey, I'm not complaining. I drive a BMW." Nick smiled at his own inside joke. He had not grown up rich, did not know much about what it was like to live with money. High school football coaches didn't make much money. And most of Nick's life after he left home had been spent earning his degrees. Four years of student loans, one year internship, seven years of residency. When he had finally made some money, it had no longer mattered to him. He had spent part of it on the BMW; the rest had gone home to the coach. Without Nick's mother around anymore, the money made things easier on him.

"Listen," Samantha said, leaning toward him. "I want to apologize for the way I've acted toward you. You've been a great help so far. I know I came down hard in the beginning—but you have to admit, you're a bit of a bastard."

Nick smiled, still looking out the window. That's how his mom had always described the coach. A bastard. But she had loved him to the very end. Despite the depression at a lost career, despite the pain of his joints, despite the ever-present Jack Daniel's.

"I try my best. I've never been much of a people person. Why I went to medical school."

Samantha laughed. "I do know that you've been through a lot in your life. But I couldn't take any chances with this; there's too much at stake."

Nick felt his smile disappearing. There it was again, the pity that he had first sensed in the law firm. He didn't want to get angry at her again—she was trying to be nice. But his hand had already started to ache.

"You don't have to worry about me," he said, suddenly turning toward her. "I'm not going to fuck up your investigation. I'm trying to help—and I think I'm succeeding."

Samantha blanched. There was no way to miss the venom in his voice. "That's one hell of a wall you've built, isn't it?"

The statement was simple, but got right under Nick's skin. A wall? He had built the fucking Empire State Building of walls. First a virus had taken Jennifer away. Then an accident had ruined his career. How was he supposed to act?

"Don't psychoanalyze me, okay?" He softened his tone, but didn't undo his expression. "You don't know the first thing about it."

"I know you lost your wife. And I know you got hurt. I also know you're a damn good doctor, and you've coped extremely well."

"Let's leave it at that. I'm not here to prove myself to you. I want to be a part of this because it turns me on and I think I can make a difference."

"Always the cowboy," Samantha said. There was something strange in her voice, as if the word touched off a memory. Nick couldn't stifle his curiosity.

"What about you? Twenty-five, twenty-six, and saving the world. Flying around in a Pentagon jet, playing with two hundred-million-dollar computers—that doesn't turn you on?"

Samantha grabbed the side of her seat as the jet bounced through an air pocket, then rolled her eyes. "I'm not in it for the rush. I'm a scientist, and this is the edge of science."

"But why USAMRIID?"

"Kind of fell into it," Samantha said. It was obvious she wasn't used to talking about herself. "My father was a navy pilot, and I grew up with the service as a part of my life. I went through Berkeley on an army scholarship; then I got lucky while writing my dissertation on hemorrhagic viruses. USAMRIID came after me."

"So you were a navy brat?"

"For a while. I lived with my father at his base in Hawaii until I was thirteen. Then I moved in with my mother in Cincinnati."

The tension in her voice was unmistakable. Nick knew it was time to back off, but he wanted to know more. "What made you move to Cincinnati?"

She turned toward the window, and Nick thought she was going to close down. But for some reason, she didn't. "My older brother was killed in a training accident. My father fell apart, and for a while, so did I. I got sick—it was pretty bad."

Nick wasn't sure what she meant by "sick," but he let her continue uninterrupted. "I moved in with my mother to get away from Andrew's memories. I felt very guilty about my father—I left him to deal with the pain on his own. When I was eighteen, I guess I chose the military in part because I was trying to take Andrew's place."

She turned away from the window. Her eyes were red at the corners, but she wasn't crying. She was still in control. "I did my dissertation on Ebola and Marburg, and the timing was right—USAMRIID offered me a pretty good position at their Washington headquarters. When the response team was created, I was in the right place at the right time. I went through a year of intensive training, and here I am."

Nick knew there was a lot she wasn't telling him. There was no way it was easy for someone so young—and a woman—to move up so quickly in an organization like USAMRIID. But it was obvious she was driven. Perhaps she was still trying to take her brother's place. *Now who's the psychologist?*

"In some ways," Samantha finished. "I *am* here to prove myself. I know I'm good at my job, but if this thing gets out of my control, you can bet that's not going to make any difference. My career's wrapped up in this thing too."

"So we've both got our reasons—and our scars. We should be able to keep your investigation going without killing one another."

Samantha laughed. Then she pushed her hair out of her eyes. "Nick, can I ask you a question? If you don't want to answer, you don't have to—"

"You want to know how my wife got AIDS." Nick didn't know why, but suddenly he wanted to tell her. "It was the second year of my surgical residency. We wanted to start a family. She was going to take time out of her pediatric training to have the baby. We had it all planned out."

Strange, to be talking about it. It no longer made him want to drink, or scream, or even cry. "About two months into the pregnancy, she collapsed in the bathroom. Shooting pains in her abdomen, and bleeding, lots of bleeding. I got called out of surgery, but she was already on her way to an adjoining operating room. They did an emergency laparotomy."

He remembered that she wasn't a doctor. "It was an ectopic pregnancy. The fertilized egg had lodged in a fallopian tube. The tube had ruptured. There were problems in surgery, more bleeding—extensive. She needed a transfusion."

He closed his eyes, his teeth inadvertently coming together. Yes, damn it, he was angry. It wasn't supposed to be possible anymore. Ninety-nine percent, that was what the books said. The screening process was almost perfect.

"The truth is, it still happens. Even with the new screening methods. It takes less than ten microliters of blood to transmit HIV. That's roughly the amount necessary to cover the head of a pin."

He opened his eyes, the anger subsiding. "Her weakened state made it very easy for the virus. The opportunistic infections started almost at once. She went from an HIV diagnosis to AIDS in no time at all. We never had to decide about continued sexual practices, or having the child we both so wanted, because I never got to make love to my wife again. She died a year later."

Samantha reached across the aisle and touched his hand. The motion surprised Nick, brought him out of the darkness. "I'm sorry. I didn't mean to make you remember."

"It's okay. But you understand, I don't see CaV the same way you do. I know we're fighting a war against these creatures. I know what they can do."

Samantha removed her hand from his, nodding. "Then you can be as much of a bastard as you want. We both know what the common enemy is."

The jet dipped downward, beginning its descent into Washington. Nick took a deep breath and forced the sorrow out of his mind. Samantha was honest and straightforward. He was beginning to like her. He settled into his leather chair, preparing for landing. Despite his pessimism, he couldn't help feeling a tinge of excitement as the plane bumped down onto the runway.

Twenty minutes later, Nick and Samantha stepped through the door into Stanley Preston's private hospital room.

"He's blind," Samantha said, staring at the man in the bed. "He's completely blind."

With that realization, they suddenly began to understand.

SEVENTEEN

t he helicopters come in low over the jungle. Six, camouflage green, flying in close combat formation. Their long, steel rotors rip through the glassy dawn as they bear down on the tiny village. Grass huts, oxen drinking from wooden troughs, children dancing through mud puddles, mothers and fathers working in the nearby rice paddy. Someone hears the rotors and four dozen faces turn upward, shock and fear filling Asian eyes. A young pregnant woman screams as the helicopters clear the last set of trees; she is expecting the hail of bullets, the parallel rows that will tear families apart, fling children's limbs into the mud puddles and fathers' brains into the rice paddies.

But the hail of bullets never comes. Instead, the helicopters slow as they reach the center of the village. A vent opens in the bottom of the lead helicopter. Five white pellets—each the size of a man's head—drop to the ground. Then the helicopters turn back toward the jungle, gaining altitude; a minute later, they are gone.

The villagers stare at the white pellets. They are almost spherical, with smooth, polished surfaces. One of the bolder children points and makes a joke; the American helicopters are laying eggs.

Suddenly, the child starts to choke. Then all of the villagers are clutching at their throats. Blood spurts from their mouths as the vesicles in their lungs explode. They drop where they stand, into the mud puddles, into the rice paddies. Agent MCa21— mitotoxic chloric acid—has infiltrated their respiratory systems. An airborne compound developed during the summer of 1962, in the biochemical labs at MIT . . .

"Melora, you were the only one who ever understood."

Melora Parkridge opened her eyes. She could feel the tears on her cheeks. Her father was lying on the stiff cot in front of her, his naked, withered body glowing in the high orange light. He was staring at the ceiling, his lips curled back from his darkened gums.

"You know how I suffered. Your mother never understood."

Melora nodded, lifting a wet washcloth out of a bucket of soapy water stashed under the cot, as her gaze moved around the small room. Four gray walls, an antique wooden dresser, a nineteen-inch color television sitting on top of a felt-covered card table near the bed, and the chair—shiny steel frame, oversized wheels, vinyl padded seat. The same wheelchair her father had been using since the sixties. The same chair he had sat in at her graduation from the biochemistry department at MIT. The only chair he had ever bought—to replace the one they had given him when they had brought him home from the front, half a man, shattered.

She turned toward his legs, the tears running freely. Sticklike, skeletal, the pale skin wrinkled and covered with age spots. She could still see the scar that streaked across his right hip, continuing under his body to the small of his back. The shrapnel from the experimental nonmagnetic land mine had severed his spinal column—true to the German weapon's design. His wound had changed the way American troops swept for mines; their magnetic sensors suddenly outdated in the race for better means to kill. *Progress. Science. Mitotoxic chloric acid . . .*

"Even fifty years later, every night I dream that I'm walking again. Every morning I stare at that damn chair. All I have is you, Melora."

"I'll always be here to take care of you."

"Because it hurts, Melora. It never stopped hurting."

"I know."

She knew. *The helicopters come in low over the jungle.* She had watched the scene a thousand times in her head. She did not know the name of the village, or its exact location, but she knew that it had once existed, somewhere in Laos, somewhere deep in the jungle. *Beta Run 669–7, Confidential, for Internal Use Only.* She had seen the file pictures—the aftermath. The bodies heaped together, the white spheres still decaying in the humid jungle sun. She carried the guilt with her like her father carried his shrapnel scars.

"You know how much I love you, don't you,

Melora? You've always taken care of me, even when your mother stopped. When she couldn't handle it anymore."

Melora nodded. She lifted his gnarled hand, holding it in the air as she slid the washcloth down under his elbow, gently rubbing at the flaps of aging skin. It was fifteen years since her mother had disappeared. She had been threatening to leave since Melora was a child. She had tried, at first, to be a wife to her tortured husband. But she wasn't a strong woman. She had wanted him to accept what had happened, to move on, to grow, to live. To be like the other soldiers who came home carrying shrapnel, the stiff-chinned veterans from the John Wayne movies—proud to have sacrificed for their nation, proud to have helped rid the world of Hitler, whatever the cost. Instead, Allen Parkridge had grown into a depressed, bitter old man.

Melora moved the washcloth over his chest, watching the dribbles of water roll over his wrinkled skin. She was paying for a full-time nurse, but still she bathed him herself; it was a ritual that dated back to her twenty-fourth birthday, right after she had left MIT. Her mother had called it abnormal, another reason Melora would never find a man, would never lead a normal life. A symbol of a perverse, obsessive relationship.

Perhaps the attention she paid her father *was* perverse. Melora liked to think of it as penance. Her father dreamed about his destroyed legs; she dreamed about egg-shaped white tablets. There was nothing she could do for the villagers—except suffer daily with her father. It was warped logic, but it worked. The time spent with her father was cathartic, helped strengthen her. More than that, her

moments watching his pain helped solidify her
resolve. *The thing that had taken his legs and the white
tablets she had unwittingly developed at MIT were
symptoms of the same disease. . . .*

She finished washing his chest, then dropped
the washcloth back into the bucket. She dried him
with a clean towel, then retrieved the covers from
the end of the bed and pulled them up over his
naked body. The nurse could put him back into his
gown; Melora was already running late.

"I have to go now," she said, rising. "But I'll be
back tomorrow."

"Because you care about me. You've always
cared about me."

Melora leaned forward and kissed his forehead.
It was like kissing a piece of cold chicken. She
backed to the doorway and took a last look at her
father. Only his head was visible above the sheet.
His face was still pointed toward the ceiling. He
was a picture of pure misery. And he had been that
way as long as she could remember.

She turned and headed out of his private room.
The hallway was empty and smelled of antiseptic
soap. The floor was yellowed porcelain, the walls
hospital blue. There were numbered wooden doors
every ten feet, but Melora had never been in any of
the other private rooms. She walked stiffly forward,
the tears drying on her cheeks.

She came to a pair of windowed doors and
pushed her way through into the main lobby. A
thick crimson carpet swept across a thirty-foot-wide
rectangular atrium, ending in another set of double
doors. In front of the doors was a curved reception
desk, staffed by two elderly nurses in white uniforms. Couches sat at random intervals throughout

the room, and there were three television sets hanging from racks on the walls, all tuned to the same
home shopping channel. A dozen wheelchairs spotted the lobby, and Melora tried to avoid looking at
the other residents as she headed toward the reception desk.

She hated the thought of her father living in this
place. But at eighty-three, he needed full-time care.
With the hours she was keeping, there was no way
she could leave him in her apartment. Thankfully, it
was only a temporary situation. After the Big Turn
On, she would take her father far away from here.
She had already made plans: a two-bedroom cabin
in Colorado, located next to a natural spring.
Spectacular views and no neighbors.

She nodded at the two nurses as she passed the
reception desk. They hardly acknowledged her;
Melora had not missed a visit in the year and half
since she had placed her father in their care.

She stepped through the double doors and felt
the fresh air against her face. Gothic pillars rose up
on either side of the stone front steps, backlit by a
pair of hanging imitation oil lamps. It was dark, and
she could barely make out the low curves of her
Volvo parked twenty yards away. She strolled
across the manicured front lawn, her shoulders rising under her ever-present blue jumpsuit, her arms
straightening at her sides. She could feel the energy
returning to her veins, the mask gliding down over
her face. She needed to be viciously strong, especially now, so close to the Big Turn On. She needed
to remember: *Penance.* Sharing her father's pain was
only the beginning. The event she had planned
would weigh against the monstrous sin of the white
egg-shaped pellets.

She reached her Volvo and slid inside. There was
no need for locks in this shadow of a town: Split
River, Virginia, had fewer than three thousand residents, most of whom worked at a nearby Pepsi Cola
bottling factory. She turned the key and listened as
the Volvo started up.

The Split River Home for Convalescents was
only ten minutes from Pandora's main laboratory. If
Melora drove quickly, she would arrive a few minutes before her helicopter. Then Simon would get
her back to Telecon before Teal missed her. He had
another late-night meeting planned, to once again
go over the final preparations. He didn't want to
leave anything to chance.

Neither did Melora. She had been preparing for
this for a long time.

EIGHTEEN

the eye was enormous, suspended five feet above the porcelain floor by a glowing Lucite column. A triangular cross-section of the eye was missing, a three-dimensional slice paired away to give full view of the sphere's inner workings. Different colored lights showed pathways and circuit lines, bright red diodes indicating photons, rods, and cones—the magical insides of one of nature's most amazing machines.

"The department's pride and joy," explained an overweight opthamology resident with bushy black hair and a thick Indian accent. "A teaching device for the medical students. Paid for by the wife of a senator who ran out of PC charities to fund. Bad for the baby seals and the blue whales, good for us."

Samantha paced around the edge of the teaching atrium, which housed the huge diorama, too ex-

hausted to be overly impressed—but excited enough
to be impatient with the resident's unnecessary wit.
It was nearing nine in the evening, and her investigation had suddenly exploded. She was so close she
could taste success; from the few words Nick had
offered since the discovery of Stanley Preston's condition, she knew they had found the link that would
perhaps explain it all. She just wasn't sure, yet, how
to decipher what they had learned.

But judging from the expression on Nick's face,
he had a pretty clear idea. He was sitting on the
edge of a mahogany teaching desk a few feet away,
concentrating on Stanley Preston's medical chart.
The resident was still babbling on about George
Washington University's opthamology department
and its funding troubles, but Nick was oblivious.

"There are a number of other models I can show
you," continued the resident, obviously excited by
the company. "We've got a whole slew of wonderful—"

"Thank you, we'll take it from here," Samantha
interrupted, her voice stiffer than necessary. The resident shrugged, backing out of the atrium. The door
clicked shut behind him.

It had been Nick's idea to move their discussion
to the opthamology department. Not because there
was anything they needed in that area of the hospital; it was simply a setting that seemed appropriate.
The magical natural machine represented by the
enormous diorama was the key they had been looking for.

"Cataracts," Nick stated, finally closing Preston's
medical chart. "Totally distorting his lenses, to the
point of blindness. No light could get through. No
light at all."

Samantha watched him thoughtfully. All the facts were there, she just hadn't yet made the connections. Nick was ahead of her, of that she was pretty sure, but she didn't think he had it all yet, either. Of course, he would never let that show. That wasn't his way. He held things inside as long as possible.

The conversation in the airplane had surprised her, shown her a side to Nick she had not expected. Depth, sensitivity—and in turn, he had brought her out of her own shell. She had told very few people about Andrew. She was still scared to talk about it, as if bringing it out into the open would push her back to the anorexia that had almost killed her.

She blinked, clearing her mind of the thought. Now was not the time for personal scars. "And Tarrance?" she asked. "His Marfan's screwed with his lenses as well, correct?"

"Upward displacement. Light could still get through, but distorted, diminished."

He stood up from the desk and crossed to the model eye in the middle of the atrium. "You have a basic understanding of how sight works, right?"

Samantha nodded, though in truth, "basic" was a bit of an overstatement. She had studied eyesight in the course of working on her Ph.D., but only in relation to the effects of certain viruses on the optic centers.

"Photons of light pass through the lens and hit the retina," she started, "and cells in the retina perceive that light, communicating through the optic nerve to centers in the brain."

Nick traced the track of red diodes that traveled through the diorama. "The photons hit the retina, and cells called rods and cones—mostly rods in the periphery, mostly cones in the center—react with proteins called rhodopsin and opsin. The specific wavelengths of light—by wavelength, I mean color, or spectral identification—cause the rhodopsin and opsin proteins to change shape. This change of shape causes a cascade of cellular events that leads to the opening of ion channels which in turn transmit the signal down the optic nerves."

"Ion channels," Samantha repeated, trying to dredge up what she knew about the nervous system. "Sort of the electronic wiring of the body."

"Right," Nick said, walking around the huge eye. "Ion channels allow the body's cells to communicate by regulating and transmitting electrical impulses, or packages of information. In simple terms, sight works in this way: the photons that enter the eye cause the ion channels to open in a certain manner—regulated by the shape of the rhodopsin and opsin proteins—which communicates vision to the brain."

It was alien stuff to Samantha, but she realized it was less important to understand the details than to make sense of the overall picture. *Light goes in through the lens, causes a cellular reaction in the retina, which is transmitted by means of ion channels to the brain.*

"Okay," Samantha said, crossing past Nick to the other side of the eye. They were pacing the room like two caged animals, focused on their imagined prey—which was somehow represented by the diorama. "We know how sight works. And we've got two survivors with one major similarity—screwed up lenses."

"But that's not all we've got," Nick said, stopping directly across from her, their line of sight broken by the great eye. "We've also got a few major clues to work with. Starting with the calcifying disease itself. At the autopsy, one thing that struck me was the nature of the calcification. It was not uniform."

"No," Samantha agreed. "In all the victims, the brain was the most calcified. Then the heart and muscles. The least calcified was the fatty and connective tissue."

"If I remember my basic anatomy, the brain is the area of the body with the highest concentration of ion channels. The muscles—and the heart is a large muscle—come next, then the organs and fatty tissue. Exactly in the same order as calcification."

Samantha stepped forward. Maybe it was the excitement of the moment, maybe it was the bridge they had crossed in the airplane, maybe it was the idea that they were using each other to think, to process ideas and clues—but she suddenly wanted to be close to him. "So we've got a disease that has an obvious affinity for ion channels. And we've got two survivors with disrupted sight, a process that involves an outside force interacting with—"

"Ion channels," Nick finished for her. Now they were almost near enough to touch. "The question is, what does one have to do with the other? How are the ion channels in the retina linked to the ion channels in the rest of the body?"

Samantha swung away from Nick, her hands slapping together. "CaV," she said suddenly. "A mutated rhinovirus. The CaV virus, like any virus, spreads from cell to cell. It could be the bridge between the different ion channels."

"Well, we still haven't explained where CaV comes from. Unless . . ." he paused, his face suddenly lighting up.

"What is it?"

"Hold on a second. You said before that rhinoviruses are present almost everywhere. It's quite likely that there were normal rhinoviruses present in each of the outbreak sites, right? Before the disease struck."

Samantha nodded. Nick continued on, his words coming fast. "Samantha, what is it that's been bothering us most about these outbreaks?"

Samantha answered without thinking. "The method of infection. How the disease seemed to strike nine different geographic locations in the same room."

"Right. In each outbreak, it seems like there are as many epicenters of the virus as their are victims. Well, what if that were true? What if each victim *was* the epicenter of CaV?"

Samantha stared at him. "I don't understand."

"What if a common rhinovirus was *mutated* within each victim. What if the genetic engines within each victim's optic cells—controlled by their ion channels—were spitting out strange sequences of DNA? And this DNA was interacting with the common rhinovirus, changing its genetic makeup."

Samantha realized with a start that he was right. *It was possible.* "Viruses often incorporate the DNA of cells they infect, and then, in their search for reproduction, they carry that DNA with them from cell to cell. But what if instead of a simple blueprint for replication, a virus carried along with it a blueprint for calcium production? It would travel from cell to cell, forcing each cell to pump out calcium. Not just any cells—appropriate cells. Cells with the specific codes, or receptor sites, specific to that sequence of viral DNA. In this case, cells with ion channels."

Samantha felt as if a stick of dynamite had

exploded inside her skull. She spun toward Nick and grabbed his hand. "Is this just bullshit? Or are we getting it?"

Nick pulled her across the atrium. There was a large slate blackboard attached to the far wall, twenty feet beyond the huge eye. Nick quickly found a piece of chalk and attacked the slate.

Photons, he wrote, the chalk sending up clouds as his hand moved. "Not just any photons—photons of some uncommon wavelength, or strange modulation—interact with *ion channels* in the retina, causing the transfer of *DNA* into a *rhinovirus*, which in turn spreads to affect *other ion channels* in the body—"

Samantha grabbed the chalk from him. "Trying to reproduce," she said, picking up the train of thought. "But instead, uses the ion channels to force the cells to produce huge amounts of *calcium*. And wham bam, we've got ourselves a room full of *dead lawyers*."

She stepped back from the blackboard, breathing fast, her heart pounding. She stared at the large chalk words: *Photons. Ion channels. DNA. Rhinovirus. Other ion channels. Calcium. Dead lawyers.* It looked like nonsense—but it made sense. It explained why they couldn't replicate in the lab what had happened in the law firm—the mutated rhinovirus was just a carrier; it wasn't the source of the disease. The true source of the disease came from within each victim's body, brought about by an unknown stream of photons. The theory made all the clues fit together, and the science was real, possible. Except for one thing . . .

"What sort of photons are we talking about?" she asked, turning toward Nick. "What the hell kind of light could be causing this sort of chain reaction? And where is it coming from?"

Nick cleared his throat. A dusting of chalk clung to his wild brown hair. "To answer that, we have to go back to the scenes. In each case, what was going on when the disease struck?"

Samantha took a deep breath, thinking. She had spent the past two weeks looking for links between the sites—similar travel histories, last meals, allergies, the list went on forever. But now they were looking for something specific, a link that had to do with light, with photons, electricity—she paused, startled by her own thoughts.

"We know what the lawyers were doing. Tarrance told us. "They were sitting in front of a television screen. A teleconference."

Nick looked at her. "And the sewage workers were watching a basketball game."

"Nick, what the hell is going on?"

Ten minutes later, camped out in a co-opted GW University Hospital computer room, Samantha parroted the information as it came over her secure Internet line.

"The first outbreak occurred in a graduate dorm at the University of Minnesota," Samantha said soberly. "Three students were playing a computer game against another group of students in an adjoining room. The two computers were linked by fiber optic lines—part of Telecon's beta test of the information highway."

"The precursor to the Big Turn On." Nick said. Everyone knew about the beta test; it was the news subject of the year. A few thousand lucky households got to try out the information highway before the rest of the country joined in.

Samantha paused, her mouth parched. "The second outbreak occurred three hours later at a steel factory in Pittsburgh. The victims were on a break, watching a boxing match. They were also part of Telecon's beta test. The next outbreak took place that same evening in a home in San Diego, California. A thirty-three-year-old insurance broker was telecommuting to work."

"Through the fiber optic network," Nick whispered. "Another member of the beta test, right?"

"And the next two as well. First, an architect in Oklahoma, using the fiber optic network to send video to his boss. And last, the young woman in Vermont who was watching a television sitcom; video on demand, Telecon calls it. Christ, Nick, they're all part of Telecon's beta test. We ignored it before, because we didn't see how it could be relevant."

She leaned back from her computer terminal. Her entire body felt numb. She could not believe the suspicions going through her head. Was it possible? Television sets and computer screens? Telecon's beta test?

"It's not as crazy as it seems," Nick said, though his voice seemed to doubt his words. "It's well documented that certain forms of light can have dangerous effects on human physiology. In epileptics, for instance, seizures can be induced by high intensity strobe lights."

Samantha shook her head, refusing to accept what they had discovered. A disease spread through television screens? "Nick, we're not talking about seizures."

"No," he quickly agreed. "But my point is, just because it seems insane, don't immediately assume it's impossible."

"You think something is traveling through the fiber optic lines?"

There, she had said it. She turned to see the reaction on Nick's face. She wanted him to shake his head, to swear it was impossible. He just met her gaze.

"I think we need to learn more about the beta test, about fiber optics, about Telecon before we can say for sure. But yes, this is where the evidence is pointing."

Samantha shut her eyes. It was not what she had wanted to hear, even though she agreed. A growing mountain of dead bodies, a hypothesis that involved television sets and computer screens—she was going to get laughed out of USAMRIID. *But what if they were right?*

"We're going to need replicable results before we approach anyone with this."

"I don't know, Samantha. That may not be possible, at least not right away. There are an infinite number of wavelengths of light. I don't know much about Telecon's fiber optic network, but from what I've read, the whole point of fiber optics is bandwidth—"

"Hold on," Samantha interrupted. "We're getting ahead of ourselves. Neither one of us has the expertise to figure this out. Before I risk my career, I need to know the facts—from an expert. Someone we can trust to keep this quiet until we're sure."

Nick leaned back against a computer table. "You have someone in mind?"

Samantha pursed her lips. A foolish choice, she told herself. Especially with Nick in tow. But he *was* an expert. And she had once trusted him—at least enough to sleep with him.

NINETEEN

are you sure this is the right place?" Nick leaned back against the parked limousine, a Styrofoam cup full of coffee warming his hands. Samantha nodded, beckoning him forward.

"He said he would meet us inside the lobby."

"From the looks of things, we're already in the lobby."

Nick finished his coffee and left the cup on top of the limousine. The caffeine felt good; he had been up most of the night. He didn't like hotels, and after the discovery they had made in the GW computer lab, his mind would not leave him alone. The more he thought about it, the more their hypothesis seemed correct—despite what that would mean.

He caught up to Samantha at the head of a stone walkway. They were six blocks behind Union

Station, lodged between two streets of boarded-up tenement buildings and what looked like a defunct public school. Nick slid his hands into his pockets as he surveyed what there was of the building in front of them: the FBI Center for Developing Technologies was obviously still under construction. Bulldozers and small cranes sat at odd angles in a vast mud field that surrounded an unremarkable two-story structure. Half of the windows on the second floor were covered with strips of orange canvas instead of glass, and much of the outer walls were still nothing more than bare Sheetrock.

The stone walkway ended in what would one day be a functional front entrance; a glass revolving door set in between two steel columns, underneath a bronze FBI seal. Yellow tape crisscrossed the glass of the door, and the seal was tilted a few degrees off center, as if its rivets still needed tightening. Samantha stepped into the revolving door first and Nick followed, wondering what he would find on the other side.

Samantha had been fairly mysterious about the "expert" they were going to meet: Ted Finder, a high-level communications operative with the FBI, and an old friend of hers from right after college. Nick could tell by the tension in the limousine there was more to it than that. Samantha and Ted had had a relationship of some sort. Just from looking at her, he could tell that there were still some feelings, at least on her part.

She had traded her gray power suit for a black outfit: a clingy rolled turtleneck, a charcoal Armani jacket, and black tights that made her legs seem twice as long. Her hair fell down against her shoulders, one errant lock coiling past her right eye, giving her a dangerous, sensual air. She still looked like she could rip your lungs out if you crossed her, but now the stiffness was tinged with sex appeal.

Or maybe Nick was reading too much into her demeanor. For all he knew, this Ted Finder was some pimply former classmate.

"Samantha. Christ, you look great."

Six foot three, wavy blond hair, blue eyes, line-backer shoulders, a thousand-dollar pinstriped suit—Nick suddenly wanted to throw up. Ted Finder looked like one of those guys who sold cologne in upscale department stores. No question, those teeth were bonded, nothing in nature was actually that white.

"Ted, this is Nick Barnes. Thanks so much for meeting us on such short notice."

Ted shook Nick's hand, flashing those damn teeth. He seemed to take in Nick's leather jacket, faded jeans, and J. Crew lace-up boots in one glance. "No problem, Sam. Please excuse the decor around here—the place isn't officially up and running for two more months."

He took a step back, waving behind him at the discordant front lobby. Half of the cement floor was covered in red carpeting, the other half cluttered with leftover steel beams and huge wooden boxes full of rivets, nails, and unrecognizable chunks of metal. The walls were still unfinished, with exposed wiring and plumbing tubes sticking out of gaps in the cream plaster. Two men in orange construction suits and yellow hard hats were standing by one of the gaps, working carefully to string a long, snake-like cable down the underside of what looked like a water pipe.

"For now," Ted explained, "we're running our

fiber optic cables anywhere we can. This used to be a post office, before the area went to hell. We've set up shop on the second floor while they finish remodeling the downstairs. Come on, I'll show you."

He strolled to Samantha and put an arm over her shoulders. For some reason, this familiarity tugged at Nick. Or maybe it was the fact that the guy seemed to be completely ignoring him—or perhaps it was still just the guy's teeth.

"I have to admit," he heard Ted comment as they moved through the lobby, "I was a little surprised you called. How long has it been—four years?"

Nick couldn't hear Samantha's answer. He hurried to keep up as they entered a stairwell at the far end of the lobby. They picked their way past boxes of construction material as they climbed to the second floor. A heavy, unfinished wooden door opened up into a makeshift computer lab: a sprawling, open loft with exposed wood floors, cluttered with desks and steel drafting tables. There were at least fifty personal computers in the room, with wires and cables running in every direction across the floorboards, disappearing into panels of sockets lining the cinder-block walls. At least fifteen people in white shirts and knit ties mulled around the room, some gathered in small groups around computer screens. Ted led them toward a cubicle in the back of the room. As they navigated forward, Nick couldn't help noticing that all of the computers he passed had Telecon Set-Top Boxes. He also noticed a huge coil of fiber optic cable in the far left corner of the room.

Once inside the cubicle, Ted waved them to two chairs in front of a small steel table, pulling over a wooden stool for himself. Nick found himself staring at an IBM with an oversized screen. Above the screen was another Set-Top Box, a single red word blinking across its face: READY. He was surprised by the word; his own Set-Top Box attached to his television at home was still blank, waiting for Telecon's Big Turn On, now just two days away. Then he realized that Ted's computer must be involved in the beta test. He glanced at Samantha, wondering if she had noticed. She, too, was staring at the bright red word.

"You said on the phone that you had some questions for me about Telecon's beta test," Ted said, focusing his smile on Samantha. "I must admit, I'm intrigued. You're still with USAMRIID, aren't you?"

Samantha nodded, turning away from the Set-Top Box. "Before we start, I need you to know how sensitive this is. I called you because I think I can trust you."

Ted threw a quick glance at Nick. "Of course, Sam. As long as it doesn't infringe on my commitment to the bureau—"

"It won't. Just information, Ted. Dr. Barnes is helping me in an investigation into some mysterious deaths. We think there's a possibility that these deaths are linked to Telecon's beta test."

Ted started to laugh, then realized she was serious. Still, he couldn't keep an edge of incredulity out of his voice. "Linked how? People getting zapped by their Set-Top Boxes?"

"I'd rather not get into that yet. Right now, we just need to know what it is we're dealing with."

Ted slid out of his jacket and hung it on a hook suspended from the cubicle wall. Nick was surprised to see a leather holster under his right arm.

He also noticed an ominous bulge just above Ted's ankle. He had thought this guy was supposed to be some sort of tech. Did everyone in the FBI carry guns?

"Short course or long?" Ted asked, setting back down on his stool.

"Very short, if that's possible."

"Well, I can try. I guess the shortest way to put it is this: Telecon's beta test is the first step in the biggest societal change in the last thousand years."

Nick felt like rolling his eyes, but didn't. Like everyone else, Nick had been hearing about the information highway for much of his adult life. He had seen nothing yet that had lived up to the hype. He noticed Ted was looking at him.

"I can see you're skeptical. That's good, that's what Telecon wants. A skeptical audience. It will make their accomplishment so much more enormous."

He rose from his stool and walked over to the Set-Top Box on top of the computer. "People think that the Internet is a tiny example of what the information highway is going to be like. It's not. Two days from now, society is going to change. Every television set and computer in the country is going to be linked together by Telecon's fiber optic network. Nearly instantaneous exchange of information—of any kind—will suddenly be possible."

He reached behind his computer and flicked a switch. The screen glowed blue. A menu appeared, white words scrolling in from the right: MARKET-PLACE, RESEARCH, ENTERTAINMENT, TELE-CONFERENCE, WORKSTATION, PRESS ONE FOR MORE.

He hit the number one on the keyboard. A new

menu appeared. MEDICAL, BANKING, EDUCA-
TIONAL, TRAVEL, ANALYSIS, PRESS ONE FOR
MORE.

He turned, looking at both Nick and Samantha.
"In two days, nearly every person in the country is
going to wake up to the exact same menu on his
television screen—an almost infinite number of
options, all brought right into your home by Telecon
Industries. The technology, of course, is fairly complicated: fiber optic cables running underground to
junctions in every home, more glass lines feeding
into the Set-Top Boxes—themselves a marvel of
microchip engineering and interactive software. But
the results will be like magic. A push of a button,
and every household and business in the country
will be truly interconnected."

Samantha pointed to the Set-Top Box. "And this
is all possible because of fiber optics?"

"Exactly. The keyword of the revolution is *bandwidth*. See, information doesn't move any faster
through fiber optic cable than through copper
wire—both go the speed of light. But fiber optic
cable, which is made out of super-pure glass, can
carry an enormous bandwidth—more than 2.5 gigabits per second. That's enough room to carry the
entire *Encyclopedia Britannica* at once; or twenty-four
thousand phone calls; or an entire Hollywood
movie. Around the world, in a fraction of a second."

"And Telecon runs this entire network?" Nick
asked. He had never paid that much attention to the
TV news, so he only knew the basics: fiber optics
made the information highway possible. Telecon
had built the network over the past ten years, and
had provided the Set-Top Boxes free to every household in the country.

"Well, depends what you mean by run. Telecon has been granted—grudgingly by the industry, legally by the government—a temporary monopoly on the network."

"That seems un-American," Samantha commented.

"Not really," Ted responded. "It's the same thing that happened when the telephone lines first went in. One company was given a temporary monopoly to cover the enormous start-up costs of laying all the lines. Of course, this case is a little different. Telecon took over the industry before the government even got involved. Mergers, acquisitions, a slow monopoly of the best interactive software—and then, most importantly, the encryption program that became the standard method of securing information."

"But how could they afford to lay all the fiber optic cables? That must have cost billions."

"An estimated thirty billion dollars, actually. Telecon didn't personally lay all the lines; the cable and telephone companies did much of the actual work. But Telecon used intricate corporate means to gain control of those lines; the Trojan Horse Strategy, they're calling it in the business schools. First, the dumping of the Set-Top Boxes. Nearly every household and business in the country got a free box. And then, when the government chose Telecon's encryption program as the official standard, that gave Telecon everything it needed to take control of the network. By the time the fiber optic lines were ready for the beta test, Telecon was the only company that could make the information highway work."

"And then the government jumped in," Samantha said.

"The Republican Congress, led by Speaker Tyro

Carlson, had already been leaning toward a national effort to get the highway up and running. Making one encryption program standard was the first step; they'd been working on that for years, since the failure of their own Clipper chip. Allowing Telecon to run its beta test—and then go national this Thursday—was the next obvious step. The legislation states that Telecon will amicably allow itself to be broken up into competing pieces in three years."

Nick looked at the Set-Top Box. There was something ominous about the idea of one company having so much power. But from what he understood about encryption, the fact that Telecon made the boxes and the software didn't mean it could control the information itself. The reason the government's Clipper chip failed was because there were rumors of a backdoor, which would allow the government to break the encryption codes. Telecon's encryption program was chosen because it was supposedly unbreakable.

"So that's the overview," Ted was saying, dropping back onto his stool. "As for specifics on the technology, you'll have to give me some idea what you're looking for."

Samantha glanced at Nick; she was trying to decide how much she should tell Ted. Nick was pleased by her concern. Despite whatever relationship she once had with this guy, she didn't trust him entirely.

"At this point, I have only one question. Would it be possible for some unknown, unexpected wavelength of light to be transmitted through the fiber optic network to television and computer screens at different locations across the country?"

Ted saw the concern in her face and took the

question seriously. "Well, that's really two questions. First, would it be possible for the television screens and computers to emit whatever wavelength of light you're talking about; and second, would an unknown wavelength of light be able to pass through Telecon's network without anyone noticing."

He thought for a few seconds. "My answer to the first part is a tentative yes. Although televisions themselves are only designed to present wavelengths corresponding to the visible bandwidth of light, we know that screens also give off very low level infrared rays and sometimes X rays. If an unknown wavelength was transmitted through the fiber optic cable attached to a specific television, I think it would be possible for that wavelength to pass through the picture tube and be emitted through the glass of the screen. The same goes for personal computers."

He leaned forward. "As for the second part of your question, my official answer would be no. First, the Set-Top Box encryption process makes it impossible for an unknown, uncoded wavelength to be accepted by the network or by the individual receiver at each household. Second, all transmissions on the network pass through Telecon's main complex here in D.C.; their computer monitors every single byte—I've seen it in action myself on a walk-through tour. It would be impossible for something to pass through their system without someone noticing."

Nick leaned back, frustrated. This was not the answer he had wanted to hear. Then he noticed that Samantha was focused on Ted's face. She was trying to read his expression.

"Officially, that's your answer. What about unofficially?"

Ted had suddenly become uncomfortable. The change was obvious, as he shifted against his stool. "You know this business, Sam. In the bureau, there are always rumors. Everyone loves a good conspiracy."

"Come on, Ted. This is important."

Samantha did not move her gaze from Ted's face. Finally he shrugged. "The truth is, Sam, nobody really knows what the hell is going on inside Telecon's complex. In a matter of a few years, they've dominated an entire industry. They wiped out all their competitors—Microsoft, Oracle, Netcom, Prodigy, everyone. Their encryption process is supposed to be perfect. Their supervising computer is supposed to be state of the art. But who the hell really knows?"

Nick's eyes shifted to Ted's holstered gun. "Aren't *you* supposed to know?"

Ted glanced at him, then grinned. "There are the powers that be—and then there are the *powers that be*. We would be foolish to think Telecon didn't have its secrets. We can inspect their complex; we can take apart their hardware and analyze their software—but in the end, we're still on the outside."

Nick nodded; despite his first impression, he grudgingly admitted that Ted was okay. At the very least, he was honest. Nick turned back to the Set-Top Box.

"So how do we get inside?"

Ted leaned forward. "To get inside Telecon, first you have to get past Marcus Teal."

TWENTY

Patrick Fishman stood on the front steps of the decaying town house for a good five minutes before he worked up the courage to reach for the doorbell. He had lived on Cross Street for fifteen solid years, ever since he had retired from his postal route. In that entire time, he had never visited a neighbor. Cross just wasn't that sort of street. Tucked into a forgotten corner of Washington's compact Chinatown, more than half of the old buildings that lined the small alleyway were boarded up and condemned. Patrick had been mugged twice in the entryway to his own home, just next door to where he was now standing. But for the first time in fifteen long years, Patrick had finally decided it was time to meet at least one of his neighbors—for a single, compelling reason.

The smell. It had started slowly, two weeks ago, a

sickly sweet odor—something akin to rotting meat. Over the next few days, it had grown stronger and stronger, wafting through the open windows of Patrick's second-floor apartment. Patrick had tried living with the windows closed, but his single room was like a coffin without a cross breeze, and at seventy-six, Patrick didn't need a constant preview of what was coming soon enough.

So at seven-fifteen that morning, he had finally decided to do something about it. Cross Street being what it was, a call to the D.C. police department had been out of the question. Patrick himself had a few secrets—the fact that he hadn't paid any taxes in thirty years came to mind—and he didn't see a need to get the cops involved. Instead, he had followed his nose, identifying the town house next door, number 316, as the source of the noxious smell. He remembered seeing someone moving into the previously empty town house just a week before the smell started, but he purposely hadn't gotten a good look at his new neighbor. On Cross Street, the less you knew . . .

His gnarled hand trembled as he touched the buzzer; he wasn't a social person, didn't have much family. Unless one counted that worthless daughter of his in Baltimore, who seemed to call only when she needed money for bail, drugs, or an abortion— six in five years, must have been some sort of a record. The truth was, Patrick didn't really like many people. Forty years as a postal employee did that to you. He shifted his weight from one of his Hush Puppies to the other, hoping this would be quick.

A few seconds later, he hit the buzzer again, this time leaving his finger against the cold plastic dime for a full heartbeat. He could hear the metallic sound reverberating behind the scuffed wooden door—he hoped to hell someone was home. He had put on his best shirt, his bright green Hawaiian, with the flowers and dolphins and ducks—or at least, that was what they looked like. Did they even have ducks in Hawaii?

Finally, there was a shuffling sound behind the door. Patrick crossed his arms against his chest, taking a slight step back. He listened as a bolt was pulled back, then the jingle of a chain being undone. There was a slight moment of inner tension as the door swung inward; then the feeling dissipated as his eyes settled on the little man in the dirty gray T-shirt.

His neighbor wasn't much to look at. Maybe thirty-five, with thick glasses and a piglike face. His thin dark hair was oily and sticking up from his head, and his muscular shoulders were hunched forward, his hands deep in the pockets of his sweatpants. His deepset eyes were red and glassy, and his lips were moving, slightly, as if he were whispering to himself. A strange, ugly man.

"Can I help you?" he asked in a slightly nasal voice. The skin above his glazed right eye twitched in tune to his words, and Patrick wondered if he too suffered from allergies—it had been a particularly bad ragweed month in D.C. Or perhaps he was reacting to the smell; even from outside on the steps, Patrick could tell that it pervaded the air inside, an almost numbing mist of odor.

"Um," Patrick started, his voice sounding very old in his ears. "I live next door. The brown six story. I'm here about the smell."

To the point. The piglike man just nodded, his

expression unchanged. "Yes, of course. I'm extremely sorry about that."

"It's pretty bad."

"Oh yes. Pretty horrible. The smell. I'm Ned, by the way."

With a sudden motion, he stuck out his right hand. Patrick shook it cautiously, noticing that the man wasn't looking at him, instead he was focused on a point a few inches above Patrick's right shoulder.

"Patrick Fishman. You got something rotting in there?"

A tremor moved across Ned's face, then he shook his head. "Good one, Patrick. No, of course not. It's something else entirely—something quite neat, actually. See, I'm a bit of a scientist. An engineer. Would you like to see what I'm working on?"

The request seemed totally out of character, but somehow genuine, and Patrick meditated on it for a second: did he really want to go inside the old town house? The smell was disgusting even from the outside; how bad would it be at the source? Then again, he had to admit, it was a bit intriguing. And the strange, ugly man seemed harmless. A little weird, but harmless.

"What kind of an engineer?" Patrick asked, his mind already made up.

Ned stepped back, beckoning him through the entrance. "I work at Telecon Industries."

"The Set-Top Box people?"

"Yes. I helped design the box."

Patrick stepped inside, impressed. The front entrance opened into a large sitting room with hardwood floors and little furniture. There was an old couch in one corner, ripped and fading, and a lamp that looked like it was at least fifty years old. Patrick could see cardboard boxes scattered around the room's periphery, overflowing with gadgets and wires and pieces of old computers, television sets, telephones, all jumbled and strewn randomly throughout the first floor.

"You got a lot of junk," Patrick said, as he followed Ned through the room. "You bring this stuff home from your work?"

"Some of it. Some of it I've collected on my own. Don't worry, you'll understand everything in a moment. Here we go."

He stopped in front of a heavy wooden door. There was a large brass key in a lock under the knob, and he twisted it, pulling the door open. A waft of bad air hit Patrick in the face.

"Hell," he said. "How can you stand it? Smells like a damn meat locker."

"It does smell bad," Ned agreed. "But you get used to it. And it's a necessary component of my work."

He stepped aside, pointing at the open doorway. "I've turned the basement into sort of a workshop. It's a wonderful space for my needs. But you can see for yourself."

Patrick peered past him. There was a flight of wooden stairs leading down into pitch darkness; obviously, the basement had no windows, no source of natural light. The smell wafting up through the open door was enough to make Patrick gag.

"Christ, it's just awful."

"I promise you'll understand as soon as you see what I'm up to. You'll really be impressed. And you'll be the first witness to what I've done. A historic moment."

Patrick rubbed his sweaty, gnarled palms against his slacks. Hell, maybe the ugly man really was working on something neat down there. Would it hurt to take a glance?

"Looks pretty dark."

"I promise, you won't be sorry. You go ahead, I'll get the lights. Careful, the steps are a little bit old."

Patrick started down the wooden stairs into the darkness. His arthritic knees cried out with each step, but he ignored them. The sickly, sweet smell was stronger, now, making his eyes water and his lips quiver. He couldn't see much of anything, but he could feel the cold, musty air of a cinder-block basement against his face. He took the steps carefully, moving deeper and deeper. He wondered what the hell was taking Ned so long with the lights.

He reached the bottom of the steps and felt hard cement beneath his Hush Puppies. He put his hands on his hips and frowned. "What the hell are you doing up there?" he shouted over his shoulder.

Suddenly, the lights came on. Patrick's eyes went wide and his mouth dropped open. He couldn't believe what he was looking at. He had never seen anything so horrible in his entire life. He was stunned, paralyzed—then something inside of him clicked, and he knew he had to get out of there. But before he could react, there was a sudden motion behind him.

Something sharp bit at the back of his neck, a single, sweeping motion, instantly severing his spinal chord between the first and second vertebrae. His knees buckled, his eyes still wide open, and silently, his body collapsed to the floor.

TWENTY-ONE

*W*elcome to the world of fiber optics. Please keep your hands and feet in the tram at all times."

A melodic female voice dripping with a heavy English accent echoed through the cavernous black hallway, mingling with the quiet hiss of the hydraulic tram. Nick had both hands on the safety bar, his expression incredulous; he could tell by Samantha's face that she was equally dismayed. When they had first approached the enormous Telecon complex at Third and Maryland, on the southeastern corner of Washington's famous National Mall, they had been impressed by the size of the building, but they could not have guessed at the insanity that had greeted them when they walked through the massive electronic front door.

Along with about three hundred tourists in

brightly colored clothes, they had been ushered into a roped line by uniformed employees. For nearly fifteen minutes, they had marveled at the vast front hall, with its thirty-foot ceilings and polished marble floor. The walls were covered with black crushed velvet, and huge glowing tubes crisscrossed the ceiling, spiriting balls of colored light back and forth at immense speeds. Nick figured that the tubes were supposed to represent fiber optic cables; obviously, the people who had designed the complex had taken Disneyworld as an architectural model.

When he and Samantha had finally reached the front of the line, his assumption had been confirmed: the hydraulic tram was a thing of wonder, thirty shining white cars floating a few inches above a concrete track. The track led through a brown curtain, so there was no way to predict what lay ahead. But judging from the entrance hall, it had to be something worth seeing.

He and Samantha had arrived a few minutes early for their scheduled meeting with Marcus Teal, so they had decided what the hell, they could use a little entertainment. After leaving Ted's office, Samantha had contacted Teal through her superiors at USAMRIID. Then she and Nick had reviewed their theory over a deli lunch. Nick had asked a few innocuous questions about Ted, but had learned little more than he already knew. They had once had a relationship, it had fallen apart, this was the first they'd spoken in a number of years. She had broken off that line of questioning with questions of her own; about Jennifer, about Nick's father, about his mother's death from a cardiac arrest when he was nineteen. A few hours later, they were sitting in a hydraulic tram.

"And so we begin," the English voice reverberated through their ears. "Our wonderful journey into the world of Telecon."

The tram slid forward and Nick watched as the elderly couple in the car ahead of them disappeared through the curtain. Then he felt soft material against his face and laughed out loud. "I feel like I'm in a car wash."

"Can you imagine how much this cost?" Samantha whispered back. She leaned close to him, her warm breath touching his cheek. "I remember when this building went up. They bought the spot from the Smithsonian for more than two hundred million dollars. Originally, the plot of land was slated for an American Indian Museum, but Marcus Teal had the necessary influence to make his dream come true. He wanted to be in Washington, rather than some remote location like Seattle, to be close to the communication lawmakers and lobbyists."

"Ladies and gentlemen," the English voice continued. "Telecon Industries is proud to present the greatest scientific achievement of the twentieth century. Optical fiber."

To the left of the tram, a section of the darkness was suddenly bathed in bright light. A huge column of glass sped down from the ceiling, disappearing right into the ground. The column was perfectly transparent and cylindrical, perhaps ten feet in diameter. "Optical fiber," the voice continued, "is a strand of glass five times thinner than a single human hair— yet centimeter by centimeter, this tiny strand is a hundred times stronger than the strongest steel."

"Looks like a big straw," someone in the back of the tram quipped in a heavy southern accent. Laughter rumbled from car to car.

"In theory," the narration continued, "one square inch of optical fiber could support 230 five-ton tractor trailers. It is a marvel of technology and manufacturing. And it will, no doubt, change the way we live."

The tram slid past the enormous glass straw, and another section of darkness suddenly lit up. A pyre of synthetic fire leapt toward the ceiling, causing Nick to jump back, gasping. A young child two cars ahead screamed, causing another flurry of laughter.

"The history of light communication dates back to the dawn of time," continued the voice. "Fire. Even in the very beginning, mankind realized that light was a means of transmitting information. Ancient man lit pyres to communicate across the dark plains, and a thousand years later, Egyptians used mirrors to focus sunlight at spots hundreds of miles away. We at Telecon are simply continuing in the great human tradition of communication innovation."

"That's a mouthful," Nick whispered. The elderly woman in front of him shushed him.

"Fiber optics will revolutionize the way we communicate. By carrying information stored in packets of light, fiber optic technology allows us a volume, or bandwidth, never before imagined. Fiber can transmit so much information at once, you could send an entire Hollywood movie around the world in less than a second. Two tiny strands of optical fiber can transmit the equivalent of twenty-five thousand phone calls *at the same time*."

A massive globe of the world sped through the still burning pyre of fire, keeping pace with the moving tram. "And this is not a technology of the future— this is a technology of today. If all the fiber optic

cable that has already been deployed were strung
end to end it would reach to the moon and back
forty times!"

The English woman sounded like she was about
to break into song. "It would take forty tons of copper to transmit the same information as one quarter
pound of fiber optic cable. Today we are linking
ourselves together with a means of communication
that is faster, better, and more powerful than anything in our history. We are truly creating a global
village, an information highway—an international
family!"

Suddenly, a glowing spiderweb appeared above
the tram, spreading down around them like a
cocoon. "In less than forty-six hours, ninety-five
percent of the nation's fiber optic network will be in
place. Most of the nation's television sets and computers will be linked through the Set-Top Boxes we
have provided, at no cost to the consumer. We at
Telecon are proud to share our technology with you,
our national family."

The spiderweb was replaced by a huge face. It
took Nick a second to place the striking features—
the freshly shaved head, the high cheekbones, the
startling dark eyes. Marcus Teal looked like a young
Denzel Washington, but with a brilliant glint in his
brown irises, the gaze of one of the world's true
geniuses.

"I'm Marcus Teal," a youthful voice boomed
through the air. "I just want to say thank you for
making Telecon Industries the number-one telecommunication company in the world. Ten o'clock
Thursday morning, we will all be linked together in
a way that once seemed impossible. And we at
Telecon are honored to be the company that is

bringing the information highway—and all that it can offer—to you."

Marcus winked at the entire tram. "As we like to say here in our home complex, *Turn it on, with Telecon!*"

The lights went on, and the tram slid to a sudden stop. They were in another part of the front lobby, which had opened up into a large atrium with a blue carpeted floor and high white walls. On the walls were pictures of scientists in lab coats, most likely Telecon employees. Under each picture was a line of text; groups of tourists huddled at random intervals, studying the accomplishments of men and women they would probably ignore on the street—or avoid at a cocktail party.

Nick rose from the tram and stepped out onto the carpet. Samantha slid out after him, her chunky-heeled DKNY shoes clicking as she stretched to her full five feet, ten inches. Even though they had been together for more than a day, Nick had not yet gotten used to her height.

"Well," she said. "What did you think of that?"

"Marcus and his Telecon buddies obviously think a lot of themselves. And judging from the turnout, a lot of other people seem to agree."

Samantha laughed. "This is Washington, Nick. If the U.S. Sanitation Department built a building this close to the Smithsonian and opened it to the public, they'd attract a few hundred tourists an hour. But I do admit, it was quite a presentation."

They were now halfway across the atrium, rapidly approaching a security desk in front of a huge electronic revolving door. Next to the desk stood a high Plexiglas case, containing thousands of intertwined glassy strings—another replica of the growing fiber optic web? Nick's eyes settled on a plaque under the case:

Junction to the World

According to the script underneath, the cables in the case linked the Telecon system to the national network.

"The Big Turn On," Samantha said, pulling his attention away from the case. "If our hypothesis is right—do you realize what could happen after Thursday morning?"

"That's why we're here."

Samantha stepped up to the desk and retrieved her USAMRIID badge from the inside pocket of her charcoal jacket. She handed the badge to the security guard, who was dressed in the same blue uniform as the employees who had helped them onto the tram. The guard looked over the badge, then nodded. "Good morning, Dr. Craig. Mr. Teal is very excited to meet you. If you'll just come this way."

He ushered them toward the revolving door.

Marcus Teal's office was fifty feet across and glowing, every visible surface an almost blinding shade of ivory. There was an impressive marble desk at one end, behind which stood a white leather chair. The entire right wall of the room was thick glass, with a panoramic view of the mall; in the middle of the vista stood the Washington Monument, a dagger splitting the glassy, aquamarine sky in two.

Next to the desk stood a bank of computer consoles with bubblelike screens. A flock of technicians—four men and two women—huddled in front of the consoles, working on Y-shaped ergonomic keyboards. Like every other Telecon employee Nick had seen so far, they were clad in blue uniforms that contrasted starkly with the decor.

The security guard led them to a pair of parallel white couches under the vast window. "Can I get you any coffee? How about a latte?"

Samantha shook her head, and Nick followed suit. The guard shrugged, his smile still obsequious. "Mr. Teal will be with you in a moment. He hates to keep guests waiting, but it's been a bit of a madhouse lately."

As the guard backed away, Nick leaned toward Samantha. "Polite guy," he said. "But I wish someone would explain to me why everyone's dressed like a blueberry."

Samantha chuckled, then quickly raised her hand to her mouth. "Why don't you ask Teal?" She whispered. "Here he comes now."

Nick turned just in time to see Marcus Teal breeze through the entrance to his office. He seemed shorter in person, perhaps five eight, and his uniform was different from the other Telecon employees, while still the same shade of blueberry blue. It had no collar—a sort of Nehru cum Star Trek look—and sharp, precise shoulders. There were buttoned pockets up and down the front, and the slacks were a little too long, dragging down over the tops of his shiny black shoes. Somehow, the look was fashionable; science meets rock and roll, with a little bit of Armani thrown in for good measure.

The suit went well with Teal's face. His features were as chiseled as in the projection image from the tram ride; his caramel cheeks seemed ready to leap off of his face, and his nose was perfect, impeccably situated above his movie-star smile. His gait was

determined and strong, and he strolled through the
office like the CEO billionaire he was. The technicians by the computer looked up, the expressions on
their faces something akin to awe.

Teal ignored them, heading straight to where
Nick and Samantha were standing. "I'm so sorry to
make you wait," he said, his right hand stretching
forward. "The preparations for Thursday have gotten the best of me, I have to admit."

"No problem," Samantha said, her voice suddenly official. "I don't know if I made it clear on the
phone, Mr. Teal, but we need a few minutes alone, if
that would be possible."

Teal raised his eyebrows, but his smile didn't
change. "Of course."

He turned toward the technicians and made a
quick gesture with his right hand. To Nick's amaze-
ment, they hurried toward the door—no questions,
no banter, nothing at all—just the quiet scampering
of feet against marble. When they were gone, Teal
turned back toward Samantha.

"I've never met anyone from USAMRIID
before," he said amiably. Then he shifted toward
Nick. "Nor did I realize that doctors still made
house calls. I'm intrigued."

"Mr. Teal," Samantha continued, a flick of her
eye signaling Nick to let her handle the conversation. "I'm sorry to say this isn't a social call. We
think we've stumbled onto something frightening,
and we need to ask you a few questions."

Teal beckoned them to one of the couches.
Samantha and Nick took position next to one another,
and Teal sat across from them. "Go right ahead. I have
only a few minutes, but I hope I can be helpful."

Nick let Samantha do most of the talking. She

and Nick had agreed that they would have to tell Teal the essence of their hypothesis; he had as much to lose if they were right as anyone, and only he would know how to narrow down the possible wavelength of light that could be causing CaV.

So she told Teal everything—from the very first reports of the horrible calcifying disease to the discovery of the two survivors. Nick watched Teal's face as she spoke; at first, he seemed attentive, his luminescent eyes totally focused on Samantha. But as she started in on their theories concerning the source of the disease—the idea that photons might have caused the outbreaks—his smile disappeared, and he seemed to have suddenly lost patience. When she pulled the Polaroid of the Vermont victim out of her pocket, his eyes quickly shifted to Nick, then toward the ceiling. By the time Samantha arrived at the connection to Telecon—the fact that all the outbreaks involved televisions or computers that were linked to the beta test—Teal was bouncing a manicured hand against his knee.

"If there's even a small chance that this disease sprang from the fiber optic network," Samantha finally finished, putting the Polaroid back in her pocket, "it's imperative that we have your help in determining how—"

"Hold on," Teal interrupted, raising his hands. "Let's slow down for a moment. You're asking me to believe that twenty-seven people caught a deadly calcifying disease from their television sets?"

The question was abrupt, hostile. Nick leaned forward, keeping his voice as calm as possible. "If you look at the facts, Mr. Teal, you'll see that our theory—as crazy as it seems—has merit."

"Actually, Dr. Barnes, I don't see that at all. A

'strange' form of light magically burst out of a basketball game, killing a bunch of sewer engineers? What the hell is this, some sick practical joke?"

"It's not a joke at all," Nick responded, his face getting hot. "A lot of people have died. A lot more will, if we don't figure out how this happened."

Teal crossed his arms. A corner of his upper lip twitched upward, and he chuckled out loud. Then he shook his head, turning back toward Samantha. When he spoke, his voice was full of venom.

"You folks at USAMRIID think I have time for this crap? Do you know the first thing about fiber optics, Dr. Craig? Do you have any idea what it is you're proposing?"

Nick felt bile rising in his chest. He didn't care who Marcus Teal was. . . .

But before he could say anything, Samantha's hand touched his knee. "That's why we're here," she said. "Why don't you tell us why our theory is so impossible."

Teal stood up from the couch and turned toward the window. He put his hands on his hips, staring out across the crowded mall. "As ludicrous as this is, I'm not surprised. It's human nature to be afraid of new technologies. Science has always been regarded with fear; people are terrified by what they don't understand. Science is seen as evil, dangerous. It's such a shame."

He turned away from the window, a truly stricken look on his face. "The fiber optic network is the most exciting and empowering development in recent history. We're connecting the world; we're getting rid of boundaries and offering limitless knowledge to millions and millions of people."

"Mr. Teal," Samantha said. "We have nothing

against the technology. We're simply trying to understand why these people died."

"They didn't die from my network. The fiber optic cables we've deployed carry only packets of information that pass through our central web, which is regulated here in this complex. The wavelength of light information is kept at a constant 1550 nanometers—exactly what is necessary for information to be read by our Set-Top Boxes. There is absolutely no way a substantially different wavelength could pass through our network without someone noticing."

Nick rose from the couch, unable to contain himself. "Then how the hell do you explain all the bodies?"

Teal swung toward him. "That's not my problem, is it? Listen, Dr. Barnes. I am sorry that people died. But my network did not carry the disease. Maybe their television sets malfunctioned—"

"In all the different sites?" Nick asked. "Couldn't the malfunction have occurred somewhere in the network, spitting out an unknown wavelength—"

"Absolutely not. You have heard of our encryption program, haven't you?"

Nick nodded. "I'm aware that your program is the accepted standard—"

"My program is infallible, Dr. Barnes. It is impossible for information to enter our web without carrying with it the proper encryption code, and there's no way a malfunction could emit something with that code."

Nick rubbed his jaw. An unsettling thought occurred to him. "What if it wasn't a malfunction? What if someone wanted to send some strange frequency—"

"You don't understand, Dr. Barnes. When I say infallible, I mean infallible. The encryption method was developed by some of the best minds on earth. It's called an Evolving Code; simply put, the code changes second by second by means of a random evolutionary matrix. It's impossible to break without a simultaneously evolving code breaker."

Nick felt a headache coming on. "A random evolutionary matrix?"

"Christ," Teal said, as if speaking to a child. "I really don't have time for this. Okay, I'll make it simple. Dr. Barnes, tell me the first number that pops into your head."

Nick raised his eyebrows. "Seven?"

"Okay. Now another. Don't think, just say a number."

Nick was confused, but he complied. "Thirteen."

"Fine. The code just changed from seven to thirteen. Only packets of information with those two numbers can get through the system. And the only way to know those numbers is to have a Dr. Barnes code breaker—a matrix that knows the patterns of thought that led to those two random choices."

"But if they're random—"

"Even random choices can be predicted," Teal explained, "if the exact circumstances that led to those choices are mathematically replicated. Of course, we're getting into some heavy theory here. Suffice it to say, there really isn't such a thing as random. And there isn't any way that an unauthorized transmission, or wavelength, could travel through the Telecon fiber optic network."

Teal crossed away from the window and stopped in front of the parallel couches.

"If we're quite finished here—"

"Mr. Teal," Samantha started, "I don't think we're even close to finished."

A low chime echoed through the room, and Teal looked up. He strolled to a panel attached to a nearby wall and pressed a button. "Yes, what is it?"

"It's Melora," a woman's voice responded from the panel. "I have the specs on the new audio chip. I can come back if you're busy."

Teal shook his head. "Actually, please come in. I have some people here who'd like to speak to you."

He hit another button on the panel, and the door to his office swung inward. A tall woman with short dark hair and sharp shoulders entered. She took long, determined steps, her facial features hard and extremely pale. She had a stiff manila folder under her right arm, and a partially constructed Set-Top Box under her left. She paused a few feet from the couches, glancing at Nick and Samantha. She reminded Nick of his ninth-grade English teacher: mean spirited, tough, all edges and angles.

"This is Melora Parkridge," Teal said. "She's our director of R&D. She can tell you anything more you need to know."

Samantha and Nick both rose, but the sharp woman made no move in their direction. Samantha turned back to Teal.

"Actually, we were hoping you could show us your main computer system—"

"I'm sorry, that won't be possible."

Teal walked over to his director of R&D and took the folder and Set-Top Box from her, then he headed for the door. Samantha took a step after him.

"But Mr. Teal, we're not finished—"

"I beg to differ, Dr. Craig. I've heard enough. As

far as I'm concerned, you're talking science fiction. And I do hope you've seriously thought through the consequences of the accusations you've brought up. The last thing I need, at this time, is the bad press that a ridiculous disease scare would bring."

"No," Samantha shot back. "The *last* thing you need is a massive CaV outbreak."

Teal looked at her over his shoulder. "Thank you for your concern. Ms. Parkridge can answer any specific questions you have about our technology. She'll show you out when you're through."

Without another word, he exited the office. Samantha was left staring at the empty doorway. Melora Parkridge cleared her throat. Her tone was as stiff and reluctant as her demeanor. "Mr. Teal said you have some questions for me? Please make it short; I'm quite busy."

Nick was about to ask the same questions he had asked Teal, when Samantha turned around. Her face had gone cool; she had regained her control. "Actually, we got everything we need from Mr. Teal. Thank you. If you could just show us out."

The woman shrugged, then headed for the door. Nick and Samantha followed a few feet behind. As they passed into the outer hallway, Samantha leaned close to Nick's ear. "She won't tell us anything worthwhile. I'll have my own technical team in here in an hour. We'll tear this place apart if we have to."

"What about the risk to your career?"

"We can't help that. Teal isn't going to be cooperative. And we can't replicate the disease, or come up with any new evidence, without a closer look at his system. We don't have any choice but to go through USAMRIID channels—even if it means my career."

Nick nodded. But he was worried. "Teal isn't a lightweight. A billion dollars goes a long way."

"*Especially* in Washington."

The sixty-inch high-definition television screen spat a cascade of colors across the small vault; the entire room became a rainbow, sheer sheets of steel engulfed by pixels of colored light. Marcus Teal sat in a high leather chair behind a polished glass desk, staring at the screen. His fingers were laced together on top of the desk, his shoulders hunched forward, his eyes focused on the two figures on the screen.

The woman was classically beautiful: tall, in a fashionable charcoal jacket and black leggings. The man was ruggedly handsome, dark curly hair above a solidly square face, leather jacket, jeans, dark boots. Marcus watched as they followed Melora into a hallway that led to the front lobby. He had been charting their progress through the Telecon complex ever since he had escaped from his office.

The security vault on the fifth floor of the complex was one of Marcus's many secrets. The vault was separate from the main security station located in the basement; it was wired—by fiber optic lines, of course—into its own bank of camouflaged video cameras.

Teal watched the attractive couple move through the lobby, past the glass case containing the system's main fiber optic junction, and head toward the electronic front door. His breathing remained steady, his skin cool, his heart rate normal. He imagined himself a spider, waiting quietly in the center of his web. No emotion, no anger, no fear.

Less than two days. He was a blink away from everything he had worked for. The time had been

purchased on all the networks, the news media had
been alerted. Every household in the country would
be watching as he smiled and flicked the switch.
Menus would appear on television screens across
the nation. The exchange of information would
begin. Slowly, at first. Interactive video games.
Television sitcoms on demand. Teleconferences
between mothers and sons, brothers and sisters.

The exchange would accelerate. Buying and
selling over a national, instantaneous, *frictionless*
market. Money would turn electronic as banks went
on-line. Wall Street would extend across the network, reaching the farthest corners of the nation.
The government would follow Wall Street; politics
would take on an immediate, democratic character.
American society would become one computer
screen multiplied three hundred million times.

At first, the government would be watching.
Tyro Carlson, the speaker of the House, and his congressional committee on communications would be
lurking around every corner. And Teal would be the
model corporate CEO. He would charm them with
his smile and his generosity. He would let them
carry out their inspections, let them make their
proud speeches about the new society he had created.

And then, once the system was in place, once the
country had learned to rely on the information
highway—as it had learned to rely on electricity
and running water—Teal would begin the process
of change.

He watched as the USAMRIID scientists exited
the complex through the front sliding glass door.
For a second, he felt the skin above his eyes grow
hot. He leaned back from the glass desk, his hands,

still clasped, rising to his chin. His mind was going through scenarios. Thinking ahead, contemplating possible futures. Assessing risks.

A spider in the center of a web. The web was vast and the spider was powerful. He had already eaten all of the other spiders and had destroyed all the other webs. Microsoft. The phone companies. The federal antitrust laws. The spider had risen from the depths of the ghetto, had clawed his way to the top of an industry.

The spider was not afraid of two scientists with nothing more than a theory. Marcus Teal's jaw tightened as he hastily reached for a phone.

TWENTY-TWO

this is it," Samantha said, as she stepped out of the limousine. Nick slid after her, a thrill riding through his shoulders. When she had suggested they stop at her apartment to regroup, he had been more than a little surprised; if he had made the same offer just a day ago in Boston, she probably would have laughed in his face. But their relationship had progressed; at the least, they didn't hate each other anymore.

Nick followed her up the sidewalk toward the three-story town house. Her street was narrow and lined with meticulously pruned baby spruce trees, spaced at five-foot intervals along a cobblestone sidewalk. The entrance to her building was equally elegant: wood-trimmed walls, flowing white drapes, and an oak-paneled inner door, complete with a pair of brass lion's head knockers. Nick fought the urge to comment on the knockers and instead followed her inside. A winding cement staircase spiraled upward, and Samantha took the first two steps as one.

"The first floor is empty, and I'm considering buying it as well—though I'll probably need another promotion before I can afford it. The third floor is occupied by a retired elderly couple; they throw the loudest parties in Georgetown, so don't be surprised if my ceiling caves in without warning."

Nick laughed while trying to catch his breath. The steps were high and there were too many of them, but Samantha didn't seem to notice as her long, muscular legs propelled her upward.

Finally, they reached her door. She fumbled for her keys, and then they were inside, Samantha letting him go ahead, an apologetic expression on her face. "Excuse the mess. I've been living in that limousine for the past three days."

Of course, there wasn't any mess—at least not by Nick's standards. The living room was well lit and feminine, with a cream three-cushioned sofa sandwiched between a pair of hardwood framed rockers, a drop-leaf table set off to one side and surrounded by hand-crafted black villa chairs, a number of wrought-iron standing lamps and matching wall sconces—and underneath it all, a Valencia rug, with finished edges. There were two sets of high bay windows on opposite ends of the room, casting streams of orange sunlight across the soft white walls. The room looked like something out of a Crate & Barrel catalogue.

"Now I know I can never show you my apartment," Nick said, heading for the couch. "At least not until I hose it down."

Samantha laughed, but there was tension in her eyes. Nick immediately wanted to set her at ease. "I have to say, it's been a lot more fun working with you ever since we decided to stop trying to kill each other."

"Eloquently put," Samantha responded. She slid her jacket off of her shoulders and hung it across the back of one of the villa chairs. Her turtleneck was snug against her body, and Nick quickly looked away. Samantha didn't seem to notice. "Before we get down to some serious talk, I'm going to need to make a few phone calls. I'll use the bedroom. There's a second line by the couch if you want to check your messages."

Nick nodded. Actually, Boston General was the farthest thing from his mind—but she was right, he probably needed to check in. After narrowly avoiding suspension for his actions at the law firm, he had signed out for three personal days. Even Pierce couldn't stop him from taking the short break; especially after Samantha had sent a letter to Chairman Peterson confirming that USAMRIID had temporary need of Nick's services.

"Take your time. I'll be fine out here."

"I shouldn't be long."

Samantha disappeared through a door at the back of the apartment, and Nick reached for an imitation Princess rotary on a bronzed leaf end table next to the couch. There was a slight scent of flowers in the air. Somehow, the smell made him comfortable and uneasy at the same time; he liked the idea of being in Samantha's apartment, but he could also recognize the prickles of guilt rising up his spine.

How long was he supposed to feel like this? Five

years, ten years? The rest of his life? He had been alone a long time. And Jennifer wasn't coming back. But did he dare get close to someone as alien as Samantha Craig? Was it even a possibility? They were two scientists chasing a disease; was Nick inventing feelings out of thin air?

Nick shook his head, dialing his voice mail. Now wasn't the time to complicate things. He pressed his ear against the phone and waited for the connection.

Three messages. He hit a few more numbers, and was surprised to find that all three were from Charlie Pace. Obviously, it was something important; Charlie had left his cellular phone number. Nick dialed as quickly as he could.

"Pace here."

Charlie's voice was barely audible over the sound of his motorcycle. Nick had never been able to figure out how he could talk on the phone and drive that monster at the same time—especially considering the number of motorcycle accident victims they'd worked on over the past two years. Then again, Pulse Jockeys saw so much shit in the line of duty, it was a wonder they weren't afraid to walk down the street. Nick himself had worked on three people who had been hit by falling air conditioners and a number of victims who'd fallen prey to such innocuous creatures as refrigerators, Coke machines, and beer kegs.

"Nick, finally. I'd begun to think you'd gotten yourself thrown into some southern jail—stepped on the wrong bubba, or made fun of somebody's alligator boots."

Nick laughed. He had told Charlie he was visiting Jennifer's parents in South Carolina. Though he trusted Charlie, Samantha had made it clear: their investigation had to remain a secret. Even Charlie had a family he'd want to protect. "Nothing as exciting as that. Just a lot of rest and relaxation. What's up?"

"I was going to ask you the same thing. I thought I was your friend. You skipping town without telling me?"

Nick raised his eyebrows. "What are you talking about? I'm just on leave for a couple of days."

"Well," Charlie said, shouting over the sound of his tires against metal bridge panels, "I've got news for you, Nick. I just got the new schedule for next month—and you ain't on it."

Nick felt a chill. He leaned forward, both feet planted on the Valencia rug. "I'm not on it?"

"Nope. I've been paired with Doug Garrot, the transfer from New York City Hospital. Sully's still our driver, but you're not anywhere to be seen. I looked through the whole list; as far as I can tell, you're not assigned to any team. What gives?"

"That's what I'd like to know. Charlie, I have a bad feeling about this. You talked to Pierce lately?"

Nick could hear Charlie's motorcycle slowing down. His voice became clearer. "I do my best to avoid the bastard. You think he's fucking with you again?"

Nick bit his lower lip. Pierce had tried almost everything to get rid of him, but he had never simply taken him off the roster—Peterson would never have let him do that. To fire someone at Boston General, you had to have a full hearing; you had to show cause.

"I don't know. I have to make a phone call, Charlie. Thanks for the tip."

"Work it out, Nick. I don't want to lose you. You're the best I've ever worked with. If you need me to go kick Pierce's ass, just let me know."

Nick hung up and stared at the phone. Could Pierce have taken him off the roster? The jerk had quite a grudge against him, but he'd have had to come up with a pretty good story to get Peterson to go along. Could it have something to do with the three personal days? Nick doubted it; he had worked double shifts for two years and was due some time. Besides, Pierce knew he was working with USAMRIID. It had to be a mistake.

He quickly dialed Pierce's private number, trying to calm his angry nerves. He had to try to be civil.

"Administrator Pierce. What is it?"

How pleasant. Nick clenched his teeth and kept his tone as neutral as possible. "Rudolph, this is Nick Barnes. You want to tell me what the hell is going on?"

There was a brief pause on the other end of the line. Nick's left hand formed into a fist as he struggled to control his temper. He could picture Pierce leaning back, his big feet up on his desk, his slimy blond ponytail hanging down against his chair.

"Good afternoon, Dr. Barnes," Pierce finally said. "Having a nice vacation?"

Nick started to bounce his fist against his knee. "You know that this isn't a vacation. I'm working with Dr. Craig from USAMRIID—"

"Last time I looked, you were an employee of this hospital—not a member of USAMRIID. Then again, that could change. If you'd like, I'd be happy to write a recommendation. Although you might want to look it over before you send it in."

Nick didn't have time for this garbage. He could hear Samantha's voice through the door to the other room; she was arguing vehemently about something, and he was curious what it could be. He didn't want to waste any more time talking to Pierce. "What the hell's the story with the ambulance roster? Charlie says my name's been left off."

There was another pause, and the ruffling of pages. "It seems that way, doesn't it? Well, Dr. Barnes, there's a very good reason. I received three phone calls this morning from an attorney representing Telecon Industries in Washington. They've slapped a six-million-dollar harassment suit against Boston General."

Nick gasped. Teal had sued him? And so quickly? *Christ.*

"Rudolph, I can explain that—"

"I don't want an explanation. I want your ass in my office tomorrow morning. You'll meet with our lawyer and try and figure out a way you can apologize to whomever you pissed off."

"I can't get back tomorrow," Nick started. "I need a few more days—"

Rudolph's voice rose an octave. "Unless you report to my office at nine tomorrow morning, you can consider yourself suspended. And Peterson isn't going to save you this time."

"Rudolph—"

There was a click, and then the bray of a dial tone. Nick slammed the phone down. Christ, he hated that bastard. Nick had worked tirelessly for Boston General. So he had caused a bit of trouble after Jennifer's death, and again after the accident. He had pulled himself together, had become the best damn paramedic . . .

A loud slam pulled Nick out of his thoughts. Samantha had just stormed out of the other room, flinging the door shut behind her. She looked positively dangerous; her gray eyes were like oil fires, and her nostrils flared. She stood in front of the couch, arms at her sides. Nick noticed that her hands were trembling.

"This is ridiculous," she said, flinging the words at him. "I feel like I could kill someone."

"You're not the only one," Nick responded. "I just found out that I'm losing my job. Teal sued my hospital, claiming harassment. If I don't return to Boston immediately, I'm out on my ass."

Samantha pulled her hands backward through her hair, her eyes still smoldering. "Well, you can be on the next plane out."

"What are you talking about?"

She dropped onto the couch next to him, her face slack, the exhaustion of the past two days catching up with her.

"Our investigation is officially over."

TWENTY-THREE

nick looked like a chastised puppy, his lips hanging open, his eyes wide. Samantha was so upset she almost started laughing—the two of them had been so quickly shot down by Marcus Teal's paranoia.

"That was my boss on the line," she said. "They're going to take the investigation out of my hands. He wouldn't say why—but I know it had to be Teal."

The conversation with Sydney Foster had been infuriating. Foster wouldn't give her any answers; she was simply to cease her investigation. There had been enormous pressure from above. She had tried to explain the situation with Teal, but Sydney had closed down on her. As important as it was to stop CaV, he had no choice but to put somebody else in charge.

"A couple of phone calls," Nick said, shaking his head. "That's all it took."

Samantha felt water burning at the back of her eyes, but she wasn't going to cry, damn it. She was going to remain in control. "This is appalling. USAMRIID is supposed to be above politics. It's supposed to be about science. Teal didn't refute our hypothesis—he simply killed the messenger."

Nick reached out and took her hand in his. His hand felt warm and strong. She suddenly had the urge to pull away, but she resisted.

"It was naive of us to assume he'd help," he said. "Teal told us himself—the bad press would hurt him."

"It's more than that. His reaction was too severe; he could have arranged a way for us to continue our investigation without the press finding out. He's hiding something."

"I don't know. Maybe he just saw us as an irritation—two insects tickling at him—and he moved to squash us."

"Well, that's it then. CaV's going to strike again. And after the Big Turn On, there will be hundreds of millions of televisions and computers connected to the network. God only knows how many people are going to die."

"That's exactly why we can't give up."

Samantha looked into his eyes and saw Andrew. Standing with his arms crossed on the bow of a military schooner, watching the Navy jets taking off and landing. And then the picture changed: a funeral procession, her father trembling in his crisp white uniform. A fist tightened in her stomach.

"They took the investigation away from me," she hissed, angry. "I don't have the personnel—or the money—to continue. And you'll lose your job. Nick, it's over."

"As long as CaV is out there, it's not over. And we are not going to give up."

Samantha pulled her hand away from him and looked away. She wanted to scream at him. She wanted to hurt him, to make him feel what she was feeling—the anger, the pain, the sense of loss. Her career was sliding away. She was going to lose everything she had built—and then she would get sick again.

Missed meals, salad dinners, phone calls to her father late at night to share his tears, his stories about Andrew, about his strength, his passion, his wonderful cowboy ways. Then even the salad dinners would be too much: she would need total control, she would stop eating entirely. Weakness, dizziness, nausea, hot sweats, then the chills, the blurry vision. The hospital, the doctors showing her videos and pictures of living skeletons, of what she was heading for. *Controlling yourself to death.*

"Samantha," Nick said quietly. "People are going to die. And we're the only ones who know the truth. It's Teal's network. Something deadly is traveling through those fiber optic lines."

Samantha felt the tears running down her cheeks. Damn it, why did she have to be so weak? *Why did he have to be so strong?* "You don't know when to quit."

"If I knew when to quit, I would have given up two years ago. I lost my hand, my career—damn it, if I knew when to quit, I would have given up when Jennifer died. But I didn't. I wasn't going to lose myself. I threw myself into surgery, became the best surgeon I could be. After the accident, I spent months trying to teach my other hand to hold a scalpel. When that didn't work, I found something else—the ambulances. But I never gave up. When you give up, you may as well be dead. That's not what Jennifer would have wanted. That doesn't do anyone any good."

Samantha felt her throat constricting. The tears were sprinting freely down her face, riding the high angles of her cheeks, her jaw, down her long, smooth throat. She was staring at herself in a hospital mirror, staring at her sunken stomach and shrunken breasts and bone thin legs and thinking, *This is not what Andrew would have wanted!* But it wasn't that easy. It had never been that easy.

"Nick, this is different—"

"Shut up, Samantha. For once in your life, just stop thinking."

She whirled toward him. What the hell did he know about her? She opened her mouth but before the words could come out, he was moving toward her, erasing the distance between them. His hands came out and took her by the chin, and suddenly they were kissing, fiercely. Their bodies came together and she fell back against the couch, swallowed up by him, his strength, his passion. Their tongues danced together, lips crushing lips, hands roaming. She could feel the strong muscles under his shirt—his firm arms, chest, the ridges of his flat stomach.

Then she was gasping, pulling back, her mind fighting what was going on. There had been men since Ted, but never like this, never so quickly, so spontaneously. It had to be planned, methodical, analyzed, *controlled.* . . .

Nick reached forward and slid his hands under

her turtleneck. She felt his hands running up her stomach, up between her breasts. She arched her back and he lifted the turtleneck from the bottom, revealing her smooth skin, the angle of her rib cage, her black lace demi bra. The turtleneck came off, then the bra, and she lay back against the couch, her firm breasts raised, her nipples hard, her blood coursing. Nick exhaled, looking at her—and suddenly it was too much.

Skin on skin, the hug turning savage. There was a brief second of weightlessness as they rolled off the edge of the couch—and then they hit the rug, bodies intertwined, the passion of the moment making everything disappear in a whirl of athletic sex.

Samantha lay back against the floor, her hands running through her sweat-soaked hair. Her heart was still pounding. A bright red flower engulfed her chest, her nipples pulsing, her face flushed. She had never felt anything like that in her entire life. She'd had orgasms before, of course, but never anything so overwhelming, so complete. Every muscle in her body quivered, ever neuron in her skin fired in the wake of the pleasure that had enveloped her.

"My god," she said toward the ceiling. "I guess you are good for something."

Nick laughed. "I hope the elderly couple upstairs had the television on high. If you had been any louder, we would have had the cops at our door."

"I'm sorry," Samantha said, covering her mouth, embarrassed. "I didn't know I was making any noise. I think I lost consciousness somewhere in there."

Nick ran his fingers through her hair. His body

felt good on top of hers. Still, there was a gnawing feeling in the back of her mind that she had just made an enormous mistake. It wasn't the sex—she was old enough to accept that sex was sometimes unavoidable. It was the connection she was making. She was falling for Nick, despite the fact that they were polar opposites, that sooner or later, they would hate each other again.

"Nick—"

"Don't," he said. He took her by the chin and kissed her deeply. "I know what you're going to say. But now isn't the time."

She nodded, brushing tears out of the corner of her eyes. He was right. "What are we going to do? Do we really continue our investigation—without my authority? Without USAMRIID?"

Nick ran his fingers between her breasts. "I think we have to. We can't just sit back and pretend CaV isn't going to strike again."

Samantha closed her eyes. Her mind was working fast, planning, plotting. Nick had infused her with new resolve; she wasn't ready to give up, either. She had lost control for a few minutes, but now she was thinking clearly. It wasn't over yet. She couldn't let it be over.

"First, we're going to need help. Teal might have taken the investigation away from me, but I'm still an employee of the federal government. I'm still U.S. military. I'll head over to my office and find out how thorough Teal really was."

"And then?"

Samantha knew the answer without thinking. "Teal's complex. We have to get inside. If this disease is passing through the fiber optic web, we have to go inside Telecon and find out where it's coming from. If there's a malfunction in their system, we have to neutralize it. If the disease is being deliberately fed into the network, we have to stop whoever's doing it."

"You think that's a possibility?" Nick asked, surprised. "I only mentioned it to get information about the encryption process from Teal. Why would someone deliberately spread a disease?"

Samantha shrugged. "You've never heard of serial killers? Some people are just randomly brutal. They kill without reason."

"Even serial killers have reasons, in their own minds. And this isn't like picking up a knife or a gun; this would take genius and time and probably a lot of money. I don't think Teal was lying about his Evolving Code. Maybe it's not infallible, but it's probably pretty close."

"That's part of what we have to find out. If the disease isn't coming from a malfunction, then someone did figure out how to break that code. And again, the only way we're going to know how is to get inside that complex."

Nick cupped her left breast in his hand, touching the nipple between two fingers. "Can we do that?"

Samantha thought for a few seconds. "The place has heavy security. Plus a veritable army of personnel. You saw all the blueberries."

Nick smiled. "What are a few hundred blueberries against a USAMRIID scientist and a one-handed paramedic?"

Samantha laughed. Then her face turned serious. "I think I can get us architectural plans of the complex. And if I have any pull left, I'm pretty sure I can take care of the security—high tech and low.

But I can't fix what Teal's already done. We're both going to be risking our careers."

Nick nodded. "If we don't take that risk, people are going to die. That's the one sure thing in all of this. CaV isn't going away on its own."

TWENTY-FOUR

Samantha forced her eyes straight ahead as she walked down the center of the well-lit, porcelain-tiled hallway. The air was kept at a constant fifty-eight degrees Fahrenheit, and she could feel the dry, cool air in the back of her throat. She knew that every breath brought in a half-dozen chemical antiviral and antibacterial cleansers; without a doubt, this was the most sterile building within fifty miles of Washington, D.C.

USAMRIID had three main headquarters in the eastern part of the country. First, there was the publicly known biohazard lab in Reston, Virginia. Then, the less well known analysis complex just outside the Washington city limits. And then there was the Box: a cubic, high-security building twenty minutes outside of Arlington. Samantha had done her basic virus training in Reston, but her office was in base-

ment level 3C of the Box; this was the true headquarters in the national battle against disease.

Samantha turned a corner, heading down
another cold hallway. The walls were smooth
cement, with steel hatchlike doors every fifteen feet;
some of the doors opened into laboratories, others
into offices. None of the doors was labeled, nor
were there any doorknobs. Instead, there were cameras staring down from above each hatch, hooked
into a central security network, a simple, effective
system.

Samantha hid her trembling hands behind her
back as she came to a stop in front of one of the steel
hatches. She could remember only one other time
she had been this nervous inside the catacomb hallways of the Box. Her first day, four years ago. She
had stood in front of this very same door, staring
blankly up at the camera, waiting.

There was a series of clicks, and the door slid
upward. Samantha took a deep breath and stepped
through. The floor was the same tiled porcelain, the
walls still sheer cement. The room was six hundred
square feet, with a steel desk, two steel chairs, and a
high bookshelf lined with every virology textbook
currently in print. The ceiling was one enormous fluorescent panel, humming in tune with the overwhelming air-conditioning. There was a full colored
map of the United States covering most of the far
wall, with glowing red pushpins marking the CaV
outbreak cities; a terrifying cliché, a symptom of
USAMRIID's impotence—a map waiting for more
red pushpins.

The door slid shut behind her, and she took
another step forward, her hands tightly clasped
behind her back. Sydney Foster was sitting stiffly

behind his steel desk, his legs crossed, his hands resting on the keyboard of his laptop computer. The computer was open but the screen was not lit; the laptop was on standby, and it was obvious that Sydney had been sitting motionless for a long time. His thick lips were pursed, and the scar above his right eye melded with the wrinkles of a growing frown.

He was a striking man, a sort of living monument to the military ideal; in many ways, he reminded Samantha of her father. Foster had served as a doctor in Korea and before that, in the tail end of World War II. He was a respected scientist and had written four prize-winning books on viruses in the past five years.

"I'm not surprised to see you," he said, quietly, as he shut the laptop. "Actually, I expected you to get here sooner. Please, take a seat."

"No thank you." Samantha dug the fingernails of her right hand into the palm of her left. She had to play this extremely carefully. Foster would help her—if she gave him the chance.

"Samantha, you understand that this was not my call. This is coming from above."

"Dr. Paulson?" Samantha asked. Paulson was the head of USAMRIID.

"Even beyond Paulson. The determination has been made; your investigation is floundering. You have no replicable evidence. We're no closer to understanding CaV than when you started."

Samantha felt her face go pale. She concentrated on Foster's eyes. Was there something there? It was time to take a chance. To tell him what she had found. "That's absolutely not true. I know where CaV is coming from—"

"Stop." His voice cut through the air. His eyes daggered upward, then settled on her face. The motion had been almost imperceptible, but she immediately understood.

He didn't want her to say it out loud for the microphones to hear. He didn't want her to tell him because he already knew. Either he had gotten to Ted and figured out the rest on his own, or he had other means of keeping tabs. Perhaps listening devices in her limousine or in her apartment. It didn't matter. He knew, and he didn't want her to say it out loud. Which could mean only one thing.

"Your role in this investigation is officially over," he continued. "You are not to continue researching CaV. You no longer have access to the laboratory outside of Boston, or the authority to conduct tests on the autopsied victims."

He was still focused on her eyes. She could see a fire behind his dark pupils. Inside, he did not want her to stop. He knew how deadly this disease was. He knew what would happen if she was right.

"For the time being, your promotion has been revoked."

He rose from behind his desk. He seemed massively fit, especially for his age. More than six feet tall, two hundred and fifty pounds of densely packed muscle. Like her, he was wearing a long white lab coat and sterile white pants.

"Until a decision is made as to your status, you will act as my personal assistant. I am leaving in three hours for Uganda. There is a reported outbreak of a new form of the Hantavirus. While I am gone, you will take care of my domestic needs; the Uganda project is priority one, and you are not to discuss it with anyone else. I will call you with specific questions, and you will act under my authority. Do you understand?"

Samantha nodded. Her throat was parched, and it had little to do with the sterile air. Foster reached into the inside front pocket of his lab coat and pulled out a sheet of computer paper. He stepped out from behind the desk, and handed the piece of paper to her.

"Here is my itinerary. I will call you in two days."

He walked past her and headed to the door. She stared at his wide back, then shifted her eyes to the piece of computer paper.

```
If you are wrong, it will be both our
careers.
```

TWENTY-FIVE

it was the strangest-looking helicopter Nick had ever seen: forty feet long, ten feet high, boxlike, with slanted plates of shiny black glass covering most of the fuselage, giving it a sort of ziggurat shape. It had long rotors, already beginning to blur, but the rotors seemed to be placed much higher than on a normal helicopter, perched at the top of a long, telescoping black pipe. Underneath the rotors, mounted to the top of the copter's fuselage, were what looked like two huge oil drums. A similar pair of black canisters hung from the bottom of the fuselage, directly above the landing struts. Each of the drums was a quarter the size of the helicopter itself, unmarked, made out of a shiny, smooth material Nick could not name. With the ziggurat-slanted panels and the sandwiching shiny oil drums, the copter looked like an alien beetle, squatting alone in a corner of the enormous hangar.

"What the hell is that thing?"

Nick's voice echoed off of the high curved walls. The hangar was a hundred yards long and at least as high. It had curved walls and a cement floor, stained at random intervals with oil and grease. There were a number of vehicles spotting the hangar: two normal helicopters by the front entrance behind Nick, a Humvee all-terrain vehicle to his right, three motorcycles parked together behind the Humvee, and six stretch limousines separated by orange plastic cones twenty yards to his left. One of the limousines had picked him up at his hotel two hours ago.

Still waiting for an answer, he glanced at the man standing next to him. The man was dressed in military camouflage and had a holstered revolver hanging from a belt at his waist. He was standing stiffly, arms at his sides, also facing the strange helicopter. He had met Nick at the door to his hotel room at eleven P.M., and had ridden with him in the back of the limousine; in that entire time, he had said only a handful of words. First, in the hotel: "Dress casually; athletic wear is preferred." Then, as he escorted Nick to the car: "You have been granted temporary priority clearance. Anything you see or hear is protected information. Communicating this information to any noncleared individual is a treasonable offense. Failure to comply will result in prosecution."

When Nick had asked where he was going, the man had ignored his question. When Nick had asked about Samantha—if she was going to meet him wherever they were going, if she had anything to do with this—the man remained stone-faced, staring straight ahead. The limousine had traveled

in what seemed like circles for forty-five minutes,
finally exiting the city to the south. After another
hour of painful silence, it had turned onto a
deserted two-lane highway. Ten minutes later, it
had veered onto a paved driveway. It had passed
through two gated fences, stopping in front of a
third. A soldier in a matching camouflage uniform
had poked his head into the limousine, looking
Nick over. The limousine had been waved forward,
and a few minutes later, it had entered the enormous hangar.

Still, there was no sign of Samantha. For all Nick
knew, he had been kidnapped. His eyes dropped to
the gun hanging from his escort's belt. "Am I in
some sort of trouble?"

Silence. If Nick concentrated really hard, he
could see the man's chest rising and falling—but
that was all. "Is Dr. Craig on her way here?"

Still, nothing. Nick began to get frustrated. "Are
we going to stand here all night?"

"Nick. Over here." Samantha's voice broke across
the cavernous hangar, and Nick swung around. She
was standing by the closest limousine. A smile
broke across his face as he started toward her. The
sudden excitement startled him; he hadn't felt this
way in a long time. They had been separated only
for a few hours—but it felt like days.

She was dressed down, as he was: a bulky gray
sweat suit, black Reeboks, her hair pulled back in a
tight ponytail. There was an oversized green duffel
bag on the hood of the limousine behind her. As he
came closer, she looked him over, also smiling. He
was wearing a Harvard sweatshirt, Boston College
sweatpants, and a backwards BC baseball cap. He
had finally had a chance to shave, and he looked a

lot like he had in college—athletic, boyish, ready for anything.

"Sorry about leaving you in the dark," she said, kissing his cheek. "I've been busy with the arrangements—and everything's got to move quickly."

Nick nodded, the scent of her in his nostrils, the feel of her lips still resonating through his cheek. Just a few hours ago, she had been naked beneath him, her long legs around his waist. All he wanted to do was grab her and climb into the back of the limousine. He blushed at his own thoughts. "What is this place, anyway?"

"There are a few things you can't ask me. That's one of them." She turned and unzipped the duffel bag, digging through the contents. "I told you before that the team I used to head was called Viral Response and Covert Reaction. I also told you we have the full cooperation of other special branches of the military: FBI, CIA, et cetera. Both for training, and for equipment supply. USAMRIID is fairly capable of response, but for covert reaction, we turn for help to the experts."

She pulled from the duffel bag a rolled-up sheet of thin paper. She unrolled it carefully, and spread it out on the top of the limousine. Nick saw that it was a three-dimensional, full-color floor plan.

"See, Nick, a few years ago USAMRIID recognized the same thing you realized when AIDS took Jennifer away from you. We're fighting a war. This is just one of the many places we've borrowed to prepare for that war. I spent three months here—and in the empty fields behind this hangar—preparing for that war. I'm no expert, but I am capable; hopefully enough for what we need to do tonight."

"So you *are* still in charge of the investigation?"

Nick asked, confused. "I thought we were going to have to go ahead on our own."

Samantha glanced past his shoulder, making sure his escort was still standing in front of the strange helicopter, at least ten yards away. "We are on our own. This is a one-shot deal; if something goes wrong, we're going to take the fall. As far as my superiors are concerned, this has nothing to do with USAMRIID."

Christ. Nick wasn't sure what he was getting into, but it sounded like the risk was enormous. For both of them. If Pierce really kicked him off the hospital staff tomorrow morning, he could always find another hospital to hire him; but if he and Samantha got themselves in serious trouble—he shook the thought away. He knew how important this was.

"This is the official blueprint for the Telecon complex," Samantha continued, holding down the corners of the unrolled paper. "This, over here, is the main entrance; it looks like the hydraulic tram traveled in a semicircle, arriving at the back of the lobby here. At night, the lobby doors are sealed tight by an electronic locking system. Three armed guards remain at the lobby desk until four A.M., when they are relieved by a second shift."

She shifted position, pointing at another spot in the center of the blueprint. "I'm pretty sure this is our goal. According to my FBI sources, the second and third floors of the complex contain offices, copy rooms, cafeterias. It's the fourth floor that matters to us; this cube in the direct center is the computer control atrium. It contains the main supervising computer through which all network transmissions pass."

"The center of the web."

"Exactly. The room itself is a specially made, completely self-contained unit forged out of three-foot-thick steel. The only way inside is through an outer steel chamber, separated from the main atrium by an electronic airlock. The airlock is controlled by a sophisticated computerized security system. To get inside, you must present two forms of biological identification: first, there is a retinal scanner. It measures the diameter and shape of your retina. Then, there is a voice recorder; it measures the sound frequency of your vocal chords. Both security measures are state of the art, extremely expensive, and very hard to beat."

"Sounds like we don't have much of a chance getting inside the atrium."

Samantha nodded. "But I don't think we have to."

She reached back into her duffel and pulled out a small black box with a suction cup attached to one side. "Nick, have you ever heard of Van Eck radiation?"

"I've heard the term, but I don't know what it means."

"Simply put, it's the magnetic field produced by electrical current. Every time anything electric is used, a tiny magnetic field is broadcast into the air. Every time something comes up on a computer monitor the information is also broadcast in the form of Van Eck radiation into the air. With this device, we can read that radiation and translate it into something we can understand."

"We can eavesdrop on a computer screen?"

"That's right. And we don't even have to be in the same room. The magnetic fields reflect onto any metal surface, such as heating ducts, drain pipes—

and three-foot-thick steel walls. We don't have to get inside the main atrium, we just have to get close. We'll be able to steal an electromagnetic record of anything that comes through their computer, as well as some trace of any computer action over the last few days."

She turned back to the three-dimensional blueprint. "There's a file room next door to the atrium. I think they keep disk and print records of their system in there, which might be interesting to go through as well. The security is very light, compared to the main atrium."

She rolled the blueprint back into a tight tube, and shoved it and the Van Eck reader back inside the duffel bag. Then she closed the zipper and dragged the duffel off of the limousine. It looked like it weighed a good thirty or forty pounds; Nick wondered what else she had hidden away in there. She slung it over her right shoulder, and turned toward the strange helicopter.

"So the only real difficulty will be getting inside the complex," she said, starting forward. Nick followed a step behind.

"Three armed guards in the lobby, right?"

Samantha nodded. "Our goal is to avoid contact with anybody—we can't risk being discovered—or violence of any kind. No end-zone runs this time, Nick."

She stopped where he had been standing before, thirty feet in front of the helicopter. "It turns out, the lobby isn't the only way inside the Telecon complex. There's a helicopter bay on the roof. It's outfitted with the latest in radar and engine-heat sensors. And it's connected to the complex by an automated security tunnel, stocked with motion and infrared detectors. But at night, the helicopter bay has no human security. Just the automatics."

Nick noticed the change in her voice. She sounded like a Pulse Jockey, chasing the adrenaline high. "How are we going to get past the automatic sensors? And how are we going to get onto the roof without setting off their system?"

Samantha signaled toward the helicopter with her right hand. There was a loud clanking, and a side door came open, dropping to the cement floor. There were steps on the inside of the door, leading up into the dark belly of the strangely shaped machine.

"Come on," she said simply. She bent her knees and started forward. Nick followed, sighing; this was the way she liked to do things. She always had to be in control. For now, he had no choice but to follow her lead.

Nick's stomach dropped as the helicopter shuddered upward. They had cleared the hangar doors a few minutes ago, and were now steadily climbing into the darkness, the copter jerking back and forth as gusts of cool wind slammed against the heavy metal fuselage. Nick was sitting across from Samantha on a steel bench bolted to the floor, a leather harness strapped over his right shoulder. The duffel bag was on the floor, held steady between Samantha's black Reeboks. The curved copter door to Nick's left vibrated as the wind blew through cracks at the edge of the steel. In the center of the door was a small round Plexiglas window, and Nick could see the clouds as they passed through them, wisps of gray cloth in the thick velvet darkness. Behind Samantha was a low wall that separated them from the cockpit; Nick could see the two pilots strapped in high leather chairs, surrounded by a glowing cocoon of knobs, levers, lights, and control panels.

A rough male voice burst out from a microphone somewhere above Nick's right ear: "Estimated target time, thirty-six minutes." Nick took a deep breath, trying to calm his stomach. His fingers were white against the steel bench beneath him.

"You'll get used to the jerking around in a few minutes," Samantha shouted over the sound of the wind. "Once we stop ascending and go horizontal, things will smooth out."

"You still haven't told me how we're going to get this monster down on top of the Telecon building without anyone noticing."

Samantha leaned forward as far as her harness would allow. If she had reached out, she would almost have been able to touch Nick's knees. "As I said before, the Telecon helicopter bay has two ways of tracking incoming visitors. Radar, and engine-heat sensors."

She nodded toward the side wall. "I'm sure you noticed the smooth, angled panels all over the exterior of this copter. Those are radar deflection shields. It's the same technology they use on the Stealth bomber. The panels are made out of a Dow Chemical boron fiber material called Fibaloy, sheathed with tiles made of a radar deflecting aluminum hybrid. As far as radar goes, we're pretty much invisible."

"And the engine heat?"

"That's where things get interesting. Nick, what usually happens when a helicopter loses engine power?"

Nick raised his eyebrows. The helicopter was still rising, and his stomach felt like it had been left somewhere far below. "It drops. Like a stone."

"But not this baby. Did you notice those enormous canisters attached above and below the fuselage?"

"They looked like oil drums."

"Right. A few minutes before takeoff, rubber hoses attached to tanks located under the hangar floor were connected to all four drums. The drums were pumped full of hydrogen. Which, as you know, is markedly lighter than air."

Nick's eyes went wide. He'd never heard of such a thing. "You mean we're basically sitting inside a blimp?"

"The Comanche Heliboat C49; it's still considered an experimental technology. It combines the versatility and airspeed of an attack helicopter with the engine silence of 'lighter than air' craft. When we're over the Telecon complex, the pilots will cut the engine. The Comanche will drop at just a foot per second, like a landing hot air balloon. No radar visibility, no engine heat."

Amazing. Nick stared at the two pilots beyond the low metal wall. They were punching buttons and levers on the panels in front of them. Nick could see nothing but darkness through the Plexiglas cockpit bubble in front of them; they were probably flying entirely by computer. This machine had to have cost a bundle of Pentagon money. It definitely wasn't just for USAMRIID's use. He guessed CIA, or NSA. What other missions had those two pilots flown in their invisible helicopter?

Samantha was rummaging through her duffel bag. "Once we land on the roof, we'll have to get through the security tunnel. That means we have to beat infrared and motion sensors. I've got a trick for the motion sensors, which I'll show you once we're there. I'll deal with the infrared problem in a second. Once past the tunnel, we'll have to get past their camera system."

"They've got cameras, too?"

"Camouflaged in the ceilings and walls. You won't see them, but they'll definitely see you. They use a very new technology called visual recognition—the same system we use in the lab back at the Quarantine Unit. Basically, they can track specific shades of color. The system doesn't alert human security when it recognizes those specific shades."

"The blueberry uniforms."

Samantha smiled, as she pulled two of the ugly jumpsuits out of her duffel bag.

"Where did you get those?"

"I found out where Telecon gets them cleaned and had a couple of operatives lift them for us. They'll be snug, but good enough." She handed one of the jumpsuits to Nick. Then she undid her harness, and slid across to his bench, sitting next to him. He liked the feel of her leg next to his. Then he noticed that the helicopter was no longer jerking back and forth; the roar of the wind had changed to a dull rushing, as the machine slashed forward. They were moving fast, perhaps more than a hundred miles per hour.

"I guess we should change," he said, taking off his hat and starting to lift up his sweatshirt.

"We do have to get undressed. But before we put on the uniforms, there's something else we have to do."

Nick raised his eyebrows. She leaned forward,

and pulled an aluminum canister out of the duffel bag. The canister looked a bit like a can of paint. Samantha pried at the top with her fingers, and there was a sudden popping sound. The top flipped off and clattered to the floor.

Even in the low light of the helicopter, the contents glowed; it was some sort of shimmering cream, like molten silver pudding. Samantha stuck her fingers into the canister and scooped out a handful of the thick, silvery stuff. She reached forward, and Nick jerked his head back. "What the hell is that stuff?"

Samantha laughed. "Don't be such a chicken. It's not going to hurt."

She pressed her hand against his cheek, spreading the stuff across his smooth skin. It felt cold, creamy, like whipped butter. She took another handful of the stuff and continued spreading it across his face until every inch of skin was covered. He turned and saw himself reflected in the oval window. He looked like some sort of android or the Tin Man from *The Wizard of Oz*.

"Liquid Mylar," Samantha said, going to work on her own face. "It will suppress our infrared output. We'll be able to walk right past their sensors."

"Is it safe? The skin needs to breath—"

"We'll leave a small patch at the base of our necks, like circus performers. And we'll wash it off as soon as we're back in the helicopter; I've brought along a jar of a special cleanser. It's all been field tested, with adequate results."

Again, Nick glanced toward the two pilots. "So we're going to get naked and spread this stuff all over ourselves? Right here, in the helicopter?"

Samantha didn't answer. Instead, she grabbed

the bottom of her sweatshirt and lifted the material up her smooth, naked stomach. In a second her top was off, her naked chest trembling with the rhythmic hum of the helicopter's rotors. She took Nick's hands and dipped them deep into the canister of liquid Mylar, then placed them on her breasts. He could feel her nipples harden under his palms.

"What about them?" he whispered toward the cockpit.

"They're trained professionals. They wouldn't turn around if I pulled my revolver and shot you in the head."

"You have a revolver?"

"Focus, Nick, focus. You have to make sure every inch of my chest is covered. And my stomach. My hips. My legs." She wriggled out of her sweatpants, as the helicopter sped forward through the night.

"Five hundred feet above target. Prepare to cut engines."

Nick pulled his harness tight against his chest. His heart was pounding, and he could taste the adrenaline on the back of his tongue. His skin felt strangely cool under the thin sheen of liquid Mylar, and the blue jumpsuit was tight around his waist and shoulders, making it slightly hard to breath.

He looked over at Samantha. She was back on the other bench, tightening her own harness over her blue jumpsuit. She looked like a robot or a Vegas exotic dancer, her skin shining beneath her long dark hair. Her jumpsuit was open two buttons down the front, revealing a sliver of silver between her breasts. The last ten minutes had been the most sensual of Nick's adult life. He felt charged, ready for anything.

"Engines off. Radio and air silence. Beginning, now."

Suddenly, the helicopter went dead silent. Nick glanced up through the oval window and watched the rotors slow to a stop. All the cockpit lights went off, and the interior went inky black. Then the copter began to drop. Slowly, gently, foot by foot. It was an eerie sensation. Nick was surrounded by heavy steel, but he was descending like a slowly leaking balloon.

The seconds passed in silence. Nick concentrated on his luminescent hands, meanwhile flexing the muscles in his legs and arms. There was a sudden jolt and the sound of metal scraping against concrete; then Samantha was out of her harness and moving toward the door. Nick unhooked his own harness and helped her slide the door open. She grabbed the duffel bag and quickly scampered out of the helicopter.

Nick dropped down after her, slightly dizzy as his legs adjusted to the solid rooftop. They were standing in a recessed rectangle of paved blacktop, surrounded by high cinder-block walls. There was a glass revolving door twenty feet to Nick's left, casting a red glow from within the complex.

Samantha bent low and sprinted toward the revolving door. Nick raced after her. She stopped a few feet to the side of the door and pressed her back against a cinder-block wall. Then she reached out and touched the glass with a shiny hand. The door didn't move.

"Electronic lock," Samantha whispered. She reached into her duffel bag and pulled out a small plastic device, barely the size of a packet of matches. She stretched her arm high above her head, holding the device close to the top of the glass door. Then she flicked a switch on the surface.

Suddenly, the door started to revolve. "High emission electronic pulse," Samantha whispered. "Fooled the door's wiring into thinking the circuit has been completed."

Nick started forward, but Samantha stopped him with a hand. "You've forgotten the tunnel's motion sensors," she said. "Once you step out of that revolving door, security will come running."

Again, she reached into her duffel bag. This time she came out with an opaque glass container, about the size of a jar of peanut butter. Nick looked at it closely and jerked back, startled. It looked like the glass was moving. Then he realized that it wasn't the glass, it was the dark mass inside.

Samantha stepped in front of the revolving door and held the glass at arm's length, the top pointed toward the red glow coming through the spinning glass. With one twist of her wrist, she uncapped the jar. There was a quiet buzzing, as the black mass fountained out into the revolving door. Nick gasped, taking another step back. The cloud of tiny insects seemed to get larger as Samantha shook the jar; most of the cloud went into the revolving door, but wisps of black hung back, clinging to her face, her hair. A small pocket of the insects flew past Nick's eyes, and he squinted at them, barely able to distinguish the tiny individual bugs.

"Gnats?" Nick asked "You're dumping gnats into the tunnel?"

"Specially bred by CIA entomologists. The sophisticated motion sensors are programmed to ignore insects, dust particles, anything small enough and common enough to cause frequent problems.

These gnats will fill the tunnel, millions of tiny epicenters of motion; the sensors will override themselves trying to ignore them. We'll be able to walk
right through. Just don't swallow too many of
them."

Ingenious. And fairly disgusting. Samantha slung
the duffel bag over her shoulder and dove into the
revolving door. Nick followed in the next slice, trying to ignore the buzzing in his ears. He clenched
his teeth as the revolving door spit him out next to
Samantha. The air was blurry with the insects; the
cloud of gnats had expanded to fill nearly every
inch of the twenty-foot tunnel.

Samantha slid forward, and Nick followed, his
face pelted by the tiny bugs. He could feel them
crawling in his nose, ears, on his lips, even under
his eyelids. He tried to concentrate on the tunnel
itself; the curved plastic walls, the tracks of tiny red
lights along the ceiling. But his skin was crawling,
under his shirt, in his pants, up and down his
thighs.

Finally, they reached the inner steel door. There
was a panel halfway up the steel, containing a plastic plate and a small row of buttons. Samantha
pulled something out of the pocket of her jumpsuit
and went to work on the bottom corner of the panel.
The panel clicked off its base, and she stuck something long and thin underneath, feeling around like
a dentist examining someone's teeth.

There was a quiet whirring, and the steel door
slid upward. The cloud of gnats billowed forward
and Samantha followed, waving Nick after her.

They entered a much larger hallway, with fluorescent ceiling lights and white shag carpeting. The
cloud of gnats began to dissipate as they sped ahead

of Nick and Samantha, and Nick wondered what the Telecon employees would think when they began seeing the insects everywhere.

The hallway took a sharp corner, then Samantha cautioned him with a raised finger. They could hear voices in the distance. Nick held his breath, copying Samantha as she slid along the hallway wall. What would they do if they ran into somebody? He shivered at the thought.

Samantha grabbed his hand, stopping him, and pointed ahead. The hallway ended in a wide, open room filled with twelve-foot-high plastifoam cubicles. There were watercoolers and fax tables every few cubicles, and a dull hum of clicking keyboards and hushed voices rose above the low walls. Although the place seemed quarter-occupied at best, there were at least thirty people in the vast room.

Shit. From what Nick remembered of the blueprint, the hallway that led to the file room was twenty yards past the nearest cubicle. They would have to slide along the wall in plain view; if someone chose that moment to step out for a drink, or a fax, they'd be screwed.

No choice but to go for it. He followed Samantha to the end of the hallway, and squeezed her hand for luck. They slinked out into the opening, keeping as close to the wall as possible. Nick moved slowly, taking each step carefully, concentrating on Samantha's Reeboks. At one point halfway through the room, there was the sound of a chair being pushed back in the closest cubicle, not ten yards ahead of them. Nick and Samantha froze. They were going to get caught. The cubicle worker would find them, scream, and it would all be over.

But then there was the sound of woman's laughter, and the click of a computer keyboard. Nick recognized the electronic clamor of the game Doom seeping out above the cubicle's walls; the woman was obviously just reacting to something that had happened in her virtual world. Nick squeezed Samantha's hand, and they continued forward, quickening their pace.

A minute later they turned down another shag-carpeted hallway. Ten feet ahead, Nick saw a solid gray door with a familiar locking panel halfway up its face. A few feet beyond that door was what looked like a steel airlock, with rounded corners and a Plexiglas center. Through the center Nick could make out a small steel chamber. That was the anteroom to the main computer system. They had reached their target.

Samantha rushed to the gray file room door and went to work on the panel. A few seconds later the door slid upward, and Nick followed her inside. The door slid shut behind them, and Nick exhaled, relief filling him. The lights came on automatically.

The file room was twenty feet across, containing a wall of locked steel cabinets, a pair of IBM computer centers, and a row of high aluminum shelves.

"You stand by the door," Samantha hissed. "If you hear someone coming, signal me; we can hide behind the computer counter."

Nick nodded, taking position to the right of the steel door. He watched as Samantha yanked the Van Eck reader free from the kit and quickly moved to the far wall. Nick noticed her ease of motion with awe. She could pick electronic locks in seconds, work high-tech devices, plan and stage an entire covert operation—it was a little frightening, actually. She seemed totally at home with the tools of the espionage trade. Nick was getting turned on just watching her.

She chose a spot eye-level on the wall and attached the suction cup, using her entire arm to make sure it was squarely affixed. A tiny red diode on the face of the device blinked three times; then Samantha smiled and pressed a button under the bottom edge of the black plastic.

"I'll be able to access the information with my laptop," she whispered. "We should be able to get a good idea of how the computer system tracks information on the fiber optic web—and whether or not anything strange has gone through in the past couple of days."

She yanked the device off the wall and shoved it back into her pocket. Nick looked at her, surprised.

"That's it?"

"Did you expect buzzers and bells? We still have a few more minutes before the helicopter takes off, so I'll check out these file cabinets. There might be something on the Evolving Code."

She headed toward the wall of locked steel cabinets. Again, she pulled the small lock-picking device out of her pocket.

"A thief could do a lot with one of those," Nick commented.

"Professional thieves have much better electronic kits than this. There's no such thing as hard security anymore—someone will always find a better way to break inside."

In less time than it took Nick to think of a response, she had the cabinet open and was rifling through its contents: disks, folders, fax paper.

"Anything good?" Nick asked, nervously listening at the door. He was ready to get back to the helicopter.

"These seem to be backup files for what's on the computer system next door. Nothing in this one about the Evolving Code—let me try some of the others."

She moved from cabinet to cabinet, using her electronic lock-picking tools to open one after another. "I'm cutting off their alarm circuits as I go," she explained. "So their main computers won't show anything abnormal. From what I can tell, these cabinets are seriously wired."

She had reached the last row of cabinets and had paused near the bottom right corner. In one hand she held a three-quarter-inch computer disk. In the other hand, an open plastic file folder. Her eyes danced through the first page of the file, again and again.

"What is it?" Nick asked. "Is it about the Evolving Code?"

Samantha nodded. "It's marked confidential. It looks like the preliminary outline of the project that led to the development of the Evolving Code. Take a look at this."

She crossed the room in three steps, holding the file open for Nick to see. Nick took it from her, glancing at the first page. Across the top was a banner in oversized letters:

**Project Profile: The Evolving Code—
Submitted by Co-Directors of R&D,
Melora Parkridge and Eric Hoffman. May 1987**

"Eric Hoffman," Nick commented. "I didn't realize there was a co-director of R&D."

"There isn't. I checked their company prospectus earlier today. Melora Parkridge is the only head of R&D. Perhaps Hoffman quit. If we can find him, we might get some good information—"

"Samantha, check this out." Nick had continued turning pages. Stapled to the last page of the file was a small index card. On the card were three sentences of copy. The first was typewritten:

Query: Is the Backdoor Hypothesis
feasible?

The second sentence was also typewritten, but cryptic, difficult for Nick to decipher:

Look to the Source—E.H.

The third sentence was handwritten in a scrawl of blue ink:

Discontinue research on Backdoor Hypothesis—
Teal.

"The Backdoor Hypothesis," Samantha murmured. "Were they talking about a backdoor to the Evolving Code?"

Nick had been thinking the same thing. A backdoor was a secret way through the encryption; it was the rumor of a backdoor that had ruined the government's Clipper chip. If there was a backdoor to the Evolving Code, it would mean the entire information highway was going to be built on a fallacy. Nick felt his stomach trembling.

"Well, the only thing that's clear is the last sentence. Teal discontinued research into this backdoor."

Samantha bit her lower lip, her finger bouncing against the note card. "It's the second sentence that matters. E.H. probably stands for Eric Hoffman. I don't understand the rest of it—but Hoffman's the key. If this has something to do with the Evolving Code, he'll know. We have to find him."

She closed the file and tucked it into the duffel bag.

"What about the disk?"

"It was in the file. It might have more information about this Backdoor Hypothesis." She shoved it in with the file. Then she went back to the cabinets, and began relocking the steel doors.

"I'm not sure what any of this has to do with CaV," Nick said.

Samantha shrugged, finishing with the cabinets and joining Nick by the steel door. "Maybe nothing. But it's a start. If there's a backdoor to the code, there's a way past the Telecon system."

"If there's a backdoor to the code," Nick whispered back, as the steel door slid open, "Teal is sitting on a multibillion-dollar disaster."

Melora Parkridge stared at the two figures on the sixty-inch high-definition screen in front of her as the nausea tore through her stomach. Damn it, everything had been going so smoothly. And now this.

She leaned back in Teal's high leather chair, drumming her fingers against his polished glass desk. This was his vault, his little secret—but of course Teal had no secrets from her. She had known about the vault since the day it was built. He had paid off the technician who had helped wire the private camera system to his screen—and that, of course, was his mistake. If someone could be paid to keep his silence, he could always be paid more to break that promise. Pandora did not pay the people it used. Pandora dealt with them—*anything, always, for the greater good.*

And now Pandora had a problem. Melora leaned forward over the desk, her pointed breasts pushing the material of her jumpsuit against the smooth glass, her sharp nose inches away from the figures on the screen. She watched as the man and woman navigated through the alley, barely avoiding detection; a second later they had made it to the entrance to the access tunnel, pausing so the woman could again release another jar of well-trained insects.

There was no question: even through the glowing Mylar masks, Melora recognized the two intruders. They were the same two who had been in Teal's office that very morning. He had insisted to Melora that he had dealt with them, but obviously, his methods were not sufficient.

If Simon had not been on his way to pick her up for a last-minute visit to Pandora's lab, their assault on the complex would have gone completely undetected. Simon had almost landed right on top of their peculiar helicopter, barely turning away at the last minute. He had done his best to cover up his near miss with radio chatter—pretending to be a misguided news copter nearly landing on the wrong building—and then had immediately called Melora in her office. She had headed straight to the vault.

At first, she had planned to report the two interlopers to Teal, who was at home napping, in preparation for his upcoming debut. His lawyers would have eaten them alive, and everything would have

been fine. But then the woman had found the file—
and worse yet, the disk.

Damn Hoffman, even from the grave. She had
thought she had found all his copies and destroyed
them after his car accident. Obviously, he had been
more determined than she had realized.

Damage done, she reminded herself. Now it was
up to her to solve Pandora's new problem. Teal had
failed to stop the two scientists—but Teal, despite
his billions, did not have anywhere near the
resources that Pandora commanded. There were
limits to what Teal could—and would—do.

Pandora had no limits. More importantly, neither did Melora Parkridge.

TWENTY-SIX

ted Finder was waiting for them when they stepped out of the stairwell onto the second floor of the FBI communications complex, a pot of coffee in his hand and a cigar clamped between his teeth. The room was twice as crowded as it had been the day before, still dominated by white shirts and knit ties, groups of as many as ten people standing around the glowing computer screens. Ted's shirt looked freshly pressed, and he was wearing checkered suspenders. He pulled the cigar out of his mouth and smiled, waving the coffee pot. It was the Ted Samantha remembered—handsome, cheerful, boisterous.

"I assure you, nine A.M. isn't always like this. We're closing down early today—and for the rest of the week—so they can finish with the plumbing and wiring. Coffee?"

251

Samantha shook her head. She and Nick had shared a pot at her place before the limousine had picked them up. Although they had slept only a few hours, she felt wired. Everything was happening fast—not just the investigation, but the change in her relationship with Nick. Already he had spent the night in her apartment. With Ted, it had been three months before they had even considered sex. She had been a lot younger then, but it was more than that: with Nick there was an attraction—both emotional and physical—that she could not deny.

Ted led them through the room, laughing and chatting with the other feds along the way. It was obvious that the room loved Ted Finder; that was how it had always been with him. The life of the party, with his perfect blond hair, his athlete's body, his infectious humor, his obvious intelligence. But he was also arrogant, domineering, self-centered— Samantha shook the memories away. She was being unfair. Relationships fell apart; most were not meant to last forever. The minute she had first set eyes on Ted again, she had known she had done the right thing by breaking up with him. Thankfully, he was mature enough to let the past stay where it was. He was the same old Ted: eager to please, to help in any way.

Once they were back in his cubicle, Samantha unbuttoned her black cashmere jacket and pulled the plastic folder and three-quarter-inch disk out of the wide inside pocket.

Ted took the folder from her and started in on the first page. After a few seconds, he glanced up at her. "Where the hell did you get this?"

Samantha didn't answer. Ted nodded, turning

back to the folder. In a few seconds he had read the bulk of the file. Samantha and Nick had gone through it a dozen times during the night. Basically, it outlined the theory behind the Evolving Code. The idea itself was simple: a constantly evolving matrix spat out encoded numbers at random intervals. The evolution of the matrix was guided by a series of mathematical events and obstacles, so the randomly encoded numbers were specified by how that matrix reacted to its virtual surroundings.

Obviously, none of this was new to Ted. He didn't pause until he reached the note card attached to the last page of the file. Then the skin above his eyes wrinkled upward, and his lips fell open.

"Backdoor Hypothesis," he whispered, twice. Then he cleared his throat, looking up. "Is there any more to this?"

Samantha passed him the disk. "Only this. We're guessing that the letters E.H. stand for Eric Hoffman, a former co-director of R&D. We were hoping he would be able to tell us more."

"Not likely. Eric Hoffman died in a car accident more than a year ago. He was a brilliant software engineer and programmer; I'd met him on occasion at functions over the past few years. He and Melora Parkridge were Teal's secret weapons—they were primarily responsible for the software behind the Set-Top Boxes."

"So you know Melora Parkridge?" Nick asked. Samantha was almost startled by his voice. She had noticed how quiet he had become in Ted's presence. *Male ego.* So busy pouting or chest pounding, they didn't even know when they'd won.

"Briefly. She's always around on our walk-through tours of Telecon's complex. A stiff, mean-spirited woman. Brilliant, but socially inept. And a little bit scary."

"I noticed," Nick agreed. Samantha grimaced, listening to the two of them. Melora Parkridge had been curt, and her appearance severe, but it was a male gut reaction to label women scientists in this manner. She wondered how many of her colleagues at USAMRIID called her "scary."

"Let me make a quick copy of this," Ted said, turning toward his computer counter. Beside his PC workstation was a small double-slotted plastic box. Before Samantha could say anything, he shoved the disk into the top slot, and pressed a button on the side. The device whirred for a few seconds, then the disk popped back out. Ted grabbed it and handed it back to Samantha. He pulled a second disk out of the bottom slot, patting it with his other hand.

"For all we know, this Backdoor Hypothesis has nothing to do with the Evolving Code; the note card could have been attached to the code file by mistake, or just for the hell of it. Hopefully, there's more information on this disk."

Samantha glanced toward the door to Ted's cubicle. Someone was having an argument just a few yards away: raised male voices, the clicking of computer keys. "Ted, we're still trying to keep this as confidential as possible—"

"Don't worry, Sam. I'll wait till the place clears out, in about forty minutes. I should have an hour or two before the contractors show up."

Samantha nodded, slipping her copy of the disk back into her jacket pocket. "So you said Eric Hoffman died a year ago?"

"His obituary made the *Post*. A severe car accident."

"Here in Washington?" Nick asked. Samantha wondered why that mattered.

Ted shrugged. "I don't remember the details."

"Did he leave behind any family?" Samantha asked. Hoffman's death was a frustrating setback, but it wasn't necessarily a dead end. "A wife, kids—"

"I think there was a wife. Hold on a minute." He flicked on his IBM and waited for the beta test menu to appear on the screen, as before. He leaned behind the processor and meddled with the attachments for a few seconds; a new menu took the place of the old one, and Samantha recognized the glowing FBI seal.

Ted went back to the keyboard and began a data bank search, using Hoffman's name and a series of numbers and letters she didn't recognize—probably codes for his occupation, approximate time of death, etc. A minute later a high-definition picture came up on the screen. A woman, fairly attractive, with long red hair and thin lips. Underneath the picture was a paragraph of text.

"Sonya Hoffman-Lassiter. Thirty-four, pretty, high school diploma but no college degree. She remarried shortly after Hoffman's death. Neither she nor her new husband are employed; they both still live in Hoffman's house in Arlington County. I'll print out the address and phone number for you."

He hit a key, and Samantha ripped the page out of his printer. He had also printed out the woman's picture, and Samantha folded it dead center between the woman's pretty green eyes. Then she took a pen off of Ted's computer counter and pulled a blank sheet out of the printer. "This is my cell phone number. Call me when you've had a chance to look at the disk."

"I will." Ted paused, tapping the disk. "A Backdoor Hypothesis. Christ, Samantha, if this has anything to do with Teal's Evolving Code—"

"We know, Ted. We know."

Thirty-five minutes later Samantha pulled her jacket tight over her white silk button-down shirt as she stepped out of the limousine onto a tree-lined sidewalk in Arlington County. Nick slid out after her: khakis, flannel shirt, same leather jacket and lace-up boots. She wondered if he owned anything more dressy, or if it was simply the result of a quick packing job.

"This is idyllic," he commented, brushing crumbs off of his khakis. They had shared a box of muffins on the ride over. Despite herself, Samantha had thought about each bite in terms of calories; she doubted that would ever change. But with Nick next to her, his eyes telling her how beautiful she was to him, she wouldn't stop eating. That she knew.

"Hoffman must have made a pretty good salary." The house was two stories, blue, with a two-car garage and a large screened front porch. There were wide picture windows on both the first and second floors, but the drapes were tightly drawn, revealing nothing of the interior. The front lawn was recently mowed, and the stone path that led to the porch had been recently weeded. The house was slightly larger than the others on the street; Samantha guessed the price was somewhere near half a million, if not more. This was one of Washington's prime suburbs.

They reached the stone steps to the screened porch, and Samantha peered through the interlocking hexagons of the aluminum screening. There were two rockers and a wicker couch to the right side of the inner door. A can of Raid bug spray was sitting on a glass end table between the rockers.

Nick reached forward and tried the screen door. It was locked, and Samantha searched for the buzzer. She found it halfway up the door frame, and pressed it twice, letting her finger rest a little longer than necessary.

There was motion from inside the house; then the inner door swung outward, and an overweight man with a heavy beard and thick glasses stepped out onto the porch. He was wearing a sleeveless white T-shirt and green sweatpants. He had a can of Budweiser in his left hand.

"Can I help you?"

Samantha noticed the ketchup stain in the center of his T-shirt. "Is Mrs. Lassiter home?"

"She ain't expecting no one. I'm her husband, so you can tell me what you want."

Samantha exhaled through her teeth, as she felt the man's eyes ride up and down her body. She didn't have time to explain—nor was she about to try with this Neanderthal. She reached into her jacket and pulled out her USAMRIID identification. She flipped it open, letting him see the shiny silver crest but not giving him a chance to read the words.

"We're with the IRS. We have a few questions about her 1040s."

The Neanderthal took a tiny step back, a nervous expression crossing his face. "The IRS?"

Nick took a step forward, hands behind his back. His eyes roamed around the outside of the house. "This is a nice house, Mr. Lassiter. Good collateral for almost a decade of unpaid back taxes, I'd guess."

Lassiter coughed, his fingers denting the aluminum of his Budweiser can. "Hold on a second. I'll get Sonya."

"You do that," Samantha said. Lassiter rushed back into the house, his thick thighs jiggling as he disappeared. Samantha turned toward Nick. "Nice touch."

Nick shrugged, smiling. A few minutes later, the inner door reopened. Sonya Hoffman-Lassiter stepped into the screened porch. She was markedly less attractive than her picture. There were thick lines under her green eyes, and her red hair was stringy, the ends frayed. She was wearing jean overalls and a heavy wool sweater. Her hands were jammed deep into her pockets. She stopped a few feet in front of the screened door.

"Tom says you're from the IRS? I pay my taxes on time—"

"Mrs. Lassiter," Samantha interrupted, smiling amicably. "We're not actually here to ask about your taxes. If it's okay, we'd like to speak to you for a few minutes about your former husband. Eric Hoffman."

Sonya frowned. "You ain't from the IRS."

"No, we're not. We're scientists involved with an investigation into Telecon Industries—"

"Look, I don't have to talk to you. Eric died a long time ago. I don't have anything to do with Telecon anymore."

Samantha felt the acid in her stomach. This wasn't going to be easy. "Would you mind if we came inside? Just for a few minutes."

Sonya glanced over her shoulder, then shook her head. "No, I don't think that's a good idea. It's kind of a mess inside. Tom had his poker buddies over last night."

"Then maybe we can talk out here on the porch?

It's really important that we speak to you. Please?"

Sonya bit her thin lower lip, thinking. Finally, she shrugged. "Guess I could spare a few minutes."

She put her hand on the handle to the screen door, then glanced around Nick and Samantha. "You don't see any of the little bastards, do you?"

Samantha raised her eyebrows. "Sorry?"

"Bees. I'm allergic. I stop breathing. Almost died once three years ago."

"Anaphylactic shock," Nick said. "Do you carry an epinephrine injector with you?"

The woman patted her overalls. "Always. And I try to stay inside until winter. Never be too careful. The little bastards don't give up easy."

She unlocked the screen door and yanked it open, ushering them quickly inside. She slammed the door shut, locking it. Samantha watched her from behind; obviously, the woman was not entirely together. She'd known plenty of people who were allergic to insect bites, but this level of paranoia was a bit much. Especially this late in October.

Sonya finished with the door and pointed them to the wicker couch. She sat on one of the rockers, taking the can of Raid off of the end table and resting it on her lap. "So you're investigating Telecon? What'd they do? Tell me it's something really awful."

"You sound like you don't think much of Telecon," Nick commented. The woman whirled toward him, angry.

"Bunch of home-wrecking bastards. Especially that woman, the ice queen. Melora Parkridge. And Teal, he's as bad as the ice queen. Ruined my marriage, the two of them."

Sonya suddenly realized how loud her voice had

become, and she glanced at the inner door to her house, nervous. Then she looked down at her lap, concentrating on the can of Raid. Samantha felt an instant sympathy for the woman. She had not always been like this. Samantha could tell that Sonya had once been beautiful.

"How did Telecon ruin your marriage?"

It was a personal question, but Samantha could see that the woman wanted to talk. "Eric and I met five years ago. I was working at the A&P, a checkout girl. He was this geeky scientist—I'm sure you know the type. Lots of Stouffer microwave pizzas, TV dinners, that sort of thing. Anyway, we got married a few months later. It was real love, perfect."

Samantha nodded, her eyes gentle. She didn't want to rush the woman. This was their only link to Hoffman—and to whatever information he might have left behind about the Evolving Code.

"Then he started working late," the woman continued, her fingers tightening around the can of Raid. "Meetings that lasted until midnight. Weekends at his computer. At first, I thought he was having an affair. Then I met Melora Parkridge and realized that wasn't it."

She swallowed, her voice growing thick. "It got worse and worse. Pretty soon, he wasn't coming home at all. I asked him and he tried to explain; it was some sort of project they were working on, something that was going to change the world. But I didn't care about that. I wanted a husband. My husband."

She took a deep breath, glancing at the house. "I met Tom two years ago. He worked at the place where we got our cars fixed. He was training to be a mechanic."

She raised her eyes, looking right at Samantha. "I was a widow already, long before the car accident. Tom was nice to me, cared about me—he loved me the way Eric did, before he gave me up for Telecon."

Her eyes jumped to a spot to Samantha's right. Suddenly, she whipped the can of Raid up and pressed the trigger. A spout of noxious chemicals sprayed into the air. Samantha barely had time to jerk her face out of the way. Sonya dropped the can back onto her lap, putting her hands on her knees. "Of course, the minute I married him he dropped out of mechanic school. Now he drinks all night with his buddies and I spend all my time cleaning up after him. But it's still better than being alone. Know what I mean?"

Samantha forced another nod. This was a pathetic woman. Dependent, self-hating, helpless—the kind of woman Samantha had vowed never to be. "Sonya, did your husband ever tell you what sort of project he was working on? The one that kept him at Telecon nights and weekends?"

"I don't know, I never listened when he talked his computer crap. It might have had something to do with the Set-Top Boxes—there were always pieces of them lying around the house."

Samantha's ears perked up. Nick leaned past her and asked the question. "Do you still have those pieces?"

The woman shook her head. "Some guys from Telecon came by the week after his car accident and took everything away. They even emptied the desk in his study, and the shelves in the basement. Took all his papers and notebooks. Pretty thorough bastards."

Samantha sighed. "So none of his papers were left behind?"

Sonya shook her head. Samantha was about to get up, when Nick leaned forward again. "Sonya, could they have missed anything? The people from Telecon?"

Sonya thought for a few seconds. "Well, I don't know. They got everything that was in the house."

"Did he have any papers outside of the house? Maybe something he had you hold for him, somewhere they wouldn't look?"

Sonya touched her thin lips. "It's funny you ask it like that. About a month or so before the car accident, he gave me a couple of things to put in my safety deposit box. He said they were valuable, but they weren't, really, just a couple of notebooks. I tried reading through one of them, but it was just a lot of computer crap."

Samantha's body tingled. She said a silent prayer: "Did you keep the notebooks?"

"I put 'em in my safety deposit box, like he asked. Haven't looked at them in a year. Why?"

"Do you think it would be possible for us to see them?"

Sonya shrugged. "I don't see why not."

"Could you pick them up today?"

"Well—"

"Our investigation is well funded, Sonya. We have a thousand dollars budgeted to incidental expenses. And we realize how inconvenient this is for you."

Sonya's eyes lit up. She quickly rose from her chair. "It will take me some time to find the key. But I could get over there this afternoon."

"I'll give you my phone number. You can call me

when you have the notebooks. I'll arrange for someone to pick them up."

"And you'll cover my, ah, incidental, ah—"

Samantha rose from the wicker couch, smiling.
"That's what our expense budget is for. Thank you
for your help. And I am sorry about your loss."

Sonya nodded, as Samantha handed her a blank
card with her cellular phone number written on the
back. Sonya unlocked the screen door, searched for
bees, then quickly held it open. Samantha rushed
through, followed by Nick. After the door slammed
shut behind them, Nick turned, asking a final question.

"Sonya, was your husband's car accident here in
Washington?"

It was the same question he had asked Ted.
Again, Samantha wondered why that was important. Sonya shook her head, her eyes still jumping
back and forth as she looked for bees.

"No, he was on a business trip. I think he was in
Providence, Rhode Island. Telecon had an office
near there."

"Thank you," Nick said, touching Samantha's
shoulder. "Again, please call us when you have the
notebooks."

Sonya nodded, then disappeared back into her
house. Samantha glanced at Nick as he started
down the front path. "Why did you want to know
where Eric Hoffman died?"

"Just curious, I guess. If he was in an accident in
Providence, the ambulance probably took him to
the trauma department at Providence City Hospital.
About an hour from Boston General, not including
traffic."

"It's been a year."

"Most hospitals keep X rays and other stats on file for much longer than that. If I'm lucky, I can get a friend to swing over there this afternoon, take a look around."

"You don't think—"

"It won't hurt to cover all the bases. I'll call Charlie from the limousine."

"You can't just call the trauma center?"

"I doubt I'll get anyone to do a thorough search on short notice. But Charlie won't let me down. If there's something off about the way Hoffman died, he'll find it."

Samantha looked at him, impressed. There was no reason to suspect Telecon's involvement in anything as nefarious as Hoffman's car accident, but the Evolving Code was worth billions, and Hoffman had been on the inside. There was no telling what Marcus Teal was capable of.

Samantha felt the excitement rising through her body. If they were lucky, Hoffman had left something worthwhile behind in his wife's safety deposit box. Despite the setbacks, the investigation was progressing. And she had remained firmly in control.

One hundred yards away, two men in orange Vepco uniforms sat quietly in the front seat of a parked repair van. One of the men was tall, with curly red hair and a scruffy goatee. His partner was five four, squat, with a double chin and a cigarette hanging out of the corner of his mouth. In front of the man with the cigarette, attached to the top of the dashboard, was a small television monitor. Next to the monitor was a control panel and a pair of spherical speakers.

"The limo's starting up," he mumbled past his

cigarette. The driver leaned toward the screen, nodding. He could see the limousine slowly pulling away from the curb. The shot was from a slightly elevated angle, magnified to fill the screen. The camera was a technological marvel, the size of two quarters glued together, and was located on the tip of a telescoping, centimeter thin rod of high purity glass extended fifteen feet above the top of the van. The eye in the sky, it was called. Made surveillance a hell of a lot easier.

"Make sure you've got a full radio and microwave blanket. Every frequency."

The man with the cigarette hit buttons on the control panel. The spherical speakers crackled to life. Garbled words echoed through the van. He tinkered with a few more buttons, and the words became clear: a man's voice, answered by a second man far away.

"Cell phone," the man with the cigarette commented. "Scrambled, pretty high tech. Took a full three seconds to break through."

The driver smiled. He had worked freelance for many organizations since his discharge from special forces: CIA, NSA, DEA, even the Fibbies. But nothing had compared—in technology, take home pay, or structure—to this. Whoever these people were that signed his checks, they knew their business.

He leaned back from the screen and pressed his foot against the gas. The van rolled slowly down the street, keeping roughly one hundred and fifty yards behind the limousine. They didn't need to get any closer. Every few minutes they would raise the telescoping camera and relocate the limousine, adjust direction. And even if they did somehow lose their target, it didn't matter. A similar van was parked down the street from Samantha Craig's apartment. And another a few blocks from the FBI Center for Developing Technologies.

Whoever the hell they were, Pandora was thorough.

TWENTY-SEVEN

nick paused in the doorway to Samantha's bedroom, his nostrils full of her subtle perfume. Her bed was made, but he could still see the indentation where they had slept, the afterimage of a late night of passion and emotional revelation imprinted in her cream down comforter. They had shared their scars and would, Nick was sure, soon begin healing together.

The guilt was still there, but it was muted, acceptable. Nick took a deep breath, his eyes traveling through the bedroom. The bed was large and took up most of the exposed hardwood floor. There was a polished oak desk next to the bed, with a computer, printer, and fax machine. Next to the fax machine was an antique brass-plated pharmacy lamp, sitting beside a vase full of slightly less than fresh hothouse flowers. Aside from the bed and the desk, the bedroom contained a pair of matching cream Stratford chairs, a tall chest made of finished maple, and a standing brass cantilever floor lamp. Every item was of the highest quality, mingling in perfect harmony, a bedroom to match the elegance of her well-designed living room.

Samantha crossed the room quickly, heading straight for the desk. The duffel bag from last night was beneath the desk's swivel chair, and she dropped to her knees beside it, working on the zipper. Nick sat on the bed, watching the muscles of her neck tense as she dug through the duffel's contents. He was fascinated by her body, by her length and angles and curves. He supposed it had to do with being alone for so long, but he could not get enough of her.

He had called Charlie from the limousine. Charlie had been practicing his sax in the basement of his rental home in Somerville. He had a midnight show at the Cantab Lounge in Cambridge, but he figured he could get to Providence and back with more than enough time to spare. Anything for a friend, that was Charlie's way. And he didn't ask questions. Which had made Nick feel even worse about the lies he was telling—that Hoffman had been a friend of Jennifer's parents, that there were some questions about the car accident involving a possible insurance fraud scheme. X rays, a trauma file, any autopsy findings—anything Charlie could find.

When this was all over, he would buy Charlie dinner and explain what had really been going on. He would tell Charlie everything—about CaV, Telecon, and Samantha. Especially about Samantha.

"Here it is." She pulled out the Van Eck reader,

holding it in front of her eyes. "This will just take a second."

She rose and leaned behind the computer, grabbing at wires that looped down the back of her desk. Nick wanted to help, but he was useless when it came to computers. He was the stereotypical consumer that Telecon's Set-Top Boxes were designed for. He needed it to be simple, happy, and at his fingertips.

"So what, exactly, are you going to get from that thing?"

Samantha came out from behind the computer. The Van Eck reader was in her left hand, hooked by a long black cable to the back of the processor. "Any pixel that lit up on a computer screen, any key punched on a computer keyboard. By testing the strength of the signals, we can lay out the information by time—essentially, we'll get a look at everything electronic that went on in that computer room over the past twenty-four hours."

She flicked on the computer and began to hit keys. A few seconds later, green sentences began to slide down from the top of the screen. A mixture of numbers, letters, and strange, unreadable icons. At the end of each line was a highlighted packet of numbers, next to a string of two- and three-letter abbreviations.

"Military time standards," Samantha said, pointing at the highlighted packets. "And these abbreviations look like city labels: *N.Y.*, *L.A.*, *Tol.*—that's probably Toledo."

Nick could not hide his confusion. He didn't see anything but incomprehensible code. "Where is this coming from?"

Samantha glanced at the Van Eck reader. "Screen

emissions from twenty-five feet away. There must be a rather large high-density display in the main computer atrium. It's getting a constant feed from the computer. It must be monitoring the beta test."

"So these sentences—"

"Represent the information that passed through their computer system at these specific times, between these strings of cities."

Nick watched the green lines scrolling on into infinity. "Does this mean anything to you? It's just a lot of techno garbage to me."

Samantha wasn't listening to him; instead, she was ruffling through a pad of paper next to her computer. She found what she was looking for and turned back to the screen. "Don't worry about the numbers and letters—they represent each transmission, but of themselves they don't mean anything. Remember, each bit is scrambled by the Evolving Code and can only be unscrambled when it reaches its destination Set-Top Box."

"So what good is this?"

"We can't read the transmissions, but we can read the time codes," Samantha responded, using her mouse to speed up the scroll. "If we focus on the specific time of one of the CaV outbreaks," she glanced at the pad of paper, "four-thirty Monday morning, for instance, we should be able to at least tell if anything strange went through the system. Here we go."

She slapped the space bar, and the screen froze. Then she moved her finger down the lines of code and paused.

"Look at this."

Nick looked under her finger and saw a blank line in the stream of sentences. It was as if a single sentence was missing. He shifted his eyes down one line and searched out the city abbreviation. There it was, *BOS.* On the other end of the code was another city abbreviation: *WADC.* He guessed it was Washington.

"A break in the code," he said. "Right before the Boston transmission. What does that mean?"

"I don't know. Let's try another outbreak point." She turned back to her pad of paper. "The sewer engineers were watching a transmission of a basketball game originating in L.A. at four-forty Monday afternoon."

She attacked the keyboard, letting the screen continue scrolling, searching the time codes.

"There."

"Son of a bitch," Nick said, rising half off the bed. "Another break. Right before the transmission. Try another."

He felt the excitement build as she searched for the transmission that killed the young woman near Burlington, Vermont, who had been innocently trying to watch a sitcom—the woman whose picture she still carried in her pocket. This time, Samantha did not know the exact time of the transmission; instead, she was searching for the city code while watching the approximate morning window.

Bam. She slammed her hand against the space bar, once again freezing the screen. There was another break in the transmissions. Right below the break, were the city codes. *BRL*— Burlington. *L.A.*, Los Angeles. Eight forty-five in the morning.

Nick exhaled, his stomach churning. "Samantha, you realize what this means?"

Samantha looked at him. Her eyes were wide. "It means our hypothesis is correct. There's no way this could be a coincidence. A break in the transmissions before each outbreak of CaV."

She pointed at the Van Eck reader. "This is our proof. I could take this back to USAMRIID. They'd have to listen—"

"I don't know, Samantha. What do the breaks mean? It's hard to believe they're coincidental, but we can't *prove* they have anything to do with CaV."

Samantha nodded, thinking. "The breaks could be caused by a number of things. The system shutting down for a fraction of a second before the deadly transmissions, maybe some sort of hardware glitch. Or a software manifestation, perhaps as simple as our unknown wavelength of light showing up as a blank line of code."

"It could take us a long time to figure this out on our own. And the Big Turn On is now twenty-one hours away. Even with expert help—"

A metallic ringing filled the room. Nick watched as Samantha reached into her jacket and pulled out her tiny cellular phone. She held it to her ear, anticipation obvious on her face. Then her eyes widened, and she held the phone a few inches away. The person on the other end was shouting.

"Hold on, Ted," she said. "I'm going to put you on speaker."

"That thing has a speaker setting?" Nick asked, incredulous. Samantha nodded, flicking a switch on the phone's side and setting it down on her desk. A second later, Ted Finder's voice burst through the air.

"Sam, you have to tell me where you got this disk."

Nick looked at Samantha. Ted sounded out of breath, even through the distortion caused by the tiny phone's speakers. Samantha leaned close to the desk.

"Ted, you know I can't—"

"Sam, don't fuck with me. This is important. Where did you get this disk?"

Samantha sat back, her face stiff. She looked at Nick, and he nodded. They had no choice but to trust Ted. "We stole it from the Telecon Complex."

"That's what I thought. Sam, I can hardly believe this. I've never seen anything—Jesus, I don't know what to say."

Nick couldn't contain his curiosity. Their findings from the Van Eck reader were exciting, but Ted's near delirium hinted at something much better. "What is it? Is it a backdoor to the code?"

"I better not talk about it over the phone."

"It's a secure line," Samantha reminded him.

"I don't care. You have to get over here. Right now."

"Ted—"

"Samantha, listen to me. This is bigger than a backdoor. It's bigger than the Evolving Code— Christ, you're not going to believe this."

She could hear the excitement in his voice. She could also hear something else—fear? Something on the disk had him terrified. "What is it, Ted? What have you found?"

There was a long pause. Finally, Ted's voice returned, barely a whisper.

"I think it's alive."

TWENTY-EIGHT

Samantha was the first to notice that something wasn't right. They were moving up the stone walkway to the FBI Center for Developing Technologies—racing past the parked bulldozers and the sleeping crane—when she stopped, pointing at the second floor of the building. As before, half of the windows were covered by orange strips of canvas. Next to these was a row of real glass windows, the panes glowing in the midafternoon sun. Samantha jabbed her finger toward the center pane. There was a spiderweb of circular cracks in the glass, emanating from a spot in the direct center. It looked like someone had thrown a small rock through the window.

"I didn't notice that cracked pane this morning, did you?"

"Maybe the electrical people did it."

"I don't think they've arrived yet. I don't see a van."

Nick shrugged. He didn't think a broken window was much to worry about. The building was under construction; these things happened. Maybe Ted had smiled at it and the thing had shattered from the glow.

In a moment they were up the front steps and into the revolving door. The lobby looked the same as before, unfinished wood with scattered boxes and construction equipment. It didn't look like any more wiring had been done: cables and raw electrical cords hung down the cinder-block walls, and there were still patches of exposed metal pipes. There was no sign of the electrical or plumbing contractors; nor were there any other signs of life, and Nick guessed that the other feds had already cleared out.

They headed straight to the stone stairwell and started up the steps. Nick felt the tension rising as he navigated past boxes of screws, hammers, and wooden dowels. He reached the heavy wooden door two steps in front of Samantha and skidded to a stop. His eyes widened as he focused on the knob.

"What the hell?"

The wood around the knob was splintered. The brass knob was hanging halfway out of the door, bent completely out of shape. It looked like someone had hit it with a heavy pipe. The door itself was open a few inches, spilling a triangle of orange light into the cement stairwell.

Samantha pushed him back against the wall of the stairwell, and moved to the other side of the door. Her face had gone white. Nick remembered her joke about the revolver in the helicopter.

"Samantha," he started to ask, but she shook her head, silencing him. He doubted she was armed. He had watched her change into the cashmere jacket and herringbone tights that morning, and had been with her ever since. He would have noticed if she had strapped on a gun.

She took a deep breath, and put her hand on the bent knob. Nick braced himself, ready to leap in front of her. He didn't care about her training—he would protect her at all costs.

She yanked the door open and before Nick could move, she had slid into the room, her knees bent, her head low. Nick followed as quickly as his reflexes would allow.

The room looked like the aftermath of a hurricane. Shattered glass covered the hardwood floor. Upended desks and cabinets lay surrounded by destroyed computer screens. One of the fluorescent light panels from the ceiling hung from a long frayed wire, swinging in the breeze blowing through a tattered canvas window. Nick saw Samantha's legs tremble as she crept forward, and he moved close to her, his eyes trying to take in all the corners at once. There didn't seem to be anybody else in the room.

Step by step, they closed in on Ted's cubicle. Nick's eyes widened as he saw a line of tiny holes in the plastifoam front wall; he realized they were bullet holes, from some sort of small-caliber weapon. The same weapon that had put a hole in the glass window pane.

The door to the cubicle was half open. Samantha turned the corner first, stopping dead, a thin gasp coming out of her. Nick quickly pushed in beside her.

Ted was sitting in his chair, his body bent at the waist. His head was jammed through the screen of his computer. There was blood seeping down around his neck, and two bloody holes in his back. One of the bullets had snapped his suspenders, and his pants hung low around his hips.

"My God," Samantha whispered, her voice verging on tears. Nick stepped past her, reaching for Ted's carotid even though he knew it was pointless. There was no pulse. He was about to pull Ted's head out of the computer when he stopped, staring down at the keyboard. Ted's hands were resting on the space bar—covered in thick rubber dish gloves.

Nick stared at the gloves. Slowly, he reached forward and lifted Ted's left hand off of the keyboard. Delicately, he pulled the glove free from his fingers and turned his hand over.

The tips of his fingers were covered in third-degree burns: bright red blisters and black soot spots. Nick let Ted's hand drop and stepped away, shocked. *What the hell?* His first thought was torture, but then why would Ted be wearing rubber gloves? What was going . . .

There was a sudden noise from outside the cubicle. Nick whirled around, and saw Samantha's eyes go wide. They weren't alone. There was another sound, closer, and then a metallic click. The sound of a gun being cocked.

Samantha leapt forward, grabbing Nick by the waist and sending him crashing to the floor. There was a series of muffled pops, and plumes of plasti-foam showered down on Nick's back. Samantha rolled off of Nick, her eyes wild. Nick looked up and saw a line of tiny holes in the wall a few feet above his head. *Christ.*

"Stay still," Samantha hissed. She was trying to get her phone out of her jacket, but the material was caught on the leg of Ted's swivel chair.

Nick had no intention of staying still. He reached up and grabbed Ted's body, yanking him free of the computer. The swivel chair tilted to the side and Ted's body crashed onto Nick's legs. Nick cursed, then rolled Ted over, searching. Samantha got her phone free, then turned and stared.

"What the hell are you doing?"

Nick didn't answer. First he checked under Ted's right arm—*nothing.* Then he leaned forward and felt down Ted's left leg. There it was, just as he had remembered: a leather ankle holster. Nick yanked the revolver free with his left hand, his teeth clenching. The gun was heavy, the barrel frighteningly large.

"Samantha, how many bullets does this thing hold?"

"Nick—"

"How many!"

Samantha glanced at it for less than a second. "Beretta Model 92F. Fifteen rounds. Nick, you better let me—"

Nick shook his head, scrambling toward the door of the cubicle, keeping low. He could hear quiet footsteps getting closer on the other side of the wall. He could also hear low voices, and the crackle of a walkie-talkie. Shit, shit, shit, his brain was shouting, and shooting pains ran down the back of his right hand. Maybe he should have given Samantha the gun, but he wasn't going to. Because somewhere in the back of his mind, something had clicked. His jaw clenched tight and the muscles in the back of his neck bunched up. He was scared and more than that, he was pissed. He was going to take control.

"Get behind me," he hissed back at Samantha. "When I go out that door you follow right behind. Head toward the back of the room. Find cover."

"Nick," Samantha hissed back, crawling after him. "There could be twenty people out there—"

"I know. Just follow my lead."

If there were twenty of them out there, he and Samantha were fucked no matter what they did. He stopped a few inches from the cubicle door and flexed his knees, ready. The coach's voice blared in his ears: *Action beats reaction.* Then he heard another click and his stomach dropped. No more time to waste, he had to move.

He leapt forward, leading with his right shoulder, just as the quiet pops tore through the cubicle wall. His shoulder collided with the door and his body barreled through, the Beretta coming up in a low arc. His eyes instantly took in the scene: one man in a heavy blue overcoat was standing ten feet away, a silenced pistol aimed at the cubicle wall. Another man in a leather bomber jacket and dark shades was five feet behind him, an oversized shotgun resting across his arms. A short woman in a black suit was standing by the door, what looked like a submachine gun in her hands. All three were turning toward him, shocked looks on their faces. *Action beats reaction!*

He screamed and squeezed the trigger, still moving forward, his body low, his legs churning underneath him. The gun bucked upward, an explosion crashing through the air. A computer behind the man in the blue overcoat exploded in a rain of glass. Nick squeezed again, and the man lurched backward, crashing into the man with the shotgun. There was a third explosion, then a fourth, then a fifth—pieces of the wall fountaining upward, computers shattering, tables erupting in a hail of wooden splinters. The man with the shotgun was suddenly sprawling backward through the air, the top of his head missing. The woman at the door swung her submachine gun, a lick of flame spouting from its barrel. Nick felt something bite into his right thigh but he didn't have time to scream; his finger closed on the trigger again and there were four more explosions in quick succession. The woman fell backward through the door, her lungs suddenly exposed.

Nick's body continued forward, his eyes wildly searching the room. There was blood everywhere. The two men were lying next to each other, draped over a fallen computer cabinet. The woman's shoes were still in the room, the rest of her body out in the stairwell.

"I shot them," Nick whispered, as his body finally came to a stop. Fierce pain ripped through his right leg, and he stumbled forward. "I shot them all."

"You shot everything," Samantha gasped, crawling toward him. She hadn't headed for the back wall—there hadn't been time to do anything but stare. "How did you do that?"

Nick looked at the gun in his hand. His body had started to shake. "A lot of repressed anger." Then his right leg totally gave out. He crashed to the floor, his teeth coming together. The pain was enormous. A hot knife was digging into his thigh, halfway between his knee and pelvis. Samantha dove toward him, her face filled with fear.

"Nick, you're hit."

Nick looked down at his leg. To his surprise, it wasn't as bad as it felt. The bullet had torn through his jeans, ripping through his skin, but it didn't look like it had hit the bone. He was bleeding pretty badly, but it didn't look like a severed artery.

"I need something to stop the bleeding."

Samantha nodded, racing to the back of the room. She ripped a piece of canvas out of the window and rushed back. "Will this do?"

Nick took the canvas and tied it around his thigh, pulling it as tight as he could. He tied a double knot, then twisted the knot around, lowering his circulation. It wasn't great, but it would hold. He held out his hand and Samantha helped him up. Pain tore up and down his leg, but it was bearable.

"We have to get out of here," Samantha hissed. "There will be more of them downstairs. They'll be up here any minute."

"How do you know?"

She nodded toward the two men lying in the center of the room. "The lead man was using a .22 caliber with suppresser. Behind him, a backup with a scattergun. Then the team leader, with a submachine gun. It's a classic covert action."

"You mean they're government?"

Samantha's face was white with fear. "I don't know. But they're definitely professional. This is an FBI office, Nick. Ted was set up—he was a target."

Nick stared at her. "Because of us?"

Samantha didn't answer. Nick realized that they had to move, quickly. He forgot about the pain in his thigh and glanced at the door. No way could they go down the stairwell. If Samantha was right, they'd be cut to ribbons before they made the lobby.

Nick's shooting had bought them a few minutes, but nothing more.

He turned toward the back wall, his eyes sweeping to the far left corner. There it was, just as he had remembered. A coil of thick rubber encased cable. The fiber optic line. It looked like at least fifty feet, coming out of the cinder-block wall.

"Come on," he said, staggering toward the cable. Samantha put a hand under his arm and helped him, her gaze following his. She realized what he had in mind, and quickly went to the nearest canvas-covered window. She pulled the canvas back and glanced outside.

"Looks clear," she said. "An alley, behind the boarded-up school. You think the cable will hold?"

Nick was about to answer when he heard voices coming from the stairwell. At least four people, taking the steps quickly. There was no more time for caution.

He grabbed the end of the cable with both hands and lifted it, groaning at the pain rising up his thigh and down his right hand. The cable was heavy, and seemed pretty strong. Strong enough for his body weight? There was no way to know.

Samantha helped him drag the cable to the window. Together, they lowered it down the side of the building. Thirty, maybe forty feet, to the blacktop alley. It would be a long fall.

Nick stumbled back to the spot where the cable came out of the cinder-block wall. It looked like it ran down the side of the building, all the way to first floor.

"It should be pretty well braced," Nick whispered, hoping it was true. "You go first."

"But your leg—"

"I'll be okay. I climbed ropes all through football. I can do this with one hand." Or he could—ten years ago.

Samantha nodded. She leaned forward, and kissed him. Then she went to the window and gripped the rubber cable. Nick helped her get her legs over the sill. She gave him one last look, then dropped downward, out of sight. Nick leaned over the sill, watching her progress. She was moving quickly, using her legs against the wall, her hands sliding down the cable. He shifted his eyes to the spot where it was attached to the wall, it looked good. It was going to hold.

The voices were getting louder outside the doorway. Any second, more trained killers would burst into the room. He had to buy more time.

He turned toward the half-open doorway and aimed the Beretta. Then he gritted his teeth and squeezed the trigger. The gun erupted five more times. The half-open door shattered, wood splinters clattering down the stairwell. He heard a muffled shout, then nothing. Hopefully, that had slowed them down.

He shoved the Beretta into his belt and hobbled to the window. With great effort, he lifted himself over the sill, letting his legs hang down the side of the building. The wind tugged at his clothes and his right thigh cried out. *Concentrate. Whatever happens, you've lived through worse.*

Slowly, carefully, he lowered himself down the side of the building. The muscles in his arms bulged, his lungs burned, his thigh screamed, but he moved downward, foot by foot. A few minutes later his shoes touched blacktop and he felt Samantha's hands around his waist, helping him down. He let go of the cable, letting it swing against the building. As Teal had said, the stuff really was amazing.

"This way," Samantha whispered. "I checked, the alley has a back way out. We don't want to risk going past the front of the building."

"What do you think happened to your driver?" The limousine had been parked out front when they entered the building.

Samantha shook her head, as she led him down the alley. The muscles of her face tensed. "I think they were waiting for us. They killed Ted—we can assume they killed my driver."

"These people are serious," Nick whispered. "And brutal. What do they want?"

Samantha patted her jacket. The Telecon computer disk was still in her front pocket. "I think it has to do with this disk."

"Christ," Nick whispered. "Charlie." He had sent Charlie after Hoffman's medical records. Had he put his best friend in danger? Providence was far from Washington. And they couldn't have traced the secure phone call—could they? The truth was, he had no idea what they were dealing with.

"Samantha, who are these people?"

"I don't know. Ted was FBI, Nick. They killed him in his office. If they're willing to do that, nothing will stop them. We can't trust anybody."

Nick swallowed. He prayed that Charlie was okay. His mind whirled back to Ted, his snapped suspenders, the blood running down his neck. Then he remembered Ted's fingers. The third-degree burns. The rubber gloves. He glanced at Samantha, thought about the disk in her front pocket.

What the hell was going on?

TWENTY-NINE

S uburbia. Pretty little houses on pretty little swipes of green, big family cars parked in garages overflowing with bicycles and riding mowers and skis, backyards cluttered with barbecues and hammocks and trees—so many wonderful trees. Ned Dickerson crouched in the late-afternoon shadows at the base of one such wonderful tree, his hand running up and down the rough, aging bark.

His mouth was half open, his eyes flickering upward into his head, his entire body quivering. The colored lights were blindingly strong, the feelings that tore through his groin beyond fantastic. He did not know how long he had been standing there. Nor did he know why. But it didn't matter. He was no longer in control of his body.

Is this what insanity feels like? Actions you can't

control, memories that make no sense, waking up at seven in the morning in a basement you don't recognize with your hands covered in blood and a straight razor on the floor next to the body of an old stranger in a Hawaiian shirt . . .

Ned's muscles began to contort, his spine arching back. He clenched his teeth together as a dull moan escaped his throat. The colors grew and grew—and suddenly a calmness moved through him, straightening his spine, ending the convulsions. He lowered his head, his eyes narrowing. The dead old stranger in the Hawaiian shirt was instantly forgotten. Ned's body became a willing extension of the colors. *Hardware.* He would do anything the colors wanted him to do. *Software.*

The hardware-software analogy had come to him that morning, in the basement on Cross Street. He knew, in what was left of the logical portion of his brain, that it was crazy, that the laptop computer couldn't be the cause of what was going on in his life, that it had to be something else, a disease, a fever of the brain—but the analogy had stuck. The colored lights were the software, his body was the hardware—and he was helpless, as helpless as a computer or a mechanical toy or a microwave oven.

He dug his fingers into the bark, staring up at the pretty little house. White, split-level, common for this quiet, high-priced chunk of Bethesda, Maryland. Twenty feet in front of him was the front porch—small, well-lit, bristling with flowerpots and Japanese lanterns. To the left of the porch was the living room window, burning bright orange in the late-afternoon grayness. He could see shapes within the orange, two forms intertwined on a couch. A large, overweight man and a tall, long-haired woman, their backs to the window, their faces melded together like the joints of a skeleton. Somewhere in Ned's mind, he realized that he knew the man; blonde, forty-six, more than two hundred pounds. The man's name was Emile Benson. He worked at Telecon, and Ned hated him. But that didn't matter. At the moment, Ned's body felt no hate. Hardware had no concept of emotion. Hardware followed software's commands. Without question, without thought.

The passionate embrace ended, the shapes shifting within the orange light. Benson and the woman stood, holding hands, whispering, laughing, conspiring. Ned knew they had been meeting like this for nearly two months. Sending e-mail through the Telecon network every day, e-mail that spun behind Ned's eyes as he stared through the living room window. *Insanity is seeing e-mail behind your eyes.* Benson was a father of four, two weeks from his twentieth wedding anniversary. The woman with him on the couch was his former secretary, decidedly not his wife. Both creatures were irrelevant. *Insanity is thinking of other human beings as 'creatures.'* Ned's head began to ache.

There was the click of a lock turning, and the front porch was suddenly bathed in warm light. The Japanese lanterns and flowerpots glowed as Benson lumbered outside. Ned could see the smile on his face, the bright red splotches on his cheeks. He could imagine the endorphins coursing through the man's veins, the tiny packets of chemical ecstasy—his afterglow—filling him with confidence and strength.

Benson stuck his hands into the pockets of his

slacks and sauntered down the front steps, out onto the lawn. Ned felt his muscles tense, his thighs quivering as preparatory commands slid down his spinal chord. *Software commands hardware. Hardware responds to software.*

The moment came suddenly, a flash of fluid motion. Benson was ten feet away, moving forward, unaware, when Ned leapt toward him—moving with a speed he did not understand, a strength he could not explain. It was as if every muscle had suddenly learned to work concurrently, the shared grace of a professional athlete. He caught Benson around the throat and pulled him back into the shadows of the tree, stifling the big man's voice with a stiff forearm against his vocal chords.

Ned could smell the sex on him, sweat and perfume mingled together with the sickly sweet aroma of fear. The back of his mind cried out at what he was doing—what he knew he was about to do. But the colored lights, *my god the colors*. The creature is irrelevant. The creature is irrelevant. Ned pulled the much larger man tight against his chest, his own back against the tree, and moved his lips close to Benson's right ear.

"Hello, Dr. Benson."

Ned hardly recognized his own voice, did not know how he could sound so calm, or why he needed to say anything at all. Benson wriggled in his grip, but quickly realized the futility of struggling. Although he had almost forty pounds on his assailant, Ned's formerly pudgy body had become all wires and steel.

"I'm sorry to bother you," Ned continued. "This will only take a moment."

He let up slightly on Benson's throat, allowing

him to gasp for air. "Ned Dickerson? Is that you? Jesus, Ned—is this about the Chippendale picture? It was a joke, please, Jesus."

Ned didn't respond, quietly reaching into his own front jeans pocket. He withdrew a small black device, holding it in front of Benson's face. "Dr. Benson, if you could please state your name."

Benson's face was full of confusion, as he stared at the black device. It took him a few seconds to realize that it was a miniature tape recorder. "Wha—" he started, fighting the fear. "Emile Benson—Ned, please. What do you want from me?"

Ned flicked off the recorder and slid it back into his pocket. "Thank you, Dr. Benson. There's just one more thing I need."

He tightened his grip on Benson's throat, again cutting off the large man's voice. From out of his other front pocket he pulled a wad of billowy cotton and lifted it in front of Benson's mouth. Benson struggled, but Ned forced his blubbery jaw down and shoved the wad of cotton between his teeth. Benson gasped, dull moans leaking out from behind the gag.

Ned paused, as a shiver ran up his spine. For a brief moment, his body struggled against the colored lights, his mind fought to free itself from the haze of commands. But then the colored lights surged forward, doubling and tripling in strength. The orgasmic feeling was too strong.

Ned pulled a six-inch steel tool out of his back pocket. The tool looked like an oversized set of tweezers, with sharp, spoonlike scoops instead of tips. Benson's eyes widened as he stared at the thing. Even through the colors, Ned empathized with the man; in truth, the tool was much worse than it seemed. Ned had borrowed it from the local organ transplant ward.

Suddenly, he jammed the steel tweezers into Benson's right eye. *The creature is irrelevant.* Benson's entire body convulsed upward, but Ned held on, twisting the tweezers right, then left. *Software commands hardware.* There was a quiet pop as the spoon-like scoops touched at the back of Benson's eye socket—and then the tweezers came free, trailing a string of severed optic nerve. Ned gently brought the tweezers close to his own face, making sure the tool had done its job.

The jelly orb looked strangely alive in the steel metal scoops, shining and perfectly intact. Ned nodded, holding the tweezers up and away with one hand while getting a good grip on Benson's jaw with the other. Benson's knees had gone slack, a strange sound slithering out from behind the gag. *The creature is irrelevant.* With one swift twist, Ned snapped his neck and let him slide to the ground. Then he reached into his other back pocket and brought out a small aluminum cylinder.

He flipped open the cap of the cylinder with his thumb and gingerly placed Benson's right eyeball inside. Then he recapped the container and shoved it back in his pocket. The container would keep the organ in perfect condition for forty-eight hours—which was thirty-two more than Ned needed.

Ned wiped his bloody hands on his jeans. His eyes drifted to the slack body on the ground. He would drag the body back to the basement on Cross Street. Tomorrow morning he would wake up with more blood on his hands and no memory of what had happened. Then the colored lights would return, and it would start all over again.

He leaned over Benson's corpse. *The creature is irrelevant.* He wanted to tell him that it wasn't his fault. He wanted to explain about the colored lights, about the software and the hardware. But it was too late, Benson was dead and there was no way to explain. Or apologize. *Insanity is never having to say you're sorry.*

THIRTY

i think we're going to get charged for these."

Samantha helped wrap a monogrammed towel around Nick's injured thigh. There was already a pile of bloodied linen in a corner of the small hotel bathroom, and the sink was cluttered with darkened tissues and empty antibiotic containers.

Nick forced a laugh. Samantha could see that he was trying to mask the pain; the wound to his leg was worse than he had initially thought. Although the bullet hadn't gone deep, it had nicked a muscle—and now that the thrill of their escape had faded, the pain was beginning to kick in.

"Maybe we should get you to a hospital," Samantha said, as she helped Nick rise from the toilet seat and head out into the bedroom. Nick shook his head.

"I'll be okay. The antibiotics will keep away infection. And the bleeding's pretty much stopped."

They had picked up the antibiotics at a pharmacy on the way to the hotel. The Midland had been Samantha's choice: the huge, Victorian-style convention center, complete with stone turrets and bellhops in eighteenth-century style uniforms, was two miles behind Union Station, surrounded by a smattering of brand-name hotels. It was large enough to provide adequate cover, while still close to the center of the city—in case they had to make another quick escape. Once inside the hotel room, they had headed straight to the bathroom for some field medicine.

Samantha watched Nick settle onto the stiff king-sized bed. The room was staid and shaped like an L: off to the right was a small dressing room, with ornate brass wall mirrors and a pair of silver-lined sinks. The main part of the room was mostly taken up by the bed. The headboard was carved out of redwood, and stretched halfway up the colorfully papered wall. Across from the bed was a television stand and a twenty-inch Sony television, complete with Telecon Set-Top Box. Next to the television was an antique rocking chair, and beside that a small honor bar.

"I need to call Charlie," Nick said, and Samantha noticed a slight tremor in his voice. She realized that they were both still in shock; the situation had exploded so quickly, it had caught them by surprise. Two hours ago they had been in her apartment looking at the Van Eck results, and then Ted had called . . .

Ted. Samantha felt a dull throb in the back of her throat. She had dated him for almost a year. Slept with him nearly every night, laughed with him at movies, shared his secrets. She hadn't loved him,

but that didn't seem to matter, now. He was dead—
and she had a strong suspicion it was because of
her. Although the raid on the FBI center could have
been a coincidence, she doubted it. The killers had
waited until Ted was alone with the disk. Unless
they were already after him, and had chosen that
moment coincidentally, he had died because of her.

As she watched Nick crawl across the bed to the
phone, she reached into her jacket and pulled out
the three-quarter-inch disk. Her body trembled as
she turned it in front of her eyes. What could be so
valuable that they would kill for it? And who were
they?

Professionals, of that she was sure. Nick had surprised them with his animalistic heroics, and with
Ted's gun. Otherwise, they would have killed Nick
and Samantha in clean fashion. They had used Ted
as a trap, leading Nick and Samantha deep inside.
Then they had closed in. Like professionals.

She watched as Nick dialed the phone. CIA,
NSA, some other government branch? Doubtful; no
matter how valuable the disk was, she couldn't
imagine a U.S. organization sending troops into an
FBI center. A foreign agency? Still, it seemed too
brazen, too risky. The only other possibility was a
mercenary team: paid professional killers, sent to
retrieve what Telecon had lost.

Samantha clenched her teeth as she watched
Nick dial another phone number, hang up, then dial
another after that. Red anger filled her from inside.
She was going to get the bastards who had killed
Ted. Her fingers tightened against the disk—the
first thing was to find out what was so valuable.

Nick slammed the phone down, and turned
toward Samantha. "He's nowhere. I can't reach him

on his cell phone or his home, and they haven't heard from him at work. I even tried the Trauma Center in Providence, but he never arrived."

"Nick, I'm sure he's okay."

"We don't know what sort of organization we're up against. They killed Ted. They could have killed Hoffman too. And I sent Charlie after Hoffman's records."

The guilt was obvious in his voice—the same guilt Samantha had felt when she first saw Ted. Then she had a sudden thought: What about Sonya Hoffman? They had bribed her to get Hoffman's notebook from her safety deposit box. If they were under surveillance . . . Christ.

Samantha headed toward the phone. She had discarded her cellular phone after they had escaped Ted's lab; she didn't know if the thing was somehow tapped, but she didn't want to take a chance.

She pulled the sheet of computer paper with Sonya Hoffman-Lassiter's address and phone number out of her pocket, and dialed. Her fears mounted as the seconds passed, ring after ring; of course, Sonya could still be on her way back from the bank.

"Who is it?" The voice was rough and male, and obviously upset. The Neanderthal, Tom Lassiter.

"Is your wife in, Mr. Lassiter?"

There was a long pause, then Lassiter's voice came back. Samantha noticed with a start that he was crying. "She's dead. Just got back from the hospital. She's dead."

Samantha's stomach dropped. She had been right—Ted's death was her fault. And so was Sonya Lassiter's. "She's dead?" she whispered. "How did it happen?"

Lassiter choked back a sob. "The bees. They got

her. I woke up from a nap and found her on the porch. The screen door was open. She had been stung twice on the chest. Stopped breathing."

Samantha closed her eyes. She felt Nick's hand touch her shoulder. He understood from the expression on her face.

"I just don't understand," Lassiter continued, "she was always so careful. And she carried the epipen in her pocket. But when I looked for it, it was gone."

"Mr. Lassiter," Samantha said, the muscles in her jaw tightening. "Did Sonya make a trip to her bank this afternoon? This is extremely important."

Lassiter seemed confused. "I don't know. I was asleep. She's dead. Christ, I can't believe she's dead—"

"Mr. Lassiter, please, many lives depend on this. Did she bring anything back with her from the bank?"

"It doesn't matter. Nothing matters, she's gone."

Samantha clenched her fingers.

"It *does* matter. She went to retrieve something from her safety deposit box." Samantha had a sudden thought. "Something that I was going to pay her a thousand dollars for."

There was another pause. "A thousand dollars?"

"I've got the money right here. I know it won't help your grief, but—"

"Hold on a second." She heard the phone click against a counter, and Lassiter's hurried footsteps disappearing out of the room. She was momentarily sickened by the baseness of human nature, but she had read Lassiter correctly.

"They got her too," Nick spoke from the bed. "Am I right?"

Samantha nodded. She saw the stricken look on Nick's face. He was worried about Charlie. Probably with good reason.

Finally, Lassiter returned. "A notebook. Leather bound. Probably fifty pages of notes. You say a thousand dollars?"

Samantha's head spun. It had been a long shot. How had Sonya's killers missed the notebook? "Where did you find it?"

"Me and Sonya had a sort of hiding place. In her car. A little rip in the vinyl under the driver's seat. It's where we hid our, ah, you know, pot."

It was probably more than marijuana, but Samantha couldn't have cared less. "I need that notebook. I'm sorry to be bothering you during this bad time—"

"You've got the money?"

"Right in my hand." She paused, thinking. They had to meet somewhere crowded, somewhere she could blend in. And she did not want to be seen with him in case he was being watched. She did not trust his ability to evade professional surveillance. "Tom, how quickly can you get to Union Station?"

"Thirty, forty minutes."

"We'll make it forty-five. You know where the automatic lockers are? By the tracks?"

"There are a lot of lockers—"

"The lockers are arranged by number and letter. I will leave the thousand dollars in locker 31C, by track thirty. If that locker is being used, I'll use the next locker to the right, and so on. I'll leave the locker unlocked, and I'll be nearby, watching. You substitute the notebook for the money and walk away."

Tom cleared his throat. "Is this illegal?"

This from the man who had a specific place in his car to stash his pot. "No, but there is a chance that you will be followed. You'll have to be extremely careful. Don't stop to talk to anyone. Forty-five minutes. The money will be there."

She hung up the phone and turned toward Nick. "He's got Hoffman's notebook. I'm going to Union Station to pick it up. First I've got to pick up a thousand dollars. The banks are open for only another twenty minutes, so I have to hurry."

Nick placed his feet on the carpet and started to rise off the bed. Samantha put her hands on his shoulders and pushed him back down. "You've got to rest your leg. I'll retrieve the notebook—and I'll also get hold of a computer so we can see what's on that disk."

"I'm not going to let you go alone." His voice was firm, but she could see that he was in pain. His body needed time to recoup.

"Yes, you are. You're no good to me like this. And you've got to continue trying to reach Charlie. At least to warn him."

The mention of Nick's friend made his face go slack. She was right, he had to keep searching for Charlie. He sighed, then reached into his belt and pulled out Ted's Beretta.

"At least take this."

Samantha shook her head. She knew how to use a gun, but the first thing she had learned in her training was when not to carry one. She was the hunted, not the hunter. A gun only made you over-confident—and stupid, like Nick's moves in the FBI center. If she got into a gunfight at Union Station, she would lose. And probably kill innocent civilians in the process.

"You hold on to it. And take the disk." She pulled the disk out of her jacket and handed it to him. "Don't let anyone inside. I'll be back in an hour."

"Be careful." He squeezed her hands. This time, Samantha had to play the cowboy.

East Federal Savings was a mile from Union Station, located on the corner of a crowded intersection, right in front of a tour bus stop. Three new buses sat parked in a row by the curb. Sleek and green, with oversized tires and curved glass windows. A large crowd of Japanese businessmen in blue suits huddled around the lead bus, while their guide read instructions in Japanese from a yellow pamphlet. Nobody seemed to notice the tall white woman standing in the outskirts of the crowd, a long gray overcoat draped over her body, her hair pulled back and shoved into the oversized soft velvet of an Italian-style beret. There were a few other non-Japanese in the crowd, including the tour guide and at least three drivers. Samantha was no more noticeable than the others; perhaps it was the scarf pulled high over her chin, or the thick plastic glasses above her nose.

Samantha's nerves fired off as she clenched the packet of hundred dollar bills in her right pocket. She kept her eyes pinned to the back of the Japanese businessman in front of her, fighting the urge to turn around.

She had first noticed the two men on her way into the bank; they had been standing by the foreign currency desk, pretending to breeze through investment brochures. Both tall, one with slicked back silvery hair and a green sports jacket, the other blond, wearing khakis, a checkered shirt, and a white plaster cast covering most of his right arm. They had been taking turns watching the revolving door, the angles of their backs predictable and deliberate.

It was mostly dumb luck that they had not spotted Samantha before she saw them; the disguise she had picked up along the way to the bank was weak, certainly not enough to bear close scrutiny. But she had hunched her shoulders and bent her knees at the last second, taking just the right number of inches off of her height. The scarf, hat, and glasses had been enough to get her out of the revolving door and into the withdrawal line, where she had quickly positioned herself between two elderly men chatting about basketball scores.

Then the fear had set in. It was a classic surveillance operation: teams positioned at all the local utility points—banks, airports, train stations, sometimes even supermarkets and drug stores. If she was right, and the two men were looking for her, they were part of something well organized and extensive.

She had reached the front of the line and had made her withdrawal, nervously glancing over her shoulder as the teller counted out the hundred-dollar bills. The two men hadn't moved from their post, and Samantha's knees had begun to shake; there was no way she could risk going through the revolving door again, and she didn't see another way out.

At that moment, the Japanese tour group had suddenly swarmed through the revolving door, two at a time, jabbering in loud voices. The two operatives had completely disappeared in the crowd of blue business suits, and Samantha had rushed toward the door.

To her surprise, she had suddenly found herself in the same sea of business suits; the foreign currency desk had closed fifteen minutes earlier, and the Japanese tourists had rebounded like steel balls in a Pachinko machine. She had hastily tried to shove her way forward through the mob, but had momentarily lost her footing. When she finally made it into the revolving door, she had completely lost sight of the two watching men.

Once outside, she had decided her best move was to lose herself in the crowd. As the crowd reached the parked buses, she worked her way to the direct center and nearly ran into the harried tour guide, who had been in mid-argument with one of the buses' drivers. They were loudly discussing the best way to get to the bus lot behind Union Station.

A coincidence too good to pass up. Samantha had then drifted to the back of the crowd, keeping her eyes peeled for the two men. She had caught a glimpse of them as they came out of the revolving door, harried looks on their faces. The man with the cast was scanning the crowd, and she wondered if they had seen her exiting the bank.

Not good.

She hunched forward, listening to the tour guide's Japanese. There was no way she could make a run for it. The two men were too close.

The tour guide said something and smiled, and the crowd started to file onto the first bus. The guide stood at the door, checking each passenger off of a list attached to a clipboard. He looked like a college kid, with short red hair and freckles. Samantha moved forward with the crowd, keeping her eyes pinned to the ground.

She was ten people from the front of the line

when one of the drivers climbed aboard and signaled that the bus was full. The crowd shifted,
heading toward the second bus. Samantha saw her
chance and slid quickly to the front, a step ahead of
the tour guide. She quickly scampered up the steps
of the second bus and slid inside. Then she rushed
down the aisle to the last set of seats. For a brief second, she thought she had made it unnoticed.

"Excuse me," a nasal voice came at her down the
aisle. "Are you on the list?"

The tour guide was strolling down the aisle,
followed by a line of Japanese businessmen. His
clipboard was out in front of him. Samantha swallowed, trying to think up a lie. Then she noticed the
businessman directly behind the guide—male,
maybe thirty, a smile on his face as his eyes slid up
and down her legs. She caught his attention with a
wave, smiling back at him.

"Honey," she cooed, sticking out her chest. "I
saved a seat for us."

The tour guide looked from her to the man, then
at the clipboard. Finally he shrugged and pushed
his way back down the aisle. The Japanese businessman stared at her, stunned. She grabbed his hand
and pulled him into the seat next to her.

"Thanks for not blowing the whistle on me," she
whispered, squeezing his hand. "I really need the
lift. I promise I'll leave you alone as soon as we're at
Union Station."

The man continued staring at her in shock.
"*Shitzurey shimas?*"

"You don't speak any English at all, do you?"

"*Wakarimasen.*"

"Even better. Look, I'll just sit here, you sit there,
everything will be fine."

Suddenly Samantha realized that there were a half-dozen pairs of eyes staring at her from the surrounding seats. She smiled sheepishly, wondering what the hell she was going to do now. Then one of the businessmen started to laugh, and suddenly they were all laughing, the closest few reaching forward to slap her seatmate on the shoulder. At first he looked as bewildered as she by the attention, but then he warmed to it, taking her hand in his and pumping it over his shoulder, like she was some sort of prize. She shrugged, playing the part, leaning into him, laughing with the others. *Whatever worked.*

The bus started up and slowly pulled away from the curb. The Japanese man next to her attempted twice more to make conversation, then seemed content just to hold her hand. Samantha tried to get a last look for the man with the cast or his partner, but the window had fogged up from all the laughing and talking.

The ten-minute ride was one of the most confusing, loud, nerve-racking trips Samantha had ever taken. Three times the Japanese man put his hand on her thigh, and the third time she had bent his forefinger back so far that tears had sprung into his eyes. But then he had just laughed, while his friends slapped him on the back. She couldn't begin to understand what was going on, but she didn't care. She was on her way to Union Station.

The bus pulled to a stop in a gated back lot, and the businessmen began to file down the aisle. Samantha followed a step behind her new friend, who still clutched her hand. They stepped onto pavement and she yanked her hand free. He looked at her with a crestfallen expression, and she sighed,

leaning forward. She gave him a quick kiss and then
shoved her way through the crowd. There was a
burst of applause and shoulder slapping as she
pushed free, and she couldn't help but laugh.

She entered Union Station through an arched
doorway. She found herself in the east hall, a vast
room with plaster walls and thick columns painted
to look like marble. Wheeled vendor carts filled
nearly every inch of the room, pushing everything
from political paraphernalia to grandfather clocks
made to look like the Washington Monument. There
were a few dozen people milling about the room,
and Samantha moved quickly from cart to cart, constantly watching for any sign of surveillance. She
paused at one of the carts, buying a package of gum
shaped like the president's head. She put a stick in
her mouth and chewed, calming her nerves.
Hopefully, her entrance through the tour bus lot
would give her some needed breathing room.

She avoided the main waiting room, with its
ninety-six foot gold-leaf ceiling and marble floors,
instead heading directly into the track waiting area;
the rectangular alcove was thirty-feet wide and five
times as long, running the entire length of the enormous building. To Samantha's left, the alcove was
lined with shops and fast-food restaurants. The
other side had double doors every twenty feet,
beneath gilded track numbers. Between the double
doors were row upon row of standing steel lockers.

The alcove was twice as crowded as the east hall;
Samantha guessed that most of the people she
passed were waiting for the six o'clock to New York
City. She stayed close to the brightly lit shops, where
most of the crowd huddled at high plastic patio
tables. She was counting the tracks as she went, her

eyes running over the banks of steel lockers. She knew there was a better than good chance that locker 31C would be empty; hardly anyone used the automated lockers, especially this late in the afternoon. They were more for day tourists, who took the train in for a few hours of monument gawking.

Track thirty was directly across from an imitation French bakery. Samantha found an empty table under a corner of a zebra-patterned awning, and sat down facing the nearby set of lockers. She was at least ten minutes early, enough time to make sure she was unobserved before she made the drop.

She watched the slow stream of human traffic, her eyes carefully picking through the clothes and mannerisms, searching for anything that screamed "professional." Of course, the best operatives were impossible to spot. But those sorts of operatives were not wasted on train stations and local banks.

Satisfied that the station seemed safe, she rose from the table and walked toward the set of lockers. She kept her gait steady, unremarkable, and did not turn her head to either side. She had to appear nonchalant—any sudden move could give her away.

She reached the lockers and searched for 31C. She had picked that specific locker because she had used it once before. During a USAMRIID training exercise, she had hidden a vial of fake Ebola-tainted blood inside the locker; a team of five scientists had three days to find the vial before the imaginary terrorists used it to wipe out half the city. The scientists failed, and USAMRIID received twenty million dollars in extra funding the next day.

As she had predicted, the locker was not in use. She pulled open the door, glancing into the shallow cubicle. It smelled vaguely of dirty laundry. She reached into her pocket, pulled out the batch of hundred-dollar bills, and shoved it deep into the back corner. Then she opened her mouth and spit her chewing gum into her left hand. She carefully stuck the gum under the latch of the door, so that it would not automatically lock, and shut the locker.

She quickly paced back to her seat under the zebra-patterned awning. Her heart was racing, but her face remained smooth. She dropped back into her seat and took deep breaths, steadying her nerves.

The minutes dripped by. Twice men tried to join her at the little table, and twice she politely refused— even with the glasses and the foolish beret, they were drawn to her. These were the men she would never want, the ones who approached her because of her looks, because she was thin and tall and had breasts.

There. Ambling toward the lockers, hands sheepishly in his pockets, a black backpack over his left shoulder. Lassiter was impossible to miss. He had put a flannel shirt over his stained T-shirt, but with his gut, his beard, and his conspicuous gait, there was no way he could go unnoticed. He headed straight for locker 31C, and Samantha could almost see the saliva dripping down the corners of his lips. *The bastard.* His wife had just died and there were probably trained killers watching him, and all he cared about was the thousand dollars.

Lassiter reached the locker and yanked open the door without pause. As he reached inside with his thick fingers, Samantha searched the area around him—still no sign of surveillance. But they had to be nearby. Lassiter paid no attention to his surroundings as he yanked the wad of hundred-dollar bills out of the locker, a grin erupting across his face.

He took a step back from the locker, unstrapping his backpack. Samantha's body shivered with anticipation as he pulled a leather-bound notebook out from inside and shoved it into 31C. Then he reshut the door, spun on his heels, and headed back toward the main hall of the station.

Samantha stared at the locker, counting the seconds in her head. She had to give him time to get outside, far away from her. If he was being watched, the surveillance team would have to make a decision: continue following him or try and get at whatever it was he had left in the locker. But they could not know that the locker was still unlocked, and without the proper code, it would be impossible to break inside. Drug lords and homicide suspects had been using these lockers for that very reason for many years.

All right, it has to be now. Samantha pushed back her chair and started forward. She moved quickly, her eyes scanning the alcove, her stomach churning. She was taking a huge chance, but the area looked clear. Step by step, she moved closer and closer.

She reached the locker and yanked open the door. She grabbed the leather-bound notebook, the thrill of victory rising through her shoulders. It felt heavy, the thick leather adding at least two pounds to the weight of the pages inside. She pulled up the bottom of her sweatshirt and shoved the notebook under her waistband, then tucked the sweatshirt into her pants. A smile broke across her face as she felt the coolness of the leather against her stomach. She whirled around—

And nearly slammed into the man with the plaster cast. Her eyes went wide and her throat closed. The man grinned, and suddenly there was a click and his cast clattered to the ground. There was a nine-inch serrated black-steel commando knife Velcroed to his checkered sleeve. In one motion he ripped the knife free and thrust it toward Samantha's stomach.

She had no time to react. The blade hit her an inch under her belly button and she gasped, slamming back into the lockers. The knife was sticking out of her sweatshirt and she dropped to her knees, her face white, and somebody screamed, pointing, and suddenly people were running toward her. The man with the cast looked up, thought about going for the knife for another stab, then realized there wasn't time. He turned toward the east hall and ran, ducking between the growing crowd of shocked tourists.

Christ. Samantha's head dropped and she stared down at the knife sticking out of her stomach. The funny thing was, she didn't feel any pain. She was having trouble catching her breath, and she wanted to vomit, but no pain.

She reached down with both hands and grabbed the hilt of the knife. Slowly, she wrenched it forward. It popped free. No blood. Not a single drop.

The knife clattered to the floor and she pulled up the front of her sweatshirt. There was a deep gash in the thick leather of the notebook. But the knife had not punctured the other side of the cover. Samantha felt her entire body start to shake. Hands touched her shoulder, and someone helped her to her feet.

"Are you okay?" a woman's voice asked. "Do you need a doctor?"

Samantha fought to regain her composure. There was no time for this. "Fine, thank you. We were rehearsing for a play. It was a fake knife."

The woman looked down at the serrated blade. "Doesn't look fake."

"That's the beauty of it."

Samantha pulled away, clutching the notebook against her stomach. Out of the corner of her eye, she saw a door marked "Ladies." She pushed through the crowd of bystanders, a phony smile painted across her face.

She barely made it to a stall before the first wave of vomit crashed against her teeth.

THIRTY-ONE

Seconds after Nick opened the hotel room door, Samantha tossed the notebook and laptop computer she had picked up in the hotel business center onto the bed, and fell into his arms, her hands tight against his back. She pressed her face against his chest, her eyes tightly closed, the tracks of tears already drying on her cheeks. She knew how close she had come to death. The worst part of it was the thought of being separated from him, the way she had been separated from Andrew; she could not go through that again. The minute that knife had torn through her sweatshirt she had realized she loved Nick Barnes. She didn't know how it had happened, but it was the truth.

"Are you okay?" Nick asked, his left hand touching her hair.

She nodded, pulling away. "I'm fine. There was

a bit of trouble at the train station, but I'm okay."

"What sort of trouble?"

Samantha didn't want to put it into words. She didn't want to remember it so clearly, not yet. "I'll tell you when this is all over. But I got the notebook, and I checked out a laptop from the business center downstairs."

She crossed to the bed and lifted the laptop. It was much heavier than hers, almost twice as thick. She found the cord and plugged it in next to the television. Then she placed it on the antique rocking chair and opened the lid. She watched as the Telecon operating system filled the screen with color. The machine was not the latest model, but it would be good enough. It had a disk drive and enough RAM.

"Did you have any luck with Charlie?" she asked, as she crossed back to the bed.

"Nothing doing. I still can't find him anywhere. I even called the other members of his jazz band. He missed a rehearsal this afternoon. They have a gig tonight, and they're beginning to worry."

"I'm sure he's okay." She paused. "Have you checked—"

"The trauma centers and morgues in every hospital between Boston and Providence. Nothing."

"That's promising. We just have to believe he's okay."

Nick nodded, watching as she lifted the notebook. "So what have we got?"

She had fought the urge to look inside the leather-bound cover on the way back to the hotel. She had wanted to be with Nick when she finally opened the notebook. She took a deep breath, and turned to the first page.

The chapters were handwritten in script, legible but hurried, with few curls and too many exclamation points. From the very first sentence, Samantha knew they had found the reason behind Ted and Sonya's deaths—and probably Eric Hoffman's as well.

"'I've found Teal's hypothetical backdoor,'" she read, feeling the extreme tension in the scripted words. "'He says it must remain a secret, and I understand why. But I don't believe him when he says he will never implement my theory. I believe he wants the backdoor. For himself.'"

Samantha looked up. Nick had dropped back down onto the bed. Here it was, a secret that would cost Teal his billions, a secret that would put a halt to his information highway and to Telecon's monopoly power over the industry. There was a backdoor to the Evolving Code, the accepted standard method of securing all the information that passed through the fiber optic network.

Samantha turned pages as Eric Hoffman detailed the Backdoor Hypothesis; the answer lay in the way the Evolving Code worked. The word "evolving" had not been chosen simply because it was synonymous with "changing": the theory behind the Evolving Code parroted the basic theory behind Darwinian evolution. Like an evolving genetic machine, the code's matrix reacted to a series of sensations, all the while designing a mathematical equation that spit out the code itself—a series of numbers, as Teal had explained in his office. To decode the encrypted transmission, the receiving software had to re-create the exact same series of sensations, designing the exact same mathematical equation. Two identical "evolutions," enacted almost instantaneously within the sending and receiving Set-Top Boxes.

"'To break the code,'" Samantha read, "'look to the source.' There it is again, Nick. The same sentence from the note card. But now he explains it. The 'source' of the code is evolution. The way to break the code is to use evolution to design a code breaker."

Nick looked at the notebook over her shoulder. "I'm not sure I understand what that means."

Samantha turned to the next page, skimming the small paragraphs. It was complicated, but the theory seemed sound. She knew she would never understand more than the basics. But the basics were enough. "In a way, you let the code-breaking software design itself. Look at it this way: the Evolving Code is basically a mathematical equation that is designed by letting a program roam free in a virtual world of sensations. As the program reacts to those sensations—picture primitive man learning to wear clothes in response to cold, finding shelter in response to rain—the mathematical equation changes, becomes more complicated, and specific to that virtual world."

"And this happens instantaneously?"

"Just about. Modern computers work in time frames smaller than nanoseconds. The entire history of Earth could be mimicked in a minute, or even less."

Nick rubbed the sudden wrinkles over his eyes. "Okay, so now how does Hoffman say you break the code?"

"By setting another program loose in the same virtual world. A program whose only goal is to grow with the original program, react to the same evolutionary sensations, essentially spying on the original program. And then somehow communicate the final mathematical equation back across the fiber optic lines."

"A symbiotic program," Nick murmured. "Like some sort of virus you implant in the original Evolving Code software. With its own mission, its own means of carrying out that mission. Christ, it almost sounds like we're talking about a sentient being."

The way Nick said the words ticked at Samantha's brain. She remembered Ted's final words: *I think it's alive.* She focused back on the notebook and began turning pages. More on the Backdoor Hypothesis. Engineering notes. Software specs. She reached the last chapter, a mere two pages of Hoffman's scrawl. She read the first two sentences, and then paused. She reread the sentences, her ears starting to ring.

> I have made a frightening discovery. Melora
> has taken my research in a direction I do not
> understand. I think she is trying to create
> some sort of weapon. I don't know why.

"Nick—"

"I know, I just read the same thing. Turn the page."

She flipped to the last page of the notebook. She read the words aloud: "'Melora calls it the Reaper. It is named after one of the first computer viruses. Essentially, she is using the same evolutionary model to create an unbeatable data virus. She has released a program with only two goals—reproduction and survival—into the virtual evolutionary environment. Through natural selection, it becomes stronger; weak versions of the virus are killed off, and only the better versions survive. In a way the Reaper is an intelligent program. It learns. It calculates. At some point, it is no longer just reacting—it becomes proactive. I am worried that theoretically, the final version of the Reaper will be invincible.'"

Nick touched Samantha's hand. She understood. He, too, had recognized the similarities between the Reaper and a biological virus. *Two goals: reproduction and survival.* But in the time frame of a computer processor, a virus could evolve through a virtual billion years in the space of a minute. Samantha's throat went dry, as she continued reading aloud.

"'Tomorrow, I'm going to tell Teal about Melora's project. I think the Reaper is too dangerous for further experimentation. I have loaded Melora's preliminary work onto a disk, and will deliver it to Teal along with my notes. I have made a few copies of the disk, in case Melora discovers my intentions. In truth, I am scared of her. I do not know why she has created this Reaper. I have watched her for days, but am unable to learn much about her beyond the fact that she makes a daily visit to her veteran father in a convalescent home in upstate Virginia. I also believe she has access to a private computer lab—she did not develop the Reaper in our lab, I am sure of that. Perhaps Teal will have more answers.'"

Hoffman's scrawled notes ended. The notebook felt extremely heavy in Samantha's hands, and she let it drop onto the bed. *Christ.* Her mind was fighting to digest everything she had just read.

"Teal's got a backdoor," Nick finally said. "What is he planning to do with it? He can unlock any transmission that goes through his network. Every secret in the world revealed—he could make an infinite amount of money."

"He already has enough money."

"Then power—"

"What sort of power? It's possible that he intends to use the backdoor to make Telecon even bigger, but I think it has to be more than that. He must have another agenda."

"Would he kill to keep his backdoor secret?"

Samantha shrugged, thinking of Ted and the man with the cast. "Possibly. But I'm not sure Teal is the one we're after."

"Melora's Reaper," Nick commented.

"Teal might have killed Hoffman because he was concerned about the backdoor, or Melora might have killed him because he was going to tell Teal about the Reaper. Teal could be trying to kill us because he's afraid we've discovered his secret. Or Melora could be after us because we have Hoffman's disk—with the Reaper."

At the mention of the disk, Samantha's heart fluttered. It was time to see what Ted had seen. "Get the disk, Nick."

Nick walked across the room and pulled the disk out from under the mattress. A decidedly male hiding place. Samantha pulled the rocking chair over so they could sit on the edge of the bed and still see the screen. Then she took the disk from Nick, and shoved it into the drive.

The screen immediately went black. Samantha looked at Nick. "Did you notice how fast that happened? And the disk drive didn't even seem to run."

"Nanoseconds," Nick commented. "Isn't that what you said?"

Samantha nodded. She wondered what to do next. She was about to ask Nick what he thought when she saw his left hand snaking toward the space bar.

"Hold on—"

She was too late. His fingers touched the plastic key and suddenly there was a sound like a leather belt pulled tight. Nick's body was hurled backward across the room, and he crashed into the night table, sending a lamp shattering against the wall. Samantha leapt to her feet, covering her mouth with her hand. She ran around the bed and looked at Nick, who was sprawled against what was left of the night table.

His hair was standing straight up and his eyes were wide. His left hand was in the air in front of his face, the fingers curled inward.

"Nick, are you okay?"

It took him a moment to respond. His voice was scratchy. "Jesus Christ, what happened?"

He slowly turned his hand over, and opened his palm. The tips of his fingers were covered with burn blisters. Samantha bent to her knees and took his wrist. His skin tingled.

"An electric shock. My god, you could have been killed."

"Through the keyboard?" Nick gasped. He was still staring at his fingers. "Ted had the same burns. But he was wearing gloves."

"Because he had come at the computer the same way you did—at first. Then he got careful."

She helped Nick up from the floor. He tried to pat down his hair, and she could see his hands were shaking. But he would be okay; the jolt had been quick, like placing a finger in a socket. Despite the warnings of mothers and after-school specials, that usually didn't kill you.

Nick pointed at the laptop computer with his burned fingers. "How did it do that?"

"It pulled the voltage out of the wall socket," Samantha guessed. "And focused it through the wiring of the keyboard. Your skin is conductive, and the jolt passed right through the plastic keys."

"No, I mean *how did it do that*?"

Samantha understood what he meant. She thought for a full second. "The disk was infected by the Reaper. The Reaper loaded itself into the computer. It made the immediate decision that you were a threat to its two goals—survival and reproduction. It dealt with you in summary fashion."

Nick stared at her. Suddenly, he leapt forward. He was about to use his hands to shut the laptop, then remembered the jolt that had just thrown him across the room. Instead, he lifted his rubber-soled shoe and kicked the computer off of the rocking chair. It slammed shut when it hit the floor. Not satisfied, Nick kicked the plug out of the wall. Then he brought his foot down on top of the computer, crushing the plastic. Samantha stared at him in shock.

"Nick, what the hell are you doing?"

He slowly repeated what she had just told him. "It decided that I was a threat—and dealt with me." He turned to face her. "It recognized me as a threat to its existence. Then it fired a jolt of electricity into my body, trying to eliminate that threat. The electricity was a weapon it used to try and get rid of me."

Samantha realized where he was heading. "You think it has other weapons in its arsenal?"

"Think about it. The Reaper is a computer virus

that has realized that its true enemy is outside the computer—in computerese, its user. Like a biological virus, it will do anything it can to secure its two goals: survival and reproduction. It will use everything it has at its disposal. And it will learn from its mistakes. If electricity doesn't stop me, it will find another way."

Samantha had a sudden realization. "CaV."

"I think the Reaper would have to be connected to the fiber optic network to find a source for the wavelength that causes CaV, but yes, CaV. This Reaper is like any biological weapon, like AIDS, or Ebola, except it has recognized its enemy. It knows that we're trying to stop it. It will do anything in its power to stop us."

Samantha sat down on the bed. Her body felt weak. "But it didn't kill Ted, and if it is the thing that sent CaV through the beta test, why didn't it kill more people?"

Nick sat down next to her. "Remember what Hoffman wrote. *It no longer just reacts.* It's a sentient program. It calculates—it thinks. It doesn't just want to kill a few thousand people. It wants what every virus wants: immortality—to survive and reproduce forever."

Samantha knew that he was right. They could not prove it, but she was certain they had just found the source of CaV. "So you think Melora loaded the Reaper into the beta test?"

Nick shrugged. "Perhaps in a controlled fashion, which explains the breaks in the Van Eck readings. The Reaper wouldn't want to infect the entire beta test—that would only increase its risk of being discovered. It wanted to go slow, careful."

"*It wanted?* You make it sound like Melora is a

tool of the Reaper, not the other way around."

"That's not what I mean, of course. It's just that I doubt she can fully control the Reaper. It's like the Pentagon trying to manufacture and control a biological weapon. You know, better than I, how impossible that is."

Samantha nodded. That was what USAMRIID was about. Trying to control the uncontrollable. In a sense, that was what her entire life was about. Nick rose from the bed and walked back to the shattered laptop computer, poking it with his shoe.

"It's not Teal we're after; it's Melora Parkridge. She developed this Reaper—a computer virus that has recognized who its true enemy is. A computer virus that just might have learned how to beat that enemy."

Samantha watched as Nick raised his burned fingers, waving them in the air. They must have hurt, but he didn't look like he was in pain—he was in awe.

"So how do we stop her?" Samantha asked, more to herself than to Nick. "Do we go back to Telecon?"

"I don't think that will work. Hoffman wrote that she had her own lab, so she may not even be there. And there's no way Teal's going to let us inside. He's got his own agenda to hide. Anything short of a full-scale assault on the complex will be pretty much useless."

Samantha remembered the man with the cast, the knife digging through her sweatshirt. "The minute I try to arrange another operation, this hotel will be crawling with trained killers. Whether they work for Teal or Melora, the people searching for us are organized, well funded, and determined. We need to find another way to get to Melora."

Nick pointed at the notebook on the bed. "Hoffman gave us a starting point. Her veteran father. It shouldn't be hard to locate him. There can't be too many convalescent homes in upstate Virginia. And veterans have detailed medical records, the kind of records that are easy to look up."

Samantha nodded. There was no question in her mind: Melora Parkridge was behind CaV. For whatever reason, she had created a horrible weapon. That weapon had already caused nineteen deaths. If she meant to release it into Teal's fiber optic network—it was a terrifying thought. There would be no stopping the Reaper after the Big Turn On. It would have access to every television screen and computer in the country. Samantha glanced at her watch. It was already close to ten.

"We have twelve hours," she stated simply.

THIRTY-TWO

ned Dickerson sat in the cold cement basement of 316 Cross Street and cried. He was
wearing his blue Telecon jumpsuit and a
pair of bright green sneakers that Mary
Dober had given him for his thirty-ninth birthday.
He was sitting with his legs straight out in front of
him, his shoes pointing toward the wooden rafters
twenty feet above. He wrung his hands as the tears
ran down his cheeks. Big round salty innocent tears,
the kind that come out of babies and mental
patients.

The laptop computer was on his lap, but still
closed, still off, the cord trailing to a spot two inches
from the wall socket. The cord had come unplugged
and the battery had run out, and then the colored
lights had stopped and Ned had reached to plug it
back in—and something had happened. A tiny

piece of Ned Dickerson had surfaced through the colored lights.

He had seen himself and his surroundings, and had started to cry.

My God, what have I done? How many wife murderers and serial killers and child molesters and even petty thieves had sat on a basement floor and asked themselves the same question? But the thought did not comfort Ned Dickerson. Because he knew, for a fact, he could never be normal again.

He raised his head, the tears still streaming down his face. Directly ahead of him was a large-screen television set, attached to a souped-up IBM personal computer by a series of fiber optic cables. He had made the adjustments to the personal computer himself—although he could not remember what, exactly, he had done.

But behind him were the results. Ned turned his head, slowly digesting the carnage. First, there were the small caged animals: two rabbits, a guinea pig, and a Dalmatian pup he had taken home from the city pound. Then the larger animals: a chimpanzee he had stolen from a research facility in Baltimore, and a full-grown Rottweiler he had bought at a downtown security store. Then the even larger animals: the old man in the Hawaiian shirt from next door and Emile Benson.

Except for Benson and the old man, all the bodies were the same. Ivory skin, contorted spines, bulging eyes. The caged animals had already begun to rot, the skin peeling from their bodies in stiff white sheets. Ned turned away from the corpses, his body jerking in tune to his sobs. He stared down at the laptop, swearing that he would never plug it in, that he would never look at the colored lights again. But even as he thought the words, he knew that he was lying—he could feel the raw energy building in his thighs.

The colored lights were not yet finished with him. Despite himself, his eyes flicked upward toward the wide-screen television. Leaning against the set was a long plastic case, the kind one might use to carry a fishing pole or maybe a trombone. Inside the case was a semi-automatic Armalite AR–19 hunting rifle. He had bought the gun two days ago at a sporting goods store. He did not know what the colored lights intended him to do with it, but he was certain that he would soon find out.

His eyes glazed over as he watched his hands moving toward the laptop's cord.

THIRTY-THREE

this is close to what I pictured," Nick commented as he accompanied Samantha up the manicured front lawn, the stiff grass crunching under his boots. The Split River Home for Convalescents was a hodgepodge of architectural styles, a three-story Colonial with bars on the windows, Gothic pillars backlit by imitation oil lamps, and a pair of folded-up steel wheelchairs sitting by a swinging bench in a corner of a small wooden front porch.

"Kind of creepy."

"A big old house filled with people waiting to die. Hard to think of it as a happy place."

Finding Allen Parkridge had been easier than Nick had predicted. A single phone call to a past acquaintance in the surgical department of a V.A. trauma center had gotten him a list of convalescent homes in the northern Virginia area with occupants receiving veteran medical aid. Then it had just been a matter of calling the thirty-six homes and asking to speak with Mr. Parkridge. The woman who had answered at Split River had curtly explained that no personal calls were allowed after ten P.M., that her shift was ending and she wasn't about to get into an argument about house rules—and that besides, Allen was already asleep. Still, after a short amount of needling, she had given Nick the mailing address so he could send his "uncle" a Fed-Ex care package in the morning. Of course, there was a chance that there was more than one veteran named Parkridge in a convalescent home in that part of Virginia, but Nick liked his odds.

Finding a vehicle to get them to Split River had been decidedly more difficult. According to an atlas in the hotel lobby, Split River was more than forty minutes outside the city; public transportation was ruled out by the distance, USAMRIID aid was too dangerous to arrange, and a taxi would leave them stranded or reliant on an innocent driver if the visit with Parkridge led them to Melora—or back to Telecon. A rental car was out of the question; if operatives were watching the local banks, they were probably also watching the rental car agencies.

That left Samantha's network of friends and associates, and Nick's hospital connections. They had finally decided to try Nick's connections, because it was less likely the network of operatives would anticipate his actions. A few more phone calls, and the use of Charlie's name—as much as it pained Nick given his friend's still uncertain where-abouts—had gotten them the perfect vehicle for their mission.

Nick could see the red and blue lights flickering across the manicured blades of grass around his feet. The ambulance was parked by the curb five yards behind them, its flashing bank of lights tearing a brilliant patch out of the black denim night. It was an out-of-use unit, borrowed from the mechanics' lot behind G.W. Hospital. True to their unspoken Pulse Jockey code, the G.W. paramedics had not asked Nick any difficult questions: they had simply told him where to pick up the keys, where to leave the ambulance when he was done, and what he and Charlie could expect to owe in return for the favor when he returned to Boston. The ambulance had a slightly skewed front axle and a problem with its tail lights, but otherwise, it worked fine. They had made the forty-minute drive in less than three-quarters time, using the lights sparingly to clear wide holes in the spotty evening traffic.

"I'll do the talking," Nick said, as they reached the front porch. "These places usually don't have doctors on staff, just RNs, sometimes not even that. So it isn't unusual for a private physician to make a house call."

"Even this late at night?" Samantha pulled at her light green surgical scrubs. They fit loosely under a slightly oversized white doctor's coat. Nick was wearing a matching outfit, with a stethoscope hanging over his neck and an empty doctor's bag under his right arm. One of the G.W. paramedics—a former partner of Charlie's from before Nick's accident—had fulfilled Nick's requests to the letter. For all intents and purposes, he and Samantha looked like two harried doctors making an emergency house call. The only thing out of the ordinary in their appearances was a slight bulge under the elas-

tic of Nick's scrub pants, where he had jammed
Ted's Beretta.

"I was on call, you were in surgery. This was the
earliest we could get out."

"Sounds good to me."

Nick found a buzzer next to the front door. He
gave it two quick punches, then stood back, waiting.
A minute later there was a short click, and he pulled
on the doorknob. The door came open, and he and
Samantha stepped into the front lobby. A black
woman in her mid-sixties sat behind a reception
desk to Nick's right, dressed in a stiff white nurse's
uniform. Directly ahead of him, a thick crimson carpet poured out across a rectangular open area filled
with three-seater couches, rocking chairs, and a
number of empty steel wheelchairs like the ones out
on the front porch. There were televisions hanging
from racks attached to the hospital-blue walls.

"Can I help you?" the nurse-receptionist asked
in a heavy southern accent. The wrinkles above her
round, yellowed eyes showed concern—she had
obviously noticed the lights from the ambulance
through the lobby windows, and was taking in Nick
and Samantha's apparel in quick, but exaggerated,
glances.

"I'm Dr. Barnes, this is Dr. Craig. We're here to
see a patient of yours, Allen Parkridge."

The woman raised her gray eyebrows, then
turned to a file cabinet by her desk. She pulled open
the top drawer and started to search through a
batch of manila folders. Nick bit down on his lower
lip, thinking fast.

"Dr. Craig and I are on the surgical staff at G.W.
We were asked in as consults on Mr. Parkridge's
case—"

"It says here that Mr. Parkridge's personal physician is Dr. Bruce Kestler," the nurse interrupted. "It also says Dr. Kestler was in twice last week. There's no mention of impending surgery."

"Because there's none planned—yet. We're here to determine if surgery is necessary. Kestler was in my office this afternoon, and the symptoms he described concerned me; if I'm right, Mr. Parkridge could be in immediate need of a bowel resection. Dr. Craig is our bowel expert, which explains why we're here so late. I was waiting for her to get out of surgery."

The nurse continued to stare at Parkridge's file. "I should probably call Dr. Kestler—"

"Please do," Samantha said, her voice sharp. "And explain to him that I did not have time to play games with his patient's receptionist. I have two more resections tonight, and one early tomorrow morning. Dr. Kestler can find himself another consult."

With that, she turned and walked out the front door. Nick stared after her, as shocked as the nurse. Then he realized it was a good ploy; if this nurse had been in the business long, the odds were she had dealt with her fair share of surgeons' egos. He quickly picked up the charade. "I'm sorry—a total bitch, but the absolute best at what she does. Kestler asked for her personally, and I can promise he won't be happy if we lose her."

The nurse glanced nervously at the door. "Look, it's just we don't usually get visitors this late. I didn't mean to cause a problem. Dr. Kestler's probably asleep, anyway. I'm sure it will be okay if you look in on Mr. Parkridge. I'll get the key to his room."

Nick cheered inwardly. He opened the front

door and signaled to Samantha, who had barely stepped off the porch and onto the front lawn. She winked at Nick, then strolled back up the front steps and whiffed past him into the lobby. She kept her eyes straight ahead, not pausing to look at the nurse, who was clumsily searching a rack of keys for the proper set.

"Here we go," the nurse said, nearly beaming with relief. "Room 122. It's on the first floor, just follow me."

She came out from behind the reception desk and led them to a pair of windowed double doors. The doors opened into a long hallway with porcelain floors and more blue walls. They sped past numbered wooden doors, the nurse practically running to stay ahead of Samantha's priggish gait.

By the time they reached 122, the nurse was out of breath. She fumbled to get the key into the lock, then let the door swing inward. Samantha brushed by her. "Thank you. We'll be no more than a few minutes."

"Can I help with anything?"

Samantha nearly laughed out loud. "Unless you've performed bowel resections in your spare time, I'm sure Dr. Barnes and I will be better off on our own."

She disappeared into the room, leaving the nurse standing red faced in the doorway. Nick rolled his eyes as he stepped past her. "Charming, isn't she? Just be glad you don't have to work with her."

He shut the wooden door behind him and leaned back against it, relieved. Samantha was already across the small room, pulling a stool up next to the stiff army-style bed. Aside from the bed, the room contained a scuffed armoire squatting against one gray wall, a color television with a gleaming Set-Top Box sitting on a green card table, and an old-fashioned steel wheelchair in the corner closest to the door.

"He's fast asleep," Samantha whispered from near the bed. "I don't feel good about this."

Nick stepped away from the door. Only Allen Parkridge's head was visible from beneath a long white sheet. His face was a waxen mask, gutted by deep wrinkles, speckled with brown age spots, turned blankly upward toward the ceiling in an expression of pure acquiescence. Life had destroyed this man. It had nothing to do with his age or his infirmity; it was an aura that rose from his appearance even in sleep, an almost suffocating sense of desperation. This face cried out: *victim*. Nick turned his head in disgust.

This was the reason he hated the pity so much, hated the sympathetic looks and well-meaning words. Despite what the world might do to him, he would never let himself be a victim, never let himself become the man on the stiff army cot.

"I guess we have no choice," Samantha said. She reached forward and shook Parkridge's arm. His lips curled even farther into their grimace, then his eyelids crumpled upward.

"Melora?"

The weathered voice echoed off of the gray walls. Samantha glanced at Nick, who took a step closer. It was the right Parkridge, the right convalescent home. Samantha leaned close to Parkridge's cot.

"No, Mr. Parkridge—"

"Had the dream again, Melora. The walking

dream. Like before the chair. Before what they did to me. Only you understood. Only you."

Samantha looked up. Nick touched her shoulder. He had a fair amount of experience with the different stages of age; more than half of a paramedic's calls had to do with old people, from broken hips to strokes to Alzheimer's shut-ins on the loose. "Mr. Parkridge, please listen carefully. We're friends of Melora's. My name is Nick. This is Samantha."

Parkridge didn't turn his head. "Melora never needed friends. She's always had me. Always understood."

"Understood what, Mr. Parkridge? Can you tell us what Melora understood?" Nick didn't know what he was fishing for. They needed to know about Melora Parkridge, find out anything they could. Why would she want to release a sentient computer virus into the Telecon beta test? Why did she develop the Reaper in the first place?

"She always understood *me*!" There was a flutter of motion under the white sheet, and a gnarled hand crawled out from beneath the corner closest to Samantha, pointing toward the old-fashioned wheelchair. "Understood that monster they sent me home in! Understood the pain, every day, the pain!"

Victim. Nick mouthed the word like a curse. He did not trivialize whatever injury had left Allen Parkridge confined to a wheelchair, or in a convalescent home, but he hated Parkridge for his self-pity. That was the easy way. Climb inside the darkness in your soul and tell the world to fuck itself—he was ashamed for Allen Parkridge, and he wondered what it was like for Melora to have a father like this. What it had done to her psyche.

"Mr. Parkridge," Nick said. "It's very important that you listen to me. We need to find Melora."

"She'll be here tomorrow. She's here every day. She cares—"

"And we care, too. But we need to find her tonight. Do you know where we can find her tonight?"

Parkridge stared at the ceiling in silent agony. Nick felt himself getting frustrated. He was about to try again when Samantha reached forward and touched the old man's gnarled hand.

"Melora loves you very much. She visits you often, doesn't she?"

"Every day. Twice a day. Sometimes more."

Samantha glanced at Nick. The ride from downtown Washington was forty minutes without traffic. Did that mean she lived near Split River, and stopped in on her father before and after work?

"More than twice a day," Samantha commented. "Does she travel far from home to see you?"

"Not from home. From work. She works right nearby, so she can see me. Every day."

Samantha and Nick locked eyes. *She works nearby.* Telecon was located in the center of Washington, D.C. It wasn't Telecon Parkridge was talking about; perhaps it was the private lab Hoffman had mentioned in his notebook.

"What does she do nearby? Mr. Parkridge?"

"She works so we can be together. So we will always be together—"

"Mr. Parkridge. Please, concentrate—"

"Because she understands and she hates with me, she knows why to hate and how to hate—"

"Mr. Parkridge!"

But it was no use. Parkridge's eyes were wide

open, his mouth quivering as the words poured out. Frantic, meaningless, disturbing words. Samantha rose from the stool and walked with Nick toward the door.

"It might be a false lead," she said over the din of Parkridge's monologue. "He might not have any conception of time, or days, or even weeks. She might have visited him twice in the last year."

Nick shrugged. "Maybe. Or maybe he meant exactly what he said. And Melora Parkridge's private lab is right here, in Split River."

Nick darkened the lights and put the engine in neutral, letting the ambulance roll quietly into the small alley behind the cubic building. They were at the far end of the one commercial street in Split River; a tiny two-lane stretch of blacktop embraced on either side by quaint shops with vinyl awnings and oversized picture windows: antiques, ice cream, coffee—carbon copy, small-town America. At one in the morning, the street was deserted, lit in small orange cones by poorly placed street lamps hidden behind spruce trees and telephone poles.

"This is the place," Nick whispered, pointing through the ambulance window. He didn't need to whisper, but he felt it fit the mood. They were about to break into a building for the second time in two days.

They stood before a single-story brick building; a sign out front stated simply "Mailing Center," with symbols for Fed-Ex and UPS attached across an oversized plate glass window. From the alley, the building was nondescript, with a closed accordion-style garage door next to cement steps leading up to a rear entrance.

"If there is a lab in Split River," Samantha whispered back as she pulled off her white lab coat, "the evidence will be inside this building. Some record of oversized package deliveries, or carefully packed fragile items. Any large research lab needs an almost constant influx of materials."

"The nurse said there was also a post office two blocks past the mailing center."

"Most people perceive the post office as less reliable. Besides, if Melora is engaged in secret work, the odds are she'd choose a private delivery service like UPS or Fed-Ex, rather than something linked to the government."

Samantha and Nick slid out of the ambulance and approached the rear entrance. The stone steps led up to a high wooden door. Samantha went up the steps while Nick turned to the garage. There was a steel handle where the garage door met the blacktop driveway. Nick didn't see any sign of an alarm system—not surprising, considering the locale. He dropped to one knee, and gripped the handle with both hands.

"Shit," he heard Samantha whisper. "They've got a dead bolt on the inside of this door. They must not enter from here."

Nick clenched his teeth and lifted, the muscles in his shoulders pressing out against his borrowed scrubs. There was a loud crack and then the door was sliding up. He held it at waist level, his back straining.

"It was a high school football ritual," he hissed to Samantha. "We used to pick a neighbor's garage and have a post-game party. The receivers brought the keg, the linebackers busted inside; I didn't realize until now that we receivers got the short end of

the deal. Come on and slide underneath before I
pop a hernia."

Samantha dropped to her knees and crawled
under the edge of the garage. Then Nick bent low,
still holding the heavy iron door with both hands.
His injured thigh cried out, but he managed to limbo
into the garage without dropping the door on himself, and Samantha helped him lower it to the
ground. In a moment they were standing in absolute
darkness, the smell of gasoline strong in their nostrils.

Nick took Samantha's hand and they carefully
pushed forward through the darkness. They
stopped when they came to some sort of parked van,
then used the van's body to guide them to the front
of the garage. Nick nearly tripped over a plastic
crate, his left hand catching hold of a cold wall. He
slid his hand across the wall and found a light
switch. There was a flicker of orange, then a band of
fluorescent light rippled across the ceiling.

He turned, surveying the garage. Brick walls,
raftered ceiling, oil-stained cement floor. There were
two vans parked next to one another, one dark
brown with the UPS logo along one side, the other
Federal Express. It was strange seeing the two vans
parked in the same garage, but Nick decided it was
no stranger than Coke and Pepsi machines in the
same airport terminals, or McDonalds and Burger
Kings on the same stretch of interstate.

"Nick, come on. It's unlocked."

Nick turned toward Samantha's voice, as she
stepped through the inner garage door and into the
building. He followed her inside, his stomach
churning with nervous energy. The fluorescent light
from the garage spilled out into a carpeted rear

office: walls covered with pictures of a white-crested ocean, a steel desk with swivel chair, a row of file cabinets. There were pictures of a woman and two young children in black frames on the desk, and a Nerf basketball hoop attached to a brass garbage can in the corner by the door. A manager's office; Nick felt like a criminal as he followed Samantha to the file cabinet by the wall.

The cabinets were unlocked as well, and she started at the top right corner. "Receipts," she said simply, opening one of the files and showing Nick a stack of brightly colored strips of paper. The receipts were filed by date, filling more than ten cabinets.

Together, they began to make piles of the receipts on the steel desk. Nick felt a pang of guilt as he pushed the framed family pictures onto the swivel chair to make room. But he didn't have time to worry about what they were doing.

Slowly, the piles of receipts started to grow. Most of the locations could be quickly discarded as lab suspects: a Pepsi Cola bottling plant up the main highway—the largest package customer—a local clothing store, a fudge shop, even the convalescent home. But a few of the piles were more suspicious. Something called Flantain Industries three miles north of the convalescent home. A small private school that received five oversized packages every three days. Two unnamed receivers twenty minutes down the main highway. And a storage warehouse just outside of Split River that had received a flurry of packages over the past six months, then abruptly canceled its account a few days ago. The warehouse was a division of some corporation called Pandora Inc.

After forty minutes of stacking receipts, Nick
and Samantha leaned against the cabinets, staring at
the piles on the desk. Nick felt sweat building under
his scrubs. "It's going to take some time to check out
all these places."

"If one of them is Melora's computer lab, it will be
worth it."

"And if not?"

"If not, we go back to the convalescent home. We
work on Parkridge all night if we have to. We've got
to find out about Melora before the Big Turn On. If
she plans to load the Reaper into the information
highway, we'll have to stop her—no matter what it
takes."

Nick nodded, as they began shoving the receipts
back into the file cabinets. By the time they were finished, it was close to three o'clock in the morning.
That left seven hours.

THIRTY-FOUR

for the first time in four hours, Samantha felt the frustration draining out of her as she stepped out of the ambulance onto damp grass. The air had turned from black to gray twenty minutes ago, and now it shimmered in front of her tired eyes, a strange tan color that made everything seem sharp, a little too focused. Tiny drops of dew clung to the unshorn blades of grass around her feet, and there was a thick, musty smell in the air. She had first noticed the scent when they had turned off of the main highway onto a gravel road, perhaps two miles back. As the gravel road serpentined between two fields of high, unkempt grass, the scent grew stronger, pulling at Samantha's city lungs, inciting sudden bouts of fierce coughing. She could tell that Nick was likewise affected by the thick air; he fought to clear his throat as he stepped

339

onto the grass next to her, pulling a sleeve across his lips.

"It doesn't look like anybody's been through this field in years," he commented, pointing. "I'd guess there's enough ragweed to suffocate a city of asthmatics."

Samantha followed his finger, her excitement rising. He was right, the field to their left was completely overgrown, some of the grass reaching waist height. The field stretched for miles in every direction, and the gravel road was like a tiny, forgotten scar. In fact, there was only one other sign that humanity had reached this overlooked slice of backwoods Virginia.

The warehouse was fifty feet ahead of them, at the very end of the gravel road. It was a one-story cinder-block complex with a flat roof and absolutely no windows. The high grass reached all the way to the base of the building, the long blades clinging to the walls like crashing green waves; in another year, the warehouse would be swallowed by the field, dissolved by the encroaching sea of green.

Deserted, forgotten, devoid of life—except this warehouse had been receiving periodic package deliveries up until a few days ago. Samantha had realized the minute they had turned the last corner and finally caught sight of the cinder-block building—this was their best bet so far.

The rest of the evening had been a total waste of time. They had gone from location to location, sometimes simply driving by, as in the case of Flantain Industries, a furniture factory with ugly shrink-wrapped teak couches piled on the driveway and front lawn, and sometimes stopping for a closer look. They had wasted nearly an hour at the private school; the enormous plantationlike building had actually doubled as an "adult" establishment; a fact that should have been obvious from the number of pickup trucks and Jeeps parked in the circular driveway, but wasn't, until they pried out a downstairs window screen and entered a living room straight out of Vegas, with shag lion-print carpets, a mahogany bar, and framed "menus" on the walls, complete with pictures and tip rates.

The next two establishments had used up the rest of the evening; first some sort of plastics factory that had seemed promising until they had stumbled on a bag full of discarded, mutant, miniature army men and warped hula hoops. Then a building that was completely emptied out, without so much as a pane left in a window. There was a chance that Melora had cleaned out her lab because of their discovery of Hoffman's disk, and for a moment Samantha had thought their search was over, but then Nick had found a heat-sealed balloon full of white powder underneath a loose tile in a back room. Not the sort of laboratory—or contraband—they were looking for.

Finally, frustrated, they had headed toward the last address on their list: the warehouse and Pandora Inc. It was late—they were only three hours away from the Big Turn On—but Samantha had the sudden feeling they were close to the answers they were seeking.

They came around the front of the ambulance and started up the road. The gravel crunched under their shoes, while insects buzzed through the grass on either side and wind rustled through the dewy blades. Samantha's ears rang from the cacophony. She felt as though she was walking through an agricultural orchestra pit.

The gravel road ended in a pair of huge iron double doors; above the doors was a video camera with a wide-angle lens. The cinder-block front wall continued another ten yards above the camera, topped by a low barbed-wire fence. At the corners of the building, which was more than fifty feet long, were rounded spotlights facing upward, toward the sky. Next to the spotlights were small directional radar dishes.

Samantha put her hand on Nick's arm when they were twenty feet from the double doors, stopping him. Any closer and the camera would pick them up. She pointed at the spotlights at the corners of the roof.

"There's a helicopter pad up there. Those are guiding spots. And those radar dishes are satellite uplinks. Nick, I think this is the place."

"How are we going to get past the camera? And through those doors?"

"I don't know. I don't see any windows, either. But I also don't see any real security: no electric fence, no guard posts, just the barbed wire along the top and the camera. That doesn't mean there isn't security we can't see. But perhaps Melora was relying on the warehouse's anonymity to keep her lab secret."

"Or maybe there are fifty or a hundred armed killers inside. We have no idea what sort of organization we're up against. If it's Melora chasing us— not Teal—then she's part of something big."

"I agree. But the more I think about it, the more I'm convinced it has to be a pyramid type of operation. Very few brains at the top, an army of paid mercenaries at the lower levels. It's extremely hard to keep a large conspiracy secret—especially long enough to infiltrate a corporation like Telecon. Just as Teal's probably the only one who knows about his backdoor to the code, Melora may be one of very few conspirators with knowledge of the Reaper. Remember, killing Hoffman protected both secrets for an entire year."

"Well, we still have to find a way past that camera."

"Maybe if we go around the other side of the building."

Samantha and Nick stepped off of the gravel path into the field. As they progressed parallel to the warehouse, the field became more tangled, more difficult to walk through. Samantha felt the high grass whipping against the thin material of her scrub pants. She hoped there were no snakes hiding around her feet.

There were no noticeable windows or doors on the left side of the building, just sheer cinder blocks reaching up to the barbed wire on top. They continued, Samantha feeling each breath as she fought the heavy air. The back of the building was more promising. There was a single window in the center of the wall, ten feet up. But as Nick and Samantha got closer, she saw thin steel bars on the other side of the thick glass. Without the proper tools—a diamond bladed drill, a vial of chloric acid—there was no way they were getting through the window. So close, but unless there was something on the other side . . .

"What's that?" Nick was pointing to a spot on the wall a few feet to the right of the window. Samantha stepped closer, and was surprised to see a small metal ring embedded in one of the cinder blocks. She raised her head, and saw another ring two blocks higher. And then another, the same distance above that one.

"They run all the way to the roof," Samantha said, thrilled. "And I don't see a camera. It's a way down from the helipad, in case of an emergency. See, this place is not high security—it's just well hidden. You don't secure something unless you know there are people looking for it. Come on."

She put her right foot on the bottom ring and flexed her thigh. Her tired muscles complained as she pulled herself up the face of the wall, but she ignored them. In a few minutes she had reached the barbed wire on the top of the building. The roll was about three feet high, jagged, frightening even to look at.

"Can we go over it?" Nick asked.

"No, it's too high. We have to find some way to cut through."

Suddenly, Nick was scampering down the side of the building. Samantha watched as he hit the ground and disappeared back into the field. She clung to the building alone, in silence, for what seemed like ten minutes. Then she heard rustling and saw Nick reappear. He was holding an oversized pair of iron shears in his hands. The shears were bright red and looked heavy.

It took Nick a few minutes to climb back up the building, the shears balanced clumsily under his left arm. "Standard equipment in ambulances. We use 'em with the jaws of life to get people out of wrecked cars. I used one just like it the same morning I met you. Careful, it's heavy."

She took the huge shears from him with both hands. For a brief second she almost lost her footing, but his left hand steadied her from below. She made short work of the barbed wire, clearing room for them to pass. Then she pulled herself up onto the roof.

The helipad was in the center of the roof, a bright blue bull's-eye surrounded by more spherical spotlights. Fifteen feet beyond the bull's-eye was a glass door that led into a raised stairwell alcove—access to the interior of the building.

She handed the shears back to Nick and together they hurried to the glass door. The alcove was dark, a spiral staircase leading down into an even deeper darkness. Samantha tried the door, but it was locked. She went for her lock-picking kit, and discovered, with a start, that it was no longer in her pocket. She still had the Polaroid of the Vermont victim, but the lock-picking kit was gone. She shook the loose material of her scrubs, wondering where the hell she could have lost it. Probably climbing the side of the building. If it had fallen into the high grass field, they'd never find it.

"What's wrong?" Nick asked.

"I can't pick the lock."

Nick gently pushed her aside. "Do you think there's an alarm system?"

"I don't know."

"We'll have to take the chance."

He swung the heavy shears at the glass door. The door shattered inward, shards of glass raining down the stairwell. Samantha stared at him. "You think that was a good idea?"

"We have less than three hours left. We have to find out what's going on. Besides, I don't hear anything."

It was true, there was no sound coming out of the stairwell alcove. Nick and Samantha stepped through the open doorway. They picked their way through the glass and started downward.

Each step took them deeper into darkness. The stairwell spiraled between sheer cement walls, making two complete turns and ending in a wide, doorless opening. When they reached the bottom step, Samantha flattened herself against the side of the stairwell, and Nick took position directly across from her. There was no noise coming from the other side of the doorway. Samantha counted softly to herself, steadying her nerves, pushing away her exhaustion. Then she signaled Nick with a flick of her eyes and slipped through the doorway.

Even through the darkness Samantha was struck by the room's vastness. The entire warehouse was one immense hall, with brick walls, a steel-beamed ceiling, and exposed wooden floors. Waist-high, bulky shapes ringed the hall, spaced ten feet apart in an enormous oval. Samantha counted at least fifty of the shapes that she could see, but the top and bottom of the oval were lost in the hall's dark immensity. Black, spaghettilike cables ran between the shapes, then twisted forward into the middle of the oval, melding together beneath a much larger shape, a six-foot-tall boxlike structure that rose up from the floorboards.

"What is this place?" Nick whispered. Samantha didn't answer. She was concentrating on the boxlike structure in the center of the room. She took a small step forward, and noticed a heavy scent in the air. Something bitterly smoky, like burning plastic. *Not good*. They could be walking right into a trap.

"Stay close," she whispered. "We need to find a light."

She moved along the wall, her free hand sliding

against the cool bricks. She kept as much distance as possible between her body and the oval ring of shapes; for all she knew, they were stacks of explosives. She moved ten feet before her hand touched a plastic plate attached to the wall. *Switches.* At least three, all down. She held her breath and flicked the first switch.

There was a loud metallic cough, and then the sound of a ventilation system starting up. She felt a draft of cold air and glanced toward the ceiling. She could hear a fan somewhere in the distance, and the smell of burning plastic grew stronger in her nostrils. Trembling, she flicked the second switch.

At the far end of the hall, ten feet past the last waist-high shape, a huge glass case suddenly lit up. The case was fifteen feet across and taller than Nick, and was filled with brightly colored objects.

"Let's check that out," Nick whispered, starting forward. Samantha stopped him with her hand.

"One thing at a time." She flicked the last switch. There was an insectlike hum, and then the entire hall was bathed in bright light. She blinked, her eyes adjusting, and then she quickly turned toward the waist-high shapes.

Computers. At least seventy of them, squatting on low, wheeled television trays. In the middle of the oval was a mainframe, a high-memory IBM-style monster with microchip bays running up its front. More cables connected the mainframe to the ring of computers, like rubbery spokes in a bicycle wheel.

"What's this setup for?" Nick asked, stepping forward. He was no longer whispering—it was obvious they were alone in the warehouse. Samantha felt alarms going off in her head. Why was the place deserted? The lack of security was one thing; there was no reason to secure a computer lab in the middle of nowhere. But if Melora was planning something for the Big Turn On, wouldn't someone be here?

"Be careful," Samantha said, following Nick toward the computers. "They could be booby-trapped. Or infected."

Infected. It was the right word. A sentient computer virus, a semi-alive creature that lived inside microchips and fiber optic lines. All it wanted was to reproduce and survive. No matter what happened, it would reproduce and survive.

"Do you smell that?" Nick asked, as they arrived at the closest computer.

"Burning plastic."

"I think it's coming from this computer." He walked around to the front of the screen and stopped, staring. Samantha moved to his side.

The damage was immediately obvious. The screen was covered with tiny white cracks. There was a smoky black cloud on the inside of the cracked glass, growing to a light gray in widening concentric circles. The keyboard was melted, some of the keys black and bleeding out onto the television rack. The processor was warped as if by extreme heat, like a wax candle just removed from a pizza oven. The smell was almost noxious.

Samantha immediately thought of the jolt Nick had received when they had loaded the Reaper disk into the laptop. She walked to the next computer and saw it was in the exact same shape as the first.

Computer by computer by computer; Nick and Samantha strolled in silence around the oval ring of machines, seeing the same level of destruction.

Screens cracked and smoky. Keyboards ruined. Processors completely melted. Samantha turned toward the large boxlike mainframe in the middle of the oval. She moved toward it warily. The machine did not look injured like the other computers. No signs of meltdown, no cracks or warps in the plastic case. When she got within a few inches, she noticed that one of the thin microchip decks was open. She leaned over the deck, squinting. There was an empty space where there should have been a chip. A space a little bigger than her fingernail.

She turned, her eyebrows wrinkling upward. She looked out at the ring of melted computers. Then back at the open microchip deck. Her eyes shifted up and down the mainframe. Then to the cables on the ground, the spaghetti wires that linked the mainframe to the ring of computers.

She had a sudden image of red pushpins on a map. She thought of invisible cables running under that map, cables that linked each pushpin to a central point. A point in the middle of Washington, D.C. A mainframe computer like the one she was looking at, only bigger, a supervising computer. *Jesus.*

"What is it?" Nick asked, stepping toward her. "Why is the room set up like this?"

"I think . . . a demonstration." Samantha did not know where the word came from, but it immediately struck her as correct. This was a controlled demonstration. Of something immensely powerful. A weapon—but not really a weapon, something specifically designed for one purpose.

Why? The question slammed at Samantha's mind. Why, Melora, why? Millions of dollars, probably many years of secrets, of trips to a lab in the middle of nowhere while she simultaneously worked her way through Telecon, got close to Teal, to the center of his web—why?

"Samantha," Nick said, his voice faraway. "Come and look at this."

Her concentration broke and she realized that Nick had moved across the hall to the glowing glass case at the far end. She hurried forward, passing between two of the ruined computers, her thoughts still spinning, contemplating, complaining. It took a brilliant mind to develop the Reaper. And a vicious, conniving heart to keep it a secret.

"It's like an exhibit in the Smithsonian," Nick commented, as she arrived at his side. "But totally fucked up. A selective history."

"History of what?" Samantha asked, as she peered through the glass.

"Technology."

And there it was. Carefully laid out, a structured presentation in beautiful Technicolor, a collection of artifacts, pictures, notes—*madness.* The vitriol seeped through the glass, impossible to miss. From the first artifact, an aged bow and arrow, to the next, a tiny catapult next to a hieroglyph of crushed and dying Egyptian warriors, the diorama became more and more clear. Plastic models, drawings, and pictures. Early explosive devices. The first ballistic weapons. Then the guns of the major wars in history, the muskets and repeating rifles and machine-guns. Antipersonnel mines, then nonmagnetic mines, then mines the size of pocket change. An entire shelf was devoted to the atom bomb, with a tiny replica, and a collage of pictures from Hiroshima and Naga-saki.

The exhibits moved from weapons to other forms of technological advance: transportation, manufacturing, communication. There were photographs of early motorcar accidents, of train wrecks; newspaper clippings of airplane crashes and urban fires. Pictures of the Exxon *Valdez* oil spill, of a smoggy Los Angeles morning, of impoverished children chained to sewing machines in unnamed sweatshops in unnamed cities. Next to the pictures was an article on the laying of the first transatlantic phone lines, then an actual antique phone, then a portable military phone from the Vietnam era, charred and melted, the locus of a bombing raid or a napalm morning.

From the phones, the exhibit moved to the history of biological and chemical weapons: an article about the mass genocide of Native Americans by means of disease; a picture of a World War I medical tent, full of young men dying from mustard gas; a picture of a German concentration camp, with the words "Six Million" underneath. And then something unrecognizable: two shiny, white, egg-shaped pellets, sitting next to a picture of utter carnage—a few dozen Asian men, women, and children lying in pools of respirated blood. There was a banner above the picture:

**Mitotoxic Chloric Acid. Beta Run 669–7.
Confidential, for Internal Use Only**

After the chemical weapons, taking up the entire right-hand corner of the glass case, was the final exhibit: a personal computer, sitting next to a tiny hand-held television set. And between them, a three-inch tangle of fiber optic cable. Above the cable was a small explanatory panel, the only narration in the exhibit, in bright red ink:

> The final insult. The final inhumanity. The
> society killer ...
> Our chance to strike back.
> A blow for humanity.
> A blow for Pandora.

Stunned, Samantha stepped away from the glass case. *Pandora*. That was the name of the corporation that owned the warehouse. Maybe it was also the name of the organization that was hunting Nick and Samantha. Melora could not have done all of this on her own. There had to be others—a small group of well-connected, well-funded fanatics. She looked at Nick, and saw the confusion on his face. He was still trying to take in all the exhibits, his eyes rapidly moving from picture to picture.

"What is this for? Why leave a diorama like this in the middle of a lab?"

Samantha felt her face getting hot. She was beginning to understand. "It's like leaving the murder weapon at the scene of a crime. It's an explanation, a signature. She's not trying to hide what she's done. She wanted someone to find this. She wants the world to know why. That's why there was hardly any security. That's why the place is deserted. This is her manifesto. Pandora's manifesto."

"An antitechnology conspiracy," Nick whispered. Then he turned toward the oval of ruined computers. Samantha turned with him. "You said this was a demonstration. What did you mean? A demonstration of what?"

Samantha's voice wavered. Every second, it

became clearer. "The Reaper. What it can—what it *will* do. The mainframe in the middle of the room represents the supervising computer in the Telecon complex. The surrounding personal computers symbolize the national computer and television network."

"And the missing microchip—"

"Contains the Reaper program. If Melora puts that chip in the supervising computer after the Big Turn On, this demonstration will be re-created on a massive scale. That's what Melora wants. To wipe out all the computers and televisions. Set technology back fifty years. *A blow for humanity*."

Nick leaned back against the glass case. The glass creaked under his weight, but he ignored it. "She intends to use technology to kill technology. But what about CaV—does she want to kill people, too? Wipe out a hundred million television watchers and computer users at the same time?"

Samantha shrugged. "Maybe. Melora is obviously a fanatic. And she's not alone; she's a part of some larger organization. Pandora, whatever that is. The worst kind of fanatics—terrorists armed for their cause."

"It doesn't make sense to me. Destroy the technology, okay—but kill millions of innocent people? She would have to be a monster. A genocidal monster."

Samantha had a sudden thought. "Maybe she doesn't know about CaV."

"What do you mean?"

"Look at the demonstration. Burned-out computer screens, destroyed processor. No evidence of anything worse. And Hoffman didn't make any mention of CaV. Remember, the Reaper *thinks*. It

plans, it makes strategies, it *acts*. It might have created CaV on its own. Tested it, on its own. And now
it wants to use Teal's network to attack with it—all
on its own."

Nick was staring at her. "Melora wants to use
the Reaper to wipe out technology. She thinks she
can control it, a tool for her to use. But it's controlling her."

"Not literally. Using her, more accurately. She
may know nothing at all about CaV. Or then again,
maybe she *is* a genocidal monster. She wouldn't be
the first antitechnologist with a vicious streak."

"Either way, we have to stop her from putting
that chip into the Telecon system."

Samantha checked her watch. A numbness filled
her limbs.

"We have an hour."

THIRTY-FIVE

nd one. Two. Roll." The CNN cameraman
wagged a thick finger above the high-
intensity spotlight attached to the top of his
television camera, and Marcus Teal threw
back his shoulders, a beaming smile spreading
across his face. The camera was three feet in front of
him, squatting on a telescoping tripod. The cameraman was overweight, wearing a denim jacket with
the CNN emblem on his shoulder, a black baseball
cap, and work boots. Behind him stood the spot producer in a tailored blue suit. Both men seemed
uncomfortable in the steel computer atrium, their
gazes shifting across the low semicircular computer
cabinet, the three-foot-tall high-density screen, the
hollowed-out sphere walls that rose up above. They
stood carefully on the Lucite floor, overaware of the
colored fiber optic cables that twisted beneath their

feet. But Marcus Teal didn't share their discomfort. This was his throne room, his moment—his victory.

And the camera was his best friend. He looked into the fish-eye lens and saw a hundred million faces staring back at him. The event had been building in the press for weeks: commercials, news stories, late-night comedy monologues, even the daytime talk shows. Every household with a Set-Top Box had felt the anticipation—and that meant nearly every household in the nation. Finally, the moment had come.

"Good morning, America," Teal said, his words rehearsed. He was going to be brief, because that was the tenor of the television nation, that was the tone of minds raised on sound bytes and video bits. "My name is Marcus Teal."

And I'm going to change your world. Marcus turned, waving a hand at the screen behind him. The screen was blank, waiting. Below it was a plastic panel with a single red switch. Marcus had insisted that there actually be a switch—not a computer keyboard, not a button, not a voice recognizer. This was a visual society, this moment demanded a switch. That was how it was in Teal's dreams, and that was how it would be in his reality.

"Thirty minutes after I flick that switch, the information highway will shift from theory to reality. From that moment on, you will have access to an entirely new world. A world of limitless options. Of limitless joys. A world that we will share, as equals, each and every member of our nation together like a family, a wonderful, diverse family."

Hyperbole? Teal had been fighting the accusation his entire adult life. He chose to think of it as forward thinking. In fifteen minutes, the world *would* be brought together. But the equality—that would wait for Marcus Teal to step in and use the power he had secured for himself—and himself alone. The power of his backdoor.

"At first, we will all be like infants with this new technology. Trying things out, finding out what we like and don't like. The information highway will be shaped by our needs and wants—growing as we grow, learning as we learn."

Growing, learning, changing. Becoming indispensable. And then Teal would act. He would begin the process of true change. Using his backdoor to give advantages to those who were disadvantaged. Companies he chose would rise, while others would fall. A little information, a gentle push here and there, secrets revealed and other secrets changed; slowly, he would lift entire neighborhoods with his two hands. He would have to be careful; he would have to stay invisible. But he would use his backdoor against the barriers. And slowly, the barriers would fall. Robin Hood on a massive scale. Martin Luther King, Jr., with the power of a god.

His chest swelled as he turned toward the red switch. The producer signaled with his left hand and the cameraman shifted position, widening the shot. The three of them were alone in the sealed computer atrium; Teal had not wanted anyone else present, the moment was too powerful to share. Melora was at her post, in her office, monitoring the event. Benson had mysteriously not shown—surprising, considering how hard they had all worked in the preceding weeks, but irrelevant. There were other programmers in the engineering department quite capable of monitoring the system for unforeseen glitches.

"Friends, sit back and join with me as we enter this new world of options. As we like to say here in our headquarters, Turn It On, With Telecon!"

Teal stepped forward and flicked the switch. Vaguely operatic music crashed through the steel room. Teal turned, looked directly into the camera, and winked. The producer gave him a thumbs up.

"And . . . we're out."

The cameraman stepped back from the tripod, and the producer smiled. "Congratulations. I think that went very well."

Teal nodded, turning back to the dark screen. The music had died away, and Teal's ears swam in the liquid sound of the computer fans and over-powering air-conditioning. "Thank you. I'll show you back to the anteroom. An assistant will be available, if you'd like to do any interior background shots."

The cameraman unhooked the tripod and folded it under his right arm. He hefted the camera onto his shoulder, then nodded to the producer. Teal led them toward the exit. They passed the jumble of file cabinets and computer counters that dotted the back of the atrium, and arrived at the anteroom door. He pressed his hand against the palm plate, watching it slide open. There was a security guard in a Telecon uniform waiting inside, next to the reti-nal scanner. He would escort the CNN crew out-side.

"Thank you again," Teal said, shaking the pro-ducer's hand.

"Thirty minutes?" the producer asked, as he stepped into the anteroom. "Isn't that what you said? Then the web will be up and running?"

"Precisely. There's a fair amount of self-testing

that goes on, both at the software and hardware level. But once it's started, it will go twenty-four hours a day."

"I can't wait to try it out at home."

"I'm sure there are a few hundred million others thinking the same thing."

He shut the door, and finally, he was alone. He hurried back across the atrium to his supervising computer. He stood directly in front of the screen, watching, waiting. It was going to be the longest thirty minutes of his life. He saw his face reflected in the dark screen and thought about the journey that had brought him to this point. He thought about his father, and the man who had shot him for the paltry money in his wallet. He thought about his mother, how hard she had worked every day for pennies—like so many others in that neighborhood, in neighborhoods across the country. He thought about the two gangbangers in the back row of the MLK Youth Development Center, two days ago. He closed his eyes and watched the barriers fall down.

There was a noise behind him and he opened his eyes, startled. Who dared interrupt him in his throne room? Only two people could get past the retinal scanner and the voice recognition device. . . .

"Marcus, turn around."

Icy, familiar, but with a tone of defiance Marcus had never heard before. He whirled away from the screen, and stopped cold, his eyes growing wide. Melora was standing five feet away. In her right hand was a revolver fitted with a three-inch-long suppresser.

Marcus had grown up around guns and child gangsters. He knew what the gun could do—had seen the results in the dying face of his own father.

"Melora. What—"

"Step away from the computer."

Teal saw the determination in her eyes. He took a step to his left, his arms stiff at his sides. A sweat had broken out across his back. He realized, with a start, that he was truly afraid of this woman. He did not understand her—had never understood her. And he could not control her.

She strolled forward across the Lucite, keeping the gun trained on his chest. She stopped a few feet from the screen and pressed a series of buttons on the side of a greenish-blue section of the rounded computer cabinet. One of the microchip decks whirred open. Marcus was not sure which set of microchips was stored in that particular deck— there were too many to remember without the schematic. His ears started to ring and there was a pounding above his eyes. *Make her stop!* She was violating his creation. Why? What did she plan to do? He stared at the dark barrel aimed at his chest. If not for the gun, he would have thought she was just making a final change before the system went national.

"Melora, I don't understand. It's everything we've worked for. What are you doing?"

"You're a fool, Marcus. You were always a fool."

The words were like a slap, and Marcus felt anger growing under his fear. "What do you mean?"

"Did you ever wonder why it was so easy? Why everything happened so fast? Other companies backing away. Banks and venture capitalists throwing money at you—so much damn money. Federal committees allowing a monopoly of something so powerful."

"It was *never* easy! It was a triumph of will and intelligence—"

"You were a puppet. We've been planning this from the very beginning. Unify the technology to destroy it."

She pulled something out of her pocket. Something tiny, the size of a fingernail. Then she turned toward the microchip deck. Carefully, she removed one of the microchips and dropped it to the floor. The tiny clatter echoed in Teal's ears.

"We? What do you mean—"

"It doesn't matter."

Teal's mind was spinning. *Had it come too easy?* Telecon's rise had been meteoric. Teal had bought up cable companies, telephone conglomerates, software producers—and the money had always been available, the banks and venture capitalists had always come through. Then the government had accepted the Evolving Code as the standard, and had allowed his temporary monopoly. Speaker Tyro Carlson, who had convinced the Congress to give Telecon the monopoly, had called it the most necessary step in the history of telecommunication legislation. *Could these things have been part of some plan?* Impossible.

"What the hell are you talking about?"

"In thirty minutes you'll understand."

She leaned forward and placed the thing from her pocket into the microchip deck. Then she shut the deck, and stepped back from the computer. For the first time since Teal had met her, she was smiling.

"The end of a tyranny, Marcus. A first step in the right direction."

THIRTY-SIX

ick! Look out!"

Nick whipped the steering wheel to the right and slammed his foot against the brake pedal. There was a sudden feeling of weightlessness as the ambulance lifted up on two wheels; then the tires crashed back down against the blacktop, and Nick gasped, watching the pickup truck whiz by his window. A second later and it would have been a head-on collision. Still, the fifty yards Nick had steered the ambulance the wrong way down the on-ramp had chopped fifteen minutes off their trip.

"We're okay. A few more turns and we're there."

"I hope we're in time. It could be over before we get inside—*if* we get inside."

They had lost nearly twenty minutes at a traffic foul-up on the way into the city. A multilane construction job had backed up cars for two miles; even with the lights and siren, the ambulance had inched through.

Nick tensed his fingers against the steering wheel as he took a corner at fifty miles per hour. He knew they were cutting it close. They had heard Teal's inaugural announcement on the CNN radio simulcast a minute ago. The second Teal had flicked the switch, Nick's throat had gone chalk dry. They had no idea how close Melora was to loading the Reaper into the system; perhaps she had already done so and was just waiting with the rest of the nation for the system to come alive. Literally.

"I can try to use my USAMRIID authority," Samantha said, as Nick pushed the ambulance through a red light and across a four-way intersection. "But Teal might have left orders at the desk to keep us out. We could also try to get police or federal help—"

"It will take too long to explain. And I doubt anyone will believe us, without a trip to Melora's lab. We'll have to find another way."

Nick yanked the wheel to the left, determination rising in his eyes. He was going to get inside the complex, if he had to use Ted's gun or the front fender of the ambulance. For all he knew, Charlie was dead, Melora was loading a deadly disease into the fiber optic network, and Marcus Teal was standing by in complete ignorance, his greedy thoughts focused on his damn backdoor. Nick was not going to stand by and let more people die. He couldn't stop AIDS—but he might stop CaV.

They took the final corner and Nick leaned against the brake, shutting the lights with a flick of his left hand. The Telecon complex was to their left, the massive glass entrance barely visible behind a sea of camera-toting tourists. Telecon employees were ushering the tourists into a velvet-roped corral, and there were a few dozen federal troopers milling about for extra measure. The Big Turn On had drawn an abnormally large crowd; Nick guessed there were at least three hundred people waiting on the stone front steps.

"So much for sneaking in the front door."

Samantha had her face pressed against the window. She pointed, shaking her head. "Teal certainly knows how to hype."

Above the roped-in crowd of tourists, affixed to the high glass above the entrance, was an enormous digital timer. Bright red numbers shivered across its face:

$$29{:}51$$

As Nick watched, the seconds ticked away. Fifty. Forty-nine. Forty-eight.

Christ, they didn't have much time. Nick whirled his eyes forward and saw something that made him sit up in his seat. Twenty yards ahead, parked between two police cruisers, was a pale green van. The van had the CNN logo emblazoned across its back doors.

Nick glanced to his right, making sure none of the state troopers or Telecon employees was nearby. Then he pulled the ambulance next to the CNN van, shutting the engine. He quickly slid outside and jogged around to the back of the ambulance. Samantha joined him as he opened the rear doors.

"What are you planning?"

"We can't get inside," he said, jabbing his finger toward the CNN van, "but they can."

He climbed halfway into the ambulance and opened an equipment locker. The hydraulic spreader was Velcroed next to the oversized shears they had used on the barbed wire. He grabbed the spreader and leapt back out of the ambulance. The spreader was three feet long, weighed about thirty pounds, and had two extended handles like the prongs of a shrimp fork.

"The jaws of life?" Samantha asked.

Nick nodded, heading to the back of the CNN van. Samantha kept watch while he jammed the end of the spreader into the crack between the van's two back doors. He squeezed the handles and gave a quick pull; there was a metallic groan and then a crack, as the spreader came open. The van doors swung back, the lock destroyed.

Nick handed the spreader to Samantha and climbed into the back of the CNN van. The van was full of television equipment; at least two cameras, a tripod, a number of different-sized spotlights and colored lens covers, crates filled with metal items Nick didn't recognize. There was a pile of protective clothing in the far corner, and Nick dug through, searching for anything with the CNN logo. He found a black rain slicker, two baseball hats, and a heavy gray sweatshirt. *Good enough.*

He climbed out of the van and handed Samantha the sweatshirt and one of the baseball hats. The slicker fit snugly over his shoulders, the shiny plastic material barely drifting past his waist. He donned the other hat, then pulled a heavy portable camera out of the van. He put the camera on his right shoulder and played with the buttons near the handgrip; the lens telescoped in and out. As easy as a gun, he thought to himself.

Samantha grabbed a small tripod from the van, and they started toward the front steps. Nick pulled the baseball cap tight over his hair as they entered the sea of tourists, using the camera the same way he had used the ambulance lights. The crowd split apart, letting him pass. Samantha followed a step behind, awkwardly lugging the tripod.

They passed the roped corral of tourists. A state trooper looked them over as they reached the sliding glass entrance, then nodded, smiling, when Nick pointed the camera at him, pretending to shoot. Everyone loved the camera.

The sliding doors whiffed open and Nick and Samantha stepped through. The cavernous front hall, with its walls of black velvet, marble floors, and ceiling traversed by glowing tubes spiriting balls of colored light, was just as impressive the second time. Nick's palms were sweaty against the camera handgrip, and he tried to stay calm as they moved past the line of tourists waiting to get on the hydraulic tram. The entire lobby was brimming with people; Nick guessed at least two hundred, mostly broken into families and small tour groups. Nick and Samantha passed the Plexiglas case full of fiber optic lines—Junction to the World—and slowed as they came to the security desk in front of the huge electronic revolving door. There was one guard behind the desk, his jowly face bright red, his blond hair sticking up from his head in sweaty triangular clumps. There were at least thirty people crowded by the desk, asking questions about the Big Turn On, the architecture of the complex, fiber optics—the poor security guard looked ready to quit his job. Nick and Samantha shoved through the crowd, heading straight for the revolving door.

At the last second the guard saw them and rose up from his chair. "Hold on. We've already got two of you guys inside."

"Producer wants a second camera," Nick said, still moving toward the revolving door. "Look, we're going live in two minutes for a follow-up. If I don't get this camera up to the other team, it's gonna be my job."

The guard ran a hand through his sweaty hair. An Indian man in a yellow sweater shouted a question about Teal's childhood over the desk, and the guard shouted something back, then turned toward Nick. "I've gotta find someone to escort you. Give me a second."

"We know where we're going. Our producer called from his cell phone."

"Sorry, it's procedure. Just hold on a second."

He reached for a phone, then paused as a woman holding a crying child by the hand leaned over the desk, asking about rest rooms. Nick glanced at Samantha, then back at the desk. The guard was still mid-dial, pointing the woman toward the other side of the lobby. Nick rushed into the revolving door, Samantha a step behind him. He heard a shout as the door spun, but didn't look back. He doubted the guard would try too hard to stop them; they were CNN, there were already other CNN employees inside—and the guard wouldn't want to be the cause of any press incidents.

The revolving door let them out in front of a bank of elevators. Nick hit the button for the fourth floor and shifted his weight from foot to foot, waiting. The elevator doors were covered in reflective glass, and he smiled at Samantha's reflection. Her gray eyes were tense under the dark brim of her CNN cap.

"We'll get there in time," Nick whispered. "I know we will."

"But how are we going to get inside? The computer atrium is protected by the retinal scanner and the voice recorder. If Melora is already inside, we're sunk."

The elevator doors whiffed open and Nick and Samantha stepped inside. "Then we'll find Teal. We'll make him understand. Melora is more of an enemy to him than we are."

"I don't know. If he's aware that we know about his backdoor, he won't let us go. He might help us stop Melora—"

"That's all that matters now. We'll worry about Teal when the time comes."

The elevator doors opened onto the fourth floor. Nick recognized the enormous cubicle room from two nights ago. There were men and women in Telecon uniforms everywhere: wandering past the cubicles with folders in their hands, standing by the watercoolers, leaning over the tops of their cubicles to talk with similarly confined neighbors. Nick walked along the edge of the room, mustering as much confidence as possible. Someone pointed at the camera and heads popped up above cubicle walls.

"Hey," someone called. "Get a shot of me. Hi mom."

"This gonna be on again tonight?"

"Get my best side."

Nick smiled, swinging the camera in wide arcs as he continued toward the other end of the room. He was ten feet from the hallway that led to the computer atrium when he heard a young male voice from somewhere behind him: "We'll use this as our closing shot. Full angle, wide arc."

Nick turned, his stomach sinking. An over-weight man in a CNN denim jacket was standing by the elevators, a camera over his right shoulder. Next to him was a man in a blue tailored suit, waving his hands toward the cubicles. The camera started a slow arc toward where Nick was standing.

"Shit," Nick whispered, grabbing Samantha with his free hand and pulling her quickly forward. They made it to the hallway and dove around the corner. He pressed his back against the wall, breathing hard. He didn't hear any shouts, and guessed they had escaped notice.

He carefully put the camera down on the floor, and Samantha dropped the tripod. They moved past the gray file-room door, heading toward the steel airlock with rounded edges and the Plexiglas center window. To Nick's surprise, the door was slightly open, revealing a sliver of the inner chamber. Nick pressed his hand against the door and it swung inward. His eyes went wide.

The chamber walls and ceiling were smooth and steel, painted ivory. The room had no furniture, no pictures, nothing but a plastic console attached at eye-level ten feet to Nick's left. Next to the console, an entire section of the far wall of the chamber had slid upward, revealing a bright rectangle of fluorescent-white light. Samantha touched Nick's hand.

"Why is it open?"

"I don't know." Nick stepped forward, pointing at the plastic console. There was a rubber eyepiece in a corner of the console, next to a series of digital lights. "Is that the retinal scanner?"

"And the voice recorder."

Nick shifted his eyes back toward the rectangular

light when something caught his attention. Something on the floor beneath the plastic console. Nick
crossed to the spot and dropped to one knee. He
touched the thing with his finger—and gasped,
nearly falling back. Small, round, the texture of jelly.
He did not want to turn the thing over, did not want
to really know for sure. He rose, turning back toward
the rectangle of light.

"What is it?" Samantha asked.

"I think it's—wait, do you hear that?"

Voices. Two of them, coming from beyond the
bright rectangle of light. A woman and a man. Nick
recognized both of them, and started forward,
immediately forgetting about the thing on the floor,
his blood rocketing through his veins. Samantha followed a step behind.

"Be careful. Either one of them could be armed.
And they both have reason to want us dead."

Nick slipped Ted's Beretta out from under his
waistband, as they passed into the bright light.

The computer atrium was as awe-inspiring as Nick
had anticipated. His heart pounded as he stepped
onto the transparent floor, his eyes shifting quickly
across the colored fiber optic lines under his feet.
There was a jungle of file cabinets and computer
counters to his left and right. Ahead, the walls were
white and curved inward; wrapped around the
entire front of the semicircular room was the computer system, a waist-high series of colored steel
cabinets filled with microchip decks. Above the central cabinet stood a three-foot-high blank computer
screen.

And in front of the screen stood Marcus Teal. His
spine was stiff, his shoulders back, but there was a

look of anguish on his face. Ten feet in front of him was the barrel of a gun. Behind the gun, Melora Parkridge, both arms forward, both hands wrapped around the pistol's handgrip. A shooter's stance. Teal was in the middle of a sentence, his voice angry, his body ready to move forward. Neither of them had noticed Nick and Samantha's entrance.

Nick slid quickly forward over the transparent floor, Samantha at his side. When he was ten feet from Melora he aimed the Beretta at her and cleared his throat.

Teal and Melora turned at the same time. Melora's eyes widened in shock. Then they shifted to the Beretta. "I don't know what you're doing here, but that won't do any good. It's too late."

Nick clenched his teeth. Samantha spoke for him. "We've been to your lab. We know what you intend to do—"

"What I've already done," Melora interrupted. Nick's stomach dropped.

"You've already loaded Reaper into the system?"

"Yes. I placed the chip into the computer. When the system switches on—in less than twenty-seven minutes—Reaper will be uploaded in a matter of nanoseconds. So you're too late."

"Christ," Samantha whispered. "Do you realize what you've done?"

Teal took a step toward Melora, stopping when she jerked her gun up toward his face. Teal looked at Samantha and Nick. "What *has* she done? What's this Reaper?"

"A computer virus," Melora answered, her sharp voice nearly clinical. "An intelligent, unbeatable program that will replicate itself throughout the fiber optic network. In seconds, it will destroy every computer and television screen attached to the Telecon web. I also believe it will down much of the nation's phone systems."

Her body shivered with excitement, but her voice remained steady: "The damage will multiply on itself—without computers and phones, the country will grind to a halt. All electronic data will instantaneously vanish. The economic structure of the nation will crumble; all credit cards, bank accounts, stock purchases, will become worthless. The government will cease to function. Air-traffic control will no longer exist. In fact, most forms of transportation will be utterly disabled: planes without computer guidance, trains without computer switching, roads without any form of traffic control."

Nick stared at her. He had not thought any of this through. She was right, computers were indispensable components in every area of modern life.

"There will no longer be any means of long-distance communication. Computerized manufacturing will cease to exist. Most industrialized companies will fold. Automated production will become impossible. In a matter of seconds, the entire country will jump backward in time—a hundred years, maybe more. Other economies will shatter as the concussion spreads around the world. The full effects are impossible to calculate—"

"It will be catastrophic," Teal whispered, his face slack. "Instant poverty, everywhere. Everything this country has built—"

"Gone," Melora flicked the gun in the air. "All of it, gone. Your wonderful technology. Your torturous technology. Gone. No longer will people like you violate our world. No longer will nations be forced under your chains."

"Instead," Samantha said. "They'll die. Painfully. Hundreds of millions of them."

Melora faced her. "What are you talking about? There will be a few casualties when the computers go down—"

"Not casualties," Nick said. "Mass death. Anyone in front of a computer screen. Anyone near a television set. The three of us, in this room, by that screen."

"The disease," Teal whispered. Nick could see from Teal's face that he was a beaten man, that his life had crashed down in the last few minutes. "The calcifying disease you told me about. It's real?"

Nick took a step forward, the Beretta trained on Melora's chest. Melora was still aiming at Teal, but her eyes wavered as she listened to Samantha's voice.

"Twenty-four people connected to your beta test are in USAMRIID morgues. Melora's Reaper program is a sentient virus: it reacts to its environment, fights against what it perceives as its enemy. It has perceived us."

She reached into the pocket of her scrubs and pulled out the Polaroid of the calcified woman in the Vermont cabin. She held the picture in the air. "Melora's right, it can ruin computer screens and keyboards. But it also has another way of staying alive—it kills. A freak modulation of light emitted through a television screen did this. In twenty-six minutes, there will be hundreds of millions of calcified corpses."

Melora's mouth was open, her face pale. She coughed, then shook her head. "It's impossible."

"It's not impossible—"

"The Reaper was not uploaded into the beta test. The Reaper has never left my laboratory."

Nick could hear the blood rushing through his ears. *What?* The Reaper wasn't in the beta test? Could they have been wrong? Could CaV have nothing to do with the Reaper? A coincidence? More likely, Melora was lying—or wrong. A strange thought entered his head: *Perhaps the Reaper found its own way into the beta test.*

"Can you be sure of that?" Nick asked. "Are you willing to bet a hundred million lives on that? You know what the Reaper can do. You see what CaV *has* done. You want to destroy the technology, but do you want to kill innocent people?"

Melora's arm started to shake, her gun jerking through the air. Nick took a step toward her. "Melora," he said quietly. "We've been to the convalescent home in Split River. There's a Set-Top Box in your father's room."

That did it. She turned toward him, faltering, and he dove at her. His right hand cried out as his fingers caught her wrist. Her gun spun out of her hand and clattered against the computer cabinet. Nick kicked it toward Samantha, who gathered it up.

"Quick," Nick hissed. "Take the chip out."

Melora shook her head. "That won't do any good," she mumbled, her voice confused, quiet. "The Reaper's already loaded enough of itself into the mainframe. It will deposit program building blocks in every other chip in the system. It's impossible to stop. That's the whole point—"

"How do we shut it down?" Samantha asked, grabbing Teal's arm. "Turn the whole damn thing off!"

Teal's eyes were wide. "Turn it off?"

"Damn it," Samantha shouted, aiming Melora's gun at the computer. She pulled the trigger, and there were six quick pops, followed by the high-pitched sound of metal against metal. Nick winced as something whizzed by his ear. He looked at the computer cabinet, and saw six clustered dents. Samantha pulled the trigger again, but nothing happened. She dropped the gun, frustrated.

"It's bulletproof?" She nearly screamed. "You made a bulletproof computer?"

"It's meant to withstand anything from an earthquake to a massive inferno. It's the center of the web—"

"You have to stop it!"

There was a tiny pause, then Teal nodded. Nick exhaled in relief. Teal was not a monster. In fact, neither was Melora: she had not known about CaV. The only real monster was the Reaper. Nick raised his eyebrows at the thought. Something still wasn't right. How *had* the Reaper gotten into the beta test?

"There are more than ten thousand redundant circuits," Teal was saying, sweat beading up on his forehead. "The original goal was to keep the thing running, not the reverse."

"If we can't shut it off," Samantha said, "can we quarantine it? Keep the Reaper trapped in the main system?"

Teal pointed to the colored strings under the Lucite floor. "We can't cut it off here—there are millions of cables running through this floor. But we can isolate the Reaper in this building. We just have to shut down the main fiber optic junction. In the front lobby."

Nick raised his eyebrows. "I thought that was just a display."

Teal shook his head. "It's the real thing. It's the coaxial junction that links this system to the net—the entire country is wired in through those cables."

"How do we shut it down?" Samantha asked. "Is there a switch?"

"Not a switch," Teal said, rushing across the room. "A key."

He stopped at the far wall and swung a seemingly unmarked section ninety degrees upward. Behind the section was a combination wall safe. As Nick watched, he spun the combination three times, and the safe came open. He reached inside and pulled out a transparent plastic card. The card was slightly smaller than a package of cigarettes.

"There's a slot on the back of the Plexiglas display case in the lobby. This card will open the case, and then—"

There was a sudden explosion and Teal slammed backward against the wall, doubling forward, his hands grabbing at his abdomen. Blood sprayed out between his fingers.

Nick leapt toward the floor, his body twisting in the air. He hit shoulder first, pain sparking through his body. He dragged himself along the computer cabinet, trying to find someplace to hide. He saw Samantha diving for cover behind a low computer counter. Melora was still standing by the high screen, in shock. Nick turned in the direction of the explosion.

Five feet to the left of the door, partially shielded by a steel file cabinet, stood a short, balding man with a piglike face. He had thick glasses, thinning hair, and an almost painful slouch. He was unshaven, wearing a Telecon uniform, and holding a high-powered semi-automatic hunting rifle.

He stepped out from behind the file cabinet, his thick lips quivering over yellowed teeth. His eyes were glazed and teary beneath his thick glasses. He slowly crossed to the center of the room. Melora was staring at him, her thin eyebrows sliding up her head.

"Ned?"

The piglike man looked at her.

"Yes, Ms. Parkridge." He aimed the rifle and pulled the trigger. There was another explosion and Melora's head snapped back, blood spurting from her scalp. Her body crashed against the computer screen and slumped to the floor.

Christ, Nick screamed at himself. He was in direct view, barely ten feet to Ned's left. He remained completely still, not daring to move. The Beretta was still clenched in his left hand, hidden under his body.

Ned walked across the room toward where Teal was leaning against the wall. He passed a few feet from where Samantha was hiding, then threw a glance in Nick's direction. He paused, staring right at Nick's face. Nick stared back, too afraid to do anything else. The piggish man shrugged, then turned back to Teal.

"Hello, Mr. Teal," he said, his voice strangely polite. "May I please have the card?"

Teal groaned, both hands still clenched over his injured stomach. Nick could tell the wound was serious. The piggish man bent to one knee, and pulled one of Teal's hands away from the blood. He opened Teal's fingers and took the card. Then he rose, aiming the rifle at Teal's head.

Without thinking, Nick whipped the Beretta out from under him and took aim. Ned saw the motion and started to turn, but Nick was too fast. He pulled the trigger. The gun bucked upward, and Ned spun halfway off his feet as the single bullet slammed into him. Blood sprayed out of his shoulder, the rifle clattering to the ground. There was a frozen moment, then Ned was running toward the door, clutching his shoulder with his left hand.

Samantha scooped up the discarded rifle and went after him, as Nick shoved the Beretta back into his waistband and crawled to Melora's prone body. He pressed his hand against her carotid, and felt a faint tremor, then nothing more. Dead, or dying— there was little he could do for her. He rose and ran to Teal's side. As he had guessed, his wound was bad, but hopefully not fatal; the bullet had torn right through the skin and muscles, but it didn't look like it had hit anything vital. Nick tore off a piece of his sleeve and held it tight against the wound. Teal grunted in pain, then grasped Nick's arm with a bloody hand.

"Go after him," he hissed through obvious pain. "Get the card. After you open the display case, you have to hit three switches in series. Red, green, black. It's the only way to isolate the system. Hurry, you don't have much time."

Nick didn't want to leave Teal and Melora bleeding on the floor, but he didn't have a choice. Samantha had already exited through the airlock door, and she didn't know about the three switches. He raced across the computer atrium, and just as he reached the door, he thought he saw a flicker of blue light out of the corner of his eye. He whirled back toward the computer screen—but of course, it was still blank. Then he turned back toward the door.

"Just keep your hand pressed against the wound!" he shouted to Teal as he rushed forward. "Try to keep your heart rate down!"

Ned's trail was not hard to follow; every few feet a puddle of dark red blood told Nick he was going in the right direction. As he tore through the steel chamber, and out into the carpeted hallway, he saw Samantha cutting through the huge cubicle room. Employees in blue uniforms scattered in front of her, screams and the sound of running feet filling the air as people caught sight of the rifle.

Nick moved down the hallway at a dead run, cutting the distance between them. In front of her, he saw the bank of elevators, and next to them an open stairwell door. Samantha headed for the stairwell and Nick followed, still ten feet behind her.

He tore down the four flights, his shoes slipping against the carpeted steps as he rushed to keep up. Every few steps he saw another puddle of Ned's blood—he wondered how much more blood the man could lose before he started to weaken.

He reached the bottom of the stairwell just five feet behind Samantha. The stairwell opened into the main first-floor hallway, right next to the bank of elevators. The glass revolving door that led to the lobby was directly in front of them—and Ned had just stepped inside. He turned to look back at them through the glass, a strange, helpless expression on his face. Samantha dropped to one knee, aiming the rifle.

She pumped off three shots, the sound ricocheting through the hallway. An instant later there were three soft thuds. The three oversized shells hung directly in front of Ned's face, imbedded in the thick Plexiglas of the revolving door. The revolving door continued spinning inward, and a second later Ned was gone.

"Damn it," Samantha shouted. She was up on her feet and moving forward, Nick a step behind. Then she stopped, suddenly, as she reached the revolving door. Nick nearly slammed into her.

"Why are you stopping?"

Samantha dropped the rifle to the floor. "I can't carry this into the lobby. The first cop that sees me is going to put a bullet in my head."

She was right, they'd have to go without the rifle. She entered the spinning door and Nick caught the next revolving section.

They burst out into the lobby in time to see Ned disappear through the outer sliding door. The lobby was still crowded; the panic upstairs had not yet infected the first floor. As they wove through the tourists, Nick cast a longing glance at the huge glass display case to his right; the glistening fiber optic cables glowed, and he could imagine the pulses of information sliding up and down. In about eighteen more minutes those pulses of information would pick up a stowaway, a killer virus that would reach out to every television set, every computer in the country. Unless he and Samantha could get that key.

"Come on," Samantha hissed, glancing at her watch, marking the time. "We can't lose him."

The electronic sliding door whiffed open just before they crashed into it, and Nick squinted as a blast of pure sunlight hit him squarely in the face. He whirled back and forth, his eyes wild, searching. There seemed to be twice as many people as before. He followed Samantha down the stone front steps and across the street lined with parked cars.

They were on the southeastern corner of the mall;
the carpet of manicured grass spread out to their
left, embraced on all sides by the different personalities of the Smithsonian Institute. Directly across
from them was the domed National Gallery of Art,
to their left the sloping glass Air and Space
Museum. There were people everywhere; strolling
down the paths that bisected the glade, posing for
photos with the Smithsonian buildings in the background, buying ice cream from vendors under
brightly colored umbrellas. Nick could hear Samantha's panicked breaths as she shouldered through a
group of elderly women in matching aquamarine
dresses, and then she pointed, her eyes lighting up.

Nick saw Ned lurching across the center of the
mall, his left arm limp from his shoulder wound, his
other hand still clutching the transparent card.

"Keep your eyes on the card," Nick gasped, as
he took off next to Samantha. "If he drops it, we
have to know where. If he loses us even for a second, it's over."

"Who *is* he? Why is he doing this?"

The grass turned liquid under Nick's feet as he
barreled forward, nearly upending an ice cream cart
as he fought to keep Ned in direct line of sight. "He
doesn't work for Melora or Teal."

"Well, whom does he work for?"

"Maybe he doesn't work for anybody. The
Reaper has perceived us—it has learned how to
interact with the outside world. Maybe it's found a
way to use Ned."

Samantha glanced at him, then turned back
toward Ned. The piglike man was weaving almost
randomly through the tourists, his pudgy body
jerking spasmodically as people bumped into him,

some pointing at his bloody shoulder, most stepping out of the way.

"Someone had to put the Reaper into the beta test," Nick continued, as they gave chase. "The Reaper could not have accomplished this all on its own. Someone had to be on the outside."

"You think the Reaper can somehow control him? That sounds insane."

"Maybe. But just as one certain modulation of light can set off CaV, another could sabotage thought patterns, emotional stability, almost anything. And strobe-light hypnosis is a documented phenomenon. Who knows what this psychotic we're chasing thinks he's doing? He may not be thinking at all."

Ned had reached the other side of the wide park and had made a sharp left turn. Nick and Samantha angled toward him, slowly gaining. Nick could feel the seconds ticking away as he ran, his thigh throbbing with each step. He had almost forgotten about his gunshot wound in the excitement of the last few hours, but now, with the exertion of the chase, it had flared back up. He swore at his own nervous system; he was determined to ignore the pain, no matter how bad it got.

Twenty feet ahead, Ned took a sharp right turn and headed for a series of stone steps. He passed a group of teenagers huddled around an older man with an artist's clipboard, and disappeared through a high arched door. Nick ran his eyes up the front of the building, over the jutting white rectangular pillars along its face, connecting with the huge American flag over the entrance. It was the Smithsonian Museum of American History. The front entrance was packed with people, and Ned pushed himself into the throng, disappearing inside.

"Damn it," Samantha said as she hit the bottom step to the museum. "We're going to lose him. There are too many people."

Nick realized that she was right. The front entrance was jammed; it would take a few minutes just to get to the door. *Too long.* Nick leapt up the next step and yanked Ted's Beretta out of his waistband.

"Get the hell out of my way!" he roared.

The crowd scattered, people toppling over one another to get away from the entrance. Nick crashed forward, waving the gun, and Samantha followed. Just as he hit the glass door, Nick shoved the gun back into his waistband, praying that nobody inside had seen his theatrics. He didn't have time to get arrested.

THIRTY-SEVEN

Old glory, the actual Star Spangled Banner, took up half of the far wall behind the museum's information desk, hanging in majestic repose, the stars and stripes wavering beneath a transparent protective curtain as a throng of respectful tourists looked on. Display cases and patriotic dioramas filled the great hall, glowing under ceiling spots and backlit by red, white, and blue inset bulbs. The walls were high and Gothic, the floor elegantly tiled. There was a hushed feel to the place, even though there was barely room to stand in the crush of gawkers. Nick felt the sweat running over every inch of his skin, and the sharp sting as the salty drops pooled under the bandage on his thigh.

"Over there," Samantha said in his ear, grabbing his wrist. "Right behind the pendulum."

Nick followed her gaze. On the other side of the front information desk, just ahead of Old Glory, the center of the front hall was taken up by a steel-railed inset circle, across the center of which swung an enormous, brass ball: Foucault's Pendulum, one of the museum's biggest draws. The huge 240-pound brass weight swept in long, slow arcs, affixed to a thick steel cable that was suspended from the fourth floor. Inside the low metal railing stood a ring of red plastic pins; the pendulum's arc shifted infinitesimally as the Earth spun, the red plastic pins marking the revolution as the brass ball knocked them over one by one.

Directly on the other side of the pendulum stood Ned. He was looking right at them, his body hunched forward under his Telecon uniform, the brass ball floating through the air in a perpendicular path crossing a bare yard in front of him. There was an expression of pure agony on his face—and Nick did not think it had anything to do with his shoulder wound. There was some sort of internal battle going on behind those glazed eyes.

"He's still got the card," Samantha said, moving forward.

Nick saw the card clenched between Ned's pudgy fingers. Then he moved his eyes back to the piggish face. In a moment, all that separated them was the pendulum, swinging past every few seconds with a quiet hiss.

"He doesn't look armed," Nick whispered, as someone bumped into his right shoulder.

"But we have to be careful," Samantha whispered back. "He could still have some sort of weapon concealed on him. And there are a lot of people around. You go left, I'll go right."

Nick started around the circular pendulum railing, keeping his eyes trained on Ned's thick glasses. Ned jerked his head back and forth, mechanically taking in both Nick and Samantha. His spine straightened, and suddenly he spun on his heels and ran.

"Go!" Samantha coughed, sprinting after him. Nick crashed between two college-age women carrying backpacks and swung around the other side of the pendulum, just in time to see Ned disappear through a recessed doorway in the far wall. Nick raced after him, his feet skidding against the marbled tiles.

He reached the recessed doorway a foot ahead of Samantha. The doorway opened on a cement stairwell, high steps running in both directions. The stairwell was lined with colorful framed pictures and pieces of Americana, an exhibit in progress: glowing plastic hamburgers, a neon Coca-Cola logo, a tie-dyed business suit hanging from a rubber hanger, a picture of Madonna next to a Lucite electric guitar. "Pop Culture, Up and Down" a sign declared. Nick paused in the doorway, searching past bobbing heads and saw Ned's balding pate descending past a plastic movie dinosaur affixed beneath the electric guitar.

The disjointed images blurred together as Nick took the steps two at a time. He saw Ned turn a corner ten steps below. He leapt the next four steps, ignoring the daggers of pain as his thigh screamed out, and nearly collided with an overweight woman in a polyester flowered dress. He stuck his hands out to keep his balance, catching his left wrist in the strap of the woman's vinyl handbag. The woman screamed, shoving him, and he crashed into the wall, trying to disentangle his arm. Then both he and the woman were falling, rolling the last few steps to the bottom of the stairwell.

Nick wrenched his arm free as his shoulders collided with the floor, and scrambled to his feet. The woman was shouting at him in some language he didn't understand, but she didn't look hurt—so he turned and kept moving. There were other shouts from higher up the stairwell, and he heard Samantha arguing with someone behind her. He glanced over his shoulder and saw her trying to climb over the hysterical woman; their eyes caught, and Samantha waved him forward. They were going to lose Ned if they didn't keep moving.

He burst out of the stairwell and out into the center of the first floor. He was standing at the edge of a huge, painfully schizophrenic exhibit. Above him, a colorful plaque read:

Material World

To his left and right, a tumultuous panorama rose up along the walls, showing the history of materials, from clay and stone up through modern metals—and beyond. Directly in front of him sat a full-size drag racer, made up of hundreds of different materials, from one huge Goodyear rubber tire to a crank-shaft of what looked like solid gold.

Nick spun on his heels, his eyes fighting through the glowing displays, and there Ned was, skidding past a high plastic bubble that looked to be a spacecraft cockpit. Nick barreled after him, nearly colliding with a glass case full of antique farming tools: hoes, trowels, shovels, even a steel scythe with a wicked curved blade. Ned reached the far end of the exhibit a full five yards ahead of him, and suddenly they passed from the cacophony of the Material World to a pristine modern scene, all curved walls and sci-fi lettering. Ned disappeared into a mob of moving people, and Nick rushed after him, his eyes wild.

In the center of the room was a five-foot-high stone replica of the Washington Monument, with bright neon letters wrapped around its face:

The Information Age

Along the back wall stood a glass display case charting the advance of information technology from ancient times to the present. A diorama at the far left of the room showed two Egyptian oar ships signaling one another with tiny glass mirrors across an expanse of blue plastic ocean. The chronology continued, skipping to Samuel Morse's invention of the telegraph—with Morse's actual telegraph machine clicking away inside a high plastic case—then jumping again to Alexander Graham Bell's original telephone, then to a huge section of the first transatlantic telephone cable, and on into the present. The right half of the room was taken up by an enormous stage with bold words hanging down from the ceiling:

Fiber Optics—The Future of Information Technology

Two huge television screens stood on opposite sides of the stage, connected by a thin transparent tube. Both screens were blank, and a large crowd had gathered in front of each screen, waiting. Nick's stomach churned, as he realized what they were waiting for.

Suddenly, something flashed at the edge of Nick's vision and he was hit from behind. Someone screamed as he crashed forward, colliding with a glass case and shattering through. Samuel Morse's telegraph dug into his chest as he hit the floor, the aging metal snapping under his weight.

He rolled to his left as something crashed into the floor where his head had just been. He looked up and saw Ned standing above him, a dented fire-extinguisher in his hands. Ned threw the fire extinguisher at Nick as he scrambled to his feet, the heavy metal cylinder hitting his shoulder and glancing off, sending a burst of pain up his arm. Near mass hysteria had gripped the crowded first level of the museum, as panicked people rushed away from the shattered display case. Nick could hear a police whistle from somewhere on the other side of the room, but he didn't see any security—yet.

Ned was still standing a few feet in front of him, staring dully out from behind his thick glasses. Nick's hands became fists and he lurched forward, angered by the new pain in his shoulder. Then he stopped dead as Ned's previously limp left hand whipped forward. In it was a straight razor; the gleaming blade was three inches long, sharpened to a tapered point.

Shit. Nick took a step back. He had seen many victims of razor blade fights—it was a favorite weapon of some of the most vicious Boston gangs. A straight razor could sever veins and arteries with ridiculous ease.

Ned strolled forward, the blade out in front of him, his expression still dull behind his glasses. Nick raised his hands as he backed away, and felt something hard against his shoulders. He glanced back and saw the top of the Washington Monument at jaw-level. Ned had backed him into the replica in the center of the exhibit.

Nick swallowed, looking past Ned for help. The closest people were ten feet away, pushing toward the exits. The razor blade was hidden from view by Ned's pudgy body, and nobody seemed to have noticed Nick's predicament. Nick opened his mouth to shout when he saw a familiar shape moving toward him through the edge of the crowd. Samantha, her hair wild, the Lucite guitar from the stairwell exhibit held in her hands like a weapon. Nick felt a surge of adrenaline at the sight of her, and he bent his knees. . . .

Suddenly, Ned was moving toward him, the blade slashing out. Nick cut right, his football skills barely getting him out of the way in time. Ned crashed into the stone monument with full force, and the entire thing toppled backward, slamming into the floor. There was an electric flash as the neon words burst against the polished marble.

Ned scrambled back to his feet, his eyes still pinned to Nick, when Samantha leapt the last few feet forward and swung the Lucite guitar. The guitar hit Ned in the side of his head and he toppled backward, the razor blade clattering to the floor. He landed on his knees, shaking his head, and Samantha stepped forward for a second swing. But before she could do anything there was a loud whistle from behind Nick's shoulder.

"Freeze! Drop the guitar!"

Nick whirled around and nearly slammed into a security guard holding a .38-caliber revolver. Samantha looked back at the guard, and in that second, Ned was up and moving forward. Samantha started after him, then stopped as the security guard took another step forward, his face apoplectic with anger:

"I said freeze!"

Nick looked at the .38 hanging just a foot in front of him and dove at the guard's arm, catching him just below the elbow. The guard tried to struggle, but Nick was too strong. The gun flipped out of his hand and then Nick's shoulder connected with the guard's jaw. The man slumped to the ground.

"Quick," Samantha shouted, dropping the guitar and pointing. "He's heading back toward the stairs."

Damn it, Nick thought as he took off after Ned. This was taking too long. He exited the Information Age exhibit and reentered the Material World. The room was still well populated with tourists and there was a crowd around the stairwell. He didn't see Ned, but assumed Samantha was right; Ned would be trying to get back outside, where they'd never catch him. He cut around a man shouting into a cellular phone and once again nearly collided with the same glass display case of farming tools; this time, he noticed something wrong with the case. A section of the glass had been knocked out, and one of the objects inside was missing. His stomach dropped as he realized which one.

He hit the back of the crowd at the stairwell and started to push through. He used his shoulders and his size to carve a hole for himself, and in a second he was up the first few steps. He glanced back and didn't see Samantha, but assumed she was somewhere behind him, perhaps caught in the crush of people.

He burst back out onto the ground floor, his body tense, his eyes searching. The pendulum was in front of him, the enormous flag to his left, and beyond the information desk, a constant stream of

frightened tourists evacuating through the front
door. He assumed there were security guards somewhere in the crowd, but he didn't see any close by.
Nor did he see any sign of—

There was a flash of sudden motion from his
right and he leapt back. A curved steel blade
whizzed by his shoulder. He turned and saw Ned
coming toward him, the hand scythe out in front of
him. The blade was two feet long and razor sharp,
shaped like a sideways smile. Nick backed away as
fast as he could, and found himself standing against
the circular metal railing in the middle of the room.
He could feel the wind of the pendulum on the back
of his neck.

Ned continued toward him. The stream of exiting tourists was a good twenty feet away, on the
other side of the information desk. Nick swallowed,
moving the only way he could—climbing up and
over the low metal railing. The floor beneath the
pendulum was made up of crisscrossing steel
beams, depressed about three feet. Nick heard a
clatter as he knocked over red plastic pins, and he
glanced back. The huge brass ball swung by, cutting
across the circle a few feet behind his right shoulder.

He turned back toward Ned. Ned was still moving forward, the scythe in front of him, the card still
tucked between the fingers of his right hand. Nick
tried to see some semblance of thought behind
Ned's thick glasses. All he saw was a glazed stare—
no comprehension at all.

"Why are you doing this?" Nick gasped, stepping a few inches back from the railing.

Ned paused, the scythe wavering in the air.
Then his shoulders straightened. Even though there
was blood seeping down his left arm, he seemed to

be filled with internal strength. His thick lips slid open. His voice came out in broken gasps, an exhausted monotone.

"The creature. Is. Irrelevant."

He dove forward, the scythe sweeping through the air. Nick crashed back into the depressed circle. There was a flash of black as the pendulum swung above his face, then Ned was on top of him, the scythe speeding toward his throat. He reached up at the last minute and caught Ned's wrist with both hands.

There was a frozen moment as Ned fought to bring the curved blade down. Nick used every muscle against him, his right hand screaming in pain, his back aching as the steel beams pressed into him, but still, despite his efforts, the blade slowly began to shift downward. Inch by inch, the curved steel coming closer to his throat. Nick's eyes widened and he gasped, his mind crying out. He used all his strength, but still the scythe moved toward him, Ned's thick lips curling back from his teeth, his glazed eyes locked in dull desperation.

Nick saw something reflected in those glazed eyes. Something round and shiny and growing larger and larger . . .

The 240-pound brass pendulum ball slammed directly into Ned's face. There was a sickening crunch, and Ned's entire body was tossed backward, his shoulders slamming into Old Glory. Blood spurted from his shattered face as the flag ripped free from the wall, and billowed downward over him, covering his limp, lifeless form.

Nick crawled to his feet, narrowly avoiding the pendulum as it swung back past him. Samantha was standing outside the metal railing, staring at the shape under the fallen flag. Nick looked back at the swinging pendulum, noticing its erratic arc. Then he turned back toward Samantha.

"A little push," she said. "That's all it took. Do you think he's dead?"

Nick nodded. There was no way the human skull could sustain that much damage. "He must be. Even if he's not, he won't be bothering us anymore."

"Nick," Samantha suddenly asked. "When he cornered you with the scythe, why didn't you pull Ted's gun?"

"Because—"

Nick heard shouts and running feet from the other side of the information desk, and he lunged forward. "Quick! We have to find the card!"

He pulled up a corner of the flag and began searching the floor. Samantha crawled close to Ned's crumbled body, and then jumped back to her feet. "Found it! Come on."

They headed toward the front entrance, passing three security guards who were racing toward the fallen flag. The security guards barely noticed them, in the rush to comfort Old Glory. Nick wondered what they'd think when they found Ned's body beneath the flag.

Nick and Samantha entered the crowd still streaming through the front door. Samantha came close to him as they exited onto the stone steps, passing the card to his left hand. "You're faster—but I don't know if you're fast enough."

"We'll make it," Nick said as he hit the bottom step.

"Five minutes, Nick. Not a second more."

THIRTY-EIGHT

the grass was a green haze under Nick's feet as he ran, the plastic card digging into his sweaty left palm. His muscles were pumping blind, all interbody communication long superseded by the geysers of pure adrenaline feeding through his veins. He could hear Samantha a few steps behind him, her breath coming hard. She had a runner's lungs, but he had a near-professional athlete's body, and even with his injured thigh he knew how to dig for that needed burst of game-winning speed. He concentrated on the ground at his feet, blocking everything else out, running as he had never run before.

He swung left around a German tour group, cut between a pair of hooded baby carriages, and hurdled an empty wooden bench next to a crowded ice cream cart. Suddenly he was in front of the Telecon

complex. He had outpaced Samantha by a dozen
feet, but he didn't pause. He could tell by the
swollen crowd on the Telecon front steps that he
didn't have much time. Then his eyes caught sight
of the digital display above the entrance—and his
throat constricted.

3:00

He raced up the front steps. To his dismay, there
were four armed federal troopers and two Telecon
employees in blue uniforms standing in front of the
sliding glass doors. Nick headed straight toward
them, his legs pumping, trying to think of how he
was going to get by.

"That's him!" shouted one of the Telecon
employees. "Teal said to let him and the woman
inside."

The federal troopers parted and Nick rushed by,
relief filling his face. That meant Teal was still alive.
If Teal had thought enough to make it easy for Nick
to get inside, he would probably have also cleared
out the complex so they could safely isolate the
Reaper. Nick's fingers touched the glass doors as
they whiffed open.

To his surprise, there were still a half-dozen people in the lobby, crowded around the corner near the
hydraulic tram. As he sped across the tiled floor he
realized that at least three of the crowd were wearing
D.C. paramedic's uniforms; they were hunched over
a stretcher, shouting frantic medical terms at one
another. Nick caught only a few words, "blood-
pressure falling," "perforated upper intestine," "he's
going into shock"—and then he was at the huge
Plexiglas case at the back of the room. He didn't have
time to see what was going on by the tram.

He searched frantically for a slot for the card. Directly in the center of the case was the Telecon logo: two spherical eyes connected by a lightning bolt. The logo was raised two inches off the Plexiglas, made out of a material that looked like solid gold.

Nick grabbed the logo by one of the eyes; the logo shifted, and he realized that it was screwed onto the Plexiglas. After two counter clockwise rotations, the logo came free. Underneath was the slot for the plastic card.

Nick shifted the heavy piece of gold to his left hand and took the card in his right. He heard rushed footsteps behind him, and was glad that Samantha had arrived in time to watch. He jammed the card into the slot. There was a quiet whirring, and a panel on the back of the Plexiglas slid open. A control plank stared at him, covered with colored knobs and switches. Nick fought to remember the sequence Teal had told him. Three colors. *But which three?*

It came to Nick in one burst of memory and he reached forward—when an arm whipped around his hip and there was a sudden tug at his waistband. Before he could do anything the cold barrel of Ted's Beretta was against the side of his neck.

"Samantha?"

But he knew it wasn't her. He looked up and saw Samantha running across the lobby, her face a mask of fear. Then he shifted his eyes toward the gun.

Trickles of dark blood covered most of Melora Parkridge's face. A section of her scalp was missing, and beneath the blood Nick could see the white glint of her skull. Her lips were churning, her teeth chattering together. Her eyes were glazed—the same glaze that he had seen over Ned's eyes. He remembered the flicker of blue on his way out of the computer atrium. *The Reaper.*

"Melora," he whispered. "Fight back."

There was no answer. Samantha was still moving toward him, but she was too far away to do anything. Melora pressed the barrel tighter against Nick's neck. Nick clenched his fingers against the Telecon logo. *Action beats reaction.*

Melora pulled the trigger. There was a loud metallic click—then nothing. Nick swung the heavy logo and hit her in the side of the head. She crumpled to the floor.

Samantha skidded to a stop at Nick's side, staring down at Melora's unconscious form. "Did you know?"

Nick nodded. "You said fifteen bullets, right?"

He turned back to the colored knobs and switches. His hand paused in the air, his fingers trembling.

"What are you waiting for?" Samantha said, her voice frantic.

"I'm trying to remember the right sequence."

"Are you kidding me?" Samantha shouted. "How could you forget?"

"Don't pressure me. I'll get it. Just give me a second—"

It came to him. He reached forward and flicked the three switches: red, green, then black. There was a hissing sound, and then nothing. He looked at Samantha.

"I think that was it. I was expecting more."

Samantha reached forward with both hands and pulled his face to hers. Then she started laughing.

Suddenly he was laughing, too. They had done it. It was over.

"Damn it, he's not going to make it!"

The shout filtered across the atrium, echoing in Nick's ears. He quickly pulled away from Samantha and headed toward the crowd by the revolving door. As he approached, he recognized the figure on the stretcher.

Marcus Teal didn't look good. There was an oxygen mask over his mouth and nose, IVs running into his arms, a tube attached to his nostrils, and a bag of whole blood above his right shoulder. His shirt was ripped open and the paramedics had white gauze packs affixed to his abdomen. Nick could tell, even from a distance, that the bleeding was getting worse.

Nick pushed between two of the paramedics. "What have we got?"

The nearest paramedic, a short black woman in her twenties, looked at him with raised eyebrows. He ignored her stare, leaning over Teal. "I'm a doctor."

"He's been shot, entry through the left upper quadrant, exit through the midaxillary line. From the drop in his pressure, looks like the bullet damaged his splenic artery. He's starting to crash. I don't think he'll make it to the ambulance. We're waiting for a field surgery team."

Nick touched the gauze over Teal's wound, digesting what the paramedic had told him. He knew, just from the feel of the gauze, that she was right—Teal wouldn't make it to the ambulance. In fact, Nick wasn't sure he'd be alive when the field surgery team arrived. Someone had to go inside his abdomen and clamp the damaged artery within the next few minutes. Teal didn't need a paramedic—he needed a surgeon.

A surgeon who can hold a scalpel. Nick looked into Teal's eyes.

"Just hold on," he said, his voice suddenly calm. "Everything's going to be okay."

Teal started to struggle with the oxygen mask, his face pale but his eyes fierce. Nick shook his head, amazed that Teal was still conscious. "Don't try and talk. We stopped the virus. Now we've just got to fix up that little hole in your side."

He turned toward the paramedic. "I need a sterile scalpel, two c.c.s of internal Halothane, and a Kelly clamp."

He felt Samantha's hand touch his shoulder. He didn't look back at her. He flexed the fingers of his left hand, his teeth coming together. He was going to do this, damn it.

The paramedic handed him the scalpel and threaded needle, and began to administer the internal anesthetic through the IV wire. As she plugged in the Halothane, Nick noticed that Teal was still struggling with his oxygen mask. Nick nodded at another of the paramedics and watched as the man lifted the mask off of Teal's mouth.

"I only wanted to bring down the barriers," he whispered, his voice breaking. "My intentions were good. Nobody will understand—they'll never understand."

They were the words of a man who thought he was going to die. Nick touched Teal's hand. "Just relax. You'll have time to explain."

"Either way," Teal gasped, sorrow in his voice. "It's over."

Teal was right, it was over. Nick could feel

Samantha's presence behind him, could imagine the emotions in her beautiful gray eyes. He decided that the first thing he was going to do when they got out of Washington was to take her out West, maybe back to Texas to meet the coach. He was going to teach her to ride a horse, turn her into a real live cowboy.

But first, he was going to save Marcus Teal's life. He clenched the scalpel tight in his left hand and raised it in front of his eyes, concentrating. He had been a switch hitter in college. And although surgery was not baseball, there was no physical reason why he could not do this with his left hand. To his relief, the scalpel remained steady and sure.

As Teal's eyes slid shut from the anesthesia, Nick entered a familiar, but long-neglected place. He was no longer a Pulse Jockey—now, once again, he was a surgeon.

THIRTY-NINE

Y ou want to know what I think? She's too good for you. What she's really looking for is a sax player in a body cast."

Nick laughed, the cell phone warm against his ear. Samantha sat down next to him on the edge of the bed and put a tanned hand on his thigh. Even though it was the second week of November, she was wearing a breezy summer skirt. Her long legs were sun darkened and her hair fell down against her bared shoulders.

"Charlie, you were always the better judge of people."

Charlie's laughter sounded good in Nick's ear. It was the third time they'd spoken in the two weeks since Nick's ordeal. Charlie had been released from the hospital four days ago, and Nick and Samantha had not returned to Washington until late last night.

ow they were camped out in Samantha's bedroom
they prepared for the next leg of their trip—and
ick had taken the opportunity to touch base with
s friend.

When Nick had first heard about Charlie's acci-
ent—as awful as it had been—his reaction had
een outright relief. After what had happened to
ed and to Sonya Hoffman, his paranoid mind had
oncocted hundreds of horrible scenarios. In fact,
harlie's disappearance had had nothing to do with
andora or CaV.

Charlie had been on his way to Providence to
ick up the medical info on Eric Hoffman, when he
verved to avoid a squirrel. His motorcycle had
kidded off the highway, flipping over three times.
harlie had fractured both legs on impact, and had
ent the next twelve hours lying in a ditch, cursing
lick and his stupid favors. Finally, a patrolling
olice cruiser had noticed the skid marks and
harlie had been airlifted back to Boston General,
here his legs had been set in plaster. He'd missed
aree gigs and two weeks of work—but at least he'd
ad plenty of time to practice his saxophone.

"You stay healthy," Nick said. "I'll talk to you
oon."

"Have a good trip."

Nick clicked off and put the cell phone down on
ne table by Samantha's bed. Then he touched the
ack of her hand. She looked at him, smiled, and he
ould tell that she too was thinking about the last
en days. Absolute bliss. First the weekend with the
oach, checking out Nick's high school haunts, dri-
ing the streets of Dallas in the early evening, riding
orses at a farm near his father's house. Then the
ext full week on an island in the middle of nowhere:

sun, beach, long nights of talking, forgetting, recov
ering—and learning. Despite their efforts to block
out the outside world, by the end of the week
Samantha had been receiving almost constant faxes
and phone calls.

The fallout from their investigation into CaV had
only recently begun to subside. Three days ago
Speaker Tyro Carlson had resigned from Congress in
response to the inquiry into his involvement with
Pandora. It turned out that Carlson had been a stu
dent at MIT at roughly the same time as Melora Park
ridge; he still had not admitted anything, but there
was a good chance he was part of her antitechnology
conspiracy. Meanwhile, the popular media had been
having a field day guessing about other possible con
spirators: presidents of banks, CEOs of major compa
nies involved with Telecon's quick rise—nobody was
escaping scrutiny. It was certain that a tremendous
amount of money had been involved, along with a
number of highly placed political insiders. There was
also the possibility of a foreign connection; less indus
trialized nations had an enormous amount to gain
from a massive technology crash.

Melora Parkridge had been moved to a psychi
atric institution in Baltimore, where various experts
were still trying to bring her out of a glazed, semi
catatonic state. Nick had read the autopsy reports on
Ned Dickerson while sitting in a hammock on Grand
Cayman. The pathologist had found a marked hyper
trophy, enlargement, of regions of his cerebellum
and motor cortex. And the opposite, hypotrophy, of
his amygdala. Nick had been thinking about what
the finding meant for the past few days. The cerebel
lum and motor cortex were responsible for muscle
control and involuntary reflex, while the amygdala

as the center for emotion and personality. Nick had concluded that—as insane as it sounded—Ned's brain had somehow been "reprogrammed." His body had carried out commands that had not come from voluntary thought. How the Reaper had accomplished this feat was yet another mystery, one that Nick realized he'd probably never figure out.

The one thing that was certain was that the Reaper no longer existed. The Telecon complex had been immediately quarantined. Six separate USAMRIID teams working in conjunction with FBI computer experts and CIA technicians had sanitized every inch of the complex; then the building itself had been torn down, to make way for the Native American Museum that had originally been slated for that spot.

Nick couldn't help but feel sorry for Marcus Teal when he thought about the fall of Telecon Industries. Although Teal would probably avoid legal repercussions—he was still a billionaire, and his possession of a backdoor was not a crime in itself—he had watched the collapse of his company from the television in his private hospital room. CNN, after all, had been carrying the story twenty-four hours a day.

Nick turned Samantha's hand over in his, forcing his thoughts away from Teal and Telecon Industries. "Charlie says hello. He can't wait to meet you."

"It's a short flight from Boston. And there are a lot of good blues bars in Washington. When his legs have healed, the three of us can go out to dinner."

Nick smiled. He had not missed Samantha's point. "You sound pretty certain I'll be hanging around."

"It's a good offer, Nick. A chance for us to work together, and make a difference."

Nick nodded; she was right, but in truth he still

hadn't reached a decision. The idea of working wit
Samantha was thrilling—but he wasn't sure he wa
ready to leave Boston permanently. Even after tw
weeks of near bliss, there were issues he still neede
to work through. Not so much guilt anymore, but
sense that Jennifer was still inside him, that she'd k
with him no matter how close he got to Samantha. H
assumed that was normal. But before he signed on a
Samantha's partner on the USAMRIID Respons
Team, he wanted to be sure of his feelings, really sur
that he was ready to move on with his new life.

"So I guess it's time we got going."

Nick could hear the tension in Samantha's voice
The next leg of their trip had been her idea, but sh
was nervous. She had not seen her father in a lon
time. And she had not been back to Hawaii sinc
her brother's funeral. But now, with Nick by he
side, she wanted to go. *Putting the past in the pas*
Another of the coach's life slogans. In football, as i
life, you had to get beyond the losses.

Nick watched Samantha rise from the bed an
cross to the brand-new large-screen television tha
was standing where her desk used to be. The telev
sion had been a gift from her superiors at USAM
RIID, and had been waiting in her apartment whe
they had arrived back from the Caribbean. Afte
everything that had happened, Nick had at firs
thought the gift to be in incredibly poor taste. But h
had finally agreed with Samantha that they coul
not blame the technology for what had happened
That sort of logic was the reason Melora Parkridg
was in a psychiatric institution.

Samantha paused in front of the screen, her fir
gers hitting a series of colored buttons. Nick watche
her, a surreal feeling spreading through his mind.

The Set-Top Box on top of the large screen TV was much sleeker than the Telecon version. The edges were angled out like the fins of rocket, and here were nearly twice as many buttons on the slick silver control panel. The revamped Microsoft logo covered the entire right side of the box—complete with a glowing hologram of the company chairman's face in the center.

Nick had been as surprised as anyone when the newly structured Microsoft announced its plan to replace all Telecon Set-Top Boxes with its own version—at absolutely no cost to the consumer. And like everyone else, he had reacted with apprehension when it became known that Microsoft had already turned its formerly defunct complex outside Seattle into a new center for the fiber optic infrastructure. But while debates raged in the media and in Congress, the simple truth was the technology was ready. The fiber optic network was waiting. And even if the Evolving Code was flawed, there were other encryption programs in the wings. In fact, Microsoft's Wincrypt, which came with every Microsoft Set-Top Box, was considered the top contender.

Samantha finished punching buttons and dropped back onto the bed next to Nick. He put his arm around her shoulder, staring at the dark screen. Next to the screen was a small fish-eye camera, also sporting the Microsoft logo. In a few seconds, they were going to travel to Hawaii. Samantha's father would look at them through the screen, and hopefully he would like what he saw. Because if Nick had anything to do with it, someday soon they were going to be family.

There was a sudden click, and the screen glowed blue.